# THE SOUL OF THE ROSE

This Large Print Book carries the
Seal of Approval of N.A.V.H.

# THE SOUL OF THE ROSE

## RUTH TRIPPY

**THORNDIKE PRESS**

*A part of Gale, Cengage Learning*

GALE
CENGAGE Learning·

Farmington Hills, Mich • San Francisco • New York • Waterville, Maine
Meriden, Conn • Mason, Ohio • Chicago

# GALE
## CENGAGE Learning·

LIBRARY OF CONGRESS CATALOGING-IN-PUBLICATION DATA

Trippy, Ruth.
    The soul of the rose / by Ruth Trippy. — Large print edition.
      pages ; cm. — (Thorndike Press large print clean reads)
    ISBN-13: 978-1-4104-6754-6 (hardcover)
    ISBN-10: 1-4104-6754-6 (hardcover)
    1. Single women—Fiction. 2. Choice (Psychology)—Fiction. 3. Massachusetts—Fiction. 4. Large type books. I. Title.
PS3620.R58S68 2014
813'.6—dc23                                          2013049667

Published in 2014 by arrangement with Abingdon Press

Printed in Mexico
5 6 7 18 17 16 15 14

Nevertheless, he later observed that the first great problem in life is how one could fit romantic longings of the heart together with the robust intellectual quests of reason. This was certainly Lewis's desire: to find the object of his deepest longing and have it be intellectually coherent and satisfying.

— Dr. Jerry Root
"The Spiritual Journey of C. S. Lewis"
*The C. S. Lewis Bible, NRSV*

# ACKNOWLEDGMENTS

My heartfelt thanks to my Critique Group, who read every word of The Soul of the Rose and gave generously of their time and expertise in making this a better novel: Laurie Fuller, Donna Lott, LeAnne Benfield Martin, and Gloria Spencer. They are wordsmiths and treasured friends. And the story is better because I wanted to keep them entertained from chapter to chapter.

Readers gave me valuable insight and encouragement from their overall view of the novel: Dr. Terry Ensley, Gayle Corrigan Esman, my parents Wayne and Jereen Folkert, my sister Rose Moore, my aunt Anita Van Wyk, novelist Meg Moseley, and the person who gave the final reading on its fine points, my sister Jan Whitford.

So many cited on this page prayed for me and this manuscript, one of their best gifts. Candy Menedis also read the manuscript, but she most encouraged me with her faithful prayers.

Some people read those all-important opening chapters, some at the very inception of this book, giving valuable advice and encouragement: Brenda Thomas, Rachael Boudreaux Novak, Haywood Smith, and particularly when I needed a good word, Chris Roerden, who said she liked the sensibilities of my characters.

Thanks to my photographer, Dianne Kern, for the pictures on the website. I loved her passion for capturing something she "saw" with a camera.

I am grateful to my editor, Ramona Richards, who discovered me while judging for a little writing conference in South Carolina.

And this book would not be what it is without my wonderful agent, Natasha Kern, who pressed me to make it better.

Thanks to both of my beloved children, Anne and Matthew, who gave such encouraging words while reading the book, and who believed God would someday see it published when we drove by a certain street in Asheville named "Celia."

Lastly, to my husband, Ernie, a man with a surprising feel for story, who as a youngster spent hours in the movie house each Saturday, and then later listened to his father critique plots and characters. Who would have known when I married him that he would become so valuable to me in this respect? God's vision for our lives can be inscrutable and enigmatic, but it is always superior to our own, and often shows a sense of humor.

My deepest thanks goes to the Lord, who put "the writing" in me — after I desperately needed encouragement for my life and got it reading a historical romance published in 1867. This novel, St. Elmo, was the very book Celia's friend dropped in the mud and what started Celia on her journey to the bookstore in Massachusetts.

# 1

*Massachusetts, 1876*

Celia glanced at the dim light in Mr. Chestley's back office. Surely, her employer wouldn't mind if she examined the Tennyson a few moments longer. The hand-tooled leather volume had arrived at the bookstore by post that morning, all the way from London. Who would order such an expensive item? She opened it at random.

And the soul of the rose went into my blood —

The Tennyson line touched a chord in her. How musical — rich and true. She supposed every woman's heart longed to be like that rose whose soul got into a man's blood.

Stretching, she turned up the gas lamp overhead, then set herself in front of the counter and paged to the poem's notes.

— an over-wrought youth in love with a girl whom he is prevented from marrying by difference in social position.

A sudden thought stabbed her. Her beloved friend would never read words like these — never be that rose . . .

She pushed the sorrow aside. She must. Why else had her parents sent her to work in this new environment? Her eyes scanned the shelves of books. The week she'd spent here had afforded her a reader's paradise. A well-stocked bookstore this far west of Boston was a delight. The place with its paradox of stimulation and soothing quiet ministered to the deep parts of her soul. How glad she was to spend her working hours here among these books rather than in the kitchen or at the sewing box.

She looked down and turned to the Tennyson's Table of Contents. The scent of its dark red leather mingled like fine perfume with its newly cut sheets. Carefully fingering the pages of beautiful print, she scanned the contents then glanced to the end of the column, "In Memoriam A.H.H." Next, a picture of Tennyson greeted her, a brooding sort of fellow, hair and beard bushing around his face, yet she knew his contemporaries adored him, calling him *the bard.*

Footsteps echoed from Mr. Chestley's office. Celia quickly closed the book, placed it on the counter, and began opening the other packages. Maybe she could examine it later.

Her portly employer appeared beside her. "Ah, the Tennyson. I hoped it would come before this evening."

"Is it for someone special?"

"Oh, yes. I think it best you know about Mr. Lyons before he arrives. A man of decided learning, he comes every fortnight — either to purchase or order something new." He pursed his lips. "And as unapproachable as Mr. Lyons makes himself, he still gets the community tongues wagging. But I don't pay mind to the gossip, and don't you either. He's one of our best customers. He usually comes Friday nights when we stay open late. If I'm unavailable, treat him with utmost respect." Mr. Chestley bestowed a grandfatherly smile on her. "Of course, you will. You're an exceptional girl."

Celia felt herself glow at the unexpected praise.

"Now, as for the rest of these books, you can arrange them in the display window. I'll be busy in the office."

Of course, she would do what he said, but

13

after he walked away, she couldn't help opening the Tennyson again.

Self-reverence, self-knowledge, self-control,
These three alone lead life to sovereign
    power.

Mr. Chestley and she had discussed such a thought this week, had disagreed about its view of man and life. She hadn't expected a differing opinion from an old family friend.

She allowed herself another few minutes with the Tennyson, then gathering the books, headed for the display window, glimpsing the cavernous aisles of book-shelves. Here she would discover new worlds. The bookstore would afford her not only a new environment, but a little adventure as well.

Maybe a wonderful, hearthside adventure. How she loved to read. She looked at the books she carried and clasped them hard against her. Would she ever again find another soul mate in this, considering what had happened last year? However, she did have her father and mother. She couldn't have faced the past few months without them.

Before stepping up to the window, she glanced back. Each bookcase had a polished

14

mahogany end, the one nearest the door carved with representations of music, art, and writing. Over the years, Mr. Chestley had lovingly added a touch here and there of Old World beauty. He not only viewed literature as fine art, but believed the place his books resided should evince an artistic spirit as well.

Edward Lyons paused in the shadow of a tree near a lamppost. Not until a lone horse and buggy passed and turned the corner did he cross the deserted, gas-lit street. The brisk air forecast a soon-to-arrive autumn. He halted in front of the glowing bookstore window.

A shipment must have arrived recently because all the titles were new. The display had an artistic touch he'd not seen previously. That edition of Plato looked interesting. He'd examine its footnotes; it might be a possible purchase.

A glint of pale yellow inside the store caught his eye. A woman's flaxen hair, or was it a girl's, shone in the lamplight, artfully coiled in a braid at the nape of her neck. He wondered what manner of face —

She turned to examine something on the counter, her oval countenance displaying classic features. Ah . . .

15

But what about her mental acumen? Working in a bookstore, she would be bound to have some, unless hers was a clerk's mentality.

However, for him to deal with a stranger? His first spark of interest died a quick death. Accustomed to Mr. Chestley as he was, he didn't want his ordered bookstore world upset. Besides, he was done with pretty women. The last one had nearly been his undoing.

Still, he would ask to see the Plato.

The door's brass bell jangled. Celia looked up.

A man with an imposing frame entered, wrapped in a large overcoat. His hat brim pulled low, a wealth of brown hair cascaded around his neck, covering most of his visage. He removed his hat. Celia startled with recognition. The man was Tennyson come to life — with the same bushy hair and beard.

Just then, another customer appeared from one of the book aisles, an older woman enveloped in a tented gray coat, holding high a volume. "I knew this was somewhere. Last week I saw it on the shelf above." The woman plunked the book on the counter. Her large knit hat framed plump, rosy cheeks. "I told Mrs. Divers about this; she'll be glad I found it."

Celia saw the gentleman pivot and quickly enter one of the aisles, but not before the voluble customer noticed him. She stared at his retreating figure, then bent close to Celia and murmured, "Be careful of that one, Miss. He's a bad sort. The woman I'm companion to — she was his mother-in-law." Then in a louder tone, "Let me introduce myself. I'm Miss Waul, dearie." The woman opened her purse and offered a gold dollar. "Here. This ought to take care of it."

"More than enough. I have your change right here." Celia lifted a box from underneath the counter.

While Celia wrapped the purchase in brown paper, the woman flapped her coat lapels around her neck. "I should have taken my long scarf to tie up my collar. Didn't realize it would turn so cold tonight." She leaned in again and asked in a whisper, "Is Mr. Chestley around somewhere? I wouldn't want to leave you alone with . . ." Her head tilted in the direction of the bookshelves where the other customer had disappeared.

"Mr. Chestley is in his office in back." Celia kept her voice low.

"Good. Well, good night then."

The door rattled when the woman

17

slammed it shut.

Celia's eyes swept the bookcases where she'd last seen the stranger. He was nowhere to be seen, so she bent down to replace the cash box.

The Tennyson was underneath the counter. The poet had lost a close friend unexpectedly. Like herself. Somewhere in one of his poems he'd expressed that. She hesitated, then decided to open the hand-tooled volume once more.

Was it the poem "In Memoriam A.H.H"? Yes, here it was.

As she read, the immortal words brought comfort. She felt herself still inside, the self-recrimination, the guilt, eased. She would read a bit further. She grasped the page to turn it —

"Huh-hum!" A throaty growl pierced the silence.

Celia started violently, her hand jerked and she heard the paper tear. She looked down in horror. Her stomach sickened. For a moment she couldn't move, then glanced up at the large man looming in front of her.

She let the book stay underneath the counter, then slowly rose to face the customer.

"I thought I heard —" He stopped, looked at her more closely, then asked instead,

18

"Has my order arrived? It's a special edition of Tennyson poetry."

The Tennyson was *his* book? A terrible dread took hold of her. How could she tell him? But she nodded, sank down to retrieve the volume.

What could she say? What *would* she say? She closed the book, unable to bear his first sight to be a ripped page. Then rose.

Silently, she handed him the Tennyson.

"Good. I've been waiting some time for this edition."

"It is a beautiful book," she said, her eyes downcast. She cleared her throat. "But something happened a moment ago. I accidentally ripped one of its pages." The last words were almost a whisper. Her gaze rose reluctantly to his, bracing herself for his reaction. "It *was* an accident. I am *so* sorry."

He looked at her, then looked down at the book, comprehension dawning on him. "That was the tearing sound I heard?"

She nodded, mute.

"Which page?" Anger punctuated his voice.

"I'm not sure. I was looking at In Memoriam A.H.H."

He found the Table of Contents, located the page number of the poem, then opened to it.

The rip streaked down a third of the page.

His dark eyes looked up, piercing her like an arrow. "What were you doing, reading this? It's a special edition. I only order the best and expect mint condition."

"Sir, I didn't mean to. Truly! I would never *dream* —"

"But you did. Does your employer allow you to tamper with special orders?" His mouth set hard. "What are you going to do about this?"

Celia stared up at him. "I don't blame you for being angry." Her voice had sunk again. How could she assuage him? "I'm sure Mr. Chestley will have me order another one for you. I will, of course, pay for it out of my wages. I would never allow Mr. Chestley to cover the cost of my mistake." As she said the words, she was wondering how many weeks or months, it would take her to pay for the expensive volume. The Chestleys gave her room and board with only a small stipend for necessities, maybe a little left for nonessentials. She took a deep breath. Somehow, she *would* do it.

"Is something wrong here?" Mr. Chestley rounded the corner of the bookcase. "I thought I heard your voice from my back office." He addressed Mr. Lyons.

Neither Celia nor Mr. Lyons said anything.

Mr. Chestley turned to Celia and looked at her questioningly.

Dread filled her. She would have to tell him. She started to open her mouth —

"No," Mr. Lyons said. "Nothing is the matter. Your assistant just gave me the Tennyson I ordered."

"I was sure I heard your voice raised. I want to make sure nothing is wrong."

"No. Just excited, that's all."

"Well, then." Mr. Chestley's countenance cleared and he looked from one to the other. "Let me introduce you. Mr. Lyons, this is my new assistant, Miss Celia Thatcher. Her father and I are longtime friends."

"Celia," he nodded to the big man, "this is Mr. Edward Lyons, a valued patron of our bookstore."

The man bowed slightly, stood silently for some moments, then finally asked, "So you just arrived?"

Celia felt the forced interest of his question. "Yes, the beginning of the week, but I've been coming here for years."

Should she explain? She thought she should. "My parents' home is nearly forty miles away, but our family visits every year.

21

Time spent in the bookshop has always been a highlight."

"Yes, Celia is quite the reader," Mr. Chestley interjected. "In fact, we've had one good discussion already — about Emerson's *Self-Reliance.*"

Mr. Lyons expelled a long, deep breath then said, "Self-reliance over conformity, the individual over society. I believe his thinking on individualism reaches as far back as Plato."

"Yes. Much to admire in the man's writing," Mr. Chestley said. "A great deal of truth. However, my assistant takes issue with him. What did you say a few nights ago?" The proprietor turned, his smile encouraging Celia to speak.

She hesitated. "Well, sir . . . as much as Emerson is respected in certain circles, I question his repeated idea of 'trust thyself.' I believe he has too heartfelt, too wholesale a trust in himself." She glanced at Mr. Lyons before continuing. "On the one hand, I believe each of us is created uniquely, given a particular message which is ours alone, and should not be smothered by society's dictates. On the other, we can be deceived about ourselves. Pride can cloud our vision. Emerson relies too heavily on his own ability to discover truth."

"Emerson challenges us to 'live in truth,' "
Mr. Chestley said, "to speak and act in a
truthful way with our family and friends.
Where is the fault in that?"

"On the surface none, but can one trust
*oneself* to always know the truth? Do the
right thing toward God and man?"

"I grant you Emerson would think so."

"I'd term that monumental pride."

Mr. Chestley laughed. "You see, Lyons,
what I'm up against?"

Celia glanced again at the customer, who
gave no indication of whether he agreed or
not.

"As I said —" Mr. Chestley cleared his
throat, "— we had a most interesting discussion on the subject. Now, Mr. Lyons, you
mentioned Plato. We have a new edition in
our shop window."

"Yes, I'd like to look it over."

"Good. Miss Thatcher can assist you. I'm
in the middle of examining my accounts. If
you need any additional help, I'll be in my
office."

Mr. Chestley turned to leave, and Celia
quickly stepped from behind the counter
and walked to the front window.

She leaned over the display and reached
for the Plato. Turning around, she again
noted the customer's shaggy appearance.

Yes, his resemblance to Tennyson was remarkable. She walked back and offered him the book.

"Thank you." Mr. Lyons reached for the Tennyson, and taking the two volumes, disappeared behind a bookcase. The aisle held one of several chairs placed around the shop so customers could peruse materials at their leisure. Celia concluded Mr. Lyons felt quite at home.

After half an hour, he approached again. The Tennyson lay open in his large, finely shaped hand. *That* didn't accord with the rest of his unkempt appearance. He laid the book on the scarred oak of the counter with the title "Oenone" printed at the top of the page.

"Before you say anything," Celia began quietly, "I repeat, I will order a new book. And pay for it myself. I am so sorry about the ripped page."

He looked at her pointedly. "No. You will not. And you will not tell your employer. We will let this go — as if it never happened."

"But it did. I was looking at the book when I startled and ripped it. I loved the red leather binding and have been reading it since its arrival."

"Have you read quite a bit of Tennyson?"

"I particularly enjoyed 'The Lady of Shalott' and 'Idylls of the King.' Also, 'In Memoriam A.H.H.,' I found comfort."

His look was quizzical. He pointed to a particular line. "Perhaps you are aware this quote represents Tennyson's philosophy of life."

Celia bent her gaze to note the place his finger indicated. She read aloud:

Self-reverence, self-knowledge, self-control, These three alone lead life to sovereign power.

She looked up. "I came across those exact phrases this afternoon when I unwrapped the volume."

"From what you said about Emerson, I take it you would not be in agreement with England's poet laureate."

"Self-reverence, self-knowledge, and self-control are important. But whether they alone lead life to sovereign power is another question." She hesitated, then gently added, "No, I don't agree. But I think Tennyson had more of God in his life than the quote suggests."

Mr. Lyons stood in silence, yet when she glanced up at him, she caught a sharp, direct glint in his eyes. She decided not to press the discussion further.

"I'd be obliged if you'd wrap the books well," he said, his tone clipped. "My house is some distance and I came on foot."

"Of course."

She felt him watching her in a brooding sort of way, and her fingers fumbled with the paper.

Without another word, the transaction was completed. When he opened the door to leave, a draft of cold air sent an involuntary shiver through her. The door shut with a thump. He was gone. After some moments, tears welled up in her eyes.

# 2

That evening Celia arranged the last plate on the table and glanced at Mrs. Chestley bustling about the stove, preparing to take the celebratory roast out of the oven. The kitchen's pale yellow walls breathed light, an airy background for the display of sundry plates in shades of blue and gray. On the wall above the table, an oil painting of fresh peaches whetted the appetite. She inhaled deeply. The aroma of the roast, surrounded by tender garden carrots, pungent onions, and browned potatoes, wafted from the oven. Solid food, Mrs. Chestley had said. Comforting food, Mr. Chestley had replied.

Celia put the finishing fold to the napkins. The lady of the house insisted they use the soft linen reserved for company. "To celebrate your first full week at the bookshop, my dear." She added that anyone who got along with her *lion* of a husband deserved a reward — a family joke, since Mr. Chestley was the most amiable and mild-mannered of men. Celia found him very similar to her father. In her estimation, though, her father spoke his mind more vigorously.

Mrs. Chestley stepped up to Celia and put her arm around her shoulder. "You know, we're glad to have you live with us. Are you feeling better after these last months?"

Mrs. Chestley's motherly gesture warmed Celia's heart. "Yes, I am."

"Good. Then I'll dish out the roast and vegetables onto our blue willowware. Won't that look lovely?" As Mrs. Chestley reached for the large fork, she added, "Let's call my husband. And turn up that lamp as well."

Mr. Chestley took his seat. "A feast for the eyes as well as the palate." After savoring a few hearty mouthfuls, he caught his wife's eye. "Celia did very well her first week. The front window display she arranged showed superior artistic talent, in my opinion. Then she adroitly handled a difficult customer. Now I can go back into my office and hole up whenever one darkens the shop door."

"Celia, that's wonderful." Mrs. Chestley beamed.

"And, Mary, with such an able assistant, you and I should be able to take that day outing you've been longing for. In fact, I think before winter sets in, we should hire a buggy and see the colors. A little honeymoon, if you will."

Mrs. Chestley put down her fork, rose, and hugged Celia. "See, dear, you've already brought blessing into our home."

"Madam! You are supposed to embrace *me*. I am the person who arranged for this child to come and the one who proposed the fall outing."

"Of course, dear." Mrs. Chestley dutifully slipped to his side of the table.

What good fun, Celia thought, and sweet. She was glad, too, their attention was diverted from herself. After she'd damaged Mr. Lyons's book, she felt she hardly deserved such goodwill.

"Oh, Mary, I forgot to tell you, Mr. Lyons picked up his Tennyson tonight. He seemed rather pleased with it."

"I'm sure he was, the way you described its lovely red leather cover."

"I was also glad Celia could assist him. Didn't you think he was pleased with the book, Celia?"

At the mention of the Tennyson, Celia's guilty thoughts rose in a flood.

"I — I," she floundered. Mr. Lyons had told her not to say anything. But she couldn't — she just couldn't. One hand tightly grasped the other in her lap. "I have something to tell you . . . I accidentally ripped a page of the Tennyson."

Mr. Chestley started from his chair. "What?"

"Mr. Lyons said not to say anything, but I had to tell you."

Mr. Chestley sat very still. "How did it happen?"

"I was reading the book underneath the counter. When he appeared suddenly, I startled and jerked, ripping the page." Celia looked at him apprehensively.

Mr. Chestley stared at her, as if he didn't want to believe it.

"I offered to send for a new book and pay for it myself, but he wouldn't hear of it."

Finally, he said, "I've heard he has an extensive library. And beautiful. He's very particular what he includes in it. Are you sure he wasn't upset?"

"Well, he was at first, very much so. But when you came up and asked if anything was wrong, he suddenly changed." Mr. Chestley's eyebrow cocked. Celia could see he was puzzled and surprised. "What should I do? The book *is* damaged. And I don't see how the page can be repaired."

Mr. Chestley sat some moments longer. "I still can't see him suddenly dropping the subject. As I said before, he is so particular."

Celia looked at him apprehensively. "I'm very sorry I ripped the book. I should have left it alone."

"Yes! I'm glad you realize that." He pressed his lips together. "I'm trying to think what should be done."

After some moments, he said, "If Mr. Lyons *did* say to forget it, I think that is what we must do, whatever his reasons. He is a man of decision, and we need to comply with his stated wish." Mr. Chestley shook his head. "Knowing how much his books mean to him, this shows him to be more of a gentleman than I thought — considering the rumors that have circulated about him."

Celia looked a question at Mrs. Chestley.

"You see, Celia, since his wife's death, he's become the town hermit and rather unapproachable." Mrs. Chestley paused, her forefinger drawing a circle on the table cloth, as if she was trying to decide whether to say more.

"Mary —"

Celia glanced at Mr. Chestley and saw his warning look to his wife. Would anyone say anything, explain a little more? She ventured, "A Miss Waul was in the bookstore. She warned me away from him."

"She would." Mrs. Chestley took her

31

napkin from her lap and very decidedly folded it and placed it next to her plate. "No wonder he goes out and about — at night."

Celia wasn't sure where Mrs. Chestley was going with her comment. Mr. Lyons did look a veritable curmudgeon with that bush of hair and scraggly beard. But he had overlooked her accident, forgiven it so quickly. The thought struck her forcibly.

"What we could say," Mrs. Chestley began, "is that Mr. Lyons's wife died in unhappy circumstances. Quite young, and Mr. Lyons has never been the same."

He has a broken heart then, Celia thought. After some moments, she asked, "Was his wife in ill health?"

"Some might say that," Mrs. Chestley said. "Of course, no one is sure, although the mother-in-law intimated her daughter had suffered tremendously. And the rumors — one didn't know whether to believe them or not."

"Well, as noted earlier," Mr. Chestley said, "I have chosen not to believe them."

"That is the Christian thing to do," his wife said. "Still, where there's smoke, one wonders if there's fire, as the saying goes."

"It's none of our business, my dear, and 'tis now in the past. Marguerite died — has it been two years?"

"Two at the turn of the year. I remember leaving the Christmas wreath on the door longer than usual. To give added cheer. The cold winter seemed especially chill after news of her death."

For some moments, the three of them sat quietly.

"I'm sorry, dear." Mrs. Chestley leaned forward, her hand grasping Celia's arm. "I wanted this to be a celebratory meal and instead we've turned it into — well — our dessert ought to change all that." She rose. "Stay seated, Celia. You are the guest of honor tonight. From here on, we'll forget Mr. Lyons, the ripped page, and anything else connected with him."

Returning to the table, Mrs. Chestley held aloft a white cake. A large candle glowed in its center, and she started singing, "We're glad you are here," over and over to a tune of her own making. Her husband joined in as best he could. She set the cake on the tablecloth with a flourish. "I chose a white one with cream frosting to symbolize your youth and freshness. And, of course, the candle represents your light in our lives. Now, to cut it." She handed the first piece to Celia.

Celia looked up at Mrs. Chestley, grateful

33

she was turning the meal into the celebration all of them had looked forward to. She began to feel more lighthearted.

Celia closed her eyes, savoring her first bite of the cake. It was thoroughly moist, the creamy frosting the perfect complement. "If the saying is true the way to a man's heart is through his stomach, this would be just the right finishing touch to any wife's meal."

Mrs. Chestley laughed. "I'll be glad to give away any culinary secrets." She looked over the top of her glasses. "By the way, what is this about a man's heart? Is there a young man in your life?"

A mischievous urge bubbled up in Celia. "Well, Jack from home is an old friend. We've been pals since childhood."

"Any sign of *more than pals*?"

"He was the love of my life in second grade. Of course, he was more interested in tadpoles and fishing."

"Any signs of interest lately?"

"At the last church social, he did come and sit beside me. And he was rather sad to see me leave." Celia contemplated Mrs. Chestley's question. She suddenly wondered if she could possibly be the rose that would get into Jack's blood.

"Sounds as if things might be warming up

a bit." Mrs. Chestley's eyes twinkled. "We'll keep our eye on him. Nothing like the possibility of romance to get the blood racing in these old veins."

"Don't start planning the wedding yet, my dear," Mr. Chestley said. "Celia just arrived. I don't want some young man carrying her off when she just began work. Besides, now that she's come to live with us, I must approve the young man. Only exceptional men need apply. We will have no dealings with mediocrity."

Mr. Chestley savored another mouthful of cake before continuing. "You know, Celia, something's been on my mind for a while. What would you say to starting a book discussion group? Perhaps once a month?"

"Oh! Next to reading, discussing what I've read is one of my favorite pastimes."

"Good. We have that area near the stove where room could be made for a discussion group."

Celia sat straighter. "To get people thinking, on the door we could post the title of the book with a few key questions. And then I could do a presentation about the author. My father always said a book in some way reflects an author's life and thinking."

"Excellent! You see, Mary, I told you she was exceptional." Mr. Chestley put down his fork. "And speaking of exceptional, Mary my girl, we will have to give you a blue ribbon for this dessert."

"Would you like another piece?" Mrs. Chestley reached for the knife.

"I would love it, but I'm portly enough."

"The more to squeeze, my dear. You're so very comfortable to put one's arms around."

Mr. Chestley's mouth twisted into a deprecatory smile. "Ha! I don't believe my new assistant is accustomed to such talk. You must forgive us, Celia. My wife and I are alone so much, we get rather free with one another." His smile widened. "But I think it's also a tribute to how comfortable we are around you."

He stretched his arms over his head. "This feels good after that big meal."

"Well!" Mrs. Chestley rose suddenly. "Celia, would you please help me clear the dessert dishes? And then you may dry while I wash. You and I need a little time together after my husband retires to the sitting room."

She picked up the dinnerware. "I want to hear more about this young man back home. My mother always said doing dishes provided one of the best times to talk with her children." She smiled. "Now, I have an opportunity to put to use all that good wisdom from Mother."

# 3

Mrs. Divers heard her front door open and with difficulty rose from her easy chair. This arthritis was such a bother. She shuffled out of the sitting room.

"Miss Waul! I'm glad you're back." A shiver coursed through her. The outside air had chilled the entry with Miss Waul's entrance. Mrs. Divers tightened the shawl around her as Miss Waul took off her heavy coat and placed it on the coat tree. "Did you get my book?"

"Oh, yes." Miss Waul leaned over to get it from her carryall.

"Then let's go right to the sitting room where it's warm. I'm beholden to you for going to the bookstore tonight."

Mrs. Divers lowered herself slowly into the stuffed chair by the fire, and then thumbed through the volume. How tempted she was to begin reading right now, but since her companion had gone to all that trouble, she would wait to start it after she retired for the night.

"Here, let me stoke up the fire a bit." Miss Waul took up the poker. "Would you believe I found the book in quite a different spot? Completely out of alphabetical order."

"Well, Mr. Chestley is getting older. I guess he can't be expected to get everything right." Mrs. Divers reached up and repositioned a loose hairpin in her bun.

"But he has help now. A young lady."

"Oh?"

"Yes. Looks the quiet type." Miss Waul put the poker back and plumped down into the horsehair chair on the opposite side of the fireplace. "She appears bright enough, though."

"Goodness knows, not a bluestocking, I hope. A woman like that can be downright irritating."

"She doesn't look at all bookish. In fact, she's very pretty."

"Pretty?" Mrs. Divers's interest picked up.

"Yes, her hair strikes you right away, wheat-colored and braided fancy-like. Wound at the back of her head in a sort of chignon." Miss Waul put her hand up to her hair. "I might try wearing my braid back like hers. Make my face appear less round, you know, instead of circling my head."

"Don't be silly. Your arrangement is nice and sensible. I don't want you changing on me."

"You don't think I should try something new?" Miss Waul eyed Mrs. Divers with a pleading look, then after a moment shrugged her broad shoulders. "Well, whatever you say — but I fancy the girl's hair would be like a sheaf of wheat when down, real pretty like. And you should see her lips. Red as a rose." Her lips suppressed a smirk. "Didn't know I could be poetic, did you? — but I wonder if she doesn't color them." Miss Waul smoothed her skirt. "That one won't have trouble getting a man. Finding a good one around here is the problem. If she wasn't dressed so properly in that dark brown, I'd say she looked a bit of a hussy."

"Miss Waul!"

Miss Waul tittered. "The old maid coming out in me, I guess."

"You're not old yet."

"But past my prime, I'm sure. Why, see how my hair has begun to gray these last years." She paused, then cast a pointed look at Mrs. Divers. "Worrying over Marguerite."

"Marguerite?" Sorrow or anger rose up in Mrs. Divers — she wasn't sure which. Perhaps it was both.

"Well, yes. You know she was one to need

lots of attention. 'Course she didn't get much from us after she married, but before that she took a lot."

"What do you mean?" Mrs. Divers's lips set firmly. "What would somebody expect with her so delicate? I didn't spoil her, mind you!"

"I didn't mean to say you did." Miss Waul's shoulders heaved a sigh. "But I miss her."

"Yes, my heart aches, even yet." Mrs. Divers plucked at her shawl, drawing it closer round her shoulders. "Our one and only. It hasn't been two years. I can't forgive that man!"

"I know. Well, I did the new girl one favor. Warned her away from him."

"*He* was in the bookstore?"

"Yes. Came in while I was trying to find your book. He slunk back in the shelving as soon as he saw me. Like the snake he is."

"Not a snake, Miss Waul." Mrs. Divers felt her ire rise. "A grizzly is more like it."

"A grizzly?"

"Yes, a big grizzly bear. They're unpredictable, you know. Come at you without warning." Her arthritic fingers gripped the chair arms. "He was cruel to our Marguerite, Miss Waul. We must never forget that. If I have anything to say about it, he'll never be

41

happy again."

"He seemed none too happy tonight, so comfort yourself in that. His hair's grown out like a bush. A body can't even see his face."

"Ashamed he is."

"I hear he goes around at night. Never notice him during the day."

"Good! The few times I do get out, I don't want to see him. Just thinking of him makes me —"

"Now, don't upset yourself, Mrs. Divers. You've had enough of that man for a lifetime. Must put him out of your mind."

"How can I, when he lives so near? Whenever I leave our home, I don't even look off to the left for fear of seeing his house through the trees." Mrs. Divers shuddered. "If I'd ever suspected my dear girl would have such a hard time with him, I'd have taken her away — far away, even though I've lived here for years. Yes, I would have." Tears started clouding her vision.

"Calm yourself, Mrs. Divers. Please! Here, use my hanky. I shouldn't have brought him up. The whole business is painful to us both." Miss Waul hoisted herself up from the large chair. "I'm going to get some milk for you now. Good, warm, calming milk."

Mrs. Divers dabbed at her eyes. Drat! Her nose was runny. She dabbed at it, too.

"Now, give your nose a good blow," admonished Miss Waul.

"Oh, I hate sounding like an old goose. I've got a terrible honk."

"I know that. But it makes no difference. If you can't feel comfortable with me — after all we've been through together —" Miss Waul leaned over and gave Mrs. Divers an awkward little hug.

Mrs. Divers realized, for maybe the hundredth time, how Miss Waul could comfort a soul. "Maybe you need some milk, too. You've been out in the cold this evening."

"Thank you, Mum. That would be nice."

Celia stepped outside the bookstore to better inspect the display window. She'd substituted a gold-colored cloth in place of the off-white fabric as a backdrop. This looked richer against the red and black covered books. Arranging items in an artistic manner satisfied something deep within her.

She turned to enjoy the outdoors for a few moments. Though the sun had set, the air was still comfortable, the Indian summer keeping it balmy. Even in this dusky light, the maples in front of the shops across the street showed brilliant red, and beyond them glowed golden yellow sassafras. A slightly acrid, pungent scent wafted in with the slight breeze. How she loved autumn. With all the activity of summer gone, she would have more time to read.

Farther down the street, lamps burned brightly in little houses, hinting at quiet activity within. Tied to a white picket fence, a chestnut horse stood quietly. Celia watched as two boys scuffled up the street, stopped near the horse, and crouched. She wondered why they weren't already home. Their mothers would be fixing supper.

Mrs. Chestley was sure to be doing so. Celia anticipated gathering around the evening table. The meal might be simple, sometimes only johnnycakes and warm milk with sugar sprinkled on top, and a piece of cheese with tea. But the company would be delightful.

Afterward the Chestleys and she might go for a walk. The three of them made an agreeable little group. Once, she'd gone by herself. They had smiled their approval, but told her to keep to nearby streets.

Celia enjoyed walking by herself. Though she loved being with family and friends, she could think more clearly and notice things better without the distraction of conversation shuttling back and forth.

44

*Bang!*

Celia startled. The loud report had come from the direction of the horse. His hooves pawed up the dust as he tried to back off from the fence where he was tethered.

*Bang! Bang! Bang!* A series of loud explosions pierced the air. The boys rose and started to run.

Snorting, the terrified horse tried to rear up. The fence shook. He backed off, kicking up dust.

Out of nowhere, a large man crossed the boys' path and rushed to the frightened animal. Just as he reached the struggling horse, the wood of the fence cracked and the reins snapped from their moorings. As the leather straps whirled through the air, the big man caught them.

The animal lunged, trying to bolt, but the man braced himself, holding the bridle fast, compelling the horse to quiet. The horse reared again, but the moment the hooves descended, the man grabbed its mane.

Celia watched, hardly realizing she held her breath.

The horse circled its backside around to better swing its head away from the man trying to master it. But the man hung close, forcing the horse to calm, gentling the animal with his voice.

45

Two men ran out of the house, but stopped short at the gate as the man jerked his head, cautioning them to stay away while he soothed the horse. Celia couldn't hear distinct words, but she could see they had a wonderfully calming effect.

Reaching up to give the horse a final caress, the man finally held out the reins to the horse's owner.

Celia watched the men step out the gate and shake hands. The big man pointed to the spot where the boys had crouched. What had they been about?

Finally, her breath began returning to normal. How fortunate the terrified horse had been calmed — but only thanks to the gentleman who acted decisively, so quickly. And with such strength.

At that moment, he separated from the other men and started walking in the direction of the bookstore. Celia slipped inside, hoping she hadn't been noticed. Thankfully, the incident had happened quite a ways down the street.

But how unexpected. She had thought to enjoy the tranquil night air, but the incident had frightened her, reminded her of — she shook her head as if to dismiss the picture that came to mind.

Bending over to pick up the pile of books

she'd removed from the window, she decided to go to the back of the store. She would calm her emotions by returning to everyday chores.

She clasped the books close as she walked. Later, she would display the books at advantageous spots around the store, giving the public another opportunity to see the newest offerings. But for the moment she'd spread them on a small table in the rear of the store, near an easy chair.

The bell on the door jangled. Slowly, but purposefully, she walked back through the stacks to see who entered. As she rounded the end of a large bookcase near the front door, she saw Mr. Lyons.

Mr. Lyons! Her stomach did a turn. Now she recognized his large figure in the light of the store. So he was the big man who quieted the frightened horse. She debated what to say, then said, "Outside — I saw what happened. You came in the nick of time."

He acknowledged her comment with a nod.

What were those boys doing? She had to ask. "Those loud bangs —"

"Firecrackers. Probably left over from the Centennial celebration. Pure mischief, especially around a horse."

"Certainly!" She swallowed, calmness still eluding her. "Firecrackers — the Fourth a short time ago — yes. How fortunate you were nearby. I had visions of a runaway horse bolting past me, with me unable to do anything, and I was absolutely rooted to the spot. But you seemed to know just what to do."

"My grandparents kept horses at their summer place. I grew up riding as a boy." A ghost of a smile turned up the corners of his mouth.

That seemed a happy memory. Celia felt her equilibrium returning. A moment of comfortable silence passed between them. "So, may I help you?" she offered.

He glanced in the direction of the window display. "Earlier, I noticed a book in the window. It's not there anymore."

"I placed the books on the back table. What was its title?"

"That's all right. I'll browse through the lot of them." He turned and strode into the nearest stacks.

Celia looked in surprise at the disappearing figure, puzzled by his sudden departure. She had felt a sympathy between them those few moments. The mention of his grandparents' summer home, and she had to admit, the incident with the horse seemed to have eased any feelings of constraint caused by the damaged Tennyson. But now she wasn't so sure. Her ears strained to hear what he was doing. Mrs. Chestley had been right: he was assuredly a curious sort.

She heard a rustling of pages and wondered which book had caught his fancy.

Sometime later, he approached the counter and set down a volume.

Celia's eyes flicked to it. Washington Irving's *Tales of a Traveller.*

Before she could comment, he reached into his pocket for the money. "The Plato I bought last time had good print. Very readable."

"I'm glad it suited."

"I think that's the correct change." His long fingers put an additional nickel on the counter.

"Thank you." She deposited the money into the metal box under the counter, then looked up at the bushy visage. "I'm sorry again, about the Tennyson."

"No need to say anything more. I've put it behind me."

How quickly he'd forgiven. Not like herself with Trudy. She felt ashamed, then quickly rallied. He was obviously a man to know better, and undoubtedly had a fine mind. She wondered if she dared ask his opinion, then plunged ahead. "Do you have a favorite passage or poem from Tennyson? One especially meaningful?"

He looked at her sharply as if unwilling to say, then finally quoted,

But the tender grace of a day that is dead
Will never come back to me.

She hadn't expected that selection. "Is that from — ?"

"Break, Break, Break."

"A rather sad thought." She wondered if it had to do with his wife's death. But plainly, this man and she both had experienced the death of someone dear. Her heart went out to him.

His eyebrow raised. "Nevertheless true. It is a boon how great poems, like great books, express one's thinking so well."

"A good book is like a friend in that regard." She smiled at the pleasant association. "I have many such friends."

"That is fortunate, although I imagine you have friends of flesh and blood as well."

"Thank you." A compliment from an unlikely source. For a moment, she scrutinized the bristly face across the counter and considered the scrap of poem he shared. Surely, there was more to this man than most people saw or understood.

He turned to leave.

Suddenly she felt moved to ask, "Did you see the flyer?"

He turned back. "The one on the door?"

"Yes, Mr. Chestley posted it last night. He's wanted to start a book discussion for some time. I hope that we'll attract a nice group for the evening. And some good insights from those who attend."

"I don't know if people here will provide much lively discussion. Most think alike."

"I thought *one* person might challenge our thinking."

He didn't reply, but observed her with thoughtful eyes.

"At least, my impression when I first met you — that we were quite at odds on how we viewed things."

"Did I say as much?"

"It was what you didn't say."

"Ah . . ." A glint of amusement shone from his eyes.

"You are coming?"

"I'm not sure."

The bell jangled. A well-dressed woman paused inside, then headed straight for the counter.

With some alacrity, Mr. Lyons turned to leave.

The woman flashed him a look of approval. "Mr. Lyons!"

He gave her the barest of nods.

She watched him swing open the door and turned to Celia. "My, that man is always in a hurry."

Celia had met Mrs. Adams only once, and now the widow's eyes were alive with interest. The woman smiled confidentially. "I saw your flyer on the door. I hope you invited *him*. It's about time he rejoined society."

# 4

Mr. Chestley stepped outside the bookstore, looking first one way down the street, then the other. Shops stood closed, but a bright light shone from his own store as a welcome. Four people had already gathered for the literary meeting. A nice *select* group, he would term it, but he was hoping for a few more.

That afternoon he had rounded up twelve chairs. He tried first one arrangement then another, fussing like a mother hen he supposed. The space didn't afford much room for variation, but he finally settled on two semi-circles of six with a small table and chair at the front for the discussion leader. He himself would begin the meeting then ask Celia to give a presentation of the author.

Ah! The widow Adams was approaching from the left. Undoubtedly, this was her destination. As he greeted her on the step,

53

he noted she looked particularly well, the bloom of youth had returned to her cheeks. The Harrods rounded the corner from their fashionable street. The lawyer and his stylish wife would certainly add to the occasion. And there was Celia, coming up the road with that little old lady she befriended last week. What was her name? She walked with a cane and seemed a quiet, shy sort of person. Mrs. Smith. Yes, he remembered now. That would make eleven with his wife and himself. Just one chair remained for a latecomer.

Mr. Chestley rubbed his hands together. As he let his breath out in a satisfied sigh, a white puff accentuated the nip in the night air. The little gathering looked to be a solid success. He stood another minute welcoming each arrival, and when the Harrods neared the bookstore, stepped down to greet them.

After closing the door, he approached the semi-circles. Celia was seating the elderly woman beside Miss Waul, who said in a loud whisper, "I came tonight in place of Mrs. Divers. She's a great reader, you know, and would have liked to come, but her arthritis is acting up. 'I should stay home and take care of you,' I told her. But no, she wanted to know how the meeting went and

I am to report back."

"I hope this evening lives up to your expectations," Celia said.

"I'm sure it will, I'm sure it will." Miss Waul's ruddy cheeks accentuated her wide smile.

Mr. Chestley gazed over the group, his hands clasped behind him. "We're about to begin. I hope everyone is comfortable." He smiled. The store door opened once again. He could not see the door from where he stood, so waited patiently for the newcomer to appear. Then he nodded as the person slipped into the vacant chair in the back. A soft gasp sounded from Miss Waul.

"Welcome, everyone," Mr. Chestley said. "We are pleased you came to discuss Hawthorne's *The Scarlet Letter*. When I mentioned the possibility of a book discussion group to my new assistant, she seconded the idea. For those of you who haven't met her, let me introduce Miss Celia Thatcher." He nodded in her direction. "Her family comes from a long line of distinguished scholars. I've asked her to introduce the author and indicate how his life influenced his writing. Afterward, I'll pose questions I hope elicit an interesting discussion. Now, Miss Celia Thatcher."

Celia felt the deft little pat Mrs. Chestley

55

leaned over to give her and glanced to see the proud look in the older woman's eyes. Mrs. Chestley had helped her choose the dark skirt and cream-colored blouse for the evening, deemed the long, flowing bow down her front "just right." Mrs. Chestley also insisted on fixing her hair into a knot of curls in the back where a braid usually coiled.

Celia approached the table, notes in hand. More nervous than expected, she kept her eyes fastened on the bookcase in back. "It is interesting —" she cleared her throat, "— how an author's writing flows out of his thinking, his life experience.

"This is no less true of Nathanial Hawthorne. A striking aspect of his early years was his solitary life. He once said to his friend Longfellow, 'I have seen so little of the world that I have nothing but thin air to concoct my stories of.' "

Celia smiled. "Surely, this is an exaggeration. Rather, I submit the reflective quality of his life helped him make the most of what he saw and experienced. He delved beneath the surface of people's lives to show us the workings of the human will and heart. Why?" She paused to let the question sink in. "So that we might better see our own."

She went on to describe Nathanial Hawthorne's background.

Not having dared to look over the group, Celia had concentrated instead on what she was saying. Now, however, she stopped to examine those assembled in the two semi-circles. Her eyes were immediately drawn to the place where the latecomer had seated himself. The large frame of Mr. Lyons sat somewhat apart from the others; apparently, he had moved his chair. But he had come after all.

She turned back to her notes. "As it says in the gospel of Matthew: 'For out of the abundance of the heart the mouth speaketh.' I believe we can paraphrase this author's life: 'Out of the abundance of his inner experience, his pen speaks.' " She finished her comments and resumed her seat.

Mr. Chestley stood. "Thank you, Celia. That was most enlightening. Most of us don't see so direct a connection between the author and his work. But even if a reader doesn't know anything of Hawthorne's life, the beauty and power of this novel is apparent to anyone giving it a careful reading. Let us now discuss key elements of the story and its characters."

He lowered himself into the chair by the table. "Now, would anyone care to give us a brief summary of the story?"

A silence followed, one glancing covertly at another. Mrs. Chestley looked around, then said, "I will." Sitting a little taller in her chair, her dark amethyst dress setting off her silver hair, she told of the young woman, Hester Prynne, giving birth out of wedlock in the old Puritan community of Boston. As punishment, Hester had to wear a large scarlet A on the breast of her dress.

Mr. Chestley said, "It's interesting, isn't it, that the author chooses to not say much about the adultery itself, but instead dwells on how this sin affected the four main characters in the story. Which character do you feel was most severely affected?"

Miss Waul raised her hand. "To me, it's pretty obvious it would be Hester Prynne. After all, she had to live outside of the community and wear the scarlet letter the rest of her life."

Mr. Chestley next acknowledged Mr. Harrod.

"That may be true," the lawyer said, "but the woman in question had salved her conscience by an open admission of guilt. The one who really suffered was the Rev. Mr. Dimmesdale. Because of his revered place in the community, he couldn't bring himself to confess being the child's father. That transgression continually gnawed at

him, especially when members of his congregation told him they thought him a
saint."

"But —" Miss Waul interjected — "I think
he deserved to suffer. Think of the child
who didn't have a father and wanted one.
The Rev. Dimmesdale was selfish to think
more of his position in the community than
the needs of his own child, not to speak of
the shame Hester endured standing alone
on the scaffold before the community."

"Talking of selfishness," added Mrs. Harrod, "one might think of Hester's husband,
Mr. Chillingworth. He was a lot older than
she, ugly, and added to the minister's grief
by trying to unearth the child's father and
constantly referring to the sin. I think if
we're going to talk about selfishness, it
began there."

"I think now it all goes back to Mr. Chillingworth," Miss Waul said. "He should have
never persuaded the lovely Hester to marry
him." She turned to look at Mr. Lyons.

Celia felt an uncomfortable silence settle
in the room. She searched for something to
say, and finally asked, "Yet even with all this,
don't we find a symbol of hope in the story?
In the form of a flower?" The room remained quiet, but Celia could see the
group's attention steered in a new direc-

tion. Mrs. Harrod was the first to speak.

"Might you be referring to the wild rose outside the prison?"

"Yes," Celia said. "Do you all remember how the beauty of this flower struck a contrast with the gloomy prison and its surrounding weeds? That brings up the question, why do you think Hawthorne included the rose in his story?"

Several in the group started to speak at the same time. Relieved, Celia could see the discussion was off and running again.

After everyone left, Mr. Chestley said to his wife, "The discussion ended on a happy note. Leave it to Celia."

"She is lovely, stood out so amongst us oldies. I overheard Mrs. Harrod say she thought Celia is like the wild rose of the story, bringing beauty into any gathering. Mrs. Harrod invited her over for lunch next week." A little crease formed between her eyes. "You know, Celia was the only young person present."

"Well now, I wouldn't call Mr. Lyons old. He's — what would you say, in his forties?"

"Oh, no!" His wife laughed. "That growth of beard makes him look older. That, and his serious demeanor. He's middle to late thirties."

"And there's Mrs. Adams. I believe she's about his age."

"True," agreed his wife. "In fact, I noticed them talking together after the discussion. The way she leaned toward him, I could tell she was very interested in what he was saying." A little laugh exploded out of her. "I never thought of this before, but do you think they might make a couple?"

"Mrs. Chestley! You and your romantic notions."

"Did you notice how beautifully she was dressed? She could help him with his appearance. I think he needs a wife."

"Well, he didn't stay long after that."

"No. But still, I hope he appreciated the discussion."

"I think so," Mr. Chestley said. "A man gets hungry for stimulating talk."

"I feel rather sorry for him. I hope he comes again."

"But he won't be forced. He has a stubborn streak, as strong as that imposing physique of his. You know how Boston Brahmins are. Maybe that was . . ."

"Was what?" Mrs. Chestley caught her husband's arm.

"It just occurred to me — maybe that was Marguerite's trouble, pressing him where she shouldn't have —" He shook his head.

"Well, let's not gossip."

Mrs. Chestley wrinkled up her nose. "But it's so much fun talking about him. He's such an interesting man."

"There's more to him than meets the eye. If only people in this town could see that. Most never gave him half a chance."

"He hasn't helped by holing up the way he does."

"True. Maybe in some ways he's not the wisest of men. Somewhat of a mystery as well. I hope Celia gave him something to think about tonight. If there's anyone that could pierce that hard hide of his, I think it's our little girl."

"Don't give her too big a job, Mr. Chestley. She's young and such a dear. She needs to enjoy life."

"And not get mixed up with the town hermit." Mr. Chestley placed his forefinger on his wife's lips. "Now, we won't talk any more about him. Even if it's the most interesting tidbit in our neck of the woods. And don't scrunch up your nose at me again, Mrs. Chestley. It's far too pretty."

# 5

For a moment Edward Lyons sat back and gazed at his library. Books with their dark red and brown leathers and the occasional green or blue warmed the walls of the room. The heart of his home, he would say. Gazing at the rows of volumes brought the bookstore sharply to mind — with its discussion of *The Scarlet Letter.* Attending the affair last night had been out of the ordinary for him.

What had Miss Thatcher said about Hawthorne? Something about his delving beneath the surface of people's lives to show their hearts, so that we might better see our own? Hang that Miss Waul, turning to look at him when she said Chillingworth should have never married the lovely Hester.

Why had he gone to the book discussion in the first place? That day he had gone about his habitual activities, dressing and dining as usual with no real intention of attending, but with the thought at the back of his mind, all the same. He knew what this new venture meant to Mr. Chestley who had been his quiet, staunch supporter these last hard years.

Considering this, he had decided to bestir himself. He would go for his old friend. And, he had to admit, a glimmer of curiosity existed for Miss Thatcher, how she would conduct herself and what she would bring to the discussion. When it came down to it, he was interested to hear someone's thoughts besides his own. Miss Thatcher had shown a vigorous turn of mind at their first meeting.

But he would be the last to arrive. If no seat were available, he would stand unnoticed behind the gathering. However, a chair was open on the back row. Too late, he noticed Miss Waul a few seats over, and her startled look at him. He had moved the chair then turned slightly so as to keep her from his peripheral vision.

A soft, but peremptory knock sounded at the library door.

For some moments he sat in silence.

The knock repeated. This time slower and more deliberate.

Finally he said, "Yes?"

His housekeeper, Mrs. Macon, appeared.

A thin, almost gaunt woman, but capable nonetheless. She remained in the doorway.

Perversely, now that she appeared, he felt impatience rise. This was a fine state of affairs, trying to talk across the length of the room.

He gestured to the spot directly in front of his desk.

She approached quietly, but it was clear from her demeanor she had business to discuss, business that could not wait.

"What is it?" He let his voice have just enough edge to communicate his displeasure at being interrupted.

She smoothed her apron. "Sorry to bother you, sir. But remember you told me to avail myself of any herbs from the greenhouse? Well, when I entered this morning I noticed one of the windowpanes broken. Like a ball had gone through it." She looked at him expectantly. "At the back."

"When did you discover this?"

"Just now, sir."

"Do you have any idea who did this?"

"No. However, I do have my suspicions." She pursed her thin lips. "You know that boy who used to come here occasionally —"

"What boy?"

"Dark brown hair. Ten or eleven. Goes by the name of Loydie. Our neighbor, Mrs. D

— would occasionally send over things with him while your wife was alive. He's a mischief maker."

"I remember your saying something of the sort." Edward frowned. "I'll take a look at the greenhouse to see what can be done. Thank you."

She turned to cross the room and soundlessly closed the door.

He settled back into his chair, looking around the room again, his sanctum where he escaped everyone — even his housekeeper, except today. Mrs. Macon had learned to do her cleaning when he went out for a walk. For a good many years, no one had set foot in his library except Mrs. Harrod's father. Now, there was a man who appreciated a good library. That reminded him of the quote he wanted from the Plato.

He wheeled around in his study chair, and turned the key to his glassed-in bookcase, home to his most valued collection. The Plato rested there, right beside the Tennyson. He extracted the desired book and placed it on his desk.

Sitting up in his chair, he leafed through it. His finger located the passage he needed for his article, "And this, O men of Athens, is the truth and the whole truth; I have concealed nothing, I have dissembled nothing. And yet, I know that *my plainness of speech* makes them hate me . . ." He copied the last of the quote. He'd ask his friend at the Athenaeum in Boston if this article would suit *Harper's Monthly Magazine.*

Hmm . . . he stroked his beard . . . some in this town would say Plato's defense applied to himself. Maybe that was why he seldom spoke his mind nowadays. They didn't want to hear an opposing opinion. Yes, he'd kept quiet, all because of —

Suddenly, he closed the Plato and rose. Strode out his study door, down the hall, and snatched an old coat at the kitchen door.

He circled the greenhouse. There it was — a large hole toward the back. He would place a blanket over it for the time being. He didn't want his prize plants threatened with the cold nights they'd been having lately. His handyman could take care of the window.

Involuntarily he glanced at his neighbor's property. What had his housekeeper said about his old mother-in-law sending things over with a boy? It'd be like her to send over a mischief-maker.

He turned on his heel. After his marriage, the woman had been trouble from the start. The old screech owl. He should have heeded the inner prompting when he first heard her shriek at the household help. She had been quick to recover, and he never heard her speak in such a way again — until after he married.

Why had he married Marguerite? She was beautiful. Snow-white complexion with dark, curly hair. He'd let her lovely features fool him into thinking her more than she was. And then how quickly he tired of her.

Just days after the wedding, the rude awakening erupted. Marguerite wanted her way, and let him know it in no uncertain terms. She was her own mistress and there was her mother to back her up. Next door, no less.

He jerked open the door to the greenhouse. After that, his marriage became one harsh jolt after another. He'd felt it to the depth of his soul.

The faint smell of earth and luxuriant plant growth met him as he stepped inside, fragrance to his earth loving soul. He made his way between the plants to the new tea rose bushes at the back. The offending ball had bent one of the canes. He stooped for the ball, then rested the wounded branch over a thicker, stronger one.

Ball in hand, he opened the kitchen door, but Mrs. Macon was nowhere in sight. Placing the ball on the counter, he was half a mind to march over to Mrs. Divers and demand an explanation, ask the identity of the boy. Do something.

The other half told him he was in no frame of mind to see to her at the moment. He would undoubtedly say things he'd regret.

He needed to regain his composure.

Sitting down again at his desk, he took up the Plato. The book still had the pleasing smell of new leather. He felt its fine grain. Handling the book reminded him of that first night he saw it in the bookstore window.

And the fair-haired woman inside.

Instinctively he'd withdrawn from her — despite her beauty — or maybe because of it. He remembered feeling — fear? Or was it anger at having a stranger enter his world at the bookstore?

But Miss Thatcher had proved herself different from the start. She hadn't come seeking him in the store when he sat browsing through a few books. He remembered his relief at being left alone in peace. He sensed her respect for his maturity and learning.

That first night, when she had ripped the page in his Tennyson, his blood was up. He was going to demand she order a new book. But then he saw in her eyes a look that brought him up short, a look that she understood. Oh, yes, there was chagrin, more than a little. But she also felt *for him,* aware of how it felt to have a treasure damaged. He'd never seen that in his wife. He wondered if he'd ever seen it in his mother. That spark of understanding had turned his intention, so when Mr. Chestley arrived on the scene, he found he couldn't make the girl's way harder. He wanted to make it easier, so he'd made an about-face.

Still, her fingers had trembled wrapping his package. She had feared him a little, despite her brave words. But, after all, hadn't he wanted to be feared — and left alone?

His mind darted back to the previous evening. He could not say, even now, why he had spoken during the book discussion, in fact, beforehand had decided not to, though he knew Miss Thatcher would expect it. Was it Miss Thatcher and her introduction of the author that had stirred him? He had felt his interest awaken in discovering how Hawthorne's early life had influenced his writing.

So, late in the discussion he found himself speaking, impulsively entering the fray, if fray might describe so decorous a gathering. Only a few words. Yet for him, it had seemed a fray — so much had he kept to himself these last years. The town had all but ostracized him. But then, Mrs. Adams had caught him just as he was leaving and engaged him in conversation. That was kind of her. And she had given him her full attention. Yes, very kind of her.

He looked up and stared unseeing across his study. His present life had a dark tone — like the overriding darkness in *The Scarlet Letter.* If Miss Thatcher had been there alone, he might have brought up the point. Later she talked of the terrible isolation guilt imposed, and the resulting dark thoughts. Something had stirred in him, but he'd refused to examine it. Even now as words started resurfacing, he downed them. He would think of something more pleasant in the story.

The rose, for instance. He sat back, deep in his chair, tenting his fingers. Miss Thatcher had drawn a picture of the rose's beauty and how it contrasted with the gloomy prison and its weeds. Her words had awakened in him a desire for beauty to come back into his life. Beauty in one form or another.

The other week in the bookstore, they had talked of friends. He had Plato, Tennyson, many others. Even Darby at the Athenaeum.

But might there be something more?

Hadn't Miss Thatcher said the rose lived, flowered, even flourished amid dark circumstances? He thought of his darkened life, ostracized from the town. Yet, the widow Mrs. Adams had showed him kindness. Was the tide about to turn?

Such a rose, could it be his? Could such beauty enter his life? The smallest of hopes began to stir within him.

Celia knocked on Mrs. Divers's door. Mr. Chestley had given her directions. This house sat off by itself, white with black shutters. It had to be the one.

The door opened and Miss Waul appeared. "Well, Miss Thatcher, what a pleasant surprise."

"I found this scarf in the bookstore last night and wondered if it was yours."

Miss Waul looked at it. "It's certainly the same color, but I have mine here hanging on the coat tree. You are most kind to ask."

"Who's at the door?" a querulous voice asked from inside.

Miss Waul looked back inside the house. "Miss Thatcher from the bookstore."

"Well, invite her in. Invite her in!"

"Of course. Do you have a few minutes, Miss Thatcher?"

"I don't think Mr. Chestley would mind."

"Please!" Miss Waul held the door open wide. "Let me take your coat."

A minute later, Celia settled herself into an overstuffed chair. The adjective certainly applied to the parlor furniture with its amply upholstered chairs and sofa. Knick-knacks sat on doilies, filling every available nook and cranny.

"Now set a pillow for her back, Miss Waul," Mrs. Divers instructed. "Something firm. My, you seem such a mite in that chair, Miss Thatcher. I hadn't realized you were so reed-like."

"But a very graceful reed," Miss Waul said.

"Of course, of course. You look every bit as lovely as my companion here described."

"What a nice thing to say."

"I'm sorry I didn't get to your book discussion. My arthritis, you know. But Miss Waul told me all about it."

Celia smiled at Miss Waul. "I hope you enjoyed the discussion. *The Scarlet Letter,* for its short length, provokes a lot of thought."

"I certainly did. Mrs. Divers and I were discussing it a while ago. I told her that Chillingworth was my least favorite character."

"Mine, too."

Mrs. Divers harrumphed. "I wouldn't have thought a beauty like Hester would marry an old wizened man like him."

"At least he realized the mismatch, if too late. Remember what he said? 'Mine was the first wrong, when I betrayed thy budding youth into a false and unnatural relation with my decay.' But then to compound the misfortune, after their marriage he spent most of his time in his study, not doing his duty as a husband."

"Reminds me of someone else I know," Mrs. Divers said.

Miss Waul's hand went to her mouth. "Oh! I hadn't thought of that."

Mrs. Divers nodded triumphantly to her companion before turning to Celia. "Forgive us, my dear, just a little private observation. So we're all in agreement about Chillingworth. Now, what did you think about —"

For the next quarter hour, they discussed the book and its characters. Celia looked from one woman to the other. These two seemed to love literature as she did. Could they be soul mates?

"The child Pearl was my favorite. Puts me in mind of my own daughter," Mrs. Divers said.

"I don't know about your daughter," Celia said, "but while the child Pearl was a fair sprite and her mother loved her, the little girl was still an anguish to her."

"As mine was to me, Miss Thatcher, as mine was to me —" Mrs. Divers stopped, seeming to lapse into reverie. Celia hesitated and looked to Miss Waul for help.

Miss Waul caught the look. "Yes, Miss. Marguerite was the apple of her mother's eye, that she was. And beautiful, too. So beautiful she caught many a man's eye. But it was our neighbor, Mr. —" she dropped her voice — "Mr. Lyons, who finally got her."

At the mention of the name, Mrs. Divers bestirred herself and blurted out, "My Marguerite suited him just fine before they were married. But after the knot was tied, it was a different story. And he let her know it. Oh, it was a sad affair, Miss Thatcher, a sad affair."

Celia wondered if she should try to redirect the conversation into other avenues.

"Marguerite was bright, sensitive — but delicate of health — that's why I encouraged the marriage. I could see Mr. Lyons was big and strong. And rich. He would take care of her. But she was bright only those early months, then her brightness began to fade, especially after that first year. I didn't see her much after that. Why he'd hardly let her out of the house. He was severe, Miss Thatcher. He was that severe!"

Celia looked to Miss Waul for confirmation or help, she didn't know which — but had she had it all wrong? Apparently, Mr. Lyons wasn't grieving for his wife after all. He was — how had she so misunderstood the situation?

Miss Waul rose and smoothed Mrs. Divers's hand. "Now, we're getting ourselves all worked up. And here we invite Miss Thatcher in and don't even offer her some refreshment."

Mrs. Divers roused herself. "You must forgive me, my dear, going off on a tangent like that. I missed the discussion at the bookstore, and you being so kind to bring it right here into my parlor, yes, most kind. And tea, yes, let's have some tea. That would be the very thing."

Miss Waul saw Celia to the front hall. "I'm sorry we got into all that, Miss Thatcher. But you see how this family has suffered." She handed Celia her coat. "I'll accompany you to the road. I'd like to stretch my legs a bit."

As they stepped out on the porch, Celia looked off to the left. She'd noticed a large house showing through the trees on her arrival.

Miss Waul took hold of the hand railing and carefully let herself down each step. "That's Edward Lyons's house. You see how near he is. When my mistress leaves the house she shields her face with her hand, doesn't even like to glimpse it. Now with the leaves falling, a body can see it quite well. Otherwise, during the summer, the trees hide it."

Celia tried to say something noncommittal. "It must be a cool, shady place during hot days."

"Yes, except there's a large spot in the back cleared of trees. Sunny for a garden. I hear he grows flowers. Our little Loydie says he's never seen so much color. Doesn't seem like a man that somber would have a garden." She stopped at the road. "I haven't been in the back, just up to the front door, like most people. Well now, you be careful on your way home." Miss Waul waved her off and turned back to the house.

Celia couldn't help be curious about Mr. Lyons's house, but took care not to seem to do so, allowing herself only a few glances. The dark-red brick structure had steep roofs and gables with trim and window casements of forest green. Evergreen shrubs and landscaping were tastefully laid out — what one could see of them. The whole front had a rather dark aspect, however. Like its owner?

But he had a flower garden. That was a surprise. She loved flowers, her one passion besides books and reading. What kind of blooms would he favor? If he was as interested in flowers as in books, he might have interesting varieties. Maybe some that were rare.

She quickened her pace to the bookstore. But how had he treated his wife? What Mrs. Divers said sounded threatening. Yet, he had been kind to her regarding the Tennyson.

What should she think? The man was a living oxymoron. A person with such a severe streak who loves flowers? And when she thought of that hulk of a man tending delicate blooms, what an unlikely picture *that* presented.

# 6

Celia lifted the linen cover. "These rolls smell heavenly." The warm yeasty aroma reminded her of home.

"My cook is a master baker," Mrs. Harrod said. "Take more than one. Your figure can well afford it. And remind me to send some to the Chestleys."

"I wouldn't dream of disappointing your cook." Celia laughed.

"You are a woman after my own heart."

Mrs. Harrod's sunny expression lifted Celia's expectations for the luncheon. They were already high from the moment she entered the large, graciously furnished Tudor house. When ushered into the conservatory with its multitude of yellow and burnt orange mums amid the lush green plants, she felt positively sunny as Mrs. Harrod introduced her to members of the Floral Society. Each lady wore a hat with a flower pinned to its brim. Mrs. Harrod had set a table for eight in her spacious conservatory.

Mrs. Adams leaned over to Celia. "Your book discussion came off famously."

"You are very kind." Celia's heart warmed at the thought of that enjoyable evening.

Mrs. Adams took a bite of salad before continuing. "I was so glad my friend Mrs. Harrod attended. And I suspect she invited you today because you, too, have a particular interest in flowers —"

"Of course," Mrs. Harrod interrupted, "I suspected Miss Thatcher cherished a strong attachment the way she brought up the rose in the book discussion. I just knew we wanted to know her better." Mrs. Harrod's eyes twinkled at Celia. "When I informed my husband I was having the society for lunch, I told him I was willing to bet on you." She laughed. "Not that I'm a betting woman. But Miss Thatcher, you looked such a flower at the discussion with your creamy bowed blouse and your hair tied up in curls. You reminded me of a peony, my dear. You had that same classic beauty with a flowery little fluff."

"Mrs. Harrod, your descriptions!" Mrs. Adams laughed, then looked at Celia. "Don't let her extravagant talk embarrass you, Miss Thatcher. Amongst us women, she can be quite the flibbertigibbet. In mixed society, she is more circumspect. But never dull, I warrant you."

"No, indeed," said a small lady with a huge yellow mum overloading her straw hat. "In fact, you must take what she says as a compliment. It means you've all but been accepted into the inner circle. And, my gracious, in the space of just a few minutes!"

"But only if you *do* love flowers." Mrs. Harrod adopted a severe air. "*Do* you?"

"Yes! Would you like to know my favorite?"

Mrs. Adams held her fork in midair. "That's what we're waiting to hear, my dear."

"I'm afraid such aficionados as yourselves will find me rather unimaginative, for it's the well-loved rose. But I have a passion for roses in all their forms, from the simple five-petal variety to the huge, multi-petaled blowsy ones."

"I knew it," Mrs. Harrod said. "A classic, that's what you are."

"How appropriate." Mrs. Adams put down her cup. "And now you must hear our favorites."

The ladies readily chimed in with a lively recital of flowers, from the wild blue bachelor buttons to fragrant lilac shrubs.

Finally, Mrs. Adams lifted her teacup to

Mrs. Harrod. "Now our hostess will tell you hers."

"Miss Thatcher might have already guessed." Mrs. Harrod's eyebrow lifted archly as she paused dramatically. "The peony, of course! In all its fulsome, many-petaled splendor. And now you know the compliment I paid by comparing you to my luscious flower."

"You can readily see," Mrs. Adams said, "with our specialized interests, we don't cross pollinate or step on each other's toes." She chuckled at her pun.

"Especially during the flower show," the lady in the straw hat added.

"Oh, yes, we wouldn't want to run off with each other's prizes." Mrs. Harrod laughed. "We are a smart set of little ladies."

Celia giggled demurely. How delightful to be accepted into such a lively group.

The ladies went on to talk about the flower show. When Celia asked when it was held, Mrs. Harrod said mid-June, then asked her what she might contribute. Celia said that Mrs. Chestley had climbers that had done poorly the last few years. Maybe she could coax them into a prize.

Mrs. Adams then asked about Mr. Lyons, for she had heard he had a garden bar none. She leaned over to address Mrs. Harrod.

"He and I had a nice little talk after the book discussion. Don't you think we could prevail on him to enter this year?"

"Well, we'll have to see what can be done about that," Mrs. Harrod said gaily. "He did come out of his shell to attend the discussion. Yes, Mrs. Adams, you and I together, we just might be able to manage it."

Celia turned from Mrs. Harrod's drive into the "Avenue," the street with the town's grandest homes. The early afternoon sun warmed the air. Its brightness pierced intermittently through the golden leaves of the overarching elms, hitting Celia's face in staccatos, adding verve to her walk. The sparkling conversation of the ladies at the luncheon had energized her, too, their liveliness contagious. Most of the time she involved herself in serious pursuits, so her time with the Floral Society had been a pleasant surprise. What an absolutely congenial luncheon. She felt on top of the top.

At the end of the avenue, she turned left to the town's small business district with its cozy assortment of shops and houses. She had just reached the general store when out the door bolted a boy of about ten. Looking back over his shoulder, he plowed right into her.

Celia grabbed the boy to keep from toppling over. "Whoa, there!" She regained her balance just in time.

"Sorry Miss, but I gotta go, I'm late!" He grabbed at her to steady her, then pulled away and raced down the street. Celia slowly straightened herself, her hand instinctively clutching her leg.

The door opened a second time. A bushy-haired gentleman exited.

"Blasted boy!" Mr. Lyons reached out to her tentatively, then dropped his hand. "Are you all right?"

"I'm a little shaken, that's all."

He looked hard at the running lad. "Did he apologize?"

"Well — in a manner of speaking."

"That boy's like a wild animal, he needs disciplining."

"Yes, but I have a brother who runs perpetually late, getting into all kinds of scrapes. So I'm rather inured to it, I guess." She laughed, wanting to smooth over the incident, then looked at him quizzically. "Mr. Lyons! Here it is daytime and you are out and about. I thought you kept to the night shades."

He looked at her sharply. "Business. Well,

if you're all right then —" At her affirmative nod, he tipped his hat and started off before she could say more.

She looked at his huge retreating figure in surprise. Such a sudden departure. Had she said something ill-advised? Now that she thought of it, she probably sounded impertinent with her last remark. What had come over her? Fallen in with the Floral Society's spirited ways, that's what — and not appreciated by the likes of Mr. Lyons.

Yes, he was Tennyson to the life. She'd finally told Mr. Chestley how Mr. Lyons resembled the picture of Lord Alfred she'd seen in the volume of Tennyson poems. Mr. Chestley laughed and said, "The resemblance doesn't end there." He had bent over confidentially. "Mr. Lyons is known to be about as dour, brooding, and unapproachable as Tennyson was reported to be for much of his life."

At the moment, Celia couldn't agree more. She gazed after the disappearing figure, letting some distance grow between them before she started in the same direction. After all she'd learned about him, that was surely best.

Edward Lyons took to his woods. Tramping into the forest, he put distance between himself and civilization. The only movement he wanted to see was a leaf falling, the only sound, a squirrel cavorting through the forest, rustling fallen leaves. He wanted to be quiet and alone. Alone!

Hard to believe one of the few times he ventured out in daytime he had to meet that young woman. Looking as fresh and lovely as a — rose. But that was hackneyed. She deserved better than that.

Glancing out the store window, he'd seen her walking up the sidewalk. He'd been putting on his gloves when that boy sped past him out the door and all but knocked her over. He'd jerked on the rest of the glove and rushed out.

Had the boy no manners? To top it all, he was sure the boy dropped a piece of candy when he knocked against her. Probably filched from the penny candy.

His eyes narrowed. Hadn't he seen that boy somewhere before? He tried to remember back to any recent — the horse! And the firecrackers. That boy was one of the two that set off those firecrackers. The rascal.

He tramped a good ten minutes through the forest before he felt himself calm down. His fighting energy dissipated, he hunted down a recently fallen tree he'd discovered last week. The trunk was huge. He wondered why it had fallen until he examined its base and saw the rotten inner core. Farther up the trunk where he chose to sit was solid enough.

How he loved these woods. Precious little else he loved these days. But he'd come to accept that, tamping down each day's circumstances to the back of his mind like a pipe smoker presses down tobacco in his pipe. Besides, as soon as he began to read he lived in another world. Was that how he could remain in this town after Marguerite's death? Surely any other man would have left. But he was just stubborn enough to stay. His mother had suggested he return to Boston, to the ancestral domicile. But no, he'd never live in close quarters like that again, even though eminently historical and elegant. Once he'd tasted the outdoors as a boy at his grandparents' summer place, the open air had to be part of his life. And here, except for his neighbor and their past, he had the best of both worlds — a refined, comfortable home with a library to stimulate his soul and a forest with enough acreage to provide an outlet for physical exertion and mental contemplation. Without these woods, even stubbornness wouldn't have tempted him to stay.

He gazed around him. This autumn the woods blazed with enough color for any man's hungry soul. Burnt oranges, sunny yellows, and his favorite, bright scarlet. An evocative word, that last. Was it another reason the book discussion had drawn him?

For some minutes, he sat in silence. Here in the woods, things would get unstirred. Wordsworth said it well, no matter that he talked of spring instead of fall:

I heard a thousand blended notes,
While in a grove I sate reclined,
In that sweet mood when pleasant thoughts
Bring sad thought to the mind.

To her fair works did Nature link
The human soul that through me ran;

So much beauty in nature. Such harmony. He felt a solid connection to Wordsworth; the man, like himself, had experienced disillusionment, but had found sustenance, spiritual comfort in nature.

And much it grieved my heart to think
What man has made of man . . .

The beauty in the poem underscored the sad thought of man's unfair treatment to his fellow man. The figure of Mrs. Divers thrust up suddenly. And her treatment of him.

Was the woman his Chillingworth?

Suddenly he rose. He wouldn't think of her. Instead, he would focus on the beauty of the nearby trees, one to his right particularly, its wonderful golden leaves scintillating in the bright sunlight.

A stream rippled nearby. A splash of water on his face would refresh him. He was feeling uncommonly warm.

With an easy pace, he covered the last hundred yards, over the rise of forest floor before it gentled down to the water.

But what was *that* by his stream? Two boys with fishing poles.

He barged down the embankment, stirring up dried leaves, not disguising his advance. Both youths glanced over their shoulders, then hastily rose. He recognized one of them. The firecracker boy who had run into Miss Thatcher. He quickened his pace. Up ahead he spied a spot cleared of underbrush, laid out for a fire. Fire! Anger licked through him.

Only a few moments the boys stood frozen. "Loydie!" One of them grabbed their basket. "Let's get out of here!" Without looking back, both fled along the stream, then scrambled up the embankment.

He almost pursued them, but they had too good a start. Instead, he stopped at the unlit fire ring. Kicked it. Kicked it thoroughly, scattering the wood. Then kicked leaves, twigs, and moss over the dread spot. Kicked until there was no trace of the intended fire.

A fire on his property? A thousand times no!

Smoke! Edward coughed and coughed. Heat scorched his face. He buried his face in his pillow to escape the heat and suffocating fumes. When he raised up, he saw orange and white flames licking round his bedroom door.

Shouts. Screams. Where were they coming from? Below his window? Voices yelled at him to wake up, to get out of the house.

He struggled with the bed covers, flung them off.

Cold air hit him.

He opened bleary eyes to a dark bedroom. What?

Fire. Where was it? The smoke? He rose from his bed, groping his way to the washstand and doused his face with cold water. Doused it again and again.

After drying his face, he walked to the window. Darkness and utter quiet met him.

He crossed the room and opened his bedroom door. Shadowy silence reigned in the hall. He stood still for some moments, then shuddered in the cold gloom.

Gradually the brightness, the noise, the fire of the dream subsided. He heaved a great sigh.

The sense of being trapped, that night long ago — had returned with a vengeance. Would he never forget what happened to him as a boy in his grandparents' home, his cherished boyhood summer home — going up in smoke?

Another shiver shook him.

# 7

Celia watched Mr. Chestley open the big black portfolio.

"I sent for these art prints from Boston. You know how I like adding to the store's Old World ambiance. I think something should be framed for that wall near the book discussions. Would you give them a once-over, Celia?"

Celia felt a surge of interest. "How many are there?"

"A dozen or so. I asked for a selection of country scenes from different seasons. Take your time."

Celia bent over the large folio. The top print was a large pasture of grazing sheep with rolling hills in the distance. Charming. She turned over one after another, each reminiscent of earlier centuries in England or Europe. The last three showed winter scenes, the first with figures skating down a frozen river with little cottages near the water's edge.

But this last — how different. Radically pruned trees lined a country lane, their knobby ends sprouted straight slender branches — black and brown strokes against a gray-white wash.

Just then the door opened, the little bell jangling. Celia looked up to see Mrs. Smith enter. "Can I help you?"

The old woman's face brightened on spotting her. "No, I just dropped by to say hello." Approaching the counter, she craned her neck. "What are you looking at?"

"Art prints. We're going to choose one to be framed for the store."

"May I see?"

"Of course. Look at this one, a country lane with the pruned trees. It's most unusual."

Mrs. Smith gazed at the picture. "Oh my, I don't think I've ever seen the like. Strange, isn't it?"

"Yes, the subject is very different." Celia looked up to see Mr. Chestley rounding the bookcase.

He stopped by her side. "Celia, I was waiting to hear your reaction on that one. The French countryside in winter. We don't prune our trees in that drastic fashion, do we, Mrs. Smith?"

"I should say not. The picture looks sad. I can't abide anything sad since I lost my husband."

Mr. Chestley glanced at Celia. "What do you think of it?"

"It is stark, yet there's beauty in the starkness. But a bit of hominess, too. The little cottage at the end of the lane with its lone cow conjures up a picture of a family living a simple life, maybe eking out a living. The colors and subject of the piece do complement each other."

"So you like it?"

"I find it intriguing. Something about it stirs me."

Mr. Chestley smiled his approval. The bell jangled again. "Ah, Mrs. Adams. Welcome this fine day. Would you come here and give your opinion of this most unusual print?"

"Of course." She walked over to the group and looked at the picture. "My! What are you going to do with it?"

"Well, nothing right now. I'm just getting various people's opinions."

"If you must know, I think it's most strange. Not at all beautiful. I don't see how anyone would want to purchase that."

Celia looked at her. She was rather surprised a woman who loved flowers, didn't see some redeeming quality in the picture.

94

"You and Mrs. Smith agree on that," said Mr. Chestley. "We have other prints here. I'm going to choose one to frame for our bookstore." He turned to Celia. "Before I send them back to Boston, why don't we show them at our next book discussion, and see if anyone else wants to purchase one for framing. I'm thinking particularly of Mr. Ellis at the jewelry shop."

"The viewing might draw in a few more people to the discussions. Shall I work up notices to post around town?"

"An excellent idea."

"I doubt if many will find this French winter scene appealing." Celia held the print up again. "Yet, I'm glad I can look at it before it's returned."

"Now you see the advantages of being my assistant? You never know what might come your way." Mr. Chestley nodded to the other ladies. "Would you like to see the rest of them? If so, when you're finished, tell me which one you'd like for our bookstore."

Mrs. Adams declined, saying she wanted to find a certain book.

A few minutes later, Celia saw Mrs. Smith walk to Mr. Chestley's office while she was helping Mrs. Adams with the purchase of her book. "You said you wanted to start reading this today?"

"Yes! For once, I have almost nothing to do. I'm especially interested in it as Mrs. Harrod said it was one Mr. Lyons particularly favored."

Just then, Mrs. Smith approached the counter. "Well, I made my choice, so I believe I'm about ready to go. You leaving, Mrs. Adams? If you're going my way, we can walk together." She looked at the woman expectantly.

Mrs. Adams stared at Mrs. Smith. "Oh . . . but I just thought of something I need to do. Thank you, Miss Thatcher," and she hurried out the door.

My, that was sudden, Celia thought, and not even said kindly. It was almost as if she didn't want to associate with — She felt a flicker of anger against the woman, and then looked at Mrs. Smith to see how she took the snub.

Mr. Chestley approached the counter. "Celia, I just remembered, Mr. Ellis particularly wanted to know when these prints arrived. Would you mind running over to tell him?"

Celia placed the change box under the counter. "I can leave right now. And, Mrs. Smith, would you like to walk with me?"

"I'd appreciate the company. Thank you."

"Well, of course!" Celia walked over to

the coat rack and after buttoning her coat, pulled a cherry red hat over her head and wrapped her neck with a matching scarf.

Celia held the door. As Mrs. Smith walked through, she looked up at Celia. "That strange print made me think of my husband. Have I ever told you about him?"

"I don't believe so." Celia could see the woman was in need of a good hen talk. She reminded Celia of her grandmother, although Grandmother had a much livelier view of life. What Mrs. Smith needed was some old-fashioned kindness.

Celia took hold of Mrs. Smith's arm as they walked. The air was fresh and brisk. When they reached the jewelry store, the old woman had begun telling about her courtship. "You know," she said, "my husband would stop here before we were engaged and point out my ring. Can we look in the window before you go inside?" Mrs. Smith grasped Celia's arm. "See, there's a ring similar to mine. That one on the top row, three from the right."

"I see it."

"Isn't it romantic looking at jewelry, Miss Thatcher? Do you ever daydream — about a young man?" Mrs. Smith had an interested gleam in her eye. "You do have a young man, don't you?"

"Well, I don't know. There's Jack back home."

"Jack? Why haven't we seen him yet? You're such a pretty thing."

"Jack wasn't in favor of my coming here. He wanted me to stay home with my parents, said we should go on like usual. But he has sent a couple of letters."

"Is that all? And you've been here almost three months? He isn't angry with you, is he?"

"I don't know; I never considered . . . I just thought . . . well, I don't know what I thought, to tell the truth."

"Going home any time soon?" Mrs. Smith peered up at her. "There's nothing like talking things out, face to face."

"I'm going home for Christmas, and that's only a month away."

"Don't press him, of course. But let him know."

Celia smiled.

"So, how long will you be gone?"

"Mr. Chestley is letting me stay a week."

"That'll be nice. But we'll miss you."

"Well, thank you, Mrs. Smith." Celia's lips widened into a grin as she looked down at the old lady. Mrs. Smith was rather a sweetheart after all. Who would have guessed such a romantic hid behind a

98

wrinkled old face and frizzy gray hair.

"Ah, Miss Thatcher!"

Celia turned to see Mrs. Harrod hailing her. A tall, young man walked with her.

"Excuse me for shouting." Mrs. Harrod approached with alacrity. "But you're just the person I want to see."

Celia looked first at Mrs. Harrod, then at the man at her side. "Mrs. Smith and I were doing a bit of daydreaming in front of this window. She found a ring similar to the one her husband gave her. The jewels are beautiful, aren't they?"

"Yes! This is one of my favorite shops. Early in our marriage, Mr. Harrod and I lived on practically nothing. Jewelry, such as this, came later. And the time will come, I predict, when they will grace your person as well." The vivacious woman laughed. "But say, I want you to meet someone." She looked up at the slim, fair-haired man, fondness in her eyes. "Miss Thatcher, let me introduce my son, Charles Harrod. Charles, this is Miss Celia Thatcher, the new assistant at the bookstore. And you remember Mrs. Smith."

Celia smiled. "Pleased to meet you. I've heard quite a bit about a certain prospective star of the legal profession."

Charles tipped his hat to both ladies.

"Miss Thatcher, I can hear you've been listening to some of Mother's stories. She spins them off with aplomb — as of yet, I'm afraid I have yet to prove myself in the legal world."

"Son, your professors seem to think otherwise, at least that's what they've told your father and me. And what's a mother for, if not to build up the reputation of her son."

"Mother!" Charles's cheeks flushed.

Mrs. Harrod laughed. "Celia knows I like to spark off occasionally. And make the grand gesture. We've become good friends since that first book discussion." She turned to Celia. "Isn't it wonderful Charles came home early for Christmas? Now he'll be able to attend one of your discussions."

"I hear you're discussing Dickens's *Christmas Carol*," Charles said.

"I thought it would be just the thing to inject a little holiday spirit." Celia turned to Mrs. Smith. "Don't you think that's a good idea?"

"Yes, my dear." Mrs. Smith shivered. "But now if you'll excuse me, I'm getting a mite cold."

"Of course. It was nice to see you again," Celia said.

As Mrs. Smith walked away, Mrs. Harrod startled. "Now, look!" She waved to a large

100

man walking up the street in their direction. "Mr. Lyons!" she hallowed. "Join us, please." As he neared them, "You remember my son, Charles?"

Mr. Lyons touched his hat to the two ladies. "Yes, I well remember Charles." He held out his hand. "I heard you're attending Harvard Law School. You always were a bright young man, taking after your grandfather and, of course, your father."

"That is a compliment I don't take lightly, Mr. Lyons. I remember how well Grandfather spoke of you, how complimented he felt on being invited to view your library."

"He had a rare mind."

"How nice of you to say so," Mrs. Harrod said. "I always thought my father an exceptional person." She cocked her head appealingly. "By the way, I'm giving a little holiday dinner on the twentieth, in honor of my son's visit. Mr. Lyons, would you honor us by attending? And, Celia, you will come, of course." Mrs. Harrod placed her hand on Celia's arm. "I can already see acceptance in your eyes, my dear. Now, Mr. Lyons . . ." She looked up expectantly at the gentleman.

"I don't know what to say, Madam."

"Why, you'll say 'Yes,' of course. It's time you showed yourself in society again. Remember you were every hostess's favorite bachelor? Now, you will be everyone's favorite widower."

"I'm afraid you are sanguine in your appraisal of my present stance in society, Mrs. Harrod."

"Nonsense! Besides, there's no time like Christmas to break the ice. Everyone is in such a holiday — welcoming mood. Furthermore, our gathering will be little more than a family party with a few friends. My other son, George and his wife and children, will be there. Do say you'll come."

Celia saw such misgiving in his eyes and Mrs. Harrod must have seen the same for she laughed. "Mr. Lyons, you do very little credit to your name. The lion is the most feared animal in the wild, the king of beasts. You must step forward for the occasion and help me out. Now that I've invited Celia, I'll have an uneven number at table and *that* will never do. You must be the chivalrous, lion-hearted Richard of old, and help a damsel in distress."

The beginnings of a smile played over Mr. Lyons's lips. "You are a hard woman to say no to, Mrs. Harrod. The men in your family aren't the only lawyers." He cleared his throat. "For you, then, Madam, I will come."

Mrs. Harrod impulsively laid her hand on

his arm. "I'm delighted. And I know my husband will be, too. We dine at seven. Do come early."

# 8

Edward Lyons reached for the knocker. What had he let himself in for? It had been so long since he'd attended a dinner. Remembering Mrs. Harrod would have everything up to snuff for the holiday season, he had donned his best suit. Not formal wear, because his hostess had said no to that, but he'd opted for the best he had without resorting to evening dress. And he'd had his hair and beard trimmed. The barber said he looked more civilized.

When he passed the bookstore and the Chestley home, he wondered about Miss Thatcher. Maybe he should have offered his escort. The evening was pleasant enough for walking, but somehow he hadn't felt free to make the proposal. At the book discussion, when describing Scrooge she had glanced at him. Quite directly so. What *did* she think of him? If Mr. Chestley had walked her down tonight, maybe he would offer to accompany her back.

A servant opened the door. Ah, Hatfield.

"Good evening, Mr. Lyons. Please come in."

The vestibule smelled pungently of evergreen. Garlands festooned the staircase railing and doorway entries. Mrs. Harrod could be depended upon to fill her home with the holiday spirit. He remembered she was a great champion of plants and flowers of all varieties.

"May I take your coat, sir?" And then, "Would you follow me?" Hatfield led the way to the first doorway on the left. Voices raised in appreciative laughter. Edward stopped on the threshold. "Thank you, Hatfield."

Edward surveyed the assembled party searching for his hostess. Mrs. Harrod came forward immediately. "Mr. Lyons . . . Edward. So good of you to come. How distinguished you look. You bring credit to my drawing room." She took his arm. "This is like old times, isn't it? Let me introduce you." She gently guided him to the edge of the gathering and called for everyone's attention. "It's been so long since we've had the honor of Edward Lyons's presence, I want to make certain everyone knows him and that he feels a warm welcome."

Edward nodded at each introduction. Mrs. Harrod had been true to her word. The gathering consisted mainly of family with three or four others in attendance. "Edward, you know Mrs. Adams, of course. We've enjoyed the book discussions together." Next to Charles sat Miss Thatcher, his head bent attentively to hers. Now he rose, and Miss Thatcher looked up. She was dressed in a simple dark dress that hung gracefully about her person. Pearls encircled her neck and her hair coiffed into an elegant chignon. When Mrs. Harrod made the introduction to Miss Thatcher, her eyes looked up into his.

Mr. Harrod approached and held out his hand. "Lyons, glad you could come. Want you to have an opportunity to talk with our new neighbor, Judson Darrow. He and his wife are newly arrived from Boston." Mr. Harrod drew him off to the side where an elderly gentleman sat. "Darrow, I'd like you to meet a Boston Brahmin who has decided to grace our fair town, Mr. Lyons." With that, the three of them talked agreeably about the old days in Boston where Mr. Harrod had taken his law training.

"Dinner is served," Hatfield announced.

Mr. Harrod approached his new neighbor's wife, offering her his arm. Mrs. Harrod motioned for Mr. Darrow to escort Mrs. Adams, and then approached Edward. "Would you escort me in, please?" They led the way, the others pairing off, following suit. Leading his hostess to her chair at the foot of the gala table, Edward noted his name card placed to her right. His confidence rose. Mr. Darrow was seated on her other side. Charles escorted Miss Thatcher to the seat next to the new neighbor and then sat by her. Mrs. Adams was seated on Edward's right.

"Your table is beautiful, Mrs. Harrod," Celia said. A pair of porcelain angels stood either side of the scarlet poinsettias in the table's center. All else was white napery, crystal, and silver.

"Thank you. The poinsettias were an offering from Mr. Lyons. He sent them on ahead — from his wonderful greenhouse." Edward looked at his hostess and smiled, then glanced across the table at Miss Thatcher. Her eyes had an appreciative glow.

After everyone quieted, Mr. Harrod gave a hearty welcome and offered grace. Two servants carried in the first course, a delectable terrapin soup.

Mrs. Harrod turned to Mr. Lyons. "Are you remaining here for the holidays? Or will you visit your mother?"

"She's invited me to see the new church in town, hoping my interest in architecture will lure me to Boston."

"Are you referring to Trinity Church?" his hostess asked. On Mr. Lyons's nod, she continued, "Charles said it's been completed, but won't be consecrated until next February. He said it's quite the marvel." She looked over at her son. "Didn't you say no pillars obstruct the congregation's view of the preacher?"

"Yes, Mother. It's all quite beautiful. I especially like John LaFarge's painted murals and decorations. They will be completed by the Consecration. I believe people from all over will come to visit. The preacher, of course, is very popular."

"Isn't that Phillips Brooks?" Celia asked. When Charles smiled his assent, she added, "I understand he's written the words to that new Christmas carol, 'O Little Town of Bethlehem.' "

"I think you're right."

Edward noted the warmth in Charles's tone as he answered Celia. Edward watched her quiet animation. She *was* lovely. He would offer to walk her home.

Celia held her soupspoon in midair. "I believe he visited Bethlehem a number of years ago during the Christmas season, and later wrote the poem for the children of his church to sing during their annual program."

Charles offered, "He exchanges pulpits with Boston ministers of other denominations. Is ecumenical in that regard."

"I heard him speak at the Chautauqua Institute," Mr. Darrow said. "He certainly has a way with words, a most able speaker."

"Ah, Chautauqua, that new summer institute for vacationers who want to improve their minds by studying history, art, and literature," Charles quipped. "I heard one of the topics was 'The Importance of Science to the Religious Thinker.' What do you think of that, Mr. Lyons? You keep up on that sort of thing, don't you?"

"I try. I subscribe to *Popular Science Monthly*."

"Oh, do you?" Charles laughed. "Quite the radical publication, isn't it?"

"It is an active advocate of the scientific method."

"Yes, but I also understand the editor denigrates manifestations of popular religious belief. Calls anyone who attends a camp meeting an 'ignorant blockhead.' " Charles's mouth crooked a grin.

Edward glanced at Miss Thatcher. She sat

up straighter. Was she perturbed? He answered, "At times Youmans can be rather extremist in his views. But the intent of the magazine is to obtain the most accurate knowledge of our known universe."

"And that includes expostulating on Darwinian theory?" Charles asked. "Some consider that a dangerous idea."

Edward hesitated. "Possibly. Yet I believe one needs some knowledge of it." Edward sat back in his chair, feeling the slightest bit of annoyance. It was the host or host's son's prerogative to steer the conversation. Still, he felt an edge had been introduced and wasn't sure he liked it. He had come with the intention of smoothing away any controversy regarding himself. And here he was, exposed in a touchy subject.

Mrs. Harrod put down her soupspoon. "I wonder what the Reverend Brooks would say about this new thinking in science?"

"Well, Mother, he's a learned man, so I believe he keeps abreast of it. But I've heard he's decided not to enter the debate. He emphasizes the love of Christ, asking his congregation, instead, to devote themselves to improving the lives of the poor."

"Which is as it should be," Mrs. Harrod said. "And in view of the Christmas season, I think we can honor him later on by singing his Christmas carol. Now Celia, how did you come by that interesting tidbit about his writing the words?"

Edward was grateful his hostess directed conversation to less controversial matters.

At the end of the meal, he rose with the rest of the company. Mrs. Harrod had been right. He needed to venture more into society. The meal was delicious and the company first-rate. Except for that one conversational snag, the dinner had gone well. He felt his soul taking wing.

This was a good home. Charles and his brother were fortunate to have this with such parents. Edward's memory flitted back to his own youth. His father had kept his nose close to the business grindstone so he'd seen little of him. And his socialite mother — well, Boston had a strict social code, and Mother was its obedient servant. *How* he'd learned from her. Though he now saw the need to venture out, it would be on his own terms.

As he entered the drawing room, Mrs. Adams beckoned him to her side. They had talked extensively about one of his favorite books at dinner. But it was a pleasant feeling, being thus summoned. "Please sit, Mr. Lyons, at dinner I didn't have an opportunity to express how I felt on the subject of the new science. I agree with you . . ."

A few minutes later, the Harrods permitted two of their grandchildren to join the after-dinner socializing. Edward looked across the room. The children surrounded Miss Thatcher, dancing around her. The little girl then asked to sit on her lap and Miss Thatcher readily agreed. Miss Thatcher must have begun a story because the boy leaned against her listening. His arm crept up to encircle her.

A scene from *The Christmas Carol* came forcibly to mind. Scrooge, with the spirit of Christmas Past, stood watching children run laughing around the older daughter of the household, lovingly tugging at her dress and person. Edward found himself echoing Scrooge's sentiments:

What would I not have given to be one of them! . . . As to measuring her waist in sport, as they did, bold young brood, I couldn't have done it; I should have expected my arm to have grown round it for a punishment, and never come straight again. . . . I should have liked, I do confess, to have had the lightest licence of a child, and yet to have been man enough to know its value.

"Mr. Lyons! I don't believe you've heard a word I've said this last minute," Mrs. Adams accused him, smiling, "Is there more interesting sport across the room?"

"My apologies, Ma'am. I've been so little in society these last years, I'm easily distracted. You were saying —"

"Yes, as I was saying . . ."

A while later, Edward noticed a chair vacated near Miss Thatcher. He talked a little longer with Mrs. Adams, wondering in good conscience when he could excuse himself. Nearby sat Mrs. Darrow. He hadn't yet asked her how she liked their town after residing in Boston. Maybe he could make his way to her and afterward — suddenly Mrs. Adams excused herself. "Our talk about poinsettias has been most interesting, sir. The ones you brought Mrs. Harrod were just beautiful, but I've monopolized you long enough." She laughed, her eyebrow arching provocatively as she left him.

"Thank you, Ma'am," he murmured.

On the way across the room, he stopped to make a few comments to his host, decided against engaging Mrs. Darrow in conversation, and adroitly stepped to the empty chair he had spied earlier. Here he could seem to be part of a larger group around Miss Thatcher.

As he sat, he quietly assessed the situation. Near her, he felt reticent yet strangely energized. She was a mere girl, yet he felt her to be his equal. Her handling of Dickens at the book discussion proved that. Afterward he would have liked to have stayed and talked with her, but she was busy with people buying books. He had paused, instead, to glance over the art prints Mr. Chestley had displayed around the store. The French winter scene — with its row of trees with their gnarled, pruned limbs had drawn his interest. How deeply scarred they were. Yet new life sprouted from the limbs. . . .

"I see you're stopping at that picture," Mr. Chestley had said. "Does something about it particularly catch your attention?"

"The colors suit my mood."

"Our Celia was intrigued by that one. She looked at it for some time. And now I notice every once in a while, she'll stop and look at it."

Edward stirred in his seat and looked closely at Miss Thatcher. He'd like to know her thoughts on the print. That would be something they could talk about. Before he could approach her, Mrs. Harrod suggested charades. First, the children must be sent upstairs.

The charades were Christmas carols. After that, Mrs. Harrod said they must all gather around the piano and sing carols. "Let's begin with 'O Little Town of Bethlehem'."

Everyone sang with good cheer. After singing several others, the party broke up.

Edward looked over at Miss Thatcher, alone for the moment. Just at that juncture, she glanced over at him and smiled. He quickly rose and approached her. "Did you enjoy the evening?" he asked.

"Oh, yes! It isn't often I do something like this. It'll provide memories for many days to come and has begun the holidays wonderfully for me."

"I'm glad to hear that. It has been some time since I've done something like this myself."

"I know Mrs. Harrod was gratified you accepted her invitation."

Edward acknowledged the delicate compliment with a brief nod. "We haven't had an opportunity to talk much this evening. Would you allow me to escort you home? I noticed the weather was unusually mild on my walk here —"

"Mr. Lyons!" Charles interrupted as he stepped near. "I'm sure your offer is appreciated, but I've just ordered the buggy for Miss Thatcher."

Edward hesitated before speaking. "I'm sure that would be pleasant for Miss Thatcher."

"Well, I thought I'd take her on a little ride as well." Charles smiled. "Something to finish off the evening."

Irritation pricked at Edward. Then he remembered he was in the home of the Harrods and this was their son. He should have first preference.

"Certainly," he said. "I hope Miss Thatcher enjoys the ride."

"Thank you for your kind offer, Mr. Lyons," Celia said.

"If you'll excuse me, then." He bowed formally and crossed the room. He would thank his host and hostess and then leave.

Within a few minutes, he stepped into the hall. Hatfield would bring his coat and hat. Somehow, he felt discomposed, but did not stop to analyze it. He just knew he was ready to go home.

# 9

Celia closed her valise, excitement welling up. She was going home! How she looked forward to seeing her parents, brothers, and little sister.

And Charles had offered to bring her to the train station. How flattering. When he took her home last night, he tucked the traveling blanket carefully around her knees. Said he wanted to make certain she was warm and comfortable. She wondered. . . . A knock sounded at the front door.

"Celia!" Mrs. Chestley poked her head into the room. "That must be young Mr. Harrod. Mr. Chestley will take your portmanteau."

Outside Charles took the luggage from Mr. Chestley and strapped it to the buggy. Mrs. Chestley took Celia's arm. "Now, are you going to bake my cream cake for your family?" She glanced to the back of the buggy and said a little louder, "Make it for that young man, Jack, it'll put him on his knee in no time."

Celia felt herself blushing. "Mrs. Chestley!" she whispered.

"Don't worry, dear," Mrs. Chestley whispered back.

Charles came around the buggy. "I heard that bit about the cake, Mrs. Chestley. Before you go pairing off Celia with some young man, don't you think I should have a sample? Might give me ideas, too."

"We'll see!" Mrs. Chestley looked archly at Charles. "Now, let me hug you, Celia."

Mr. Chestley followed suit. "Give our regards to your family."

After Charles handed Celia up into the buggy and she settled herself, she wondered what they would talk about, but then their conversation took off. Charles told how he loved to travel, and after he graduated and passed the bar, hoped to go on the Grand Tour. Then he'd join his father or try a firm in Boston. He caught her eye. Too bad she wasn't delaying her trip until after the holidays, then he could accompany her as her hometown was right on the way. "Do you go to Boston much?" he asked.

"No, I've been only once in my life and that was a family excursion. We looked forward to it for a whole year."

He laughed. "To hear you talk, you make it sound as if you had planned an extended trip out West, or some such."

"Well, it was special, because usually we made our yearly trip in the opposite direction to the Chestleys. That's how the opportunity came for me to work in the bookstore."

After he settled her on board the train, he stood on the platform and waited until the train left the station. How nice to be attended by such a personable young man. She wondered if they'd become better acquainted, for by the time she returned, he'd be back in law school. Their conversation on the way to the station had been perfectly entertaining. Last night, too, when he had taken her home after the Christmas dinner. Then she remembered Mr. Lyons's offer to walk her home. She wondered what they would have talked about.

If truth be known, she longed for a long, serious conversation. She was tired of talking about the weather and surface topics. She wondered if people thought her too serious — a bluestocking. How she had wanted to interject her thoughts during the serious talk at the Harrods' Christmas dinner, but had refrained. Then afterward, she entertained the children. Delightful in its own way, but after a while she longed for some adult to approach her. She caught herself glancing at Mr. Lyons conversing with Mrs. Adams. They talked at length, the woman very animated. My, she had already sat with him at dinner, and here she was, claiming his attention again. She wondered if Mrs. Adams's mind had that fine edge that Mr. Lyons would appreciate. Celia rather doubted it, the way she had brushed off the French print.

Celia caught herself up short. Why was she being so critical of the woman? It showed a marked degree of unkindness in herself — just because she had slighted Mrs. Smith? There might be another explanation for her behavior. Celia should give her the benefit of the doubt.

Her mind veered back to Mr. Lyons. Even though he had a reputation as a curmudgeon — and she believed it after what Mrs. Divers had said — Celia still felt some connection with him. Knew that when she went into deeper waters, he could follow. The certainty of this satisfied something fundamental within her.

She gazed out the train window. The miles were sweeping by in a succession of rolling hills. Trees dotted the frosty landscape, their black branches like fine lace against the blue gray sky. She was going home! To a father and mother with whom she could talk as seriously as she liked and not feel constrained to contain herself. Her soul rose like a fish to bait at the water's surface.

As the train neared her hometown, she sat up straighter, straining to see familiar sights out the window. There was the church spire where she would worship Sunday with her father preaching. Her eyes moistened and a happy tightness welled up in her chest. Snow must have fallen the night before because a lovely dusting covered the fields and roads. Never had home looked so beautiful.

"Father!" Celia threw her arms around his neck. She noticed one old matron staring at her open demonstration of affection, but she didn't care. She absolutely did not care. How wonderful to see Father again.

"Mummy!" Her mother's face lifted in delight at Celia's kiss.

"My eldest is back in the nest, at least for a week." She held Celia off. "You look wonderful, my dear. We've all missed you."

Celia looked around at her younger siblings who quietly waited their turn for hugs. Joe, Eric, and Euphemie. She embraced her little sister extra-long.

"We promised we'd drop by Grandma's on the way home," Euphemie said. Mother nodded and added, "She's all eager to see if her oldest grandchild has changed in four months."

"Here, you two," Father beckoned her brothers, "carry Celia's portmanteau between you. Celia, I'll take your valise. Euphemie, take my hand. Celia, you can walk with your mother. She wants first claim on your time. You and I will have a good talk in my study later on."

The others groaned. "Aw," Eric complained, "I want to hear what she has to say, too."

"Well then, if you all feel that way, the first night will be a family time in the study."

Celia looked from one face to another. How bright and fresh they all appeared; she hadn't realized what a handsome group they made. They might not be rich, but they were a grand-looking family.

The second she walked in Gram's door, the smell of freshly baked cookies met her — with all the attendant memories. Every Sunday they had walked to Gram's for a visit, and at the end were treated to sugar cookies.

Gram gave her a long, hard hug. "You've been away too long. Come to the kitchen table, we'll visit there." She set down a blue plate piled high with the fondly remembered sweets.

"Do we get more than one?" Joe asked.

"Of course! We're celebrating Celia's homecoming." Gram tweaked Joe's nose.

Celia looked at her grandmother. She was as warm and sparkly as ever. One never left Gram's without sustenance for both soul and body.

"Jack has been asking after you," Gram said as Celia took her second cookie. "You know, there's nothing I'd like better than to have my oldest grandchild settle down close to me." She reached over and hugged Celia again. "It feels like you've been gone an age. So what about Jack? Or is there someone else?"

Celia laughed. "Let's see, how many suitors have I corralled in four months?" She held up her fingers. "There's Johnny, all of nine years old. And there's . . ." she laughed, "a quite charming young man, a future lawyer I met a few days ago. However, he'll be back in Boston before I return, and a five-day acquaintance is rather quick to decide such things, don't you think?"

The next morning Celia and her mother stood over the kitchen stove, brewing a batch of spiced apple cider. Cider was one of the things Celia had missed at the Chestleys'. She smiled at the little painting of the Chestley's bookstore and street she'd drawn as a child. It still graced the wall by the kitchen table. What a happy thought that was, her life with them. And now here she was in this dear kitchen with her very dear mother.

Her father stuck his head in the door. "Smells inviting."

"Well, my love, you're not invited yet," Mother said. "But you will be duly so when Celia and I make doughnuts this afternoon, then we'll have Grandma over."

"Celia and I need to talk."

"Certainly. After I have her to myself a little while longer." She walked up to her husband, smiled her loveliest, and shooed him back through the door. Celia saw the mischievous gleam in her mother's eye when she occasionally took over the reins and ruled her husband.

"Your father loves you and is keen to talk about serious issues, but I have something I want to ask you."

Celia sidled up to her mother and gave her a little hug. "A mother and daughter chat?" Her mother nodded. "How are you doing?" then looked at her closely. "You know, after Trudy?"

"Better. Much better. I'm so glad you sent me to live with the Chestleys. There's been so much to learn and meeting new people . . ."

"So you've forgiven . . . yourself?"

"Yes, Mummy." Celia held her mother close a moment longer.

"I'm glad." Her mother's face brightened. "Now, let's sample the cider." She dipped a ladle into the amber brew, then poured it into a cup. "Tell me what you think," and handed it to Celia.

"Mmm. Just right, I'd say."

"Good. You may finish that. Now, tell me something. I'm very curious about something you dropped in conversation yesterday. What's this about a budding lawyer?"

"Oh! Just what I said at Grandmother's. I'm not sure I'll ever see him again. But he drove me home after the Harrods' Christmas dinner and then again to the train station today. He's also very nice looking." Celia grinned. "Reminds me of Father."

"Well!" Her mother laughed. "I like him already."

"Me, too, but I'm not counting my chickens anytime soon," Celia said in a teasing tone. "Besides, I love my life with the Chestleys; I'm not looking to get married just yet.

I've so much to tell you." All the news she hadn't been able to convey in letters now came pouring out: the people she met, the special spots in the town she liked to walk, her job in the bookstore.

"What do you like best about your work?" Mother put down the big spoon she was using to stir the cider. "Here, let's sit a few minutes."

With her elbows on the table, Celia cupped her face in her hands. "Our book discussions. I love the fact that Mr. Chestley lets me choose the title for the month. Those times you and father talked books with me were wonderful preparation."

"*The Scarlet Letter* was your first choice?"

"That's right. I didn't know the level of thought the community would bring to the book, but wanted to choose one that brought possibility for deeper discussion. I had no idea it would stir things up so much. It's curious, Mother, but several counterparts to the characters seem to live right there in town."

"How is that?"

"One is a veritable Rev. Dimmesdale."

"Oh?"

"Do you remember my mentioning a curious man who comes into the bookstore every fortnight? The one with the shaggy

126

hair and beard?"

"Yes . . . but you might remind me of the details."

"He's something of a mystery. When I first saw him, he looked poor and unkempt, but is apparently independently wealthy and highly educated. After he married, something disturbing happened to his wife and she died. At first, when Mr. and Mrs. Chestley told me about it, and how Mr. Lyons became a hermit afterward, I thought he had a broken heart and felt sorry for him. But then I talked with his former mother-in-law, Mrs. Divers, and she thinks the worst things of him. It made me think I had interpreted the situation completely wrong." Celia scrunched her brows together. "Then a few days ago he was invited to the Harrods' Christmas dinner, and I saw he was well thought of, even sought after as a dinner guest. He seemed more refined with his hair trimmed and seeing him in their cultured surroundings."

"Have you had much to do with him?"

"Not outside of his fortnightly trips to the bookstore and the monthly book discussion. But the few times we've spoken have been most interesting. Once I asked his favorite passage in Tennyson, and he quoted two lines from "Break, Break, Break":

But the tender grace of a day that is dead
Will never come back to me.

"Hmm . . ." Her mother sat for a few moments in thought, then rose to take the cider off the stove. "It sounds as if he has suffered. I wonder what his spiritual state is, if he goes to God for comfort."

"I don't know. Our initial discussion led me to believe he and I differ on important issues such as the spiritual. I don't see him in church, although there are several in town. But I am under the impression he doesn't go, at least at this point. Remember I said he was a veritable hermit?"

"He does seem strange, doesn't he?"

"But then I can't forget how quickly he forgave me. Remember that incident I wrote about, the torn page in the new book he ordered. Ironic, isn't it, how differently I reacted to Trudy and my book? Just mentioning it makes me ashamed all over again."

"Well, maybe we should drop the subject. But with this man, I would be careful. Knowing you, I suspect you're interested in his philosophy of life, especially his spiritual state. But maybe you're not the one to do anything for him. Unless God opens the door —"

When everyone left after doughnuts and cider, Celia made a point to visit her father's study. She looked around the room as he settled himself in his desk chair. Books and papers stacked neatly everywhere. Not much in the way of decoration, but comfortable nonetheless. The wooden armchair she chose was cushioned with an old pillow. She positioned it better behind her back.

"Father, I'd like to know what you think about something."

"Certainly, daughter."

"At the Harrods' Christmas dinner the *Popular Science Monthly* was discussed. In fact, one of the guests subscribes to it and felt it was important to stay abreast of all that's happening in science. Are you familiar with the periodical?"

"Somewhat. My understanding is that the *Monthly* contains articles about natural science, and actively advocates the scientific method." He shifted in his chair. "I don't fault that. However, the most extreme advocates of this method claim that only through discovering facts can we come to any true knowledge of the universe and its origins. They propose the claims of science refute those of religion. In fact, they call religious ways of knowing the universe superstitious."

"That doesn't surprise me then. Charles Harrod, a law student at Harvard, said the editor of the *Monthly* belittles popular religious belief."

"Attitudes like that only add fuel to the debate between science and religion."

"Do you think there's a conflict between the two?"

"There shouldn't be," said her father. "I think the conflict comes in how the facts, as they are discovered, are interpreted. Proponents of Darwinian theory interpret evidence differently than someone like myself who believes God created the universe, and upholds it by His power."

"Darwin was mentioned at dinner, but wasn't discussed at length."

"Well, he has introduced a new way of seeing life-forms, of interpreting how they came into being. Some treat his theories as fact. Thomas Huxley has written a great deal about Darwin's assumptions, popularizing them, but I believe he and others are taking Darwin's theories beyond what he originally meant. I just finished reading Harriet Beecher Stowe's *We and Our Neighbors,* and she accuses the Darwinians and other scientific men of saying the Bible is nothing but, and I quote, 'an old curiosity-shop of by-gone literature.' I believe she is talking about the extremists in the scientific and intellectual community. You know, none, to my knowledge, testify to having a personal religious experience. They need something to explain the emergence of all we have discovered on the earth. So they are jumping on the bandwagon of this new theory."

Celia shrugged her shoulders. "Little wonder they put such stock in this theory, when they have so little knowledge of God."

"Exactly, my dear. Men make pronouncements about God when they have no experiential knowledge of Him. During our time, truth is being stripped of its Divine aspect, not only by natural science theory, but by present Biblical criticism. In place of the Divine, individuals in this camp pronounce that the laws of society and nature give us a secure basis for morality."

"But where do the laws of nature and society come from?" Celia leaned forward, gripping the desk with her hands. "I'll answer my own question. From God and His laws, like the Ten Commandments."

"Precisely. The question is, when one leaves out God, where is the ultimate authority to approve or punish a certain action? If morality is man-instituted, then ultimately man — and society — can, at will, change the code of morality." Her father's hand swept over his desk. "No, Celia, morality must be founded on something or Someone greater than mere man."

Celia sat back in her chair. "How I appreciate talking this out with you."

"You've always been interested in the bigger issues, daughter. I appreciate that."

"Thank you. This came up at the Christmas dinner. I wanted to say something, but wasn't sure of my ground. There seemed to be those at the dinner so much more knowledgeable than myself. Mr. Lyons, for instance. He's the man who frequents the bookstore, and he seemed to espouse the new scientific thinking to a degree."

Her father was silent before saying, "If Mr. Lyons goes along with that, his religious beliefs are on shaky ground, or at least, I'd question them."

"Mother and I talked this morning about Mr. Lyons, about his possible lack of faith."

"You said he is from Boston? If he is as educated and wealthy as you say, he is probably one of their elite society known as Boston Brahmins. Unitarianism has so taken over their churches it wouldn't surprise me he would side with the new science. This view in religion supports a rationalistic, rather cold view of God. In it,

Christ figures as a good man and teacher, but not the personal God who gave Himself for us unto death. Little wonder people like him have left the concept of God for the new science. And considering the fact Mr. Lyons is probably a Boston Brahmin, he will not easily change his thinking. Their heritage and way of thinking are a source of great pride."

Her father placed his fingertips together, his lips resting on his index fingers. Finally he said, "So, forewarned is forearmed." He gave her an affectionate smile. "This is just the sort of talk I've been missing."

"Me as well, Father."

His smile widened and he rose from his chair. "We'll talk more about this tomorrow and during the remainder of your visit. But now let's stretch our legs and invite your brothers and sister for a walk. Your mother could use a little peace and quiet." He looked at her. "It's so good to have you home."

Edward Lyons pushed open the bookstore door with something akin to impatience. He had waited a suitable time after the dinner at the Harrods. True, it wasn't quite time for his fortnightly visit to the store, but he had to come.

His eyes scanned the empty counter, the quiet bookcases. She didn't seem to be around. But he'd wait. He might peruse the history section, choose a volume and sit awhile in his favorite chair.

Someone exited the office at the back with a shuffling gait. Mr. Chestley appeared around the corner of one of the bookcases. "Ah, Mr. Lyons. I didn't expect to see you. But, of course, this is nice, very nice. I hope you're having a good holiday. A cheery season of the year, isn't it?"

"Yes, it is. I thought I'd browse your history section."

"You're more than welcome. If you need help of any kind, just call for me."

"Thank you."

An hour later Edward looked up from his book. *Where was she?* The door had opened and closed a number of times with different customers. His head jerked up at each jangle of the bell. Now, it had been quiet for some time. He rose from his chair and walked to the back of the store, his finger holding the place in his book. "Mr. Chestley, I was wondering about your assistant, Miss Thatcher. I want to show her something of interest in this book. Will she be here at some point in the afternoon?"

"Oh, Mr. Lyons, I'm sorry. Celia is gone

for the holidays. She couldn't very well miss seeing her family during Christmas, you know."

Edward felt a distinct drop in the region of his stomach. She hadn't said anything about it at the dinner. Of course, he hadn't talked with her much — which is what he had counted on today, here and now. "That's as it should be, of course. She'd want to spend the holiday with family." He paused, at a loss how to continue. He had to know more. This confounded reticence of his. He began slowly, "I had wanted to talk with her. Will she be gone long?"

"She'll return after the New Year. I might even close the store for a few days after Christmas. Take a holiday myself. I need to get those prints back up to Boston. You're originally from there, aren't you?"

"Yes. My mother lives on Beacon Hill." How could he get the conversation back to Miss Thatcher?

"She does? Well, then, won't you be going home for Christmas?"

"Well, I hadn't thought —"

"You know if Miss Thatcher had lived a little closer to Boston, I would have asked her to return the prints. She's right on the way, but I thought that would be too much to ask."

"She is? Ah, well . . . what town is that?"

"Mansfield. A pretty little town."

"I do recall that on the line. Of course, it's been some time since I've seen Mother. Maybe I should return — for Christmas." Edward hesitated once again. "If I do decide to go, would you like me to bring back the prints for you?"

Mr. Chestley's eyes had a hopeful gleam. "Would that be too much to ask?"

"No, no. I'd be glad to. It would give me something to do in the city."

Mr. Chestley rubbed his hands together in anticipation. "Why, Mr. Lyons, that would be nice, very nice of you — if you do decide to go." His eye had an uncertain look.

"Why, I think I will. In fact, I'll go to the train station now and telegraph my mother."

"If that's the case, I could wrap up the prints and you can pick them up whenever you're ready."

A plan began to form in Edward's mind. "Just give me the address of the establishment and I'll be glad to do the errand for you. By the way, which print did you decide on for the bookstore?"

"Let me show you. And Mr. Ellis at the jewelry store bought one, too. They're both to be framed."

Edward accompanied Mr. Chestley back to his office.

"You see, these two." Mr. Chestley held up first one print, then the other. "Mr. Ellis will want his frame in gold leaf. I'll have something less expensive. And look here, this is the unusual one Miss Thatcher liked so well."

"Ah, yes, the one with the heavily pruned trees. That shows a decidedly sophisticated taste in art. She would enjoy a city like Boston, I dare say. But living right on the way, she's probably already been there."

"Possibly. But surely not often. Her family doesn't travel much. Not for want of desiring to, but financial constraints, you know."

"Ah. When did you say she'd be returning?" There, he had finally asked.

"The Thursday after New Year's. In the afternoon."

"That'd be the 4:40."

"That's when the missus and I are scheduled to pick her up. We'll be glad to see her."

"I can imagine. I best be off to telegraph my message." Edward exited the office to pick up his hat and gloves from the side table where he'd left them. He clamped his lips together to keep from smiling like the proverbial cat from Cheshire.

# 10

Edward Lyons snapped his book shut. He was uncharacteristically — eager — wary, he wasn't sure. The conductor had called Mansfield. The train would be arriving in the station within a minute or two.

He purposely put his mind back on his visit to Boston. It had been good, but uneventful. Mother was in good health, glad to see him, of course. Had commented on his improved appearance. She had come to visit him once after Marguerite's death, but that one visit she'd cut short. He'd been hard-pressed to entertain her in a town so small, and in his frame of mind, with the suspicion of so many townsfolk at its height. He twisted on the seat.

The fact of the matter was that this visit with his mother was a vast improvement over the last one. Boston had provided much to do, and he was more like his old self, his mother said. He had to admit, he was feeling better.

The train's brakes screeched. He braced himself from falling forward, gripping the wooden bench. Ordinarily, he would be sitting in first class, but he didn't want to miss . . . the station came into view, neatly painted gray and green. Of course, he'd noticed it particularly on the way to Boston. A warm feeling had permeated him seeing the station and town, why he'd looked forward to his return trip, the reason he'd been so light-hearted with Mother.

There! He saw her cherry red scarf and hat wrapping her against the cold, her blond hair peeping from beneath. Suddenly, he felt shy like a schoolboy. Would she think him too forward saving this seat, inviting her to sit next to him? He would take care to keep things as natural as possible. But this was a little tricky. She had not the least idea he was on this train, could not know how carefully he'd planned his return from Boston to coincide with her leaving her hometown.

The train ground to a halt.

She was hugging and kissing her mother and father, bending over a young sister, then saying goodbye to her brothers. What a charming family picture. Suddenly, he wondered what it would be like to have younger brothers and sisters — he leaned over to see better — was it just one little sister in the group?

He wasn't that old. His bushy hair and beard only made him look that way. But that was all changing. In Boston, he had gone to a good barber and asked for the latest cut. And been fitted by the family tailor with a new broadcloth suit. Mother said he looked dapper. His mouth twitched at that. Interesting word for her to use, and she so particular. The last evening she'd asked the maid to get her jewelry box, and from it had presented him his father's signet ring. He looked down at his hand, at the ring's raised gold L in its center. His chest expanded with confidence. He would act offhand about seeing Miss Thatcher, maybe even act surprised. And he would just *happen* to have a seat free next to his. Maybe that's the way he should handle it.

He leaned nearer the window, wanting to make sure which door she entered. A young man had broken away from the group and was escorting her to the train steps. Beneath his hat, his hair showed dark auburn. Did any other family member have hair that dark? The young man gazed down at Miss Thatcher, but not like a brother. Edward's pulse jumped. Confound it!

As the young man preceded Miss Thatcher up the steps of the railway car, and held out a hand to assist her, she looked at him laughing, then stepped up as well. She was so full of life. Edward's breath arrested a moment.

The couple entered Edward's car, Miss Thatcher starting down the aisle with the young man in her wake. He held her valise with a proprietary air. Edward rose and his eyes sought hers, curious to see her reaction on first seeing him. She scanned the car for a seat, then saw him. She startled. Was it a glad light in her eyes?

"Mr. Lyons!"

"Hello, Miss Thatcher." He waited for her to approach then gestured toward the space next to him at the window.

"What a surprise to see you. Here of all places." She stopped in front of him. "I —" She was obviously wondering if she should accept the seat. She turned to her companion. "Jack, this is Mr. Edward Lyons, who attends the book discussions at the bookstore where I work." She turned again to him. "Mr. Lyons, Jack Milford, an old friend from my hometown."

Jack held out his hand first. "Nice to meet you, sir."

"Likewise." Edward knew the "sir" was

the required form of address, but somehow the way the young man said it made him feel old. The whippersnapper. "I can place Miss Thatcher's valise overhead," Edward offered.

She nodded her acquiescence.

"Thank you, but I can do that for Celia."

He called her Celia. Edward stepped aside as Jack stretched up to stow the valise. "Nice of you to help, young man. We're glad to have Miss Thatcher return; we certainly appreciate the book discussions she's begun. I wouldn't miss one." Had he said that with enough of a proprietary air?

"Book discussions? When I come to visit —" Jack looked at Celia with a decided air, "— you can let me know when you'll be having one."

"Jack, that would be lovely. I didn't know you'd be interested."

"Well, you always had your father to discuss such things with, so the subject never came up."

"True, but still —"

"Now, I'll want to make that visit rather soon, so let me know by your next letter." He touched her arm. Then reached for her hand and squeezed it.

"All aboard! Last call!"

"Thank you for seeing me onto the train,

Jack." Edward couldn't tell if her hand returned the squeeze or not. As Jack left, sauntering down the aisle, she glanced after him, a smile on her face.

Edward was tempted to take Celia's elbow and assist her to her place. But he refrained. He stepped back to let her pass.

"If you'll excuse me," she said, "I'd like to see my family one last time," and drew up to the window and waved. They all waved back enthusiastically.

The whistle blew. The train gave a warning jerk. Celia lurched and Mr. Lyons reached out to steady her. "Here, Miss Thatcher." He encouraged her to seat herself.

"Thank you. And a seat by the window, too. Are you sure you wouldn't like it?"

"I can see just fine. I plan to read so you can enjoy the view in peace."

"You are too kind."

"Not at all." Satisfied arrangements were going as planned, he took out his book.

Celia looked around the mahogany-paneled dining car. Mr. Lyons had reserved a place — she could hardly refuse in light of that.

Their table, covered in white linen and adorned with a red rose, was situated at one end with fewer neighboring tables. It was all so lovely. The waiter had called him *Mr. Lyons* so particularly. Had bowed, then asked about her comfort, if she had any special wishes. She felt rather overwhelmed with the royal treatment. Was it always this way? Or was it because of Mr. Lyons? She looked across the table at her companion with new regard. And he was looking *so well.*

"I was surprised to see you on the train. So you went to Boston after all?"

"To see my mother. Mr. Chestley decided me when he needed his prints returned to be framed. It worked out for us both."

"I know which picture Mr. Chestley chose for the bookstore. Were there others to be framed?"

"The owner of the jewelry store picked the winter scene with the skaters on the river."

"I liked that one."

"There was one which particularly caught my attention, the French countryside with the pruned trees."

She couldn't resist asking, "What appealed to you?"

He laughed. "The gnarly old trees!"

She joined him in laughter. "They *were* rather strange looking. Now, tell me why."

A few moments passed, the laughter in his eyes fading. "For years those trees marked the way down the lane — protective, stalwart hardwoods. . . ."

She leaned forward, encouraging him with her complete attention.

"In those old hardwoods, I saw the shoots of new growth sprouting from the old as if new hope had begun. . . ."

She didn't want to pry, but the picture seemed to speak so personally to him. Did he see it as somehow representing himself? "That's — that's so interesting. You saw hope in what some would declare a somber picture."

He laughed again. "You have an unusual way of putting it."

"My father has made the same observation about me." She smiled and looked up as the waiter set down their teacups, the teapot, then plates of delicious looking sandwiches and tiny pastries. "How delightful. And this hot tea is just what a doctor would order on a cold day."

After the waiter left, Mr. Lyons said, "Your friend Jack alluded that you talk with your father about books. What else do you talk about?"

"Just about everything. This visit we talked a lot about science and religion, the subject touched on at the Harrod Christmas dinner." She stopped a moment. This seemed a natural entrée into discovering what Mr. Lyons thought about science and religion, where he stood on matters of faith. "I know you read *Popular Science Monthly*. Tell me more about it."

"As I said at the Harrods' dinner, it's a publication that advocates the scientific method, the study of facts. Today, scientists want the most accurate knowledge available about the order of the universe."

"I've heard Thomas Huxley also elevates the scientific method."

Mr. Lyons's eyebrows raised. "You've heard of him?"

"My father and I discussed his ideas briefly."

Her companion took up his fork and tapped its end on the white napery. "Then you might know his first article of belief is that man is obligated to pursue truth, no matter where it may lead — if necessary to the utter destruction of his most cherished doctrines and institutions."

Celia took a bite of a diminutive chicken sandwich. She swallowed, then began slowly, "I don't take issue with scientific discovery or people searching for facts. That sounds noble enough. But don't you think it's important how facts are interpreted? How application is made?" She paused.

"Hasn't Mr. Huxley excluded religious belief from his interpretations of the facts?"

"I believe he has."

"If he has no knowledge of God," Celia took a sip of tea before driving home her point, "then he has no religious experience with which to measure his facts."

"You mean to color his thinking, his interpretation?"

"I mean with which to *interpret* the facts." She looked Mr. Lyons directly in the eye. "As Job said so long ago, 'I know in whom I have believed.' "

"So you propose blind faith?"

"If I were Mr. Huxley, I suppose it would be blind faith. But my faith is based on facts."

"Facts?"

"The facts of Jesus' life. His death. His resurrection."

"But suppose all that is myth, that it never occurred? Modern criticism negates the Bible as being wholly factual, so therefore, how can it be totally trustworthy?"

"You think the disciples, the early believers, were willing to die for what they knew to be falsehoods?"

Mr. Lyons sat back from the table, motioning her to continue.

"Who are these people who have the

temerity to throw God out of their assessment of the universe? Questioning His reality? Doubting His ability to answer prayer? Skeptical that Scripture can resonate with Truth?"

She took another sip of tea, then held the cup in her hands to warm them. "I venture to say it is because they have little or no experience of God. That they, in fact, spend more time trying to poke holes, find fault with Holy Writ than they do giving it an honest reading."

Celia put down her cup and asked Mr. Lyons if he wanted more tea. He nodded his acceptance. "I am sure Mr. Huxley and those of his ilk are brilliant men. But a brilliant man can fall in love with his own brilliance. He can come to trust too much in himself and his own ability to reason things out."

Mr. Lyons's lips curved up. "I seem to remember your saying something similar in your assessment of Emerson's writings on our first meeting."

Celia felt relief seeing Mr. Lyons smile. She hadn't meant to express her opinions quite so freely while his guest at this delightful tea. He would think her a bluestocking and next time choose a more demure female for company.

"You argue a convincing case, Miss Thatcher. You must be your father's daughter. I would think you have interesting talks."

"We do, but I didn't mean to come at you quite so strong. You are a most gracious host."

"What you propose is thought-provoking. I can't say I agree with all you say, but you can certainly stir the nest."

"I take that as a compliment. Thank you." She said it softly. If only he would think about all this. Even so, she was now determined to talk of less volatile topics. She cast about for another subject. The red rose against the white napery of the linen tablecloth provided the inspiration. She mentioned its beauty and how she loved flowers, roses in particular. Mr. Lyons then began talking about his rose garden. She said she'd like to see it and asked if he would be entering some of his blooms in the community garden show in June. He'd been approached about it, but hadn't seriously considered it. He might, however. The remainder of the tea passed very comfortably.

Mr. Lyons motioned to the waiter and after paying the bill, looked at his watch. "We should be nearing our destination. Are you ready to return to our seats?"

"Yes, this tea has been lovely, I will treasure the memory. Thank you so much."

"My pleasure."

They both rose, and when she turned to the door and the car jerked on the rails, Mr. Lyons immediately took her arm. She glanced up gratefully. He smiled back and continued to hold her arm as they made their way back to their places. They were seated only a short while before the conductor announced their station.

Standing in line to climb down the steps to the station platform, Mr. Lyons insisted, "Let me precede you, Miss Thatcher." On the platform he put down his case and her valise, then stepped up to take her arm, grasping her gloved hand to ease her down.

"Thank you, Mr. Lyons."

"No trouble at all."

"Celia!" Mrs. Chestley ran out the station door. She flung her arms around the girl.

Mr. Chestley soon followed and shook Mr. Lyons's hand. "Did the framing go all right?" At Mr. Lyons's assent, he added, "I'm surprised you ended on the same train as Celia. How fortunate."

As they entered the station through the double doors, Celia saw a familiar face staring at them. "Hello, Miss Waul."

"Hello. I take it you had a nice time home

150

for Christmas. I'm here to collect a parcel for Mrs. Divers."

Celia couldn't help glancing at Mr. Lyons. He nodded courteously at his neighbor, but his lips pressed together.

# 11

Mrs. Divers looked up as Miss Waul rushed into the room. "My! I haven't seen you hurry like this in a long time. Are you suddenly getting younger?"

"A spurt of energy." Miss Waul huffed. She handed Mrs. Divers a package, then sat down in the armchair opposite. "You'll never believe who I saw at the train station."

"I'm all ears. It's been so quiet around here with you gone, to say nothing of our neighbor's absence." Mrs. Divers sat back in her easy chair, but something in her companion's expression made her ask, "It's not about him, is it? Hasn't gone off and died and brought us relief?"

"Oh no, he's very much alive. I saw him step off the train just minutes ago." Miss Waul's eyes were unusually keen. "Can you guess who was with him?"

"Well now, how would I know that?" Mrs. Divers couldn't help feeling exasperated.

She didn't like guessing games. "I don't keep up with all his acquaintances, if he has that many. You know I don't get around town like I used to. That's why I sit looking out my window, to see what's passing by."

"If you won't give us a little fun and guess, I'll just have to come right out and tell you. It was," Miss Waul paused for added drama, "Miss Thatcher."

"Miss Thatcher!" Mrs. Divers sat up in her chair, frowning. "You mean they were *with* each other?"

"Well, he helped her off the train. Took her arm and hand all cozy-like. I can tell you, it was more than a friendly hand down. It seemed . . . well . . . *intimate.*"

"So, you think they had been sitting and talking with each other? They couldn't have been *traveling* together."

"I don't know, all I'm telling is what I saw."

"Let's see now." Mrs. Divers figured the possibilities. "Why was he on that train? It was Christmas. Where does that line go?"

"Boston, I think. Yes, that line goes to Boston. His mother lives there, don't you remember?"

"Of course, I remember. I also remember how she looked me over the first time we met, and remember her so stiff-like at the

153

wedding, all Boston Brahmin-like." Mrs. Divers harrumphed. "But back to the train — does Miss Thatcher live on the line to Boston? Did she go away for Christmas?"

Miss Waul sniffed. "Well, she must, don't you think? What else would she be doing?"

"Of course, she must have been visiting her family. Any other thought would be most unkind, and unlikely. But Miss Waul, we must find out more. How could Miss Thatcher be thrown in his way like that? All that man deserves is a greeting in the bookstore. That's all!" Mrs. Divers's index finger tapped hard on the stuffed arm of her chair. "If it's more, we must do something."

"But what?"

"Well, get us some tea, and we'll talk about it."

The nip in the air invigorated Celia. Mr. Chestley had encouraged her to take a short, brisk walk during lunchtime. All morning she'd worked hard to change the displays in the bookstore, freshening them up for the new year.

Last night's conversation with the Chestleys had gone past their usual bedtime. How hungry they'd been to hear news of her family. They laughed together as she told them they might not have recognized her, playing in the snow like a child. Midway through her visit, a storm had brought a big snowfall and she couldn't resist getting out in it. That last afternoon she sledded down the hill at Grandma's with her brothers and sister and felt the fun of being a young girl again — and she at twenty! Her two brothers ganged up on her, smothering her face with cold, loosely bound snowballs. When younger, she would have yelped at being bested. Now, her cry was pure joy at being teased by very dear brothers. She had missed them more than she realized.

As she walked along, she felt something sweet, yet melancholy, deep inside. Often on a Sunday afternoon, she had this same feeling when the week's activities had stilled. Times like this, life seemed a mixture of the happy and the pensive. She would wonder about her place in life — was she doing what she was supposed to?

Sharing this with the Chestleys, she was quick to assure them she wouldn't trade her present life for anything. But it had been delightful to be home. She glanced at Mrs. Chestley and noticed a questioning gleam in her eyes.

"What is it?" Celia asked.

"I was wondering about Jack."

"I saw quite a bit of him. He helped my brothers in one of our dastardly snowball fights. And I went to his family party where I felt as welcome as ever. There, are you satisfied?"

"My dear," Mrs. Chestley said, her face suffused with a merry smile, "you know I like to hear of any progress with him — or with any other young man, for that matter."

Celia approached the jewelry store. Mrs. Chestley had a decidedly romantic turn of mind. What did Celia herself think of Jack? He'd insisted on seeing her to the train with her family and said he'd come visiting. She inwardly shrugged, not sure how she felt. Well, maybe when he came to visit, when she saw him in these new surroundings, she'd know more.

Glancing inside the store, she saw Mr. Ellis hanging his newly framed print. Mr. Lyons had probably brought it over that morning. He hadn't delivered the picture for the bookstore yet. She turned and glanced back down the street at the store, making sure no one of his description was approaching. When he brought the print, she wanted to be present.

He had been the perfect gentleman on the train. Her heart warmed at the thought. She'd felt so cared for, and he looked so distinguished. As they walked down the aisle, she saw the respectful glances from other passengers. Curious that he should be sitting in coach; she would have thought he'd be in first class. In fact, it was strange she had seen him on that train at all. But then he said he'd visited his mother in Boston, and it was reasonable to return after New Year's like she had. Well, the coincidence was all to her good. What an absolutely delightful tea he had treated her to. She had felt like a princess — no, that showed her girlishness. But she had felt like someone very much valued.

And what an opportune time to plumb his views on science and religion. After her discussions with Father, it seemed the perfect opportunity. But then, she'd done most of the talking. Had she foiled her own curiosity by waxing passionate? She thought back . . . he had said a number of things, asked questions in such a way as to give her a fair picture of where he stood. He had quoted Thomas Huxley's first article of faith. *What faith,* she grimaced. Huxley's faith in *himself* was more like it. And it was clear Huxley had no compunction in destroying others' cherished doctrines and institutions. That kind of hubris reminded her of Emerson.

Oh! And then, Mr. Lyons's crack about *blind* faith. How revealing. She stopped a moment, lost in thought.

She began walking again, careful of the snow on the sidewalk. Here, it hadn't been cleared off quite so well. Mrs. Smith's house was coming up and this would be the farthest she would walk. When she had talked with her father, he'd said Mr. Lyons was in the camp of those not only questioning their faith, but losing it as well. It looked as though her father was right. She wondered about Mr. Lyons's experience with God, that he could so readily question Him.

Ah, here was Mrs. Smith's house — she would turn back. She definitely felt loosened up after a long morning rearranging books. Not only did Mr. Chestley like to have the window display changed weekly, but various books placed full face on the shelves so that different titles caught a browser's eye.

She entered the bookstore at the rear door to shed her coat and boots. Voices could be heard at the front so she walked through the stacks to the counter. Mr. Lyons's large bulk and Mr. Chestley's smaller frame bent over a large rectangular object. Mr. Chestley looked up. "Celia! Our picture has arrived. Tell me what you think."

At her name Mr. Lyons turned around, a

smile warmed his face. "How do you do, Miss Thatcher?" He stepped aside.

"Very well, thank you." She looked at the picture. "But this isn't the frame you chose, Mr. Chestley." Wood carved in graceful, elongated curves framed the peaceful scene of pastured sheep and rolling hills. A feeling of loveliness washed over her. "This frame complements the print so much better than the simple wood one I thought you ordered." She looked up at her employer.

He was smiling, but his look directed her to Mr. Lyons. "We have a benefactor."

Celia's gaze shifted to Mr. Lyons. He had a twinkle in his eye. "It's beautiful, sir, much more than I could have thought possible. The carving is exquisite."

Mr. Lyons's smile widened.

Her eyes began to mist. Celia pulled a handkerchief from her pocket. "Now, look what you've done." She laughed through the tears. "I never expected a picture to do this."

"Then my instinct was right," Mr. Lyons said. "The simple wood frame would have served well, but the shopkeeper showed me this, done by a woodcarver from Germany. It had been ordered for another picture, but the matron decided she didn't like it for hers after all. The frame was priced lower

159

than I would have thought. I couldn't *not* buy it."

"Celia, he made up the difference and won't tell me what it is."

"It's too good of you, Mr. Lyons. We shall all enjoy it so much."

"Well, I will also benefit, coming here on a regular basis as I do."

"It will hang where we have our book discussions, so it will be enjoyed by many. But still," Mr. Chestley shook his head, "I can't imagine such a frame being inexpensive, even under the circumstances you described. We owe you a debt."

"Just a debt of thanks."

"My wife will be thrilled as well."

"Speaking of that good lady, I'd like to celebrate our good fortune and invite the two of you to dinner." He turned to Celia. "And you, too, Miss Thatcher."

Celia smiled her acceptance. Her inclusion seemed almost an afterthought, but that was as it should be. The Chestleys and Mr. Lyons were old friends.

"I'll convey the invitation to my wife," Mr. Chestley said. "She'll be delighted. What day were you thinking?"

"Would a week from Saturday suit? Say seven o'clock? That would give you time to close the bookstore."

"I think that will work."

"Good. I'll send the carriage round for you."

"Now I know we're celebrating. I don't believe I've seen you use a carriage since I've known you."

"It was sitting in the stable when I bought the place. Ned, who tends my horse, will take care of the arrangements. Expect him shortly before seven, if that's all right."

"That will be fine." Mr. Chestley held out his hand. "We should be having you over for dinner. I don't know what Mrs. Chestley will say."

Mr. Lyons shook the offered hand with decision. "Just have her say yes. And I have something to show you, too." Celia looked up at him, but he didn't elucidate. "Now, I must be on my way. After the trip to Boston, affairs at home need to be attended to. If you'll excuse me."

He bowed to Celia. As his head lifted, his eyes rested on her.

She felt his kind regard and it warmed her heart. "Thank you, sir; we will all look forward to the dinner."

After Mr. Lyons exited the shop, Mr. Chestley turned to her. "Better put your coat and boots back on. My wife would be upset if I didn't let her know about this invitation the minute I heard." He looked at Celia more closely. "My dear, no one, and I mean no one is ever invited to Mr. Lyons's. I hardly think anyone knows what the inside of his house looks like. This is most unusual. I wonder what prompted it."

"Well, to celebrate the pictures, dear Mr. Chestley. As I passed the jewelry store, I noticed Mr. Ellis hanging his."

"I wonder if he's invited to dinner as well."

"I wouldn't know!" She laughed. "You sound like a typical woman, all in a tizzy."

"Forgive me, my dear. It's just — this is so unusual. You cannot know." He looked down at the picture. "The carving is skill-fully done, very refined, isn't it? We'll hang this after you get back from Mrs. Chestley." He shooed her along with both hands. "Now, get along. News like this can't wait."

# 12

Saturday evening arrived and Celia gave a last look in the mirror. She had taken special care to arrange her hair in a twisted coil at the nape of her neck, something she thought different and elegant. The dress Mrs. Chestley approved was the same dark one she'd worn to the Harrods' dinner, but with the addition of a lace collar Grandmother had given her at Christmas. The collar was wide and draped down the front. Then, as she was about to leave that last day, Grandmother pressed a small box into her hand. "Something Aunt Hattie gave me years ago; they're larger than the ones from your grandfather. Their size will balance well with your wealth of lovely hair, my dear. There now," she said in a half-whisper. "I don't see you half as much as I'd like. Whenever you wear them, think of me."

Pearl earrings! Perfect with her present dress. When Mrs. Chestley saw them, she pronounced them the finishing touch. And now, as Celia stepped out her bedroom door, she caught Mr. Chestley's eye as he waited for his wife.

"Celia!" He looked her over approvingly. "You do these old eyes proud. I couldn't be more pleased with you, if you were my own daughter."

"I'm sure Mr. Lyons's home is all that is gracious. I want to do it credit."

"Oh, you'll do more than that, my dear. You'll be the jewel in the setting. Mark my words! And I think *you* had something to do with our invitation."

"You and Mrs. Chestley are the ones he really meant to invite. I was just an after-thought."

"I'm sure. I'm sure," he said with a twinkle in his eye.

After reaching for a blanket from the guest bedroom closet, Mrs. Divers temporarily placed it on the bed. Then she looked out the window. This second story gave her a better view. Of course, she knew just seeing Edward's house would upset her, but she supposed looking was force of habit.

But what was this? She craned her neck.

As fast as she could, she hobbled to the bedroom door. "Miss Waul! Miss Waul!

164

Come here — to the guest bedroom. Quick!"

A few moments later, her companion lumbered up the stairs.

"Look! Out this window and tell me what you make of it."

Miss Waul huffed her way across the room and peered into the darkness. "Well, if Mr. Lyons's house isn't all lit up. Usually it's dark as a tomb."

"Yes! Not only are the front rooms lighted, but the drive is marked by lanterns. I've never seen the like. What do you make of it?"

Miss Waul shrugged her shoulders. "What time is it?"

"I think it's near seven o'clock."

"Well, it's obvious he's going to have some kind of company. Unless they've already arrived."

"Let's keep watch a bit," Mrs. Divers insisted.

"Of course."

"I'll stand a few minutes. Then you take your turn. We'll drag over that chair for one of us."

"All right. Would you like some tea, something to warm you?"

"That might be good. Why don't you go down, fix some, and bring it up."

Miss Waul turned and crossed the room. Just as she exited the door, Mrs. Divers called, "Come back! A carriage is turning into the drive."

Miss Waul hurried back to the window. She stretched her neck. "There's just enough opening in the trees to see. It's pretty dark, though."

"But we'll be able to see *something*. There's enough light with the house lamps and all."

"To be sure."

Mrs. Divers all but held her breath as she observed the driver get off his perch and climb the steps to the front door. "Ah! That's Edward coming out. I'd know him anywhere. Look, he's accompanying the driver down the steps. I can't see them now. They're on the other side of the carriage." She felt her insides quiver with excitement. "Now look, Miss Waul, Edward is escorting one of the ladies up the steps."

"And there's another man who's helping the other lady."

"Can you identify anyone?"

"The portly man — I think that's Mr. Chestley. Don't you think?" Miss Waul asked.

"I think you're right. And if that's Mr. Chestley, one of the women has to be Mrs.

Chestley. And the slender one — would have to be Miss Thatcher."

"I think you've solved it, Mrs. Divers. In fact, I'm sure you have. Come to think of it, who else could it possibly be? That man doesn't socialize with anyone. The only place I know he goes besides the grocers is the bookstore."

"And out to hunt," Mrs. Divers added. "I saw him just the other day. Took that big bow of his." She shuddered.

"There!" Miss Waul said with finality. "Everyone's inside. I would think they might have been invited for dinner. If so, they'll be there for a while and we can relax some. Would you like me to get that tea?"

"I would think we could go downstairs, sit by the fire as usual, then come up here for a spell."

"We could take turns standing by the window."

"Exactly, Miss Waul."

Mr. Lyons gestured to the middle-aged woman in black with a white apron who stood waiting at his side. "This is Mrs. Macon, my cook and housekeeper. She'll take your wraps." He helped Mrs. Chestley with her coat. Celia noticed he helped the older lady first. How correct and gentlemanly of him.

Her eyes scanned the front hall. Its rich dark wood embraced a spacious foyer whose various doors and arches led to other rooms, but its striking feature was a wide staircase that mounted up to an airy second floor.

Mr. Lyons gestured to an arch to their left. "Would you like to sit in the drawing room? Dinner will be ready shortly."

Celia saw Mrs. Chestley's eager look. What fun they'd have talking over the house when they returned home. Mr. and Mrs. Chestley preceded her, and Mr. Lyons stretched out his other arm to encourage her to enter, almost touching her. Celia smiled up at him. He was so deferential in seeing to their comfort. She felt his care once again, and a certain protectiveness. Involuntarily she remembered his wife and her thoughts clouded. What had gone wrong?

As they entered the drawing room, Mrs. Chestley turned to their host. "What a beautiful room." Sand-colored walls gave the room a lighter appearance than the great hall. A large tapestry depicting a medieval hunt dominated the wall opposite the fireplace. Chairs and couches upholstered in shades of brown and crimson, their dark woods complementing the door and window frames. Drapes at the windows were deep brown velvet.

Sitting down, Celia felt the room's comfort, yet also its lovely formality. A luxurious, masculine room.

"I've never been in this house," Mr. Chestley stated. "Wasn't it built by one of the town's benefactors? At least, that's what I heard after my wife and I arrived as newlyweds."

"Yes, the man who built this house gave a large sum of money to the local Congregationalist church for their present building. I understand he was a member who originally hailed from Boston. Years later when his wife passed on, he put this up for sale. I heard about it through a mutual friend in the city, and on seeing it, decided on its purchase. Suited me admirably. He didn't build this on Elm Street, like the Harrods, where most of the town's larger homes are built. He wanted to walk out his back door and hunt the fields and forests — like myself."

"Are you a sportsman then?" Mrs. Chestley asked.

"Bow and arrow. As a boy, I used to pretend I was Robin Hood. Made up all sorts of stories as I trekked through the

169

woods at my grandparents' summer home. The memory of their house spurred me to purchase this."

"Are you still able to visit the house?" Mrs. Chestley asked.

"It burned to the ground."

"How terrible!"

"Yes, it was."

Celia thought a shadow passed over his countenance. Could she lighten the conversation? "Playing Robin Hood, did you have your band of merry men?"

Mr. Lyons smiled at the remembrance. "As a matter of fact, I did. Summers at my grandparents, I joined the local gang of boys. We built forts, played cowboys and Indians. But our favorite game was Robin Hood. Most of us had read the story in school, I guess. That summer we used imaginary bows. Next Christmas, I begged my parents for a bow and arrow. They thought it better than a gun. So the following year I took my bow to the grandparents' and started a local craze. From then on, we boys had archery contests and the like. I've never lost my love of the sport. Even here, I go out on a regular basis."

"Sportsman as well as literati," Mrs. Chestley said. "An unusual combination."

"I believe one balances the other."

The conversation continued on surface topics: the weather and Mr. Chestley's plans for the bookstore. In a few minutes, Mrs. Macon appeared in the doorway, announcing dinner. Mr. Lyons held out his arm to escort Mrs. Chestley, and her husband followed suit by offering his to Celia.

When Mrs. Macon brought out the first course of cream soup, Celia couldn't help smile. She knew Mr. Chestley would consider it the epitome of comfort soup, just enough substance to make one feel fed, but not too filling before the more substantial main course to follow. She fingered the thick, yet soft damask napkins and gazed at the centerpiece of crimson roses.

"*Général Jacqueminot*, from my greenhouse," Mr. Lyons said, nodding to the flowers. "I took care to cut them nearer the bud stage when their color is a bright red. When they are fully open, their color takes on a purple hue. If you like, I'll send them home with you."

Celia could see care had been taken in every detail; everything spoke elegance, yet masculinity prevailed.

"Ah!" Mr. Chestley exclaimed when the main course arrived. "Are my eyes deceiving me, or is that crown roast of pork?"

"Yes," Mrs. Macon assured him. "And I've

taken care to make sausage from the trimmings and put it in the crown to flavor and moisten the roast."

"Mrs. Macon, Mr. Lyons, you are spoiling us," Mrs. Chestley said.

"It was my intention to treat you as the valued friends you are." Mr. Lyons directed the conversation in pleasant paths, very much the master of his house. He told them about Christmas observances in Boston, then asked how their families celebrated. Celia found him especially interested in her family and what she had done during her visit. As dessert was served, he asked, "And what about that young man who escorted you onto the train? He said he would be paying a visit."

"Oh, he's an old friend. We've known each other for years. In fact, we went to school together."

"Is that Jack?" Mrs. Chestley asked. "You didn't tell me he was coming for a visit."

"He didn't make any specific plans. Just said he'd come *sometime.*"

"Well, be sure to let me know if he does. I'm glad to hear he's doing *something.*"

Celia felt herself blushing and involuntarily glanced at Mr. Lyons. His dark eyes met hers.

"After dinner, I would like to show you

172

my library," he said. "I think you'll find something of interest."

"We'd be honored," Mr. Chestley said.

Mrs. Macon entered just then and asked if anyone would like more dessert. "Speaking for myself, I don't think I could eat another mouthful," Mr. Chestley volunteered. "It was all delicious, simply delicious."

Mrs. Chestley turned and beamed at Mrs. Macon. "My husband gets considerably simpler fare at home."

"Thank you. It's been a pleasure to prepare a meal for more than one person. The cook in me has taken wing."

"Then we'll have to do this again sometime," Mr. Lyons said. "Now then, if we're ready, shall we go to the library?" He rose and pulled Mrs. Chestley's seat back for her. Then he held out his arm to escort her. Celia followed with Mr. Chestley.

Mr. Lyons led them into the hall and turned toward the back of the house. A door on the left opened into a brightly lit room with a crackling fire. Books lined the walls. Various niches held marble busts that Celia thought might be authors, but her gaze was immediately drawn to a picture on the far wall, above his desk.

"Mr. Lyons!" Her voice caught. "The

French print!" She crossed the room to the picture.

Mr. Lyons moved from Mrs. Chestley's side to stand near Celia.

"I can't believe it! You framed my picture," she accused. "I am envious!" She turned to him. "But I couldn't be more pleased. The frame suits it perfectly, the curves and scrolls in brushed gold is exquisite."

"Your reaction is reward in itself," he said in an undertone. They stood for some moments together, quietly looking at the picture.

Mr. Chestley came to stand beside his wife. "Look, my dear, how handsomely framed. An unusual piece for your library, Mr. Lyons." He turned and looked around. "But look at all you have here."

"Yes, besides books, I've collected other items that caught my eye over the years." He turned to guide them around the room. Gesturing toward the busts, he said, "Here is Cervantes. This next, Dante." He proceeded from one object to another. Celia looked at each piece with interest, noticing how often he looked at her when explaining an object. She felt that while he included the others, somehow, he wanted *her* to see all he had.

In one corner of the room, under glass,

stood a display of quills, ink pens, and other writing paraphernalia. "See this quill," he said. "It is said to have belonged to Benjamin Franklin. Some of the others belonged to my great-grandfather who was a great one for journaling. I occasionally read one of his journals. He comments on much that happened in his day. It's been instructive to read his philosophy of life and see how similarly our minds work. The journals are kept in my mother's library."

He turned to Mr. Chestley. "You, sir, would find the bookcase behind my desk of interest. Miss Thatcher, I dare say you will as well." He led them to his desk, and sitting in his chair, took a key out of the top drawer and unlocked the cabinet directly behind it. Pushing a glass panel to one side, he extracted a volume and handed it to Mr. Chestley.

Mr. Chestley looked at the spine, then opened to the title page. "A first edition. Remarkable! Do you have others?"

"Oh, yes. Sit here in my chair so you can better see. And, Mrs. Chestley, here is a book with illustrations you might find interesting." He handed her a volume before rising. "Why don't you come over to the settee in front of the fire. I'll stoke up the flames. And Miss Thatcher, feel free to browse wherever you like."

Celia wandered from section to section, amazed at the variety and scope of the library. She wondered if Mr. Lyons would be willing to lend her a book occasionally.

Sometime later, Mr. Chestley said, "I would need hours to appreciate all of this."

"Well then, you must return."

Mrs. Chestley rose, looking at her husband. "My dear, if you would like to return at a later date, then we should go now. It is getting late, and," she smiled at their host, "Mr. Lyons has been most gracious."

"You don't have to stand at that window any longer, Miss Waul." Mrs. Divers covered her mouth in a yawn. "We're both getting tired. Maybe I can send off to his housekeeper tomorrow to make sure who was there."

"It's a shame, us waiting all this time and not to know." Miss Waul shifted her weight onto her other foot. "But wait! Someone is coming out of the house."

"Oh!" Mrs. Divers bounded out of her chair and crowded her companion at the window.

"Why!" Miss Waul burst out, "jumped like a cat, you did. I didn't know you could move so. Up in a jiffy."

"Neither did I. My excitement superseded my arthritis." Mrs. Divers put her hand on her hip. "I think I overdid it. My achy old bones! I'll pay for it tomorrow." She adjusted her spectacles. "We could see better if you dimmed the lamp in the hall. Leave just enough light to find your way back."

"All right, but I don't want to miss a thing."

"Hurry, then."

As soon as Miss Waul returned, they gazed at the scene playing out through the aperture in the trees.

"Yes," Miss Waul said, "that rotund figure is certainly Mr. Chestley."

"Then we know the others. Well, I'm surprised Edward invited them." Mrs. Divers rubbed her hip, feeling cross. "Or had anyone over, for that matter."

"Me, too."

"Well, it really is time we go to bed. I'm a' aching and a' paining all over. Tomorrow is time enough to discuss all this and if there's anything we can do about it."

# 13

"Celia, dear! Mrs. Adams and I are here to deliver a little something." As Mrs. Harrod closed the bookstore door, she motioned her friend to the counter where Celia stood. "Look what I have — a package for you. Can you guess who sent it?"

Celia looked up smiling at one of her favorite people. Mrs. Harrod never failed to bring lighthearted gaiety wherever she went.

Mrs. Harrod hid the package behind her back. "Now guess."

"Let's see . . ."

"I'll give you a hint. It's from Boston."

"Boston! That couldn't be your son?"

"One and the same." Mrs. Harrod produced the brown-wrapped parcel from behind her back and laid it on the counter. "Do open it now. I'm sure Mr. Chestley wouldn't mind. I can't wait to see what Charles sent you."

Celia reached for the scissors beneath the

counter to cut the twine. "Whatever do you think possessed him to send this?"

"Oh, I might venture a guess."

Celia glanced up to see a pleased little smirk on her friend's face and felt a blush warm her cheeks. It didn't take much perception to see where this mother's thoughts were going. Celia had thought Charles terribly interesting, but hadn't a notion to hear anything from him. Yet a letter had followed a week after her return from home. And now this.

"This doesn't surprise me in the least," Mrs. Adams said, "when I saw the gallant way he escorted you home after the Christmas party."

Celia felt it necessary to downplay the romantically intended hint. "It looks like it might be a book, don't you think?"

"I wouldn't be surprised," Mrs. Harrod said. "Charles would be sure to send something that pleased."

Just then, the bookstore door opened. Celia glanced up while Mrs. Adams turned around and exclaimed, "Mr. Lyons!"

"Oh, do come and join us, Edward," Mrs. Harrod said. "Christmas isn't over yet. See, Celia has received another present." She nudged Mrs. Adams aside, making room for him at the counter. "Celia thinks it's a book. And I'm inclined to agree."

Mr. Lyons took off his hat, smoothed his hair, and approached them.

Celia took off the last of the wrapping and turned to see the cover. "It's a novel. *Jane Eyre.*"

"*Jane Eyre?* Oh my. Did he include a note?" Mrs. Harrod leaned over to see, then laughed. "My gracious, I'm nosy as can be. What do you do with someone like me, Edward, who wants to know all her son's doings with an attractive young woman?"

A sealed note fell from the pages. Celia felt her blush deepen.

"Well, good. I'm glad he had the manners to include a note. A mother likes to see her son follow through on the niceties." Celia held it up, hesitating, and Mrs. Harrod quickly said, "But of course open that later, my dear. You're going to think me meddling, and I won't have *that.* But I hope you like the book. The binding is unusual — blue. It might match your eyes. What do you think, Edward?"

"Mrs. Harrod!" Celia remonstrated.

"Oh, just a little fun. Look at Edward, Celia. And hold up the book."

Celia did as she was told. After a long moment, her eyes flicked down from the intensity in his.

"It is a near match." He held out his hand for the volume. "Let me examine it. The binding doesn't seem original to the book." He opened it. "See, several pages at the front and back don't quite match the rest. Charles has had it rebound for you, Miss Thatcher."

"There!" Mrs. Harrod crowed. "I knew he would make it special."

"It is absolutely lovely," Celia said. "I will enjoy owning it. I read the story some years ago and look forward to reading it again."

"Well, we won't tell Charles you've already read it. I would think he would be much chagrined."

"But this story bears up under a repeated reading. It will be a pleasure."

"Good. I hope you don't consider it forward, my dear, his giving you that particular book. Such a story!" She looked at Mr. Lyons archly. "What do you think, Edward?"

"I don't know if I have any particular opinion to express. Not to you ladies, at any rate."

"That sounds a little — mysterious, don't you think, Mrs. Adams? Like he's keeping something rather important from us." Mrs. Harrod looked at Edward more closely, then turned back to her friend. "You know, I think he'd make a perfect Mr. Rochester. Maybe a young Mr. Rochester, since he's trimmed his hair and beard, but certainly the same large, dark figure I envision."

Celia looked at Mrs. Adams to see her reaction. The woman was positively glowing. "I think you've caught him exactly," she said excitedly.

Celia contemplated Mr. Lyons some moments. Yes, he did look the part. Even acted the part.

"And," Mrs. Harrod suddenly laughed, "they even have the same first name. Oh, dear! Edward, I do believe I have stumbled onto something. You can no longer be that hermit who lives across town. You will now be the enigmatic Mr. Rochester."

"I hope you won't spread that around, Ma'am. I'm enough of a curiosity in this town without adding fuel to the fire."

"Just as long as you don't have a deranged wife in that second-story turret of yours."

"That I can assure you, Madam, I do not."

Celia noticed Mr. Lyons's brows gathering in a frown and Mrs. Harrod must have as well, because she quickly added, "Don't worry, Edward. I was just joking. You know me!" She said this last lightly with the particular feminine sprightliness she was known for. "And now that I've delivered the present, I must go. Oh, by the way, just a reminder. Edward, we hope you're planning to enter the flower show this year. Celia, he will have some beauties."

Celia almost said he certainly did, if the roses on his dining room table the other night were any indication. But for some reason she hesitated to reveal she'd had dinner in his home. Of course, the invitation had been primarily to Mr. and Mrs. Chestley, yet she felt it too — privileged or private a thing to reveal — she wasn't sure.

At Mr. Lyons's silence, Mrs. Harrod said, "Well, of course, you will enter. It will be another excellent opportunity to become reacquainted with the town. Won't it, Mrs. Adams? Now, we truly must be off. Celia, I will see you next week."

"Thank you for delivering the package."

"No trouble at all. I was dying of curiosity to see what was inside. You were very sweet to open it in my presence. Now, Mrs. Adams —" She fluttered a little wave before preceding her friend out the door.

Celia turned to Mr. Lyons. "Thank you for waiting. Is there something I can help you with?"

"Well . . . I . . ." He looked rather chagrined, Celia thought. "I'm wondering if my offering will be anticlimactic, after that."

"Oh, please don't think so."

He grimaced slightly, then opened his coat and took a small book from an inner pocket. "I meant to lend this to you after dinner the other evening."

Celia held out her hand for the little book. *Lyrical Ballads.* She opened to the title page. "There is no author; what is this?"

"Actually, two poets collaborated on the work. This first edition came out anonymously. Look through it and see if you can guess the poets."

She scanned the various titles. "*The Rime of the Ancient Mariner.* Ah! Coleridge, isn't it?"

"Correct." He smiled. "Now, can you deduce the other?"

"Here's *Tintern Abbey.* That is familiar." She pressed her lips together in concentration. "Oh! I almost have it. . . ."

"If you're acquainted with Coleridge's history, you'll remember these two became friends, took long walks through the hills of their region, and evolved theories of poetic diction — which resulted in this joint publication."

She looked up at him. "This is like a mystery. I'll guess Shelley. Or Keats?"

"No to both. But you're in the right time period."

"Can you give me another clue?"

"His name starts with a W."

"Wordsworth!" On his nod, she laughed, feeling quite sheepish. "A rather obvious clue. But I needed it, I'm afraid. I'll never forget the poem's author now."

"The collection of poems was published again and attributed to both writers. But this is a rare volume and I was curious to see if you could guess the authors."

"In that case, I will be certain to treat it with extra care. You are very good to bring it."

"You know, I invited the Chestleys and you to use my library whenever you like."

"That was most kind. I wondered if we would take advantage of your offer. Not that we wouldn't have wanted to, but you must realize most people are rather in awe of you."

"I don't know if *awe* is the right word."

"Well —" She stumbled a bit. "One certainly doesn't dream of taking advantage of you. Or even want to appear to do so."

"If I was apprehensive about that, I wouldn't have extended you the invitation."

"Thank you." Celia smiled. She felt the compliment. "It will have to be at the Chestleys' convenience."

"I understand." He stood looking at her a

moment. "I was thinking, if the Chestleys are too busy, who else might accompany you? That older woman from the other side of town who attends the book discussions?"

"Mrs. Smith?"

"Yes, do you think she would enjoy the library?"

Celia laughed. "I'm not sure how great a reader she is, but for the pure triumph of saying she'd been in your house —"

"Is it as bad as that? Well, maybe we'd better limit the invitation to Mr. and Mrs. Chestley for the present."

"Maybe so. It will be the greatest of pleasures."

"And please don't wait on ceremony. Or on another dinner invitation. What say you come on a Sunday afternoon? That should not interfere with work."

"If it's too early, it might interfere with Mr. Chestley's Sunday afternoon nap. But later, he and Mrs. Chestley usually take a walk. If they were to extend their walk to your house, maybe I could accompany them."

"That would be good." He looked at her a long moment, inhaling a long breath, then exhaling as if deeply satisfied. He stood at the counter some moments longer. To bridge the quiet, Celia said, "I can't help but second Mrs. Harrod's invitation."

"What?"

"The flower show."

"We'll see. I don't know if you realize it, but at the back of my house is a freestanding conservatory. When you come on a Sunday afternoon, early enough for a good bit of daylight, you might see that as well."

"I didn't realize you had a conservatory. Mrs. Harrod never mentioned it."

"Probably because hers is superior."

"Have you seen hers?"

"Just once."

"She's enlarged it recently, probably since you've visited. It seems the only thing left to add is exotics from different countries." Celia wondered if she should offer, then forged ahead, "I might mention you would be interested in seeing her conservatory again, if that would afford you the slightest pleasure."

"It would."

"Then I will suggest it."

Another long moment of silence ensued.

"Well, I'd best be off then," he said. "Keep the book as long as you like."

"Thank you. It was most kind of you to bring it, to even think of it."

"No kindness at all. I assure you."

But as he closed the door, she thought it

surely was. It gave her pause. He who was known to be a hermit, of sorts, making a special trip to the store . . . and then, offering free access to his library to the Chestleys and herself. . . .

In her mind's eye, she could visualize the richly appointed library: its volumes of thought, books of faraway places, and stories of varied experiences. She could see herself while away many an hour in one of the comfortable chairs near the fireplace.

Would Mr. Lyons be present? Would this give them more opportunity to talk — of religion, of his beliefs. She — she wanted to do so. He had such a fine mind, she didn't doubt his keen interest in examining the issues of the day, but he also seemed to have left the moorings of his faith. The thought of him teetering between belief and unbelief distressed her. Didn't Mr. Lyons too clearly demonstrate the thinking of many in these times?

Her father had said how quickly man resorted to his own devices, came to his own conclusions — mistakenly searched for answers to the great questions of life apart from God who had given that life. She thought back to her first conversation with Mr. Lyons about Emerson, on this very spot.

Celia folded the wrapping from Charles's gift, then put the twine in a box under the counter. Reaching for the scissors, she looked down at them. Such a useful item. Yet how easily she could cut outside prescribed lines and cause a defect in the object, even ruining it.

Just so with her budding friendship with Mr. Lyons. Didn't it need thought and care? She thought back to their time in the library after dinner, how they had enjoyed looking at the French print together. Two like minds, two similar sensibilities. Had she such affinity with anyone else?

Her father. She and her father were closer, they agreed on more and years had formed their relationship. She trusted him implicitly. Could she trust Mr. Lyons? She felt the underlying conflict in their beliefs, in their views.

Yet, there was something with Mr. Lyons she didn't have with her father. Her memory relived the scene in the library when they gazed at the French picture. She and her father had looked at art once in a gallery. But that had all been rather intellectual and impersonal compared to this instance. Mr. Lyons had bought the picture and had chosen the frame himself. He liked the picture, knew she liked it. Did that enter into his decision to purchase it, hang it in his treasured library and then make certain the Chestleys and she saw it? That *she* saw it? She remembered standing with him in front of the picture, standing close: pleasuring in the beauty, in the meaning of the loneliness and harshness of the scene. Sharing it . . . together.

"Oh!" A quiet gasp burst out her parted lips. Her deep enjoyment reliving those moments shocked her. She stood quietly, hardly breathing. Yes, she saw the need for care with Mr. Lyons, the need to be circumspect. That she should be careful not to engage too much of his time or interest, or her own. The books lined up on the bookshelves suddenly came into focus. She was back in the bookstore. How had her mind wandered so?

She must get busy. To that end, she took a turn around the store. When she reached Mr. Chestley's office, she had a sudden idea. Knowing he would be gone for a couple more hours, she decided to tidy up his place. She wouldn't disturb his papers, just give them a bit of straightening. Then dust the surfaces. Giving him the semblance of orderliness would brighten his day. She went in search of the feather duster.

Opening the little cupboard for the duster,

her mind flitted to *Jane Eyre*. How thoughtful of Charles to send it. When she'd mentioned on the carriage ride to the train she was in the mood for a good story, she never dreamed he'd do such a thing as buy her a novel. And, as his mother said, *such* a novel. But Mrs. Adams had said more than Celia thought appropriate or necessary. She was sure the woman was nice enough, but to have said what she did *out loud* —

Then she remembered Mrs. Harrod's reference to Mr. Lyons resembling Mr. Rochester. She wondered she hadn't noticed before his resemblance to the fictional protagonist.

As her hand found the feather duster, she forcibly stopped her woolgathering. She would start reading Charles's gift tonight after work. Oh, and read his note. That would be something to look forward to. Then finish with a poem from Mr. Wordsworth. Both readings would enrich her life. And what about the men? Would they both enrich her life as well?

Then, there was Jack.

Oh dear. Life was getting complicated.

Well, she loved to read, and one of its delights was to provide an escape from the real world — at this moment, her very real world.

# 14

Edward felt the snow scrunch under his feet as he walked a field edging his forest. He looked up at the somber, slate gray sky. An early morning hard frost had eased, so he had decided to go outdoors for a while. Bow in hand and a quiver of arrows strapped to his back, he stopped to pick his target. He spied a sapling at some distance, reached for an arrow and inserted it in the taut string. Left arm raised, he steeled it and pulled the arrow to his cheek. Aiming for a spot center and chest-high on the sapling, he let the arrow fly. In the quiet morning air, he heard the vibrating thwack as the steel tip struck the tree. It looked as if it hit dead center. A brief flicker of satisfaction warmed him. He inhaled the cold air before his eye narrowed on another target farther into the woods. He raised the bow once again, confident he would hit the mark.

It felt good to be sure of something. His

mind darted back to yesterday when he'd given Miss Thatcher the book of poems. He hoped the book had hit its mark as surely as that last arrow. He took a few steps, chose another tree, and let go another arrow, feeling a sudden rush of desire to hit the mark of her heart as surely as that arrow hit its target.

He knew she realized the value of the little book. He chose it to pique her interest. If she loved the poetic strangeness of the French print — he remembered her gazing at the print in his library — surely, the poems would pierce her sensibilities.

As of yet, though, he knew there was a part of him that was testing her. He needed to know the depth, the sensitivity of her mind. Did she have a true interest in what he valued? He felt she did, but had to know for certain. He couldn't bear another Marguerite. Just thinking the name brought a dull pain. It had been well over two years since her death. How could her memory yet stir such darkness in him?

He would dwell instead on yesterday's pleasure. Celia's eyebrow had a particular arch whenever she wondered about something — his heart quickened to remember it — he could see that delicate brow raised above that blue, blue eye. Charles had caught its perfect azure for the book cover. Confound the cub! Would that make any kind of lasting impression? He sincerely hoped not. Edward believed he was the only man to truly appreciate her, if all he surmised about her was true. Granted, she was a woman of set belief, of strong religious conviction, yet he also saw her mind wonder and leap at new thoughts and ideas.

How he would like to travel with her, see the marvel and delight in her eyes. Surely, travel would suit her. She had ventured from her parents' hearth and home to work in a town some distance from her own. A spirit of adventure must reside deep within her.

He spied another good target, notched an arrow, and lifted the bow. For a few moments he arrested his motion, his mind contemplated his next move: the following arrow he would aim at Miss Thatcher — no, *Celia's* — sensibilities. Of course, he had planned the dinner at his house for her, the introduction to his library, and most of all, the framed picture, all meant as arrows to her soul. He let the arrow fly. At the moment of its release, Charles came to mind again.

The arrow hit slightly off its mark. Drat him! How had it happened they had both given her a book the same day, and Charles's such an engaging story to boot? A bright boy, that lawyer in training. And young. Nearer her own age.

Yet surely, not so much younger than himself. He stretched his arms wide, felt the power and prowess of his own physique. Ah, he could sweep her off her feet and hold her close if he wanted. The suddenness of the thought, the desire, startled him. Surely, he was running ahead of himself.

Yet, if she was as he thought, as he envisioned her to be — the thoughts came thick and fast. He began walking quickly to keep pace with them.

In his heart, he craved a companion who shared his deepest longings, who understood him. With Marguerite, he had a mate for — what? She had been beautiful, engaging — at first. Had he married her only to satisfy fleshly desire?

How foolish he'd been. What he really desired was a mate for his soul. The sharpness of the realized hunger startled him. He stopped suddenly atop a mound of frozen soil. Had this need been lying dormant all this time?

Looking at the scene before him — the bare trees, the brown earth peeking through the clumps of snow, the sparsity of color —

he thought suddenly of the French print. The browns, blacks, and gray-whites. It could be termed a lonely scene and the colors only emphasized it, intensified it. Yet there was that little house in the distance, a wisp of smoke coming from its chimney. Life was inside. He liked to think the life of a man with his wife. And child . . .

But he must be careful. His heart could not afford to make another mistake.

He strode across the ground separating him from that last arrow. He'd gather his arrows, pull them from the trees. The exertion would do him good. He felt the need to make an effort, to expend this sudden burst of energy.

His thoughts drifted back again to the library. He'd felt himself drawn to Celia as a moth to a flame. But he had to make sure he wouldn't get burned. Once before he'd been burned — and badly. It was imperative he keep his senses about him, see what she was made of, for his own sake. And hers. For he would not hurt her for the world. The thought struck him as rather novel. He hadn't cared if he hurt Marguerite, at least at the end.

Edward yanked the last arrow from a trunk; it proved the dickens to extract.

Thinking of Celia had sparked off this

restless energy; he decided to venture farther into the forest. He would walk a while, hard, then make for the spot where he had hung a target. By then he'd be ready to shoot again. Hiking through this part of the forest was harder, but that was all to the good. He crashed ahead, soon feeling the sweat break out underneath his garments. After a half-hour of good hard striding, he slowed his pace. Calm returned. His lips pulled into a grin. He didn't remember the last time he'd been so boisterous. Yet the results of the walk were worth it; he felt more in control, more his old self.

The limb from which he'd hung the target was in a clearing another couple hundred feet ahead. He'd sit with that tree at his back. A good-sized depression near the base of the tree was filled with water. It made a natural clearing in the forest across which to shoot his arrows. The open area also attracted the slightest of breezes. That was good, making the target like an animal, which invariably moved — though now he didn't go after animals much, unless he had a taste for game.

He approached the glade quietly. The natives had surely settled around this water. For some reason he adopted their ways when he entered these grounds. Once he'd found several arrowheads. Rather a thrill. If he'd been a boy, he could imagine how ecstatic he'd have been. As he came in view of the tree, he heard voices — boys' voices.

"Old hermit" caught his ear. Involuntarily, he smiled. Were they talking about him? He looked around. They must be sitting on the other side of the tree. He sneaked closer, curious to hear what they'd say.

"Yeah. I saw him walking to the bookstore yesterday."

"He's awful big."

"But I'm not scared of him."

"Says you!"

"Shucks. I even snuck into his house once."

"You did not!"

"I did so!"

"When was that?"

"Aw . . . a couple years ago, I guess."

"What for?"

"Wanted to see his old lady."

"That old housekeeper?"

"No! His wife."

"But she's dead."

"I know that! It was before she died."

"I don't get it. Where did you see her?"

"In her bedroom."

"Cripes!"

"Yeah, I snuck up the stairs 'n' everything."

"You didn't! What'd you do that for?"

"Had to see how she looked. And she looked real sick. Mrs. Divers put me up to it."

"And you never got caught? How'd you know where to go — in the house?"

"Had a map in my head. After I got by the old housekeeper, it was easy. Yeah, that lady was sick, real sick. No wonder she died."

"My mom said it was *that devil* who killed her."

"The devil?"

"The hermit! The fellow who owns this property! Suppose he catches us here?"

"I'm not afraid of him."

Edward didn't know whether to rush the boys and scare them off his property or just leave. The thought of Celia stopped him, he didn't want anything coming to her ears.

So after a moment, he turned and quietly retraced his steps, picking up the pace when he got out of earshot. When he reached the edge of the woods, he stopped to gaze over the open field. But he felt like a hornet's nest had stirred up inside him. That boy sneaking into his house? And Mrs. Divers? What had she been up to? He thought the whole affair between Marguerite and himself had pretty much blown over. He'd been getting out into society, attending the book discussions. But apparently, parents were still telling children tales.

And what about Celia? If the townspeople, many of them, still regarded him with suspicion, how would this affect her opinion of him? What would the townspeople think of her if she associated with him too closely? He gripped the bow. Scowling, caught up in dark thoughts, he marched home.

Several days later, life had calmed down enough for Edward to appreciate the felicity of Mrs. Harrod's invitation. He stopped in front of her door and rapped briskly. She had let him know Miss Thatcher — *Celia* — would already be present. He had hoped to drop by the bookstore and escort her. Now he would have to content himself with Mrs. Harrod's arrangements. Yet, he had looked forward to this; he must not forget that. He determined to walk Celia home. Would that cause too much of a stir?

"Good to see you, sir," Hatfield said upon opening the door. "Come right this way. The ladies are expecting you. May I take your coat?"

The butler led the way to the rear of the

house. It had been some time since Edward had entered here. It looked much different without the holiday greenery to enliven it, but the immaculate appearance of the home gave its own welcome. A subtle smell of lemon and beeswax pervaded the air. A large container of flowers sitting on a lace runner graced the hall table. The womanly touch. His housekeeper was an excellent cook, but lacked that trait. Maybe he had been too strict in the appointments of his house, too ready to remove everything after — He heard women's laughter. Light-hearted, ebullient. Life was here, feminine life. He felt himself brighten.

As Hatfield ushered him into the conservatory, he took in everything at a glance. Here all was green and airy, a contrast to the browns, whites and blacks of winter outside. Pots of flowers tucked between the surrounding plants brought splashes of color. The glass panes overhead let in plenty of light, yet shades unfurled here and there protected delicate plants from the sun. He smelled the spicy fragrance of verdant greenery and blooming flowers. Summer in winter.

The ladies sat in wicker chairs surrounded by ferns. Their apparel made splashes of color against the green foliage, Celia's dress a dusky red, Mrs. Harrod's golden yellow.

"Mr. Lyons," Hatfield announced.

Edward smoothed his hands over the front of his tweed jacket and walked forward with anticipation. Mrs. Harrod stood at once, holding out her hands in welcome. "My dear Edward, how good of you to come. You must forgive my tardy invitation — of course, I knew you would enjoy seeing the new addition to our conservatory. I'm indebted to Celia for bringing it to my attention. Will you forgive me?"

"There's nothing to forgive, nothing at all." He took both her hands and bowed over them briefly. "I am just happy to be here." He smiled on straightening, looking at Miss Thatcher. He involuntarily glanced at the hand at her side. She did not offer it.

He looked up again, caught her smiling eye. "I must thank you for your suggestion. Mrs. Harrod is known for being the queen of hostesses, but this time I am indebted to you for suggesting the idea."

"You are most welcome, kind sir." Celia curtsied playfully. "Actually, I haven't been here recently, so am delighted to come as well."

"Then we're all in one accord, which suits me exactly," Mrs. Harrod said. "I was never one to like discord. My husband calls me

202

the peacemaker. I leave all the arguing to him and my son — I wouldn't have the least inclination to be a lawyer."

"But that's what makes you such a refreshment to come home to, I'm sure," Edward said. "Just now when I entered your house, I could sense the feminine good cheer. The light, the airiness, the welcome in the air. It was enough to make me desirous for the same in my home."

"Well, being by yourself in that big house, I don't wonder. But I'm glad you felt the welcome, and *you are* welcome, most assuredly." Warmth suffused Mrs. Harrod's face.

"I am sorry about one thing," she continued, "Mrs. Adams was also to have joined us, but she is under the weather today. I know you became friends after my Christmas party, and she's a fellow plant enthusiast. I hope Miss Thatcher and I can contrive to keep you entertained."

"I can't think of anything more delightful than the two of you."

"Good! Well, then, follow me, and I'll show you the latest addition to my conservatory. Of course, you remember this room we're in."

"Yes, but not this seating area or that table and chairs over there."

"No? Then you haven't been here for

some time. I added the furniture a couple of years ago. Just about the time of — well, no matter." Her hand dismissed the subject with a little flutter. "We shall have tea here later. But now, let me show you my exotics. The room is kept extra warm and moist, imitating the tropics. I am most fortunate; when I want something showy for the house when we have guests, Hatfield takes them out of their hothouse, returning the little Cinderellas at the stroke of midnight."

Edward opened the door for the ladies and followed them into a room filled with ferns, broad-leafed potted plants, and a rubber tree.

"My husband was most generous on my last birthday," Mrs. Harrod said. "Otherwise, this room would be quite empty."

Edward examined several orchids peeking from the greenery. "You have some noble specimens. I've never tried raising them. They have a reputation for being difficult."

"Not if you choose the right varieties. I started with *cattleyas* and *phalaenopsis*. Most orchids love humidity and good air circulation. But I believe these varieties could be grown at normal room temperatures with moderate humidity. This is to say, you wouldn't necessarily have to have a special room for them like I do."

"I still think it'll be some time before I grow orchids. When I do, I'll come to you for advice."

"And I'll be glad to give it," Mrs. Harrod said laughing. "Look here, I have a fan back wicker chair off to the side, behind this fern. Anyone can sit here and pretend they're in the tropics."

"Move from summer to the tropics, all within the space of two rooms. And in a New England winter to boot. Quite an accomplishment."

"Thank you. Now, take your time looking at the various specimens. When you're ready we'll return to the main part of the conservatory for refreshments."

Later, partaking of tea and cakes, Edward felt himself swelling with congeniality. He wasn't often in the company of ladies, especially two such charming ones.

After tea, the three of them walked around the main room of the conservatory, Mrs. Harrod proudly showing off a rose she had trained into a climber. "*Céline Forestier.* It's usually a large, loose shrub. An excellent repeater, otherwise, I doubt if it would bloom this time of year. Smell its fragrance."

"A delicious scent," Mr. Lyons said. "Pale yellow with hints of buff, apricot, and pink. Beautiful."

"If you'd like a cutting, it's easily propagated."

"Thank you. I have a special fondness for the rose." He looked at Miss Thatcher, wondering if she was enjoying this as much as he. "In fact, the rose is something of a specialty of mine. A favorite is the *Centifolia*. I wonder, Miss Thatcher, if you know to what I'm referring. The Dutch flower paintings from the seventeenth century onward?"

Celia laughed. "For once I can make an informed comment because my grandmother raises them. Its common name is cabbage rose, isn't it? I've always loved their enormous, full-bodied flowers with hundreds of petals."

"Bravo, Miss Thatcher." Edward tipped his head approvingly. "To me they are a queenly flower. Because of the size of the bush, most are in my yard. However, in my conservatory, I have a white one that I am working on to force earlier than its usual blooming time, which is late in the season. Do you know which variety your grandmother has?"

After half an hour of such talk, Edward reluctantly looked at his hostess and suggested it was time for him to leave. "Mrs. Harrod, you've been a perfect hostess. It's been a pleasure to talk with someone as informed as yourself. Miss Thatcher has had to listen all this time to two plant enthusiasts." He smiled at Celia. "More than you bargained for?"

"I had no idea the two of you were so knowledgeable. I caught only about half of what was said."

"But Celia is a quick learner." Mrs. Harrod took Celia's arm. "If she likes, she can come back when you return, Edward. And you must return."

"I will look forward to it." He looked at Celia. "May I escort you home, Miss Thatcher?"

"I'm sorry to disappoint you," Mrs. Harrod said, "but you can't. I'm keeping her a little longer. I'm hoping to prevail on her to accompany me to Boston."

"Boston?"

She laughed. "I declare, Edward, you should see your face."

In truth, for a second his mind had gone blank with surprise.

Mrs. Harrod continued, "I've asked Celia to accompany me on my spring shopping trip. I need someone's advice on what looks best on me. She said she'd stay and advise what in my closet could be donated to charity." Her eyes twinkled. "I have another idea what might be done with a few of those clothes."

"Well, ladies — Boston! I was just thinking of all you could see. Miss Thatcher, you must visit the Athenaeum. You will not find a better library anywhere."

"Of course, you would suggest a library!" Mrs. Harrod quipped.

"This one has some unique displays. I will be sure to procure you an introduction and a specially guided tour. It is a privately owned collection, you know."

"Well then, that might be nice." Mrs. Harrod held out her hand. "You would know what is most interesting to see, having grown up there."

Mr. Lyons took her hand and bowed over it. Then it struck him — they would be sure to visit Charles, might be entertained by him. That was an unpleasant thought.

He let go of Mrs. Harrod's hand, then looked at Celia. "Miss Thatcher?" Hogwash with convention that dictated a lady offer her hand first. He extended his. She followed his lead and lifted hers. He grasped it, bowing over it, held onto it longer than was strictly necessary. If he could not walk her home, he would have this small piece of her. And impress on his memory the feeling of her slim hand in his.

# 15

Celia fastened the top button of the silvery-blue walking dress Mrs. Harrod had given her a few weeks ago. She had never owned anything so lovely. The tiny pearl buttons down the front and a pleated flounce highlighted its beautiful bustle. She had dressed her flaxen hair in a sophisticated braid curled at the nape of her neck. Absolutely, she felt the height of fashion.

"If you're going to accompany me to Boston shops to give counsel on my new outfits, you must look the part," Mrs. Harrod said. The other outfit and dresses she gave Celia out of her closet had been altered to fit her figure.

Celia looked around the hotel sitting room for what seemed the hundredth time. The Louis XIV furniture fitted exactly her idea of elegant feminine appointments. How had this happened? It was all due to this extraordinary lady who had befriended her. Celia felt the honor of it, the privilege. As Mrs. Harrod brought delight into her life, Celia wanted to be a delight to her.

"My dear, are you ready?" Mrs. Harrod sailed into the room. "I declare! After that meal last night, I hope I retain something of my girlish figure. The waiter *would* tempt me with all those delicacies. What was your favorite? Mine was the lobster bisque. Oh dear, I do want my measurements just right for today's shopping. Of course, you don't have to worry. You have the tiniest waist."

"This beautiful outfit you gave me accentuates it. I've never had anything so elegant."

"And it looks perfectly ravishing on you. It didn't fit me anymore, so I'm glad I found someone who could wear it." She smoothed the front of her dove gray suit and picked up her handbag. "Now, let's be off. We have a lot to accomplish before we meet Charles this afternoon."

Celia was unaccustomed to walking into the type of shop Mrs. Harrod apparently frequented. The one time she'd been to Boston, she remembered glancing into the windows of refined establishments like these, never thinking to enter one. Now, she quietly followed her companion, letting her take the lead, being introduced as her particular friend, and sitting in a comfortable chair while Mrs. Harrod was shown pictures of the latest fashions from abroad. Swatches of material were brought out, and Mrs. Harrod kept looking to her for an opinion. Celia smiled to herself. The lady had some pretty definite ideas as to what she liked and what would look good on her. Only once did Celia offer a dissenting view that a more subdued green would look more elegant in a particular afternoon dress.

Mrs. Harrod held off the swatch, closed one eye to better visualize it against the picture. "I absolutely agree. Now, do you see why I brought you along? My husband will thank you, too, for keeping me from making such a costly mistake. He tells me when I enter a room and open my mouth to speak, I exude color enough." She laughed. "I see now if I wore that bright green, I would absolutely overwhelm people. Now, let's finish our business here and have a quick bite of lunch before we meet Charles. I don't know what he has in mind, but if he wants to take us around Boston, we'll just have to think about shoes tomorrow."

After ordering lunch, Mrs. Harrod asked the proprietor if he could procure them a buggy or some such vehicle, to drive them to her son's school. "He wants us to meet him at this address; he said two o'clock."

A pleasant ride through Boston ensued with the driver, acting as impromptu guide, pointing out several landmarks. When Mrs. Harrod complimented him on his knowledge, he answered, "Drivers of any hack know something of the city's history. And such a history, ladies. It's fortunate you came at a pleasant time of year." After they crossed the Charles River into Cambridge, he looked back over his shoulder. "Harvard University just ahead."

The ride fascinated Celia. She sat forward in her seat, eagerly taking it all in. The area here in Cambridge was more open than Boston. Trees had begun to bud, some to leaf, creating clouds of fairy green.

The driver nodded to a red brick building. "Now, there's your address." He lowered himself off his perch and held out his hand to help them down.

When they entered the hall and were just about to ask at the front desk, a familiar figure bounded out of a nearby alcove. "Mother!" Charles cried, "So good to see you." He hugged her hard. "Celia, how wonderful you've come." His eyes welcomed her.

Celia couldn't help note how fine Charles

was looking — and such a gentleman.

"I've set aside the rest of the day for the both of you. But before we go, I have a little surprise. Back of here, we're allowed to play different outdoors sports. If you'll follow me. . . ." He led them down the hall to the rear of the building, then out and along a walk to an archery range on the fringe of the property. A young man stood at some distance from a target, shooting arrows.

"Charles! Have you taken up your boyhood sport?" Mrs. Harrod asked.

"Wait until you see, Mother." Charles led them across the grass. After introductions were made, Charles's shooting companion said, "He has quite the upper hand of me, Ma'am."

"Well, I must say I am surprised. I can't wait to see a demonstration."

Charles smiled at Celia and after taking up a bow and a quiver of arrows, turned to face the target. She watched him, interested. He raised the bow with assurance and let go an arrow, hitting the center circle, exactly alongside his companion's last arrow. Both ladies clapped.

"Not perfect, but that will do for starters. My colleague has agreed to have a little competition," Charles said.

An agreeable rivalry followed. The men

each shot three rounds. Mrs. Harrod declared herself vastly entertained, especially when Charles's final shot hit dead center. She clapped again and Celia enthusiastically followed suit.

Charles took off his arm guard and handed his bow to his companion. "Would you be so good as to take these? I'm escorting my mother and Miss Thatcher on a tour of Boston. Mother, I've hired a carriage for the remainder of the afternoon."

Minutes later Charles handed his mother up to her seat.

"Let me arrange myself a moment," she said. "Charles, you and Celia sit opposite me."

Charles smiled and held out his hand to help Celia, then settled himself beside her.

"Something occurred to me just now, seeing you shoot," Mrs. Harrod said, looking at her son, "I'd like to include an archery contest as part of our flower show this June. It would draw more men, make it more of an event. Don't you think so?"

"Your shows are always an event, Mother, but if you'd like to add archery, why not?"

"Well, I'd want you to help me."

"In June, you say? When I come home next, just tell me what you want done."

"Thank you!" Mrs. Harrod leaned over to

pat her son's knee.

"Now," Charles turned to Celia, "did you do anything besides shopping this morning?" On Celia's shaking her head, he said, "I thought not. Mother is an indefatigable shopper. Since we're on this side of the river, I'll show you Harvard. There," he pointed, "on our left is the School of Divinity. You know, these last decades it has become quite the bastion of modernism. Thoroughly Unitarian, I'd say."

"My father said as much," Celia said. "It is sad, considering the first two hundred years it was a stronghold of Puritan, then later Calvinistic thought."

"Why do you say sad, my dear?" Mrs. Harrod asked. "I was never clear on what Unitarians believed."

Celia leaned forward. "They deny the doctrine of the Trinity and hold that God exists in only one person. Jesus, therefore, is not divine. But they do accept his moral teachings."

Charles looked at Celia. "I suspected you would be well-informed on the subject. Then you also know that Boston and nearby Concord and Walden Pond were the seats of Transcendentalism. And I know you don't agree with that," he said, laughing.

"True." Celia smiled.

"I find transcendental thinking interesting," Charles continued, "an idealist's view of life. Not too many years ago, it was thought radical, but opposition has lessened considerably, especially around these parts. You might be aware Harvard's embrace of liberal Christianity and Unitarianism has made it possible for Transcendental theologians to make their philosophy more acceptable. When we drive back to Boston, I'll take you by Emerson and Thoreau's homes."

"You sound like a thoroughly modern thinker."

He sat back with his arm draped over the posterior of the seat. "It behooves one to know the different systems of thought, and at this point, I think one way seems as good as another."

Celia glanced at Mrs. Harrod. Wasn't she disturbed by her son's talk?

"Relax, my dear Miss Thatcher, I haven't turned heathen yet. Sit back and enjoy the ride. That's better. Now, before we leave Harvard Yard, look around this corner at that large clapboard house. It's known as the Wadsworth House. Washington slept there."

He laughed at his mother's skeptical look. "He really did!"

■ ■ ■ ■

Late the following evening, Celia took off her wrapper and climbed into bed. Sitting up, she turned and placed an extra pillow behind her. She wasn't ready to sleep yet. What a lot she had to think about. Charles's stance yesterday about spiritual things disturbed her, yet it hadn't seemed the time to provoke an open discussion. And then, the luncheon this noon with Mr. Lyons's mother. Something there had piqued her interest — disquieted her, would be a better description.

The day had started innocently enough. Escorting them shopping this morning, Charles had asked, "Didn't you say you wanted to see the Athenaeum? We won't stop now, but this afternoon you can certainly visit." He then took his mother to her favorite shoe shop and they spent an hour ordering three new pairs to go with the dresses she'd ordered yesterday — a new pair for each outfit. Celia wasn't used to such extravagance. She had one everyday pair and another for Sunday. Mrs. Harrod certainly lived on a different economic scale than she did. Yet, Celia felt herself to be her equal.

That may very well be, but she had met her match at lunch today. She turned to plump up the pillows. Before she left for Boston, Mr. Lyons had paid her a visit in the bookstore and said his mother had extended an invitation to lunch. He'd already arranged it with Mrs. Harrod. Celia's first thought was that she didn't merit such attention, and her next was of his extreme generosity. That quickly followed with curiosity to see his boyhood home.

Charles had stopped the carriage in front of a red brick townhouse, the façade a restrained Greek Revival. *"Ma mère et mademoiselle!"* He gestured with a flourish. "I let you off in arguably the most prestigious address on Beacon Hill — Louisburg Square. Do not let the modest exteriors fool you; inside, I hear, is a completely different world. I envy your invitation to the crème of Boston society."

"I'm sure Mrs. Lyons would include you in our party if she knew you were with us," his mother said. "I could ask her."

"Absolutely not! I wouldn't disarrange Mrs. Lyons's plans for the world. But I will depend on you to tell me about your visit. Now both of you have a good time. I'll be along to pick you up at two o'clock."

When he handed them out of the carriage, he purposely took Celia's arm, catching her eye. "Now, my dear, you are not to ogle too much. Edward Lyons's home might be ancestral, but it's mere side entertainment. Your real interests lie with our party."

His comment took her by surprise. He had said it with a chuckle, but she heard the serious undercurrent.

The butler opened the door and showed them into the drawing room. Oriental rugs had the same warm reds Celia remembered in Mr. Lyons's house. Grand landscapes in gilt frames surrounded the marble fireplace — how these paintings must have nurtured Mr. Lyons's love of nature. And the crystal chandelier sparkled from both the gaslight and natural sunlight from the windows. Richly ornate and dignified described the room.

They had been received with perfect cordiality. Mrs. Lyons, patrician in both look and mien, inquired after their health, then asked how they had left her son.

"Oh, he's quite the most robust man I know," Mrs. Harrod said. "He has added much to our circle of society. But only recently."

"I surmised as much."

Celia smiled at the delicate reference to

219

his hibernation.

"And I must add," Mrs. Harrod said, "Miss Thatcher has had much to do with his coming out of his shell. She has the most fascinating book discussions."

"Book discussions! Did I hear someone refer to book discussions?" An older gentleman with white hair and a goatee hurried into the room.

"Let me introduce my brother recently arrived from St. Louis," Mrs. Lyons said. "Herbert, this is Mrs. Harrod and her friend Celia Thatcher. They both live in the town in which Edward now resides and have been most kind to him."

The elderly gentleman acknowledged the introduction with a courtly bow. "Honored to meet you." He looked at Celia with a spark of interest in his eye. "Edward wrote me around Christmas — I suppose he thinks it his duty to write his uncle at the holiday — and he mentioned with more than the usual enthusiasm a couple of book discussions he attended." He smiled. "And now I think I know why."

Sitting in the drawing room, Celia couldn't remember most of the small talk Mrs. Lyons introduced, but she did notice the uncle kept glancing at her. He kept moving impatiently in his chair and seemed to want to speak, then thinking better of it, letting his sister direct the conversation.

Lunch announced, they were ushered into a dining room hung with ancestral portraits. A polished mahogany sideboard and china cabinets displayed a wealth of blue and white Chinese porcelain. Mrs. Lyons had seated Celia to her left and Mrs. Harrod on her right. She politely asked them a number of questions and seemed impressed with Mrs. Harrod. With Celia, she seemed particularly interested in her employment and family. Celia wondered if there was a discreet mental cataloging of favorable and unfavorable. Uncle Herbert, on the other hand, had a genial, forthright manner. He asked about the book discussions and encouraged Celia to talk. When he spoke about himself, he led the conversation into his adventures in the west, drawing her into the web of his stories. "Would you be frightened of a huge rodent that had presented itself on your front porch?" he asked.

"I'm sure of it! A tiny mouse can leave me quaking in my shoes."

He laughed. "Said like a true bit of femininity. My first sighting of the rodent — when I moved west — I thought it must be a rat. Dusk had fallen and it was rather hard to see. Its body was about ten inches long and his tail the same."

"Twenty inches! But it *does* sound like something my brothers would handle with aplomb. Isn't that what brothers are for?"

"Charmingly put," he said in an undertone, then more loudly, "Fortunately, in due time I discovered my visitor was a muskrat, which seemed rather more intriguing than frightening."

Celia glanced at her hostess. Mrs. Harrod had asked Mrs. Lyons a question about the Chinese porcelain and they had become engrossed in their own conversation. She turned to the uncle and even though she tried to bring up more serious topics, he very determinedly kept the conversation on light, provocative fare. Finally, she gave up and returned his jests with her own. He chuckled. "My dear. You are delightful. I will have to write Edward and tell him so."

After that, conversation became general, shared amongst the four of them. Mrs. Harrod commented on the portraits adorning the walls. "Oh, we have our requisite ancestor who came over with the Mayflower," Uncle Herbert quipped. "That dour-looking fellow over the buffet." He turned to his sister. "But I forget, he was from your side of the family, wasn't he?"

"Yes." Mrs. Lyons directed her gaze at

Mrs. Harrod. "Herbert treats our ancestors rather lightly."

"But, of course, one cannot give them too much reverence," he said.

Mrs. Lyons glanced at him with a combination of disapproval and affection, but she proceeded to tell about the other Lyons forbears. After the last one had been introduced, Uncle Herbert leaned over to Celia. "The more recent family pictures are in the parlor. You must see the one of Edward when he was younger."

After coffee and dessert, they did just that. While Mrs. Lyons led Mrs. Harrod out of the dining room to explain the history behind additional porcelain in the drawing room, Uncle Herbert detoured Celia to the family parlor. A rose silk-draped table covered with photos sat at one end of the divan. "Here, this is the one I want you to see." He held up a framed picture of a beardless young man with high cheekbones and a sensitive mouth. Idealism shone from his eyes. Celia startled. Without his beard, Mr. Lyons was one of the most handsome men she had ever seen. A curious little feeling welled up within her. She found herself staring at the picture, wanting to commit it to memory.

"You are speechless, Miss Thatcher."

She looked up at the uncle. He smiled knowingly.

She tried to make her voice noncommittal. "If you saw your nephew today, I believe his eyes would show a more guarded look."

"But *your* eyes, they are shining like the proverbial stars, my dear." He put down the picture. "Handsome devil, isn't he?" He looked at her again. "And has he played the devil?"

"What do you mean?"

His voice lowered confidentially. "I refer to his deceased wife, of course. Do you know anything of that affair?"

She looked at him a long moment. "Only that she died a sad death. At a young age."

"Yes." He paused. "This is a rather difficult question for me to ask, but as a family member I feel I must know. Do you have any idea if Edward was responsible in any way?"

Celia's hand fluttered to the brooch at the throat of her high-necked dress. "There *are* rumors, but I know nothing of substance. I am new to the community. And you know, in a small town the least bit of gossip can fan itself into fact."

"Just so." His lips pursed. "But I've never been satisfied on that score. Edward was an only child, and only children can be rather self-absorbed. And she being an only child, as well, it didn't surprise me that the marriage turned out to be an unhappy one. But for it to end as it did!"

He cleared his throat. "But enough of that." He held out his arm to escort Celia. "If Edward doesn't enter the lists for your hand, I will. You are too delightful to lose to someone else's family." A gleam brightened his eye. "Besides, we need a Beauty among our staid and dreary wall of family portraits. Now, my dear, shall we join the others?"

Celia removed the extra pillow from behind her and nestled under the bedcovers. That Uncle Herbert was a character. She bubbled up with laughter at the remembrance. Hopefully, she could sleep. The day had certainly been thought provoking.

# 16

The train pulled out of Boston, its whistle sounding distant and muffled from within the Pullman car's maroon and gold fitted interior. Celia looked out the window to see Charles walking and then jogging alongside. He threw a final, flamboyant kiss.

Mrs. Harrod turned in her seat to see the last of her son. "Just like Charles! He's terribly engaging. Don't you think so, Celia?"

"He is one of the most charming men of my acquaintance. I believe he has some of his mother in him."

Mrs. Harrod laughed. "You know how to curry favor. Shameless, girl!"

Celia smiled and settled back in her large, luxurious seat. She looked out the window for a minute, then glanced at Mrs. Harrod poking about in her satchel. That dear lady had spared no expense for this trip, and Celia appreciated it more than her friend could ever know. The Harrods might be accustomed to such things, but for Celia, everything was new and exciting — even her clothing. Today, she was dressed in a smoke gray traveling suit with onyx buttons and a matching plumed hat. Another of Mrs. Harrod's castoffs that no longer suited her, or so she said. The woman was as generous as she was charming. Celia hoped she would be as open-handed, if ever in a position to do so.

She gazed at the luxurious compartment and thought back to Christmas. On the train from home to the Chestleys, she had come upon Mr. Lyons, sitting in coach. She had wondered about it at the time, thinking he would surely travel in first class, but then had thought no more of it. But now, after seeing his home in Boston, she knew beyond a doubt that *coach* would not have been his usual accommodation.

He had been sitting, apparently perfectly content, reading a book when she walked down the aisle. She remembered him rising with alacrity, offering a seat beside him. Maybe it was Jack with her, the introductions and all, that had occupied her thoughts and made her so unaware of this oddity. No, he certainly would not have been riding in coach. Not with his home, his former home, on Louisburg Square. He must have purposely sat there so as not to miss her.

How kind and gentlemanly of him. It bespoke warmth of friendship on his part. A friendship she now gladly acknowledged to be one of her most precious gifts. She would say this despite his lack of belief in God, despite the dark mystery that surrounded his wife's death. Indeed, to think of him sitting in coach on that hard bench when he could have been sitting here, spoke the depth of his regard, his willingness to sacrifice —

Mrs. Harrod straightened in her seat. "I've decided to read a book to while away the time. See, I am taking my cue from you. You already have yours. But first," she dropped the book on her lap, "tell me what you thought of our time in Boston."

"There's so much to tell."

"Start with your overall impression."

"Well, I feel as if I've had a 'coming out.' " Celia clapped her hands twice, quietly, so as not to attract too much attention. "Just like the girls from fine families in Boston who have a cotillion. Or like a young woman in Regency England coming out into society with all the new dresses, parties, and such. Those girls couldn't have felt more special than I do now. The clothes you've given me, Mrs. Harrod! And this wonderful trip seeing the sights with Charles." She warmed to her topic. "Going to dinner with the two of you. Taking in the play. All of it. I feel older, more experienced, not so much a girl. More like a woman."

"I accomplished all that? How delightful! I wanted you to have a wonderful time, but had no idea all this was taking place."

"Oh, yes." Celia turned slightly to give her friend her full attention. "But enough about me. What were some of your favorite times?"

"Well, shopping would have to be first. Then spending time with Charles and seeing how special he thinks you." She poked a finger on Celia's arm. "And to actually have an invitation to Louisburg Square. I've always wondered what the inside of those homes looked like. Now I feel I've quite arrived. Mr. Lyons — Edward — was most gracious to arrange it."

Celia's mind flitted to the luncheon. As Charles had said, the home was ancestral, as evidenced by all those portraits. Mrs. Lyons took an obvious pride in her heritage, for it was her family that had come over with the Mayflower. Her husband's family had crossed later, and he being a maritime lawyer had bought all the beautiful Chinese porcelains.

Mrs. Harrod continued, "I got along

famously with Mrs. Lyons. And you seemed to do well with Uncle Herbert."

"I enjoyed meeting him." Celia felt herself glow. Uncle Herbert was absolutely breezy compared to Mrs. Lyons.

"What did he show you in the parlor? I didn't say anything at the time, but you had such a look on your face."

"I did? He just showed me a picture of his nephew when he was younger."

"Edward as a boy?"

"No, as a young man, but clean-shaven."

"Without his beard? Now that would be interesting."

It certainly had been interesting. Celia had noticed every detail. The wavy brown hair, the high cheekbones, the lips, the light shining from his eyes, and committed it all to memory.

As she and Uncle Herbert walked out of the family parlor, he had nearly proposed, or hinted that his nephew should. Of course, he was joking, but how absolutely feminine and attractive the old gentleman had made her feel. Just the way a girl — any woman — would want to.

She arched her back and looked up at the beautifully decorated ceiling. How wonderful she felt.

■ ■ ■ ■

Mr. and Mrs. Chestley stood on the station platform; Celia saw them scanning each window looking eagerly for her. After all the new places and adventures, how nice to see home folks.

"Oh, there's Mrs. Adams," Mrs. Harrod said. "My husband wired me in Boston that he couldn't meet me. Said Mrs. Adams had volunteered to come. But Hatfield is with her. He'll take care of everything."

Mrs. Harrod lightly grasped Celia's arm. "Let's be extra nice to her. The poor dear was terribly disappointed to learn I hadn't invited her to accompany us to Boston. Said she'd had given her eye teeth to see Mr. Lyons's home. I believe she's interested in him."

Celia looked at Mrs. Harrod, questioningly.

"Well, you know, they are about the same age. And both from a similar social strata — they might do very well together. I had thought of inviting her, but you know after Mrs. Lyons invited us to lunch, I just didn't feel right asking her." Mrs. Harrod released her arm. "But I will be sure to tell her *every* detail."

Stepping off the train, Celia glanced at Mrs. Adams before Mrs. Chestley folded her to her ample bosom.

"Dear, it's so good to see you again. I would hardly dare embrace such a sophisticated-looking lady, but I know it's our dear Celia. I was telling Mr. Chestley how empty the house felt with you away."

"Let me take your valise," Mr. Chestley said, beaming.

Mrs. Adams greeted Celia, but her eyes belied the welcome. "Miss Thatcher, you look quite the —"

"For Charles, you know," Mrs. Harrod said in an undertone, "for Charles. I'll tell you all about it." Then she turned to Celia. "Let me hug you goodbye. We did have an absolutely delightful time, didn't we?"

When Celia entered the Chestley home with the older couple hovering over her, she couldn't help but see how very modest it was in comparison to all she'd seen in Boston. Yet how comforting as well. She looked forward to her own little room. It might be rather plain, but it provided that quiet solitude she often craved.

"We're having my special potato soup for supper," Mrs. Chestley said. "I know it's a favorite, and I want you to feel as if you are coming home."

"I do!"

"Well, change your clothes. No, don't worry about helping with supper tonight. Mr. Chestley said he would. You are the guest of honor. While we eat, you can tell us all about your trip." She reached out her arms to give Celia a spontaneous hug. "Oh, and I almost forgot, you have a letter. I put it on your dresser." Mrs. Chestley's eyes twinkled up into hers.

"I'll change my travel outfit directly." Celia hugged Mrs. Chestley hard in return.

As soon as Celia entered her room, she walked to the dresser. She looked at the name on the return address: J. Milford. Jack! What did he have to say? She dropped into the chair near the window and opened the envelope. Was it what she hoped? Yes, he had written asking permission to visit. He'd finally taken her up on her invitation. How delightful. He mentioned a date two weeks hence. So that's what made Mrs. Chestley's eyes twinkle. Celia smiled. From the first, Jack had had the inside track with Mrs. Chestley. Dear Jack. There was nothing like home folks.

Supper was a cozy affair. Mrs. Chestley insisted Celia swallow a few mouthfuls before telling them anything. "You must get

233

up your strength, dear. Traveling can be so tiring."

If the Chestleys had seen how Mrs. Harrod traveled in such comfort and luxury, they would have a hard time believing travel was tiring.

Her homecoming wouldn't have been complete without seeing Mr. Lyons. He came to the bookstore the very next day, earlier than usual. When he came through the door, Celia looked up. But it was like seeing him through new eyes. Was Mrs. Adams interested in him?

"Ah, the traveler has returned," he said, holding out both hands in greeting. She reciprocated by extending hers. He took them warmly, gently in his. "Welcome home." He held them a moment longer before releasing them. "I take it Boston was all you hoped."

"More than I hoped. One of the highlights was time spent in your home. It was most thoughtful of you to arrange a visit."

"I trust Mother was well."

"She was. And very proper, of course. I would have felt overwhelmed, but for someone present who blurred the lines of propriety." When he looked at her expectantly, she tipped her head and whispered, "Uncle Herbert."

"Ha!" He laughed. "I heard he was to arrive around the time of your visit. You have met the family maverick."

"If Uncle Herbert hadn't been there and taken me under his wing, I would have been quite overcome. Louisburg Square, no less!"

"Mother is proud of the family. I'm sure you were given a tour of the family portraits. But I hope she didn't intimidate you."

"She and Mrs. Harrod got along very well together, and Uncle Herbert took it upon himself to entertain me, telling about his life out west."

"I've heard many of his tales. Some of them rather tall. I hope he didn't say or do anything to make you feel uncomfortable."

"Oh no. In fact, he was an excellent host." She paused. "One thing was quite interesting. He did show me a picture of you when you were younger."

The corner of Mr. Lyons's mouth twitched. "Ah, that must have been before I had a beard. What did you think of it?"

"It was — surprising." She looked at him a long moment. Yes, she could see the young man in him, even now. And better yet, his eyes were more like those of the picture, less guarded than when she'd first met him.

"So did you think — anything in particular?"

A bubble of laughter rose. "Oh! I could just imagine all the females dangling after you."

"That uncle of mine. He usually has some mischief up his sleeve."

She laughed outright at that.

"What made you laugh?" he asked.

"When we were speaking of the family portraits he said I would make a lovely addition to the gallery."

"That *would* add some interest. The group is rather sober, isn't it? Did he propose how to accomplish that?"

"He said he would offer for my hand, but thought a younger man would do better."

"The old codger."

"I was flattered. Of course, I knew he was joking. By the way, he said to give you his regards."

"Thank you. Well, it sounds as if you survived Uncle Herbert. Now, how did you like Boston's Athenaeum?"

"It was beautiful! I couldn't believe all the books. And the paintings on the walls. I felt like I was in a hallowed sanctum. Your friend who gave us a guided tour said that Emerson, Hawthorne, and Whitman did their research there. Think of it!"

236

"Ah, now I see you are developing a proper respect for Emerson. I dislike reminding you how little you thought of him when we first met."

"Oh, yes," she said, "our discussion of his *Reliance.*"

"I grant you, some people think he's rather progressive with his transcendental thinking. But I predict he will influence the way men think for decades to come."

Celia looked at him quizzically. "How would you characterize the Transcendentalists?"

"In simplest terms," he said, "they are idealists. They believe, along with Kant and Plato, there are truths that dawn on a person from intuition rather than from our senses such as sight, touch, hearing." His eyes questioned her, apparently assessing whether he should continue. She nodded enthusiastically. He smiled. "I know many literary critics maintain Emerson's 1836 work *Nature* as the founding document of Transcendentalism, but the Rev. William Ellery Channing, a Unitarian, preached a sermon, 'Likeness to God,' that started people thinking even earlier. In it, he said there is a single spiritual entity present in all of us — what Emerson later called the Oversoul — which is outside ourselves and yet part of us. Channing said the best place to study and observe this spiritual unity was in nature."

"You said the sermon was titled 'Likeness to God'? So where does God's Word come in all this?"

"I don't know that it does."

"Now that stands to reason," she quipped, "trying to discover God without reference to His personal Word about Himself."

"I don't know if *personal* fits into their idea of God. They think more in terms of a relationship with the universe."

"Ah!" Her eyebrows lifted. "Seeking after the universe when they could know the God who made the universe." She couldn't believe what she was hearing.

"Huh-hum," he cleared his throat. "That's one of the things I like about you, Miss Thatcher; you think. But I hope we may agree to disagree. Here, take my arm. I want to show you something."

There seemed nothing to do but follow his lead. He led her to the place in the store where they had the book discussions.

"Now," he said. "Look at the print Mr. Chestley recently hung with all the surrounding books. Of what does it remind you?"

"Oh! The Athenaeum. In a small way, of

course."

"I'm glad you see it, Miss Thatcher. I think that's one reason I like this bookstore. It reminds me of where I spent so many happy hours during student days."

"Thank you for the recommendation to see that place. Mrs. Harrod was most impressed with your connections there. Between that and your home, her already high estimation of you climbed even higher." She gave him an arch look. "Considering Mrs. Harrod is the social hub of our small town, I would call that a master stroke of yours. Win the queen, and the subjects will follow."

"That may be true, but I am particularly interested in one of her subjects." His eye effectively nailed her as his object. He bent his head down to hers. "May I call you Celia? Miss Thatcher seems too formal somehow for such friends as we've become."

Celia hesitated. "I suppose that would be proper enough."

He smiled. "And you must call me Edward."

She took her hand from his arm. "That would seem too familiar for me, I'm afraid, especially in front of others."

"Well then," he paused, "maybe only when we talk by ourselves, or with close friends."

He looked at her searchingly. "You will, won't you?"

She didn't know how to deny him. "If you wish."

"I do."

Celia felt warmth rise to her cheeks. She sought a subject less personal. "Did I mention I had news from home?" Her lips couldn't help curve in a smile.

"No, but you are obviously bursting at the seams."

"I had a letter waiting me when I returned. From an old friend who's coming to visit."

Edward walked down his drive and turned onto the road. He decided to proceed past Mrs. Divers's house then onto Main Street. He felt restless. Ordinarily, he would walk in the fields or the woods in back of his house. But today he wanted to be around people. He wanted to talk with someone. The discussion he'd had with Celia about Transcendentalism a couple weeks ago had started him thinking along those lines again. She had been very quiet as he defined the movement and its thinking. Under his breath, he quoted Emerson's *Nature:* "The foregoing generations beheld God and nature face to face. . . . Why should not we also enjoy an original relation to the universe?"

Yes, he thought, an original relation to the universe. Why adhere to the rigid orthodoxy of the Puritans, the Calvinists? Most of his contemporaries derided Puritan belief that saw man as weak and a sinner. They thought these old belief systems encouraged flawed societal strictures. He thought of the Salem witch trials to the north of Boston nearly two centuries before. And the persecution of the Quakers.

Yet, he had to be just and try to understand the opposing viewpoint, how there must be some merit in these systems of belief. He thought back to the Puritans who first landed at Plymouth, just south of his home in Boston, who taught a person must not only *understand* his religion, but *feel* it as well.

He found the intellectual and emotional sides of Puritanism confusing. How did the two fit together to make a coherent faith? Couldn't men walk down different paths to find the truth? Some, like his grandfather, embraced Unitarianism — which some said was so highly intellectual as to not seem a religion at all. But it suited him better than the emotionalism of the more evangelical faiths. Maybe that was why Transcendentalism appealed to him. He could rely on himself to find his own relation to the universe. And thereby, he hoped, to God.

He was approaching the bookstore. Without consciously admitting it, this was where he was heading.

But what was this? Beyond, at the jewelry store he saw Celia looking in its window with a young man. His step slowed.

At first, he didn't recognize the young man, but as he drew nearer, the man at Celia's side heard his footsteps and turned so that Edward could see his face. Jack! Celia's old friend from home.

Edward didn't know what to do, but felt an overwhelming impulse to impose his will on the situation and on Jack: *This far, and no farther.*

He came upon them rather abruptly. Celia turned and her countenance brightened on seeing him. The iciness that had taken hold of his heart melted somewhat.

"Hello," he said. "I was just out walking."

"I am so glad you happened by." Celia gestured to the man at her side. "You remember my introducing you to Jack? He was the one who escorted me onto the train at my hometown."

Jack smiled, hesitated, then held out his hand. Edward shook it belatedly. For the life of him, he couldn't initiate the handshake, give the welcome as was expected. "So are you here for long?" he blurted out.

"As long as Celia will allow that I'm not in the way."

"Where are you staying?" Tact had deserted him.

"Mr. and Mrs. Chestley have made room for me in their sitting room. I have a pallet. It'll be comfortable enough."

If Edward remembered rightly, the two bedrooms opened directly off the sitting room. Just a door separating this young man from Celia, from where she slept. He might even hear her moving about. It was not *proper,* Edward's mother would say.

On the spur of the moment, he said, "That's all very well and good, but you need better accommodations. I have a large home with several bedrooms that are unused. I insist you use one of them."

Celia looked at him, surprise written across her face. "That's too kind of you. I would never have thought to ask such a favor."

"I know it's not my usual manner, but I insist." He directed his look at Jack.

"Well," Celia turned to Jack, "it will be much more comfortable than your present accommodation, I can assure you. And his

243

house is down the road a ways, around that corner."

"First-class accommodations," Mr. Lyons said with forced heartiness. "I have a house-keeper who cooks for me. She can give you breakfast or whatever other meals you need. Believe me, she is itching to get her hands on another person to feed. Living by myself, I am woefully inadequate for her ideas of cooking and hospitality. And I've been thinking of having the Chestleys and Miss Thatcher over for a meal. That would help everyone all around, wouldn't it?"

As he walked away he wondered at what he'd said, where it had all come from. He certainly was going against the Boston Brahmin grain to invite a stranger into his home. His mother always said, "We never know anyone unless we've 'always' known them." However, he was personally begin-ning to feel better, setting some parameters on this Jack person.

Turning the corner into his own street, he thought, I'll take the young man hunting, sound out his mind. He remembered read-ing Clemens's article, "Old Times on the Mississippi," where *mark twain* sounded the depth in which to safely navigate a steam-boat. He doubted Jack's mind would sound a *mark twain* and prove a safe or desirable depth for Celia.

He felt like a bear about to protect its cub.

# 17

In the coming days having Jack as a guest gave Edward ample opportunity to be both subtle and direct. Never had he felt his powers to persuade and cajole more in evidence. If his father, the lawyer, could have seen the way he cross-examined this young man, being both conniving and open, he would have been well pleased.

Jack and he sat over coffee one morning. Edward asked him, what had he read recently? What did he think of this particular scientist? Did he have any intellectual interests outside his religion? But on this last Edward hit a rock he hoped wouldn't prove to be his stumbling stone — for he saw that Jack and Celia shared the same beliefs.

Other than that, Jack showed himself to be an ordinary American, the kind who was not a scientist, a philosopher, or even much of a reader. He was familiar with only a few books beyond the Bible. Edward could see he was practical rather than speculative. In fact, Jack was little concerned with intellectual questions of any kind.

Could Celia be trusted to see this?

A week later when Jack was to leave for home, Edward offered his carriage for the ride to the train station but decided not to accompany him. He must leave Celia to say goodbye in private. Then, after she saw Jack off at the train station, Edward had arranged for her to come to his home. He wanted her to preview what he hoped to enter in the flower show. Already blooms were showing themselves in the conservatory.

When the carriage finally arrived, he did not wait for it to stop before he was out the door to assist her down. She was looking uncommonly well, in a dusty blue full-skirted frock with matching wrap. His heart gave an uncomfortable lurch. She had taken special care in her dress and appearance to see Jack off. Descending the carriage her eyes were friendly as they looked up into his, but was there a trace of sadness, of melancholy perhaps?

"Thank you for inviting me to a preview of your roses," she said. "In your conservatory?"

He thought her quite businesslike in her

address. This did not bode well for finding out what was really in her heart. He offered his arm. "Before we go into the greenhouse, I'd like to show you the roses at the back of the house."

"You have roses in both places?"

"The flowers for the show will probably come from the garden. But to cover my bets, I grew some in the conservatory."

"Ah!" She laughed. "You will be a hard man to beat."

"Competition raises my blood. You are entering, of course."

"Mrs. Chestley has a climber that's done middling in past years. She said I was welcome to it if I could make it flower better. I think one of her problems is that she seldom fertilizes. Too busy. I asked one of the farmers at church to bring me some manure; in addition, every once in awhile I throw dishwater over the plant. Now the climber is doing so well, I'm hoping for some satisfactory blooms."

"Good for you. I'm not entering a climber, so we'll not be competing against each other."

Walking around the back of the house, Celia stopped at roses growing up a couple of pillars.

"You have climbers?"

"No, Stanwell Perpetual, a scraggly bush which can be useful as a pillar rose."

She leaned toward the flowers. "Pink, like a shell. With a strong, sweet fragrance."

"Be careful. They have thorns."

"Oh, I see!"

"The advantage to this flower is its early blooming and then continuously flowering until early winter."

"I like its fragrance."

"I'll cut a few for you to take home, though I warn you, the flowers won't last."

"But the fragrance will last in my memory."

They stepped into the conservatory, and because she no longer needed assistance, he reluctantly released her hand from his arm. However, they remained close, seeing the constraints of the path size. Each time her skirt brushed his leg, he felt the contact.

"Here is a famous rose, a soft flesh pink. If I told you it was named after the country house of Napoleon's Josephine, could you guess its name?"

*"Malmaison?"*

"Yes. *Souvenir de là Malmaison.* This rose fares better in hot, dry climates, but I like a challenge. Besides, its beauty and name appeals to me."

She looked around, pleasure on her expressive face. "And these other roses, you have so many colors. How delightful."

"I like diversity. I'll cut several varieties for you to take home."

"Mrs. Chestley would love that."

"I hope you will, too."

"Oh yes!" Her smile was pure sunshine.

After a tour of the conservatory, he asked, "Won't you come to the house for tea? We can put the flowers in water temporarily, then wrap them in damp cloths for you to take home."

"I don't know. Mr. Chestley is expecting me."

"We'll do the abbreviated version of tea." He wouldn't take no for an answer. He reached for shears and cut several blooms. With a decisive move, he opened the door of the conservatory, then walked to the back of the house and cut a few blooms of Stanwell Perpetual. Then he led her around the front of the house and into the foyer and placed the flowers on the hall table.

"Here, let me assist you with your wrap." She turned to let him lift it from her, and his fingertips touched her shoulders. He was sorely tempted to wrap his arms around her, but that would surprise, shock her. He must be circumspect. Besides, he still didn't know where her affections stood regarding Jack.

Last night Edward had seen them laughing together in his drawing room. Celia hadn't meant for what they shared to be a private joke, but Jack did. As they walked into the dining room, Jack placed her hand on his arm and then put his hand possessively over hers. Later in the foyer, Edward had seen him stand closer to her than was necessary.

Just now, she turned around, her eyes thanking him for taking her wrap, then took off her gloves and handed them to him.

He draped the lot on the hall chair, then reached for the flowers.

"Before you remove them, let me smell the Stanwell again," she said. "I love its sweet fragrance."

He loosened it from the other roses, but the pink cluster accidentally fell to the floor. She quickly knelt to pick it up.

"Oh!" A large bead of blood formed on her finger. "How clumsy of me."

Edward immediately put down the other roses and took a cambric handkerchief from his pocket. "Here," he held it out to her, "press this against the puncture." When she hesitated, he took her hand in his and pressed the cloth against the finger.

"I didn't want to soil your handkerchief."

"My housekeeper is adept at such types of

cleaning. When I come in from hunting, I occasionally give her opportunity to show her skill. This is nothing." He continued to press her finger to the cloth. Her delicate hand in his emboldened him. "I hadn't asked about Jack's departure. Did he get off without incident?"

"The train was on time and everything went well."

He hesitated only a moment. "I imagine you will miss him."

"Yes. People from home are special."

That sounded quite matter-of-fact. He felt hope expand within him. "What I meant was — has he wanted to become more than a friend?"

She blushed. "Well, he did ask to come again. I said I would welcome him as a friend. But nothing more."

His hand involuntarily closed on hers. He couldn't help asking, "Was he disappointed?"

Her gaze shifted away a moment. "Yes," she said softly.

"As should be expected." He smiled. "With such a prize to be gained."

She glanced up, her eyes widened. "Maybe I'd best go after all."

"I shouldn't have — pried," he said quickly. "I'll have Mrs. Macon put these flowers in water and make tea for us. It'll only take a few minutes. Besides, I have something in the library I want to show you. Two or three books came to my attention I think you'll be interested in."

He should have realized that in dismissing one suitor so soon she would not be ready to entertain another. For now, to be with her would have to be enough.

When he escorted her into the library and they began talking about books, he could see her begin to relax. Then when Mrs. Macon brought tea into the drawing room, he made a point of including the house-keeper in the conversation. A third party made things more comfortable — and proper, as his mother would say. When Mrs. Macon left, he shared a funny story, asked Celia what she remembered being humor-ous about her childhood, was careful to keep the conversation on a friendly, imper-sonal level. But he didn't know when he'd enjoyed a tea more. He was loath to see her leave, but he had promised an abbreviated teatime.

"Would you like the carriage, with all these roses to carry?"

"Oh no. It's such a short distance, I'd rather walk. If the flowers are adequately wrapped, I should have no trouble with them." She laughed, glancing at her finger.

Minutes later, he watched her walk down his drive, and waved when she turned onto the road. He resisted the urge to keep watching her. He must not seem to hover.

But wait until the flower show, my dear Miss Thatcher, and the archery contest. I have a little surprise in store for you. Something, I hope —

The flower show was just a few weeks away. He could wait that long.

Celia hadn't progressed more than a short ways down the road when a carriage drove up from behind. She had been so occupied with thought, she hadn't noticed its approach. Had the occupant seen her exit from Mr. Lyons's drive? Celia felt the slightest tinge of apprehension.

"Miss Thatcher. What a surprise." The familiar voice of Mrs. Adams spoke from the depths of her conveyance.

Celia turned and put a pleased smile on her face. If there was one person she didn't want to see at this particular juncture, it was this woman. "Hello, Mrs. Adams. A pleasant day to be out, isn't it?"

"Oh my, what roses! And what a lot to carry. I'll give you a ride."

"Thank you, but I'm fine. The flowers are

wrapped up well for carrying."

"But I insist. Here, give them to me and James can assist you up." As Celia started to shake her head, Mrs. Adams held out her hands for the flowers and James had already jumped from his perch.

Celia felt the ungraciousness of a further refusal so gave Mrs. Adams the roses. When she settled herself on the seat, the woman buried her face in the blooms.

"What heavenly fragrance! All these intermingling scents. You won't mind if I hold them a little longer, will you?"

The buggy started with just the slightest of jerks before Mrs. Adams continued, "What a fashionable outfit you are wearing, my dear. And so feminine."

"Thank you. Mrs. Harrod graciously had one of hers made over for me."

"Oh, yes, she told me — Charles —" Mrs. Adams broke off smiling. "I know Mrs. Harrod hopes — well that's none of my business." She turned just slightly — Celia felt her full attention. "But didn't I just see you coming out of Mr. Lyons's drive? Are these his roses?"

"Yes, he was kind enough to cut them for me."

"How generous. I can't believe he already has so many flowers in bloom. Did he do the same for everyone else?"

Celia felt sudden heat rise to her cheeks, "I was the only one."

"How unusual for him to single someone out." At Celia's silence, Mrs. Adams's mouth opened, but then closed it again. A pregnant pause followed. "But you don't mean . . . you weren't there by yourself?"

Celia tried to formulate words that would mitigate the situation. "I had just seen Jack, my friend from home, to the train station, and Mr. Lyons invited me to see his possible entries for the flower show." Celia tried to make it seem as casual as it had first appeared.

"Still," Mrs. Adams continued, "you know how these things can look. I wouldn't want any gossip — Mr. Lyons being a particular friend of mine who's had such a time of it since his wife's death, and for your sake, too, my dear. Well, I guess, especially for you." Mrs. Adams released one hand from the roses to place sympathetically over Celia's. "Don't worry. If anyone should say anything, I'll be sure to tell them how innocent it all was."

She took her hand away and once again grasped the flowers. "You're so young, you might not realize what you've done." Then she looked at Celia more closely. "But it *was* innocent, wasn't it?"

"Of course! Mr. Lyons and I are just friends. And being that we both have an interest in flowers . . ."

"I'm sure. But I being older, and more knowing in the ways of the world, I want to warn you. Please, my dear, don't let it happen again. Always have someone accompany you, like Mr. or Mrs. Chestley." She paused. "Now that I think more on it, going over there for any reason might give the poor man ideas. I'm sure he was hurt by his wife, contrary to rumors, and a man alone like that — after he's been married — will get lonely, hungry even, for female companionship. You might give him ideas, ones which we wouldn't want him to have. It would be most unkind to *him.* You understand, my dear?"

Celia felt a sickening shame settle on her. Saw how it might appear to anyone seeing her come from Mr. Lyons's house alone. She hastened to say, "Thank you for your warning. But let me assure you again, we are just friends."

The carriage had come to a stop. Mrs. Adams glanced out her side of the carriage. "Ah, the bookstore."

Celia looked over at her flowers. Mrs. Adams seemed loath to hand them back. The woman held them off to better view them. "What a beautiful profusion of color. Of course, I'm sure Mr. Lyons would have given his blooms to anyone present. Why don't you first step down from the carriage, my dear? Then I'll hand them to you." She smelled their fragrance again.

Celia stepped down before James could assist her, and held out her hands for the roses. If Mrs. Adams called her "my dear" one more time, she would — well, she didn't know what she'd do.

Celia picked up an entry form from the counter. Mrs. Divers said she wanted one, but neither she nor Miss Waul had been by to pick it up. And today was the final day to enter the contest. Well, she would deliver it herself. Mr. Chestley had told her to get some fresh air.

As she turned into the road fronting Mrs. Divers's house, she couldn't help remembering the afternoon a couple weeks earlier when she'd started down this same road with the roses Mr. Lyons had given her. When Mrs. Adams stopped her. And once she climbed into her carriage, how the woman had warned her, even chided her.

She had put the flowers in a vase and placed it in the Chestley's sitting room for

everyone to enjoy. That underlined the —
what was the word Mrs. Adams used — in-
nocence of her visit. When she passed the
bouquet, she would stop and smell the different fragrances mingling together. How
redolent they'd been of her time with Edward.

He'd been very concerned about her
relationship with Jack. Just the night before,
in fact, Jack had all but offered marriage.
But she hadn't let him say the words. It
would have spoiled their beautiful, light-
hearted friendship. During Jack's visit, when
she had tried to talk about serious subjects,
books for instance, he seemed only mildly
interested. Did he ever think deeply? She
knew she would tire of the same round of
small talk. Talk that centered largely on
himself. As entertaining as that could be, it
would take a woman in love to enjoy hearing about him on such a continual basis.

She wasn't in love with him. How could
she be, when she had so eagerly accepted
the invitation to take the carriage to Edward's home? She'd so wanted to see his
roses. And he was so generous in giving her
his best blooms from the conservatory and
that cluster off the pillars at the back of his
house.

But thinking back on her time in his foyer,

she had felt herself walking on eggs. When he helped her with her wrap and his fingers touched her shoulders, she felt a tingle go through her. And then her foolish carelessness in pricking her finger. How could she know he'd hold her hand, and she wanting him to. She could have pressed the handkerchief to her own finger, but she'd let him do it. She was rather shocked at herself, to give in to temptation when she knew there could be nothing further between them.

Finally, when he said something about her being a prize to be gained, she came to her senses and righted things. He took the hint and acted the perfect gentleman, in the library and afterward at tea. Like two old friends. Thank goodness. These last two weeks she'd disciplined her mind to hardly think of him. Or rather, dwell on him.

She lifted her skirt as her foot found the first step up to Mrs. Divers's front door. During this visit, she was certain if the subject of Mr. Lyons was introduced, Mrs. Divers would cure her of any ills along that line, knowing her antipathy toward the man.

She knocked on the door, and Miss Waul answered.

"Miss Thatcher, how good of you to come. I've been under the weather and have just started feeling myself again. Mrs. Divers is out back inspecting her flowers. I know she'll want to see you."

Miss Waul led the way around the house. "Mrs. Divers! Look who's here."

Mrs. Divers stood with one hand on her hip, her face scrunched up, examining her flowers. "Oh, Miss Thatcher, it's you." She glanced at the application Celia held, but didn't reach for it. "Well, if that isn't neighborly of you. My hands are a bit soiled. Miss Waul, will you take that please? You can bring it into the house. I'd like a few minutes with Miss Thatcher."

While Miss Waul walked away, Mrs. Divers said in a low voice, "I'll give you a preview of what I hope to enter. Today there's just a hint of pink. I hope these buds are out in full bloom next week." She looked affectionately at the bush. "If not, the prize will go to someone else. If I just had better health, I'd spend more time out here. As it is. . . ."

She ambled over to another rosebush. "You see this one? I wish it did better. It belonged to my daughter. With its striped pink and white petals, it's a real looker. But there's not a chance of my entering *that* this year. I'd lose for sure. Only one other person in town has it to my knowledge —" She pursed her lips. "You must know I'm

261

talking about my neighbor; I will *not* speak his name." She looked at Celia closely. "But I've been hearing things, my dear, that he's been paying you attention. That you were in his house. Alone."

In the next lightning moment, Celia's mind whirled. From whom did Mrs. Divers hear that Mrs. Adams?

"I'm surprised, Miss Thatcher. And disappointed. Take it from me, don't take anything he says or does seriously. He's all out for himself." Mrs. Divers stepped near another bush, her gnarled fingers cupping a budding flower. "His constancy is like one of these. Ephemeral. Why, he couldn't be faithful for any length of time to any woman. He doesn't have it in him. He's an intelligent man — I'll give him that. But as soon as he tires of something, he turns his back on it — or *her* as the case may be. The way he treated my Marguerite."

With one part of her Celia listened to Mrs. Divers's bitter words about Mr. Lyons, the other aghast at the gossip about herself.

They turned from the bush and started for the house. As they approached the steps to the front door, Celia found herself questioning, arguing the two concerns. Mrs. Adams had said she wouldn't say anything, hadn't she? But the woman had made her extremely uncomfortable during that ride in her carriage. Uncomfortable was hardly the word.

And what did Mrs. Divers mean, Edward couldn't be faithful or self-sacrificing? Celia thought again of how he had humbled himself to ride in coach on the train after Christmas.

Celia helped Mrs. Divers up the steps. As she did so, she was at a complete loss what to say about being in Edward's house alone. If Mrs. Divers didn't say anything more, maybe the best thing would be not to say anything. Let it drop. As to her relationship with Edward, because of their disagreement over the spiritual — which she considered most important in life — she knew he could not be considered anything more than a friend.

Even this she was beginning to find dangerous. Could they remain friends with the way she caught herself thinking about him? The way she was starting to react whenever she was with him?

"Now, dearie," Mrs. Divers said, as they stopped in front of the door, "mind what I say. I only brought up the man for your own good. Believe me, I was his mother-in-law. I know what I'm talking about."

Celia grasped Mrs. Divers's arm. "Thank

you. I know you have my best interests at heart. Let me assure you, Mr. Lyons and I are only friends. And that's the way I believe it should stay."

"That's a relief to me. And *don't* you be alone with him again. I trust you, but I certainly don't trust him." Mrs. Divers reached up to squeeze Celia's hand before she turned in at her door.

# 18

Mrs. Divers looked out her bedroom window. Blue sky had begun to appear. That heartened her. She'd attend the flower show despite her arthritis. It was no fun getting old, that was for certain, but Miss Waul would help carry her contribution to the contest. Judging would be at ten o'clock with lunch on the grounds. Last year they had ribbons and streamers marking off the area for the town-wide affair, even invited the brass band from the next town to play a concert. That added so much to the festivities she hadn't a doubt they'd be here again this year. It would make for a full day. She might need to come home in between activities to rest. But then maybe Miss Waul could find them a place in the shade to sip a lemonade, rest their limbs, and she could stay the whole time.

By the time she creaked down the stairs, her knees and the steps doing a duet, she was good and hungry for the bacon she smelled drifting from the kitchen. Honestly, she didn't know what she'd do without Miss Waul. Rising to fix her own breakfast, especially early like this, was a thing of the past. Of course, she used to do it for her husband and Marguerite, but that seemed a long, long time ago. Somewhere in there, Miss Waul had come into their lives, about the time her husband took sick. He had insisted she help out twice a week, but when he died Miss Waul came to stay. She had been a loyal friend to lean on.

By the time Mrs. Divers entered the kitchen, it had begun to smell smoky. She expected to see Miss Waul bending over the stove, but no one was in the room. She hobbled as fast as she could across the kitchen to examine affairs on the stove.

"My gracious, this bacon's a-hoppin' and a-poppin'." Mrs. Divers grabbed a dish-towel, folded it over for a pot holder and slid the pan off the burner, grabbing a cover to stop the spattering fat. She had just saved the bacon and maybe the kitchen to boot. Her insides shook like jelly.

She dropped with a thump onto one of the kitchen chairs, put her elbows on the table, hands covering her face. How well she remembered that fire when she was fourteen. It was one of the horrors of her young, protected life. One day the village where she grew up was all nice and serene, everybody going about his business, and the next day that terrible conflagration left a charred house right in the middle of town. A grease fire, they'd said. The scorched, smoky remains of that blaze stayed for a long time before the town carted all the burned stuff away. All because of a grease fire! If Miss Waul wasn't careful, she would start one. Where was she?

Mrs. Divers heard the kitchen door open. Turning, she saw her companion. "Now, where in the world have you been? I came down to find the bacon smoking away!"

"I'm sorry, Mrs. Divers!" Miss Waul held out the roses. "Here. I went to cut your flowers for you. I guess I just forgot the time, even that I was cooking bacon."

"The flowers!" Mrs. Divers got up and hurried as best she could to the cupboard for a vase. "Don't you know the first thing about roses? They must go in water immediately!" She reached for the vase she thought best for the length of stem she saw in Miss Waul's hand, then rushed to a pitcher of water that had already been drawn from the well. "We must recut the stems and put them in water right away."

The next minute she worked feverishly. "Now we want to put in some apple cider vinegar and sugar. Mix them in some water over there, then add to the flowers. That'll keep them fresh."

After Miss Waul poured the sugar mixture into the water, she walked over to the stove. "You did the right thing, Mrs. Divers, getting this pan off the burner and putting a lid on it." She reached for a potholder and lifted the lid. "My gracious, this bacon was getting charred. And that fat! I ain't seen so much fat come off bacon in ages. No wonder you was peeved. I'm sorry, truly I am."

"You remember this happened before, a couple months ago? You could burn down this house."

"I know, I know. It was careless of me. I'm so sorry." Miss Waul reached for a fork and started lifting the bacon out of the pan. "But you should see it out there this morning. That orange-yellow sun shining, making everything golden. I haven't been up and outside this early for so long, I just forgot myself, off in another world."

"You'll be in another world all right, if you burn this house down with us in it. My gracious, all this before breakfast! I wouldn't have thought it."

"Now calm yourself, Mrs. Divers. We have

a lot to look forward to today. Besides the flower show, there's the archery contest at two, don't forget that."

"If *that* man shows up at the archery contest —"

"Now, don't think about that, it'll ruin your day. You know he hasn't come to the flower event since — don't know why he'd start now. Let me get up some eggs with this bacon, then we'll get dressed and get our roses to the show."

Celia walked up to the flower tables and greeted the Harrods.

"Thank goodness you're here, Celia." Mrs. Harrod gave her a quick hug and turned to her husband. "Will you double-check all is ready for the archery contest? Celia will help me make sure the flower judging gets off to a smooth start."

Celia watched Mr. Harrod pinch his wife on the cheek. "Don't worry, my dear," he said. "Everything will go fine like always." He turned, a spring in his step.

"Just seeing him walk so confidently gives me assurance," Mrs. Harrod said. "How nice to have a husband who can take charge and make sure something's done right. Such a dear." She turned to the flower tables. "Celia, look at these blooms, will you? All the colors of the rainbow. I wish I were an artist. This is one of my favorite parts of the day, seeing these beautiful flowers lined up like this." Mrs. Harrod adjusted one of the numbers in front of a bouquet. "We have the different categories nicely separated, don't we? Would you get the judges from the tent now?"

Celia gave the rows of glorious blooms a last appreciative look. "I'll be glad to. They should be finished with their refreshments."

As she walked to the tent, she breathed in the balmy morning air. The clear blue sky with the still, cool air refreshed her. And the grass was a lovely, verdant green. Earlier this morning when she cut her roses, the sun had just been peeking over the trees. How she gloried in its saffron light, gilding grass and foliage. The day couldn't have started out more gloriously. In the distance, she heard the happy sounds of children playing impromptu games before the real competitions began. Contests and games had been planned for all ages, and at the end, a three-legged race for the boys and their fathers.

"There you are, my dear Miss Thatcher." Charles walked up, a wide grin on his face. "You look perfection in that white frocked dress."

"Thank you, kind sir." She swept him a spontaneous curtsey. "Are you ready for the archery contest this afternoon?"

"Absolutely. I'm planning a light lunch so I can be at my sharpest."

"I know you'll do really well. When your mother and I saw you shoot at Harvard, I was sure no one could beat you."

"I don't know about this local competition. We have a few hunters in the group. These country boys might come on stronger than one suspects. Then there's Mr. Lyons. I wonder about his level of play. The trouble is he does nothing by half measures and just the fact he's entered should tell a person something. Have you seen him this morning?"

"No, but it's early. His contributions for the flower show were delivered before I arrived. Your mother said Mrs. Macon brought them with Ned's help."

"Well then, he might not appear until the contest itself. You know how sensitive he is about town feeling. Too bad. He's rather a nice fellow, I think. Who would have guessed his family lived on Louisburg Square? Well yes, I suppose I could have *guessed,* but to *know* rather changes things. Of course, most of that brouhaha with him and his wife occurred when I was at school."

Celia wouldn't go down that rabbit trail. Instead, she smiled and said, "I must go to the refreshment tent. I promised your mother I'd escort the judges to the flower tables."

"May I accompany you?"

Her smile widened. "I think that would be permitted. Your mother also said I might be needed for other errands."

"Lead on, fair maiden!"

Celia spent the next hour running errands with Charles, then afterward attending events with him. They laughed and clapped together at the children's races. He intimated he wouldn't have been present if it wasn't for her, certainly wouldn't have had half the fun. She told him she was flattered.

Just as he took her elbow to help her over a tree root, they came upon Mrs. Adams sitting in the shade sipping lemonade. A wave of displeasure hit Celia. Mrs. Divers's talk came to Celia's mind. Had Mrs. Adams gossiped about her? However, Celia had forgiven her — but to have these negative feelings surface so quickly Celia wondered if she'd forgiven her at all.

Mrs. Adams smiled nicely at them, and Celia made herself return the smile and comment on the lovely day. Charles was all affability. "We're off to the three-legged race," he volunteered.

"What a delightful couple you make," Mrs. Adams cooed.

Celia had all she could do to keep the smile on her face. How she hated a comment like that. The woman was obviously trying to steer her toward Charles and away from — But even as her hackles rose, Celia was determined she *would not* let the woman spoil her day. Besides, Charles was pleasant to be with.

"Now, Miss Celia," he said, after they had lunched together, "I must leave you to get ready for the archery contest. I expect you to cheer me on. I understand you are awarding the winner."

"Yes," she said laughing. "Your mother insists. I don't know why, but she said for this particular event she wanted someone other than herself doing the honors."

"Or she doesn't want to present the prize to her own son. For the awards, you and I would make a good-looking pair."

Celia blushed. "You are quite confident of yourself, aren't you?"

"Do you mean the archery contest or with you?" he asked, a light in his eyes.

"I meant the contest, of course." She felt her blush deepen.

He held out his hand to grasp hers. "Wish

me luck."

"Of course."

She hoped he did well, but as he said, these country men could spring a surprise. Then there was Mr. Lyons — Edward. She had no idea he had entered. Now that the archery contest was shortly to begin, she craned her neck looking for him, but he was nowhere to be seen.

Ah, there were the Chestleys. She would walk with them to the archery field. On the way, they met up with Mrs. Harrod. How nice to be part of so congenial a group. When they arrived, Mr. Harrod came up to them. "You ready to take your places?" Because she was to present the prizes, she, along with Mrs. Harrod were to sit in a ribboned-off section at the front of the field.

Mrs. Chestley shooed her off. "You go on, dear. We'll be just fine here to the side." Celia glanced fondly at the Chestleys as Mr. Harrod took both her and Mrs. Harrod's elbows to escort them. After she was seated, she scanned the row of contestants. She didn't see Edward. Of course, it was still a few minutes before the competition was to begin. People were scurrying around to find a place to stand. She noticed Mrs. Divers and Miss Waul finding a place alongside the Chestleys. And a boy squeezed in front with them — it was that boy that had almost knocked her over on the sidewalk last fall. He looked up at Mrs. Divers and smiled.

Celia glanced at the line of archers. Charles caught her eye and smiled. The competition would begin any minute. She turned in her chair, scanning the crowd for Edward. A tall man with a bow was advancing just behind a family of four. The size and bearing of the man proclaimed him to be Edward. But his face! The family of four passed and he was now in full view. His eyes found hers and hinted a twinkle. She stared, she was looking at the flesh and blood version of his portrait as a younger man, beardless. The same picture that had so caught her fancy — the same luminous eyes, the lips, the high cheekbones, the closer haircut that made him seem more boyish. The debonair handsomeness of the young man in the picture translated into the man before her but with more maturity. She remembered her reaction on seeing the picture and the same reaction flooded her now.

More than one person turned to look at him. She was vaguely aware of several girls whispering behind their gloved hands. If he was aware of the stir he was causing, he didn't let on. He stopped in front of her and Mrs. Harrod. He bowed briefly, then walked on to take his place with the other contestants.

"Celia!" Mrs. Harrod grabbed hold of her arm. "Such a transformation. Why, I never in my life! Words escape me."

Edward took off his coat and strapped on his arm guard, his broad shoulders and remarkable physique clearly outlined in his shirt. Celia was glad she was sitting. The sheer beauty and physical strength of the man — she was still feeling the shock of seeing the picture come to life.

Should she look away from the archers, from him? That would seem odd — to look in another direction. That would call attention to itself. What she really wanted to do was feast her eyes on this man.

But, she warned herself, they were friends only. It could go no further than that. Their difference in faith and the problem of Marguerite loomed before her. She turned to pay attention to Mrs. Harrod at her side. They could pass the time making a few choice comments to each other. In another minute, she could turn again to look at the field of contestants. However, when she did so, her eyes were only on *him.*

Why had he done it, cutting off his beard and mustache? And trimmed his hair in that fashion? The townspeople hardly recognized him. Of course, he hadn't gone into society much these last years. Had he cut his hair and beard so as not to be recognized? But, surely, people only had to ask who he was.

She was the only one who had seen that portrait and commented on it. Had she revealed how much it had stirred her? Had he — had he done it for *her*?

Thinking back on these last weeks, months, she remembered his special attentions. She had pushed them aside, not letting them mean too much. However, now that she put them along with this sudden change in appearance, it made her wonder. In spite of herself, she was flattered. No, it was more than that. She felt honored. She *was* special to him. Felt it deep within her. For a moment, she fantasized walking down the street together, in that particular way a couple does, walking close.

Heavens! She brought herself up short. Her thoughts were carrying her away. She decided to talk with the lady on the other side of her, the wife of some dignitary, and take charge of her wayward thoughts. Celia had just made an observation about the beautiful day when the announcer for the event shouted. "Ladies and gentlemen! May I have your attention please. We're about to begin."

Celia looked down the row of archers. It was a sight, seeing all those men lined up, ready to do battle. Charles's and Edward's height made them stand above most of the others.

The announcer cleared his throat. "We are happy to include archery for the first time in our town's celebration." He looked down at his piece of paper. "Archery is estimated to originate some five to six thousand years ago. It was first used in hunting, and was favored in warfare until approximately AD 1600 because of its ability to outrange the slingshot and javelin." He looked up. "Today, we are pleased to have twenty-one archers. The contest is arranged so that three will shoot at a time. At the end of round two," he continued, "we will tabulate the scores and the nine men with the highest will remain in the contest."

He stepped off to the side and the first group of three put their left feet to the line, drew back their bows and let fly. The arrows thudded into the target. Each man shot three. The scores were called out and the arrows removed. Celia watched as wave after wave of men took their place at the line. A few arrows hit wide of the target. One tall gangly youth tried his best, but two of his failed to hit the target altogether. A short girl off to Celia's side shouted encouragement. After his first round, he stepped back from the line and looked at her, shrugged his shoulders good-naturedly and rolled his eyes. Obviously, he had entered to please her.

Charles and Edward advanced to the line in different groups of three. Celia tabulated the results of both their shots. All were in the gold circle of the bull's-eye. A little thrill of excitement ran through her.

When the gangly youth stepped up to the line a second time, several in the crowd shouted out good-humored advice. He gave a lopsided smile to the assembly, then concentrated on the business at hand. Celia was glad to see he did better, apparently enjoying himself, but surely, he wouldn't make it beyond the second round.

When Charles stepped up to shoot, Mrs. Harrod took hold of Celia's arm. "He's doing well, isn't he?" Celia nodded. Next, Edward stepped up and shot all three arrows in the gold circle. Celia didn't look at Mrs. Harrod to see her reaction.

After the second round, the moderator of the games walked to front center and announced the names of the top nine archers. Just as she thought, he called Charles and Edward. The moderator thanked those who had participated and the crowd applauded. The eliminated ones broke ranks with the others. The tall, gangly youth gave an impromptu bow and everyone laughed.

"That lends a little levity, which is good," Mr. Harrod said. "However, now we'll get down to the real competition." Celia glanced over at him. He had straightened in his chair and was looking intently at the remaining men.

The third and fourth rounds would see everyone eliminated but three. As the archers began shooting, the crowd quieted. Most of the arrows landed in the three center rings. When an occasional arrow landed in the outermost white ring, a good-natured comment went up from the crowd, suggesting the archer move it over to the left or up a ways to hit the bull's-eye. Celia sat quietly, noticing where Charles's and Edward's arrows hit. A short, big-boned man also shot very well.

Mrs. Harrod leaned over to her. "Charles will make the final, won't he?"

Celia smiled and nodded. "I've added his scores along with Edward Lyons, and both are doing extremely well."

"I hope Charles wins, my dear. I would love to see *you* present him the prize. Of course, Edward is our special friend, but not as special as our Charles, is he?"

Celia didn't know what to reply so just widened her smile.

Edward hadn't looked at the crowd or her since the competition began, but every time he walked forward to shoot, she sat up straighter in her chair, tense with anticipation. One of his arrows hit dead center and someone off to her left said loud enough for her to hear, "Ah, what's that Lyons fellow doing here anyway? He should've been barred from the contest."

"You're right there," a high-pitched voice added fervently." Celia recognized the last voice as Mrs. Divers. How utterly rude to speak out so. Up until this time, Celia had felt disposed to either Charles or Edward winning. But now, she suddenly felt herself taking up Edward's part, hoping he would win. After all, hadn't Charles the approval of his parents and the whole town? He hadn't undergone suspicion, felt ostracized. She wondered if Edward heard the remark. If he had, he hadn't given indication. Just then, the fourth round ended.

"Ladies and gentlemen, some mighty fine shooting. As soon as we finish adding the scores, we'll announce the top three finalists." In the ensuing minutes, a murmur arose, the crowd speculating who would be in the final group. Finally, the announcer was handed a sheet of paper. He looked at it and nodded his approval. "From here on the old scores will be dropped, starting fresh. I will announce the names in alphabetical order." He paused for drama. "Charles Harrod. Marcus Kirth. Edward Lyons."

Celia felt her heart in her throat. Charles looked at his parents and then at her. She smiled and then glanced in Edward's direction and saw him looking back at her for the first time in the competition. She had almost missed his look when she smiled at Charles. Few, if any, would be rooting for Edward. She held his eyes with hers and gave an encouraging nod. He should know someone was cheering him on.

"The contestants will shoot in the order announced," the moderator said. "Each will go up to the line individually." He turned to one of his helpers. "Make sure each archer has a different colored band on his arrows. Each gets three."

After all was readied, Charles stepped up first, taking his time at the line. The crowd was now very quiet. He drew back his bow and the first arrow hit the bull's-eye, only an inch away from dead center. The crowd clapped. The two that followed hit inside the gold circle as well. Applause followed each bull's-eye.

"Three times nine is twenty-seven — top score," the moderator said. "Next is Mr. Kirth."

Mr. Kirth hit his three arrows also in the bull's-eye, but two landed close to the line of the red. The crowd applauded each good shot. The moderator scratched his head. "Another twenty-seven points. I would say that's about identical scores, wouldn't you?"

He nodded to Mr. Lyons.

Edward Lyons stepped up deliberately. Slowly he raised his bow, his shoulder muscles bunching up. He let the arrow go. It hit what appeared to be dead center. "Don't that beat all!" someone said. A smattering of applause followed. Celia glanced back. It was the lanky youth, his eyes gleaming in rapt admiration. Her heart suddenly glowed with affection for the young man. Someone had dared to voice admiration for Edward.

Edward's second arrow hit next to his first. "Sakes alive!" someone exclaimed in the crowd. Again, a smattering of applause. Celia felt Mrs. Harrod stiffen. She would not for the world hurt her dear friend, but she wanted Edward to win. She would not make an open show of it, but there it was.

She held her breath on the third shot. It was about an inch from the other two, about the same distance from center as Charles's arrows.

The moderator scratched his head. "Same score, twenty-seven points." He paused, then said, "With those scores, I think we need more distance lads, don't you?" He glanced around at his assistants. At their approving nods, he said, "Let's move the target back thirty feet. Make that ten paces," he added.

Two men lifted the target, counted off the paces and set it down firmly.

The announcer cocked his head. "I think that'll work."

Charles stepped up first. He drew his bow back and held it steady before letting the arrow fly. It hit inside the red circle. The crowd clapped. He shot the second. It hit just inside the gold bull's-eye. The crowd clapped again. He took his time with his third and last arrow. It hit dead center in the bull's-eye. The crowd went wild. "He done good, real good!" Celia recognized the voice of the lanky boy. She glanced at the Harrods. They both smiled their satisfaction. "That'll be hard to beat," Mr. Harrod said in an undertone to his wife.

The second archer placed his foot to the

line. He also took his time, waiting an extra second before releasing each of his arrows. The first hit the red ring to the left of the bull's-eye. The second hit the red on the other side of the gold. He steadied his bow with care for the third and it landed just an inch from Charles's last arrow in the center. The crowd applauded appreciatively. Kirth had shot well, but clearly, Charles was ahead.

The moderator nodded to Edward. He stepped up to the line. The crowd stilled. Celia's breathing almost stopped. He lifted the bow, waited, and then released the arrow. It hit alongside Charles's second arrow just inside the bull's-eye. The crowd clapped politely. "Oh, boy!" Celia heard to her side. The lanky boy quietly explained to his girl, "That's the best first shot of this last round."

Edward lifted his bow, steadied it, then let go the second arrow. It hit the center of the target, side by side, touching Charles's third arrow. The crowd let out a collective breath; everyone had stopped breathing. Celia found her hands clenched together in her lap. She didn't dare look at Mrs. Harrod. Her eyes fixed on Edward. If only, if only he could make one more tremendous shot, he would win.

He lifted his bow one last time, held it

steady, then released the arrow. It flew across the field, the sharp snap of wood cracked the air. The third arrow had split Charles's last arrow. Celia was the first to break the silence, clapping furiously. Others in the crowd joined in almost immediately. "He did it! He did it!" the lanky boy yelled. Others joined in yelling. Charles was the first to go up and shake Edward's hand. Several of the archers went up to congratulate him, then the townspeople. It seemed as if they had forgotten their ill will and now happily claimed him victor. Celia was glad. She finally looked at the Harrods. She knew Mrs. Harrod was disappointed, but saw she had quickly submerged it and was now smiling. Mr. Harrod stepped up to congratulate the winner. "First-rate shooting," he said.

Mrs. Harrod took Celia's arm. "Let's go to the table with the ribbons, my dear. You are presenting, remember?"

# 19

Celia took her place beside Mrs. Harrod at the awards table. The announcer stood at Mrs. Harrod's other side and motioned the contest finalists to line up near Celia. The crowd gathered around them. Edward had donned his suit coat once again and stood with hands clasped in front of him, his shoulders squared. He looked athletic, fit — and handsome.

"Ladies and gentlemen," the announcer shouted, waiting a few seconds for the crowd to quiet, "we now have the honor of presenting the awards to our area's finest archers. First of all, I'd like to say thank you to all who entered. It made for an entertaining match. Each of us who watched would like to say, well done!" He cleared his throat. "But now for the awards. Miss Celia Thatcher will present the prizes." He nodded to Celia, then announced, "Third place, Marcus Kirth!"

Mr. Kirth stepped up to the table and Celia shook his hand and handed him a white ribbon. Everyone clapped.

"Second place, Charles Harrod!"

As Celia presented his red ribbon with a handshake, he leaned forward and said under cover of the crowd's clapping, "If I was first place, I'd ask for a kiss." He grinned. "I might ask for one later anyway."

Celia felt her breath catch, not sure how she should respond.

When it became quiet, the announcer beckoned the winner with a broad gesture. "Finally, first place, Edward Lyons!" As soon as his name was called, Edward stepped up and grasped Celia's hand. Those assembled clapped enthusiastically. Celia was gratified the community's feeling of goodwill extended to the ceremony. Then just before Edward released her hand, he squeezed it, light shining from his eyes. Her smile involuntarily widened. She felt the special regard he had for her, which he refrained from displaying in front of the crowd. How sensitive and diplomatic of him.

The announcer looked around at those assembled. "Let's give a final applause for all the contestants!" After the clapping died down, he said, "The awards for the flower show will be next. If everyone will step over to the other side of the refreshment tent, that ceremony will begin in a few minutes."

As those assembled began breaking up, Edward leaned over to Celia. "May I escort you to the flower awards?"

Charles sidled up to them. "Ah, I was going to offer the same, but, of course, that honor should go to the winner of the archery contest." The corners of his mouth curved up as he looked at Celia. "Later, though!"

Edward held out his arm and Celia rested her hand on it. As they started to walk she said, "Your shooting was wonderful."

He looked down at her. "Your saying that means a lot." Then he grinned from ear to ear. "I take it you recognized me when I came on the field."

"Oh!" Celia laughed. "You will never know the start you gave me, the picture in your mother's sitting room come to life. You cannot imagine how I felt."

He reached up to rub his chin. "Stripped myself of the current fashion — for you, my dear."

She felt the blood rise to her face. His "my dear" felt so different. . . . She searched for words to lighten their conversation. He placed his free hand over hers, drawing her closer. In the protection of his stature and strength, she felt buoyed along. Despite his longer legs, they fell in step as if they had walked together for years.

A stream of people headed for the flower awards. Children ran hither and yon between the adults walking in pairs or trios, but Celia was scarcely conscious of anyone else. She hardly knew where Mr. and Mrs. Harrod were, or Mr. and Mrs. Chestley — even Charles. This was Edward's time of triumph and by extension, hers. For these minutes, she was his companion by right of his win. They could walk together in full view of everyone, and no one would question the propriety.

How good it must be for Edward to feel free from public shame. She had not thought much of such a thing, but now she put herself in his shoes. Particularly for a man of his background, the proud Boston Brahmin, his soul must have felt tortured under the cloud of suspicion regarding Marguerite. She didn't know what had happened, but for now, she would just enjoy these moments with him.

They approached the tables of flowers.

"Isn't that a beautiful sight?" she asked. Pinks, yellows, whites, reds, purplish blues in different shades were amassed before them. Sweet fragrance with a hint of musk and spice wafted up in the surrounding air. "A veritable Garden of Eden."

He smiled down at her. "It seems an Eden to me this moment."

His words drew her into the exclusive circle of those he respected and cherished. Her hand pressed his arm to let him know she felt the honor of it, even as he had pressed her hand minutes ago.

Looking up at him, his eyes held hers, saying something she could not read. They were like a dark pool, a place where one found refreshment for soul and body. Like the pool by the large tree in his woods, where on his urging, she and Mr. Chestley had gone one afternoon. They had walked quite a ways before coming upon it. In the lovely quiet with occasional leaves rustling, they had both become taciturn. Mr. Chestley stood on the water's edge and after a minute, told her when he was a boy, he and other lads had gone swimming in it. They tied a rope to one of the tree's big limbs and jumped in feet first. A spring fed it so that it was bracing on the hottest day.

Celia finally looked away from the steady gaze in Edward's eyes. She would like to be standing by that pool now, with only this man at her side, the two of them alone without these people around. His nearness, his warmth enveloped her. Suddenly, she wanted that warmth to surround her, his arms holding her close.

Oh dear! This was exactly what she was afraid of, the effect he was beginning to have on her.

Stirring herself to action, she slowly slipped her hand from his arm and took a step away. "Thank you for your escort," she said in an undertone.

"Ladies and gentlemen!" Mr. Harrod's voice rose over the crowd. "We're about to present the awards for the flower show. If everyone would be quiet, please."

Charles sauntered up and stood on Celia's other side, and then Mr. and Mrs. Chestley by him. Then she saw Mrs. Adams ask people to move so that she could join Edward.

"Well, Celia," Charles said, "you ready to win a prize?"

"I don't know about that." Celia looked over to single out Mrs. Chestley. "I will have to say that the climber I entered did very well despite years of neglect."

Mrs. Chestley scrunched up her nose. "My dear, that climber was all but past redemption and I never claimed to have done it any good. I told you if it could be brought back from near death, you could enter it and take the well-deserved credit."

"Thank you." Celia crinkled up her nose in affectionate response.

"And now, ladies and gentlemen," Mr. Harrod said, "let me present my wife, Mrs. Lydia Harrod, to present the awards."

Mrs. Harrod stepped up to the ribbon table and looked at the surrounding crowd, smiling. "It has been my honor to help plan this event with our garden club." She announced the ladies' names, and the audience gave a round of applause.

"Now, we have a number of categories. The spring flowers were judged a few weeks ago as their bloom time is earlier, so those winners will be announced first." She began with the spring bulbs, the narcissus and tulips, and progressed through the lilies and irises.

"This next group of flowers are on the tables for all to see. Most of these were cut just this morning for the competition." She nodded to the array of multi-colored flowers. "I'll first announce the winners of the early summer flowers; the roses will be separate."

After announcing the early summer flowers, she walked over to stand by the last group to be awarded.

"As you can see roses reign supreme, and

because there are many entries, they've been given several categories. We'll begin with the beloved *Centifolias.* We usually think of them as pink, but this winner is white: Shailer's White Moss. The grower is Mr. Edward Lyons."

Celia heard a quiet, "Oh no," and glanced back. Behind Charles stood Mrs. Divers.

Edward stepped forward to shake Mrs. Harrod's hand and collect his ribbon. One of the ladies of the garden club brought forward the blooms and set them on an empty side table.

"As you can see," Mrs. Harrod said, "we are placing each winner out front for everyone's viewing. With so many categories, we'll have 'Best of Show' announced at the end."

"Next is a China rose, a beautiful pink that is one of our most well-known and well-loved. Old Blush is the winner, entered by Mrs. Adams. The woman quickly stepped forward to collect her ribbon, and when she turned, smiled to the crowd. Celia noticed that when she stepped back to Mr. Lyons's side, she turned to him for congratulations.

Mrs. Harrod proceeded to announce the winner in the Bourbon category, and then announced the Tea rose. "This year we have an outstanding example in the climbing Tea rose. It is a buff yellow tinged with salmon at its center. The winner is *Gloire de Dijon* submitted by Celia Thatcher."

As the helper brought a large vase with the blooms dripping luxuriously over its lip, Mrs. Harrod smiled and said, "I saw this plant last year at the side of Mrs. Chestley's house and it looked terribly woebegone. A special congratulations to Miss Thatcher on her win." Celia blushed and laughed as she went forward to collect her ribbon. When she stepped back to her place, Charles reached over and gave her shoulder a squeeze. "Good for you!" he whispered loudly.

Mrs. Harrod smiled and said, "Now, we'll announce 'Best of Show.' You see all the flowers lined up on this side table. Any one of them could win. They are beautiful examples of nature that God created." She led the crowd in a round of applause.

"Now, the winner of 'Best of Show.' Let me say one reason we chose this blossom is that the particular entry is not usually seen until later in the season. This beautiful white, many-petaled flower is a descendent or sport of the well-known pink *Centifolia*. When the winner comes to the front, we'd like to hear a few words of advice on how to grow such perfect blooms so early in the season. And, of course, our winner is — Mr. Edward Lyons."

In the split-second before the crowd burst into applause, Celia heard a gasp. The next moment Edward stepped up to collect the huge blue ribbon for Best of Show, and shook Mrs. Harrod's hand. Celia heard his "thank you," and then he turned around to address the crowd of onlookers.

Before he could start speaking, Celia heard a "No! No!" from behind her. A wave of dread coursed through her as she saw Mrs. Divers break through the crowd and march, shaking, up to the front. "He shouldn't get that award!" she said in an angry, determined voice. "He doesn't deserve such recognition!"

Mrs. Harrod looked doubtfully at Mrs. Divers. For a full five seconds no one said anything, then Mrs. Harrod said soothingly, "Please, Mrs. Divers, calm yourself."

"No! It's shameful for this man to be awarded anything. That man never should have been allowed to stay in this community for the way he treated my Marguerite! He should have gone to prison!"

Celia's stomach tightened at the venom spewing from the woman. She felt shocked, yet felt for the *mother* in her as well. Then her eyes fastened on Edward, feeling an agonizing embarrassment for him. He stood silently, staring at his former mother-in-law, saying nothing, letting her speak without interruption.

"Now, Mrs. Divers," Mrs. Harrod said. "This is not the time or place to talk about this. Let's finish the ceremony."

"Yes, it is the time and the place!" Mrs. Divers's shaky voice took on a shrillness that carried over the crowd. She looked directly at her former son-in-law. "Oh, how I rue the day you ever set eyes on my daughter!"

Just then, Mrs. Adams said in an undertone that unfortunately carried, "This is terrible, just terrible." Celia stared at her. That the woman should say anything at this time, how insensitive of her. Celia's eyes flicked over the crowd. Their eyes were pinned on Edward and Mrs. Divers. They stared horrified, yet fascinated.

"You are cruel, Edward Lyons! You stand here so properly dressed, looking the part of a perfect gentleman. Why, when you first walked up to the archery competition, I hardly recognized you. What are you about, Edward Lyons? Are you out to win another woman's heart, only to break it like Marguerite's?"

Celia held her breath, her chest tightening.

At that, Charles strode up and took Mrs. Divers gently by the elbow. Before he could say anything, she shook him off. "Don't anyone touch me. I've been silent long enough. I've suffered all this time. My daughter's death never came to court. It should have! The public is here — now I will have public court. I want this man run out of town."

"Mrs. Divers!" Mrs. Harrod's hand fluttered to her throat.

"Yes! He deserves it. My Marguerite would be here today but for him. He killed her. Oh, not with a gun or knife. He didn't impale her with that cursed bow and arrow of his. Oh, no! It was subtler than that, in a manner a court of law couldn't prosecute! But he killed her just the same."

An oppressive silence held the crowd in check. Celia's limbs felt stiff, frozen. Her eyes flickered to Mr. Lyons. He stood white and mute.

Mrs. Divers shook a crooked finger at him. "You let her die. Alone! You never called the doctor. You *let* her die. *Wished* her dead. It saved you the trouble of divorcing her or killing her outright!" She stood staring at him like an old nemesis, quivering like a leaf in the wind, but determination steeling her. "You were always out for yourself and your own pleasure. You have *no honor*!"

Celia took her eyes off Mrs. Divers and looked at Edward. The hardness and coldness of his visage was dreadful. If looks could impale, his would have stabbed the old woman. Celia wanted to move, but couldn't. She wanted to bring comfort, say wise words to mitigate the hatred of the one and the cold disdain of the other, but she couldn't stir herself.

Mr. Harrod was the first to move. He walked up to Mrs. Divers with decision. "Mrs. Divers, come with me, please." His voice was gentle but brooked no opposition. "I understand how disturbed you are. Don't worry; we'll take care of this." He took her arm and firmly moved her away from the awards table. "Let's find Miss Waul." As soon as he saw Mrs. Divers's companion, he signaled her to take her friend's other side. "Let's find a place away from here."

Edward moved next. He leaned his hands on the table, looked directly at Mrs. Harrod. "Mrs. Divers is mistaken. She is mistaken!" He drew in a deep breath. "Excuse me, please." He turned to leave and the crowd parted before him. Only after he had left the area did people start to talk in low syllables.

Charles joined his mother and consulted her briefly, then looked up at those assembled. "Ladies and gentlemen, we're sorry for what just happened. If everyone will pick up his or her flowers, that would be helpful. We want to extend our congratulations to all the winners."

Celia saw Mrs. Chestley walk up to one of her friends. "Here, Mrs. Hamilton," she said, "why don't you and your neighbor go to the refreshment tent. Didn't you want a little something before the next event?" She continued to encourage one after another of the onlookers to move on. Celia watched this quiet little woman capably disperse those nearest her.

As people began to leave, Charles approached Celia. "Can I do something for you? I know this has been a shock."

She looked up at him. "Will you please help me find a place to sit. . . ."

# 20

Celia drew the bed covers up close around her head, relieved to be alone and quiet in her own room. If only she could bury herself away from all that happened these last hours. Maybe here she could think through the dreadful revelations of the day.

Charles had taken her to the refreshment tent where he found a chair away from the other guests who drifted in and out. He insisted she drink some of the lemonade he procured for her, then he drew up a chair and solicitously saw to her every perceived need. She went along with whatever he suggested. She couldn't think, truly she couldn't. Finally, she suggested returning to the flower tables to assist his mother.

"I don't think that's necessary," Charles said. "Others can help her."

"I feel I must do something." To herself she said, something mindless — but hopefully useful. She stood and Charles reached

301

for her arm. She smiled at him absently, but something in his eyes made her determine to stop leaning on him so much, to put all confused thoughts aside until she could be alone and sort them into some sense of order. She just wanted to get through the remainder of the day.

And here she was. As she quieted herself, the questions started arising. What had Edward done? What had really happened? He'd said Mrs. Divers was mistaken. Yet, the pain of that mother. The anger, all this time, festering. Unresolved. Then for it all to come out like this. Before all those people. What a hateful situation. Humiliating. How Edward must suffer. The very ill-feeling he had tried so hard to dampen down, to appease by hiding himself away from society, now was out in the open — like a freshly exposed wound. Oh, Mrs. Divers, what have you done?

Pain seared through Celia. If she suffered, how must he!

Celia got through the following days as best she could. There was that next book discussion to prepare for. At first, she didn't have the heart for it, but after she began, found it took her mind off her pain. As she delved into Pascal, and found direction for her mind, she wondered how Edward would react to this particular writer.

The evening of the book discussion — afterward, Mrs. Chestley caught her alone a moment. "That was a wonderful discussion, dear." She reached over and hugged Celia. "I don't know how you do it, choose such scholarly works and then help us get so much out of them." She turned to pick up her shawl. "I've already told my husband I'm going right home. I'm rather tired, I suppose I'm still feeling it after all that happened this week."

Celia nodded acquiescence and walked her friend to the door, then watched as she crossed the grass to her house. All were gone now except Mr. Chestley and herself. The evening had been worthwhile. Still, *he* hadn't come.

She had hoped against hope he might. But, of course, he was probably feeling . . . oh, what he must still be suffering! The sorrow, the shame, the humiliation of it all.

Mr. Chestley walked up to her. "How are you doing? That was quite a discussion we had tonight. I thought your choice of Pascal's *Les Pensées* might be a little too deep for our readers, but you managed to whet their interest for more. Bravo, my dear." He glanced down at the floor. "I see Mr. Lyons

303

didn't join us tonight."

"Yes."

"Celia, do you think Mr. Lyons has weathered this all right?" His eyes searched hers.

She couldn't believe Mr. Chestley's tender heart. It opened up the way for her to say, "He's very strong, in more ways than one. I'm sure he'll be all right." Celia heard the bravado in her voice. "That is, I hope so."

He nodded. "Let's close the shop then. I'm surprised with these long summer days, our group didn't stay longer. It's still light outside."

"I heard a number propose walks, the evening is so mild."

"Not a bad idea. You know, I think a walk would do us good. What do you say?"

"I'd like that very much."

A few minutes later, Mr. Chestley and she stood on the bookstore stoop. Which direction would he take? All of a sudden, she wondered — would it be too much to ask? His earlier sympathy emboldened her to ask if she might choose.

"Whichever way you want to go, Celia."

"Thank you." She gestured to the left, in the direction of Mrs. Divers's and Edward's homes.

Mr. Chestley held out his arm. "You are like a daughter to me, you know." As she gratefully placed her hand in the crook of his arm, he added, "This feels more companionable, doesn't it?" She nodded in agreement, wondering if the direction she had chosen had been wise.

Mr. Chestley patted her hand. "That *was* a good book discussion, Celia. I appreciated your opening quote from Pascal: that *man is but a reed, the most feeble thing in nature; but he is a thinking reed.*" He paused before adding, "I think our friend Mr. Lyons would have appreciated it as well."

Celia looked over at her companion. "It might have piqued him. Remember how section three began? *'A Letter to incite to the search after God.'* I wonder just how much Mr. Lyons searches after God."

"You've talked with him?"

"Some. Science is so important to him, its way of discovering the world and truth so fundamental. And he doesn't seem to think science and faith can agree." Celia paused at the entrance to the road where her earlier inclination had led her.

"Would you like to turn here?" Mr. Chestley asked. "It is a pleasant way."

"Yes, I think so."

He now lagged behind ever so little, letting her lead the way. They passed Mrs. Divers's house, and then as they came up to Mr. Lyons's drive, she slowed her steps.

"I was sorry he didn't come tonight," Mr. Chestley said again. She felt his questioning glance in her direction as they stopped at the entrance to his driveway.

"Might we see if he is all right?" she asked softly.

"Actually, that's just what I was thinking, but didn't know if it would be agreeable to you."

"It would." Relief flooded her. With Mr. Chestley at her side, the visit would be proper. Without him, she could hardly have gone.

They walked down the pleasant drive and up the steps to the front door. Mr. Chestley lifted the doorknocker and gave a soft, clear rap. Celia wondered who would answer, the housekeeper or Edward himself.

The door opened. Edward. His countenance looked like he was carrying a great weight. Then he squared back his shoulders.

He gestured formally like the aristocrat from Beacon Hill Celia knew him to be. "Please come in. I wasn't expecting anyone, but this is an honor."

After they stepped into the front hall, and Mr. Lyons closed the door, absolute quiet inhabited the house. The outside world was left behind.

"Mrs. Macon has retired for the night. I don't like to keep her unnecessarily on the job unless there's — good reason. Follow me, please."

The same immaculate, masculine aspect reigned in the drawing room as formerly. Celia looked around. Calm and order presided. But something was missing, she couldn't say just what.

They seated themselves, Celia and Mr. Chestley on the divan and Edward on a chair across from them. Mr. Chestley began, "We missed you at tonight's book discussion, the first one you've not attended. We wondered if you were all right."

Mr. Lyons's eye did not meet them directly, but gazed over their shoulders. "I was sorry not to be present, but you must know it was because of what happened the other day." He looked first at Mr. Chestley, then at Celia. "I didn't want to bring any negative influence to bear on your very worthy book discussion."

"We understand," Mr. Chestley said. "However, we also want you to know our concern. We realize we've heard only one side of the story."

"Thank you." Mr. Lyons was silent for a few moments as if ordering his thoughts. He clasped his hands together in front of him. "If you will allow me then . . . I'd like to say a few words about . . . this whole affair." Mr. Chestley nodded his head. Celia leaned forward.

"First of all, let me say that I'm sorry for any pain this might have caused you. You are two very dear friends and I appreciate your coming tonight." He looked down once again. "Regarding Mrs. Divers — I had realized, to be sure, that the death of Marguerite had greatly affected her. She expressed her anger to me, many times. I don't know all she said to others, but I noticed people's looks, and suspicious comments were dropped in my hearing. It didn't take long before I chose to live a more solitary life, venturing out only when others would be less likely to be around. Mrs. Divers I avoided altogether. She was a bitter old woman, disagreeable and critical before her daughter's death, and even more so afterward."

He straightened in his chair. "Early in the marriage, she influenced her daughter and it negatively affected our relationship as husband and wife. As a result, I decided to limit my mother-in-law's association with our everyday lives. In time, I discouraged it altogether except for Sunday afternoon visits and holidays. That might seem extreme with her living so near, but it was the only way to bring peace to my household. Because — after being married only a few months, peace was what I wanted more than anything else."

He paused, his eyes avoiding theirs. "I had envisioned giving my wife things out of love and the generosity of my heart, but her increasingly shrewish ways eventually dried up those inclinations. She constantly wanted something or other and felt it was her due as my wife. It was difficult to believe she'd become so different from the person I'd courted. When I didn't furnish her with her desires, she became petulant and complaining. Even waspish at times. It shocked me. I saw a reflection of the carping mother-in-law I'd come to abhor. This was outside of my experience growing up in Beacon Hill. Every woman I'd ever encountered there acted in a refined and proper manner.

"Thinking back now, I think I might have reacted too harshly. I set up parameters around Marguerite's life so she probably felt confined, especially regarding seeing her mother. But at the time, all I wanted was peace. And if I had to, in effect, strong-arm it, I did."

Mr. Lyons looked at Celia a long moment. She wondered what he was thinking. She had drawn back on the divan, feeling both shock and sympathy. Did it show in her countenance? He sounded so disillusioned. Even harsh.

"What I say next, I wish wasn't necessary . . . but in light of circumstances. . . ." He cleared his throat. "Regarding Marguerite's death, she had been ill for some time. But she'd been ill before and I found her an inveterate complainer, sometimes when nothing was wrong. Of course, she was truly ailing this time. I knew that. But the day in question, I didn't realize how unwell she was, just knew I had to get out, away from the house awhile. I'm the first one to admit I'm not good in the sick room. Maybe it's because I've been ill so little in my life, I didn't have patience with her.

"I had let my housekeeper take her usual day off, because I didn't feel she should be kept from it. She had spent time with Marguerite and needed breathing space as well."

Here he paused, an earnest, almost desperate expression in his eyes. He looked directly at Celia. "I need you to know what happened that afternoon. You must know the truth. I want you to hear it from me, not some town gossip — or from Mrs. Divers — what she supposed to have happened. No one else was present beside myself." He leaned forward in his chair, his elbows on his knees, his hands clasped before him. "If you'll allow me then." He glanced at Mr. Chestley. "I am obliged you are here to act as witness — and to protect Celia, so to speak." Then his gaze returned to Celia.

"I had been attending Marguerite all morning, had just brought up the broth Mrs. Macon made the day before. Marguerite, however, would have none of it. I was at a loss what to do, how to please or help her. I put the soup on the nightstand within her reach and started to leave the room. She was weak and sounded congested, but still managed to cry out that I was a bad husband. And after all I had done for her. I couldn't take it any longer and shouted, "Be quiet!" I went back to measure out her medicine, but she kept on, wheezing while she screamed out she was sorry she'd ever married me.

"I slammed the medicine on her bed table. She wailed, 'Get out! I can't stand you anymore.' She choked. I rushed out of the room and heard her cry, 'I want — I want to go home to my mother. And I will! I'll shame you before the whole town.'

"I couldn't leave fast enough. I wanted to

throttle her, still that querulous tongue. At that point, I was afraid . . . afraid of what I might do."

Edward stopped, swallowed. Celia took a deep breath; she had almost stopped breathing. Her eyes flickered to Mr. Chestley, but she could not tell from his expression how he was reacting.

Edward unclasped his hands before continuing. "I knew something had to be done to calm myself, to get back to a normal frame of mind, so I headed for the rear of the house. Get away and get outside was all I could think. Get to the woods.

"As I was going out the door I grabbed my bow and arrows. I knew I would need something to occupy my mind, to focus on something other than the hatred I felt for my wife. If I could concentrate on a target, aim an arrow, I hoped my equanimity would return.

"I must have wandered for a couple of hours. Marguerite was alone in the house, but I couldn't go back. Besides, I figured it was the way she wanted it.

"After a while the stillness of the woods and the physical activity quieted me. The exertion calmed me in a way nothing else could have done. I can still see the sturdy oaks all around me that afternoon.

"When I returned, however, I dreaded going up the stairs to the room Marguerite occupied. The house was so peacefully quiet.

"Oh, to keep this stillness, I thought. I couldn't check on her immediately. She must be asleep. Let sleeping dogs lie.

"So I warmed some soup Mrs. Macon had left for me, determining after I finished eating to take some hot broth to Marguerite. I cannot tell you how I wanted to prolong the quiet, the stillness I had found in the forest, the calm that had finally been restored to my soul.

"Maybe three-quarters of an hour later, I heated the broth and took the tray up the stairs. It was silent in the hall to her bedroom. Deathly silent, as I now know. I hesitated in front of her door that was ajar. I didn't want to step inside, but finally steeled myself.

"My eyes immediately went to her figure, then her face — ashen in color. My dread of just moments before changed to a different kind of dread. I quickly placed the tray at the foot of the bed.

"Her face, her mouth, was crooked. It didn't look normal. Only one other time had I seen a dead person shortly after death

313

— my father — and her face looked like that.

"I stood for a moment and sighed, in sorrow or relief, I hardly know which. I just knew there was no hurry to ascertain her condition.

"Finally, I stepped forward and took the hand on the bedspread. It was cold and stiff. Even though I knew she was gone, yet I bent over to determine if any breath came out of her open mouth. There was none. I took her wrist and felt for a pulse. None.

"I then began going through the motions of what I thought I should do. I went to get Ned, asked him to get the doctor. After he left, I stayed with Marguerite, felt it the proper thing to do. After the doctor came, he officially declared her dead, from pneumonia he thought. I then asked if Ned would send his wife for Mrs. Divers. I'll spare you the details of what happened when she arrived. I was thankful the doctor, Ned, and his wife were present. I knew I needed others nearby when she came."

Edward looked at both of them sitting on the divan, then fastened his eyes on Celia once again. "Miss Thatcher, Celia. Will you forgive me for relating in such detail, the incidents of that afternoon? But I felt you had to know — all of it. I also wanted Mr.

Chestley present to be a support to you when you heard my side of the story."

Mr. Chestley shifted forward onto the edge of the divan. "Be assured we will support you if any untoward ramifications develop."

"Thank you."

A few moments of silence ensued. Then Mr. Lyons said, "Are you all right, Miss Thatcher? I know this has been a shock."

"Yes, yes, but thank you for sharing what happened." She glanced down at her folded hands. "However, I still feel sorry for Mrs. Divers and want the best for her."

"Yes." Mr. Lyons paused again, then asked, "Mr. Chestley, would it be all right if I showed Miss Thatcher something in the conservatory? Would you mind waiting?" At Mr. Chestley's nod, he said, "Feel free to avail yourself of anything in the library."

"Thank you, but I think I'll stay right here. After a long day in the store, and with the book discussion tonight, I would welcome a few minutes of quiet. Go ahead, Celia."

Once outside the drawing room, Edward led the way to the back of the house. "You've been to the conservatory by way of the front, but this is quicker."

Celia was curious to see his conservatory

315

again — it must be overflowing with blooms — but she wondered what he could have to show her. At the kitchen door, he took up cutting shears and a basket.

She accompanied him across the grass to the glass building.

He held the door for her, then once inside, led her to the far end. Following his purposeful steps, she could not see much beyond his broad back, but once he reached the corner, he stepped aside and let her view a rose bush. A glorious bush with striped roses, crimson splashed irregularly across pale pink petals.

He reached to cut a goodly number of sprays to place in the basket, then led her to the center of the conservatory where sat a settee and two chairs. "You see I learned something from Mrs. Harrod," he said smiling. "No furniture was here the last time you came." He set the basket of blooms on the table and motioned her to the settee, then took his seat beside her.

"This is *Versicolor* or popularly known as *Rosa Mundi*. It's from an old strain of rose known as *Gallica*. The original *Gallicas* are thought to have come from Rome and were a bright magenta pink. Portraits of *Gallicas* appear etched on the walls of Roman ruins. It is a venerable class of rose. Medieval monks used *Gallica* petals to perfume soaps and salves. This striped variety is its progeny."

"The petals are so big. What a striking flower."

"Yes, the diameter of these flowers is unusually large. It is unsurpassed so I contemplated entering it in this year's flower contest. I felt it a sure winner, but decided against doing so because of Mrs. Divers. You see, Marguerite gave this to me. Though I certainly feel less than kindly toward Mrs. Divers, I would never enter a rose to cause her pain." His eyes caught Celia's. "That woman accused me of many things. Of cruelty, even! As I said before, I could have done things differently. Yet, I would not be intentionally cruel. My upbringing would not allow that. You do believe me?"

Celia's eyes started tearing up. The terrible disappointment, the questions and fears that had formed since Mrs. Divers's accusations, she had hoped against hope they weren't true. But how could they not be? And now the relief — to see evidence of his honor, his kindness — she grasped for the handkerchief in her pocket as the tears spilled down her cheeks. "I do believe you."

She saw him shudder as some great bear coming out of hibernation. He stood up suddenly and began pacing the small space available. "Celia, for me to lose your friendship, your regard — I was sick with worry and dread. Dread you had lost faith I would do good to my fellowmen. But how could I not — with you in my life? You, who have brought kindness and beauty into it?"

Her memory flitted back to the months she had known him, when she had learned his careful, kindly ways despite — on their first meetings — his bearish appearance and demeanor. How could she have doubted him? Her soul felt light, taking wing, borne up under the trade winds of those fine feelings that had been growing in her. She smiled, feeling like she was in sunlight. How different she felt from when first arriving.

An answering smile broke from his own face. "Celia, you are the reason I look forward to each new day. Bless you, bless you, my —" His hands clenched at his side. She looked into his eyes. Their dark pools held a depth of feeling that promised future sweetness. He stretched out his hands.

As she placed her hands in his and arose, she thought, this is so different from what she felt for Jack, for Charles. Why had she not seen this before? But she knew it now. The terrible disappointment she had felt with Mrs. Divers's accusations, then the at-

318

tendant pain. To have the pain assuaged as he told his side of the story about Marguerite, and now more than that, to know what she brought into his life. . . .

She wanted to stay and just be with him, to bring refreshment and nurture into his life. To be used by God to bring warmth and stimulation and rest. And she felt he would do the same for her.

He held her hands firmly, yet carefully, as if she would break. As if their relationship, restored just moments before, was too precious to handle in any way but in the most careful of manners. She let his large hands surround hers. The warmth of his touch coursed through her.

He looked down at her hands. "Yours are so tiny."

"Or, I might say yours are so large," Celia said, smiling.

"Both are true." He smiled back. "See how nicely your hands fit in mine. A hand in a glove. See, if I close mine, yours are completely surrounded."

*Protected* was the word that came to her mind.

Warm, soft breath exuded from him. It seemed almost a sigh. "I would see no harm come to you or your reputation. As much as I would desire more — time here, I should

319

take you back to Mr. Chestley."

She knew he was right because to be out here alone, even though it was a glass enclosure that could be viewed from outside, she knew the dictates of society. They had been gone long enough. Mr. Chestley might even be wondering where they were or what they had been doing.

He let her hands go, swept up the basket of flowers and led her to the door and out onto the grass. "I want you to take these home with you, as evidence of my honor."

He stopped a minute in the kitchen to recut the stems and place damp cloths around them before returning them to the basket. "Mr. Chestley can carry these for you." As they walked down the hall to the drawing room, they heard a quiet snoring.

"Bless his heart," Celia said. "The poor dear was tired, but he was kind enough to walk me here."

"I am grateful he did." Edward slowed their pace and said softly, "And I will sleep tonight, the first good sleep I've had since the flower show. Look," he said, standing on the threshold to the room, nodding to Celia's employer, "I could have kept you longer in the conservatory and he would have never noticed." Reaching for her hand, he drew her hard to his side. They stood a few moments looking at each other, then she drew away and cleared her throat to warn her employer of their entry.

Mr. Chestley startled and sat upright in his chair. "Oh! I didn't hear you come in. Was I sleeping?" His countenance looked sheepish. He glanced at Mr. Lyons. "I must have dozed off a bit. Been a long day, you know." He looked at the basket of flowers. "Well, did you accomplish your errand then?"

"Yes," Edward said. "I'm glad you came today."

"Yes, it's been most enlightening." Mr. Chestley stood up and held out his hand for the basket. "This will all smooth over in time, Lyons, we'll see to that."

Edward escorted them out the front door, then on the landing took Celia's elbow to escort her down the steps. "Goodbye then," he said, pressing her arm.

As she and Mr. Chestley turned the corner from Mr. Lyons's street to their own, she saw a carriage approach his drive. Wasn't that Mrs. Adams?

Without further reflection, she reached into her pocket and deftly let the handkerchief drop on the road. She had forgiven Mrs. Adams for spreading the gossip about her. She truly had, but she couldn't help wanting to know where she was going.

After they had gone a few steps, hoping she judged it right, she said, "Oh, Mr. Chestley, I dropped my handkerchief at the corner. I'll be just a few seconds retrieving it," and she hurried back to the corner.

She looked back down the road to Edward's drive. Sure enough. Mrs. Adams's carriage had turned and entered it. And she was alone. The hypocrite.

Celia woke the next morning, at first dreamy, with the most amiable of thoughts. The wonderful feeling of Edward's regard, the wondrous feeling of her response to him. Had it only been yesterday morning when she had lain on this same bed in shock, confusion, and despair? When she had discovered how much she had become attached to Edward and reeled with the pain of it all? But now such relief since last night's revelations.

She stretched luxuriously, reached for her pillow and wrapped her arms around it. Oh, how she would like to. . . . Yet, even as she gloried in these thoughts, on waking more, her mind suddenly cleared and two sharp, clear questions presented themselves.

First, what was Mrs. Adams doing, going to his house alone?

And second, what were Edward's intentions regarding herself and their future? She sat up in bed. What about that most important of impediments — their difference in faith? Yesterday, she had put this question far back in her mind.

But now, especially this last, a means must be devised to speak to Edward. As soon as possible.

# 21

Celia shook out the folds of her rose-colored dress. She had chosen it with care for Sunday afternoon's walk. Edward was partial to the whole spectrum of red and rose. Even now, she could feel the warmth of his hands around hers. The thought of seeing him again was welcome. No, more than that, her very soul reached out to him. However, the thought of what she must confront him with made her heart heavy. Nevertheless, it must be done. Deliberately, she took her shawl from the hook and draped it around her shoulders.

Sunday afternoons she always walked, often alone, so what she did now was normal. Mr. and Mrs. Chestley had been apprised she might be gone longer than usual, she didn't want them to worry.

She decided to walk past Mrs. Divers's and Edward's houses, not directly enter Edward's drive. Instead, she would go past

a ways and then come back. Was that subter-
fuge? In her heart, she didn't want Mrs.
Divers thinking, if she happened to be looking out the window, that she was heading
straight for Mr. Lyons's house. Instead, she
would *happen* to drop by on the way back.
Hopefully, his housekeeper would be about
the house providing some chaperonage, but
whether she was there or not, Celia had to
see him.

Twenty minutes later, she approached
Edward's house. She had meant to take an
hour walk, but couldn't delay the visit any
longer. The trees in leaf obliterated Mrs.
Divers's home from view. That was good.
She would not for anything give Mrs. Divers
and Miss Waul something to gossip about.
For who knew how this visit could be interpreted.

She walked to the door, lifted the knocker,
and rapped a firm but quiet knock. A wait
ensued. She hoped Edward was in. The
thought hadn't occurred to her he might be
out, maybe walking in his woods.

Finally, the door opened. Mrs. Macon
looked at Celia, then glanced beyond her to
see who else was present. "Can I help you,
Miss Thatcher?" Celia noted she didn't
invite her inside, but kept her standing at
the door. Edward must be out.

"I must talk with Mr. Lyons. It's very important."

"Mr. Lyons is out at present," Mrs. Macon announced formally, but then Celia saw her eyes soften. "He's been gone a while, so might return shortly. Would you like to wait for him?"

"I would appreciate that."

Mrs. Macon led her to the drawing room. "Please make yourself comfortable."

Celia chose a chair from which she could see the doorway to the hall. She wanted to glimpse Edward as soon as possible. She chastised herself for her foolishness, but there it was. She had seen him only yesterday, and yet it seemed an age.

As she sat there, she steeled herself against what she must do, even while she longed to see him. This must be done, this clarification of views. A visit like this was not customary, a woman taking the initiative in a call. Edward would certainly wonder why she came.

She squirmed in her seat. Maybe he would be upset she had gone beyond the bounds of propriety, and then she'd have to leave. If things became awkward between them, and if he never reached for her again — to hold her hands — she would have to accept that.

Celia felt herself start to tremble. The

longer she waited, the harder the trembling was to control. Oh, maybe she shouldn't have come after all.

At that moment, she sensed and thought she heard the sound of a door opening at the back of the house. Then quiet. Maybe he was taking off his boots and coat, Mrs. Macon indicating her arrival. Perhaps he would think this visit unseemly and suggest another time and place.

Then she heard his footsteps hurry down the hall, beating a quick staccato. He was wasting no time.

She rose precipitously from her chair. Edward paused for a moment at the drawing room entrance, his eyes searching hers. He was dressed in browns, casually, for walking, his shoulders nearly filling the doorway. "Celia!" Warmth exuded from his voice. He came forward. Then just as suddenly, a shadow crossed his features. "Is anything wrong?"

Yes, a lady unaccompanied, calling on a man, was most unusual. "Nothing wrong, exactly. But I had to discuss something important with you."

"Important?" He looked around at the drawing room, then apparently decided it wasn't quite the place, because he said, "Why don't we go to the library?" He stood aside to let her precede him down the hall.

Once they entered the room, he deliberately shut the door. Mrs. Macon would not be able to hear them. It relieved her, yet — alone together?

"This is an unexpected pleasure, I am gratified you came. So you need to tell me something?" He scanned her face, then led her across the room to the fireplace. As they approached the settee with chairs on either side, his hand reached out to guide her to the settee.

"I think I should sit here," she said, indicating the chair.

He took his stand in front of the settee. "This would be more conducive to — conversation." Warmth shone in his eyes.

"Thank you, but I think this would be best."

How she wanted to be near him. He suffered the same, she guessed from his manner. But she must be wise. And strong. She had always been a woman of principle. A woman of integrity. She also admitted she'd never had this level of temptation before. Temptation? As soon as she viewed it in that light, her ardor checked and she settled herself into the chair. He took the side of the settee nearest her.

She made herself look over his shoulder,

avoiding eye contact. "I was thinking of when we first met, the cold, fall evening when you came into the store for your Tennyson and we talked about Emerson. You remember?" On his nod, she continued, "What impressed me was how differently we viewed the thoughts, the writing of the man. This has to do with what I need to talk with you today." She felt on surer ground now. "Edward," looking at him now, "I need to be direct. Tell me, do you believe God is interested in your life, to the point that He would desire to have dealings with you?"

"Ah, we are serious this afternoon." His dark eyes smiled at her, yet at the same time, they were cautious. "Can you tell me why?" He was deflecting her question.

"Because it is important for me to know."

Edward cleared his throat. "All right, then. Is God interested in my life, in my affairs?" He leaned over, resting his elbows on his knees, pressing the tips of his fingers together. His face lowered for some moments, then he raised it to look at her. "I consider God a being which has a degree of influence in the affairs of the universe. I'm not quite sure how much. God seems rather too big and grand and inscrutable for mere man to know or understand. Of course, when man gets into trouble and prays, help often mysteriously comes. I can't explain that. Some connection seems to exist . . . yes, a degree of connection . . . but I think the word *interest* in my affairs or the affairs of the world in general would be putting it too strongly."

She had feared this, expected it, but recently had pushed the real knowing of it far back in her consciousness. As on her first meeting him, she felt on the edge of a precipice. She looked at him cautiously. "I wonder," she said, "how much your upbringing has influenced your beliefs. You were raised in the church."

"Yes, but a church that didn't throw man's intellect out the window."

"Well yes, that is important." She looked down at her folded hands before continuing. "If I told you I not only believe God is interested in my life, not only believe it but have a knowing deep inside of me, what you would say?"

He shifted his position, looked at her earnestly. "Celia, where does your knowing come from? I cannot imagine anyone, even a contemplative individual, able to know God in such a way. It seems wishful thinking."

Her eyes flicked away from his. How could

she explain? But she had discovered what she needed to ascertain. He didn't believe in God, didn't know God the way she knew to be essential. So where did that put their growing care for each other, her growing attraction to him?

Being alone with him worked on her sensibilities. Even this room kindled feelings for him, so evocative of their shared interests and passions: the books, the painting above his desk, the flowers — yes, the flowers! She suddenly realized what had been missing from the rooms when she and Mr. Chestley visited yesterday. Flowers had now returned in abundance. Pink roses spilled out of the silver bowl on the mantel. They told her that his soul had come out of its shock, its shame, its humiliation. He was back to his former self. She glanced at his eyes. Yes, she saw the hope there. He was watching her intently, his focus on her. Was she now going to wrench that hope from him?

All this flashed before her in a matter of seconds. She arose suddenly from the chair, walked a little way, then turned back.

He rose as well. "What is it, Celia?"

She looked at him, her eyes widened at the monumental task in front of her. Silently, she sent up a prayer.

"This knowing God," she began, "is not

wishful thinking. It only seems that way to people who have not discovered it for themselves." She grasped the back of the chair. "Let me ask this. Do you believe in the historicity of Christ? In other words, do you believe Jesus existed?"

"I know some who question it. But I believe the historical evidence is compelling, overwhelming, in fact. Ancients like Tacitus and Josephus and others all attest to Jesus' existence. Yes, I do."

"I'm glad, because He is the kingpin in my case for knowing God. You see, if a person wants to know God, Jesus provides the way. Jesus was God's Son. He claimed to be so. Do you have a Bible here, Edward?"

"Yes, in that section of books to the right of the fireplace. Third shelf up, in the middle." She turned, searched the shelves, then reached for it.

He gestured her to sit with him on the settee. "We can look together," he offered.

She hesitated. But it seemed the obvious thing to do, so she settled herself next to him. She opened the Bible, thumbing carefully through the pages. "Consider this passage from the gospel of John." Handing the Bible to him, their hands touched. The inner warning she felt in deciding whether to sit next to him was immediately confirmed, but she went on calmly. "Here, the ninth verse of the fourteenth chapter." She leaned over and pointed to the spot. "Start reading in the middle of the verse. Jesus is speaking."

*"He that hath seen Me hath seen the Father."*

"See how closely the two are identified with each other? Look a few chapters back to John 10:30."

He turned a few pages and read, *"I and my Father are one."*

Celia's eyes lifted from the Bible and looked directly at Edward. "Not the typical statement a great teacher or even a prophet would make. Don't you agree?"

"Christ was a great teacher. Or a prophet. We both know this," he said evenly. "But God? No. In my view, that is where fanciful thinking takes over."

"Edward. Do you accuse me of being fanciful?" Her eyebrow arched playfully.

He smiled for the first time in their conversation. His hand moved as if to reach for hers. Then he arrested it. "But can you prove Jesus is Deity?"

She folded her hands demurely in her lap. "Think about His miracles. These proved He was more than mere man. He raised others from the dead. And more important, He himself rose from the dead. After His death on the cross, He came out from the grave three days later. These all testify He was God."

"If you want to believe those miracles were actually true — and His resurrection —"

"Yes, what about His resurrection?" she interrupted. "When you read the accounts of the gospels, you discover that Christ was seen alive by many after his death. The disciples, Mary Magdalene, the two men on the road to Emmaus. Paul the apostle tells us that over five hundred saw him after His resurrection."

She shifted on the settee to turn toward him. "Edward, who would die for something they knew to be untrue? Remember when we considered this on the train? Think of the lives and deaths of the disciples. All except John died hard, cruel deaths for saying they had lived with Jesus and believed Him to be God. I ask again, who would die for something he knew to be a lie?"

Edward looked at her. Was it admiration or amusement in his eye? "Miss Thatcher, you present a very good argument."

"I don't want to only present a good argument, Edward. I want you to see the truth of it as I do. This issue of God, and especially whom you consider Jesus to be, is pivotal. Jesus said, 'I am the way, the Truth, and the Life, no one comes to the Father except through Me.' "

"Celia, you cannot convince me in a single sitting. Maybe I am too set in my ways, in my thinking."

"I don't want to argue you into anything, but listen to this. I am not speaking of something I merely believe, something my parents taught me, something that sounded logical so I espoused it. No. When I was young, I wanted to know God the way my father and mother did. However, I couldn't break through the barrier between God and myself. In fact, my life, my inner life had turned bleak. I despaired of ever finding meaning to life the way I yearned for.

"One evening, however, something extraordinary, almost mysterious took place. I had finally told my father how hopeless I felt. He said, 'Why don't you tell God what you just told me. In a simple prayer. Tell Him how much you want to know Him. Confess the fact you're a sinner — like everyone else. That you know Jesus' death on the cross was to take the punishment for your sin, to reconcile you to God. Remember that Jesus said He was the Way to God, the only Way.'

"And, Edward, I did just that. I put my whole trust in what Christ had done, put my trust in Him alone. Confessed that nothing I had done or would be able to do, would find God's favor. That night something birthed in me. When I raised my head after prayer, my whole way of viewing life changed. I looked about me. Everything was alive and fresh. Believe me, Edward, I would not tell you something that was untrue. This new life with God is something real. It is something I know. I *know,* Edward. Not something I *merely believe.*"

Edward sat back on the settee. "I've never heard it put that way before. This was never part of my church's teaching."

"Maybe that's why you have so little to do with God. Religion itself can be cold and lifeless." She leaned toward him. "And you would never be party to that. You are full of life; your mind thinks, tries to get to the heart of an issue. You pursue a question to its answer. Edward, could you believe? Believe as I do?"

He crossed his arms over his chest. "But a person can *believe* anything. That doesn't make it true."

"I agree. One has to believe what is true. For example, in the time of Christopher

Columbus many believed the world was flat, that if a person sailed long enough, his ship would drop off the earth. But when explorers began to believe the earth was round, something that was true, it freed them to explore and find America. My belief is the same. It is a belief in something that exists, in a God who cares for me, and because it is true, it frees me to explore a whole new realm of the spiritual. What is this realm?" She looked at him even more earnestly. "It is this: that it is possible for humble man to know the God of the universe."

He uncrossed his arms from his chest. "Something is missing here, Celia." He leaned toward her. "Give me your hand, please." He took it gently, held it up and looked at it. "Here, you are flesh and blood." He pressed it. "You see, I can feel you. Now, here is the question. How can a flesh and blood person know something, or shall we say Someone, who is a Spirit? It doesn't seem possible." He lowered her hand and held it securely in both of his.

She smiled to herself to see her hand rest in his. How artfully he had accomplished that. She had to admit she wanted it there. Here they were, touching physically, their feelings growing toward each other, and they were having this important theological discussion. Is this how it would be with them? It seemed natural enough. Yet, she knew there could be no future with Edward unless something changed. She would let her hand rest in his for the moment, but she would not be deterred from her purpose in coming.

She took up the thread of their discussion. "Well, one instance is that the invisible God has left His mark on the visible world around us. Look at the beauty of the hills, trees, and flowers all around us. Look at the complexity of nature, how it all works together. Think of the intricacy of a single leaf, its veins bringing life to each little part, distributing sap that has come up from the trunk. Somehow, water from the ground and nutrients from the soil have formed sap to nourish that leaf.

"Here, I'd like to show you another verse in the Bible." She extracted her hand from his. "Turn to Romans." She nodded to the book. "Read verse twenty of the first chapter."

"Ah, that would be in the New Testament, would it not?"

"Edward, you're teasing me. You very well know it is. If you know that Tacitus spoke of Christ. . . ."

The glance in his eye showed mischief,

but he turned to the book and after finding the verse, read, *For the invisible things of Him from the creation of the world are clearly seen, being understood by the things that are made, even His eternal power and Godhead; so that they are without excuse.*

"See, Edward, if we take a long and thoughtful look at what God has created, we will see evidence of His power. Of His divine being in nature. The basic reality of God is plain enough."

She paused to let that sink in, then decided to drive home her point. "That's where faith comes in, but it's not the kind of faith that's a leap in the dark. It's faith based on evidence: evidence in nature, evidence in a document like the Bible, particularly the Bible. And if a person wants corroboration of the Biblical account, he can read other writings of antiquity such as Josephus — and others you've read. Beyond that, there's the evidence of people like myself who say they know God, my parents, many people in the town where I was raised, the Chestleys."

She leaned forward. "Do you believe *me*, Edward?" Her eyes held his. "You have all these evidences. Now comes the leap of faith. But, remember, it is not into complete darkness. You have evidence."

"It sounds as if you want me to make a decision now, but —" He reached for her hands again. "This is what I can see. And touch. This is what I want." His dark eyes caught hers and held them. "*Whom* I want." She felt his hands enclose hers, warm and entreating. "You are my light, my hope for a better life."

How was she to deal with him? She searched his eyes. "Edward, what I've been talking about is important. I can't tell you how important this is, of eternal importance." She glanced down at their hands. "I feel I must not be sidetracked like this."

"Celia, we've talked enough about religion for the time being." He said it gently, but firmly. "Now, I want to talk about us."

"But, Edward, there's no 'us' unless this issue of 'religion,' as you call it, is resolved. We *must* talk about it. As I said before, you pursue a question to its answer. And that's what you need to do here. This faith affects every aspect of our lives, every relationship."

"What do you mean?"

"Our relationship and relationships with others. Especially difficult ones. For example —" Here she paused. "Marguerite. Her mother."

"Enough!"

Her eyes fell, her hands clenched within

his. It was as if he'd given her a verbal slap. Had she pressed him too far?

He sat silently for some moments then let his breath out slowly. "Celia, I'm sorry I spoke so. Forgive me for being abrupt. Even if we disagree, I should speak gently, to you of all people, my d—" He began to rub his thumbs over the backs of her hands, then turned them over, opened them and rubbed her palms. She felt the entreaty in his fingers. "It's just that I felt threatened. Threatened you would use our spiritual differences to separate us. I don't want that to happen."

She looked up. "I'm sorry, Edward, for speaking of Mrs. Divers and her daughter. But that is important, too. You see, I learned — before I came here — how important it is to forgive, and to forgive quickly. The whole reason I came to work at the Chestleys was because I had not done so quickly and was suffering the effects of remorse."

She took her hands from his. "Do you remember early on in our acquaintance — when you calmed a frightened horse?"

"I remember it well."

"That incident affected me more deeply than you probably realize — because of the horse. Just a few months prior to coming here, I was given a treasured book for my birthday, the novel *St. Elmo,* which I had looked forward to for a long time. My best friend asked to borrow it, and to tell the truth, I was loath to part with it, but she *was* my closest friend. Then she carelessly let it drop in a mud puddle as we walked together after a heavy rain. I remember looking down in horror at the book, half submerged in the muddy water. I quickly bent down, grabbed it and wiped it on my skirt. I was furious, more than I can say. I cast her an angry look and ran home — fast. I cleaned the book as best I could, but the cover still showed the effects of the muddy water, and the edges of the pages were crinkly and stained brown. My beautiful book!

"I wouldn't speak to my friend for days. And then the unthinkable happened. She had an accident while riding horseback. He was frightened and threw her. When she fell her neck broke, the doctor thinks killing her instantly. That is my only comfort, because the last time she saw me, anger was written across my face. I forgave her too late."

Celia looked at Edward, tears starting to gather. "And afterward, I couldn't help but think of eternity, where my friend is now."

Edward's eyes were dark, unreadable. They were both silent long moments, then

Celia said, "What we believe about Christ affects where we will spend eternity."

She shifted her position on the settee. "Our faith — is so important. Edward, you can investigate this further, you can pray to God to reveal Himself to you. And He will — through Christ."

Celia would not let Edward's eyes stray from hers. "My dear friend, He's the only One who can make a dead religion come alive in your heart and soul. He and He alone. I am proof of that. I would not lie to you — *you* of all people."

He lifted her hands and kissed them.

Her heart bounded up.

He kept them close to his face, almost as if he was inhaling the scent of her — like fine perfume. "I'm sorry you went through that with your friend. But *we* are friends, aren't we? More than friends?"

She could see the appeal in his eyes.

He held her hands tighter, closer. She could feel the magnitude of their spiritual differences slipping away. She wanted to be touched, cared for.

In that moment, she saw the danger in remaining alone with him. "Edward, I should leave."

He looked up. "Why?"

"You know why." She tried to draw away.

"I *must* go. Please, consider what we talked about."

He stared at her a long moment, then let go of her hands. "Did you bring anything with you, something we should retrieve?"

She shook her head.

He assisted her off the settee and gestured toward the door. He opened it and led the way down the hall.

He is taking this all very calmly, she thought. She was relieved but also piqued. No, it was more than that. Hurt had started to well up in her. Could he let her go so easily?

They reached the front door. She stopped to allow him to open it for her. Instead of reaching for the door, he turned and asked, "No heartfelt good-bye, Celia? We are more than friends, you know."

She held out her hand in farewell.

His eyes glittered. "No, we must not part thus." He took her outstretched hand, grasped it and pulled her to him. His arms went around her. As he pressed her to him, she sensed his desire and felt hers rise in response. "I cannot bear to see you go without your saying a word of hope for us. Please, Celia."

Moments before, she had felt hurt and withdrawn; now here she was in his arms, desperately wanting to stay. Could she be so weak, so changeable? She clung to him a moment longer, drinking in his nearness, his warmth, his tenderness. She glanced up. His arms tightened around her. "Edward, you know I cannot. I cannot without being untrue to God." She extricated herself from his arms.

How she hated to be the cause of his hurt. No — the real cause was his own blindness, his own lack of belief.

She glanced at the door. She didn't want to walk out it alone, dreaded the coming separation, but she must. She purposefully turned to it, waiting for him to open it.

A breath of a sigh escaped him, but he opened the door, standing sentinel as she stepped over the threshold.

She walked down the steps then out onto the drive, her heart heavy, pained. But she would not look back. That would be her undoing. She *would* keep walking.

Exiting the drive to enter the road, she wondered how she could ever weather something like this again: confront him with the truth, him not receive it, and then refuse the intimacy they both wanted. Even now, she hardly trusted her strength of resolve to remain away.

When she reached the Chestleys, she

excused herself to her room. She had begun shaking. How could she trust herself to do the right thing if they were alone together again? She flung herself on the bed and buried her face into the pillow.

# 22

Edward watched Celia walk down his drive. How he ached for her, how tempted he was to go after her. But he had sensed she needed to be by herself, and had forced himself to respect her unspoken wishes. However, he could still delight in watching her sweet self, noting every movement of her arms and figure. Her mind had the same agile, quick movements as her carriage, which he valued so highly.

But how adamant she had been about her beliefs! A doubt nagged him. This whole matter of her faith seemed prodigiously important.

He respected her for that. In fact, loved her for it. He had always appreciated her fondness for engaged discussion. There was nothing settled, predictable about her. Her mind was always questing. Ah, how they could quest together!

She had reached the road. The wonder of

it was that she had come to see him at all. After what had transpired this last week, she had still come to him. He didn't deserve it after the shadow cast on his name. His once-proud name. Why had he continued to live here years after Marguerite's death? Why hadn't he removed himself to Boston? Maybe the mysterious hand of Providence had stayed him — in order for him to meet Celia — that same Providence he was uncertain with whom he had personal dealings. The very question Celia had asked, a probing question indeed.

He waited until the trees hid the last of her delightful person. She would now be passing Mrs. Divers's house. That — but no, he would not think about the old wretch, not when he had a much pleasanter subject on which to dwell.

He turned to enter his house. After shutting the door, he stood on the spot where Celia and he said good-bye. Closing his eyes, once more he felt her in his arms. She nestled just so against his chest, as if she were meant to be there.

She desired to be there. He could feel it.

It had been a long time since he desired a woman. He had blocked it off from his thinking, his consciousness. But now it was all he could do not to think of it. Celia had broken through the ice of his reserve. He trusted her. Trusted her to be good and worthy of love.

"Mr. Lyons, can I do anything for you?" Mrs. Macon was walking down the hall toward him. "You said you didn't want to be disturbed, but I was thinking the young lady might like some refreshment."

"No, you did exactly the right thing. She is gone now." He saw the question in her eyes, wondering what they had been doing sequestered so long in the library. Well, he would give her a bone. "We had a most enlightening talk." When his housekeeper kept looking at him, he added,

"About religion."

"That is a most appropriate topic for Sunday."

He could see she approved, but she wasn't sure if that was all that transpired. The devil take her, he would reveal nothing further. He raised an eyebrow and waited.

"I guess if that's all, sir, I will set out your supper and then I'll be about done for the day."

"Thank you, Mrs. Macon." He watched her walk down the hall to the kitchen.

Where was he? Oh yes, she had interrupted his thoughts about Celia. Probably just as well. He could see he would have a difficult time not letting his thoughts stray into forbidden waters. At least, waters forbidden at this point. There was that snag of religion. The topic was obviously important to Celia. And, of course, that should make it important to him. But, he smiled, Celia herself was so much more interesting. He wanted to think about her. Only her.

How long before he saw her again? Would she want to see him as soon as tomorrow, if he dropped by the bookstore? What excuse could he make? Maybe he would make no excuse, just stop by to say hello. Possibly look through the religion section. He hadn't done that in a long while. Maybe she could help him investigate it. Ah, there was a thought.

"Celia, will you help me dry dishes tonight?"

Celia looked up from the dinner table. "I'd be glad to."

"Lately I've let them air dry, but we women need time together. Just the two of us. Mr. Chestley, you can take yourself off to the sitting room and sit a spell. You've worked hard this week and deserve a rest." She winked at him. "Especially at your age."

"Now you're in trouble," he said. "I've plenty of energy for what is needed. Or for what I want." He got up from the table and hugged his wife from the back. "You remember that, Mrs. Chestley."

She turned her head slightly to better see him. He took it as an invitation and pecked her on the cheek. She laughed and blushed. Mr. Chestley looked at Celia. "Sorry for such open affection." He looked at his wife again. "But I think my assistant is accustomed to it by now."

Celia smiled at them. She would never tire of seeing their tenderness toward each other. They reminded her of Mother and Father. And what she'd had so recently with Edward.

"There now, Celia," Mrs. Chestley said some minutes later over the dishpan. "Tell me what's on your mind. You were unusually quiet at supper."

Celia put aside the dishtowel, wondering how much to say. "I would appreciate a godly woman's viewpoint. This is about a certain friendship — well, the interest goes beyond mere friendship. And the trouble is, this individual has a form of religion, knows *about* God rather than *knowing* Him. As time goes on, it's increasingly difficult to keep my perspective about him, if you know what I mean."

Mrs. Chestley washed another dish before she spoke. "This person, is it Mr. Lyons?"

351

Celia nodded.

"That doesn't surprise me, dear. I've noticed a growing interest on his part. And he is a man whose interest is not easily engaged. That is a compliment to you."

Celia smiled wryly. "Thank you, but there is the problem of his faith, or lack of it."

"Have you talked with him about it? I mean, really talked about it?"

"Yes. Or at least I've tried. He doesn't seem overly interested." Celia took up her towel again. "Oh, he's interested like he would be in any subject, but though I've tried to express how important, how really important it is to me, he brushes it aside. He hasn't grasped how vital it is to a — a deeper friendship with me."

"Or doesn't want to."

Celia turned and looked at Mrs. Chestley. "Does it go as deeply as that?"

"From what you have told me, and I know Mr. Lyons to be an insightful man, he is either brushing aside the topic or is unconsciously letting himself be obtuse about the matter. And let's remember Celia, if God is not real to him — and Mr. Lyons considers himself an intelligent man — he would wonder how God could be real to anyone else. It apparently hasn't entered his mind he could be mistaken or wrong in the matter. I think he assumes the subject will blow over in time."

"But you know it will not — not with me."

"I know, my dear." Mrs. Chestley leaned her head sympathetically toward Celia. "So, do you think you can be firm in your stance for the truth?"

Celia gripped the towel hard in her hands. "That's what troubles me." She dropped into the nearest chair and looked up at Mrs. Chestley.

"I think I can surmise what you want to say," Mrs. Chestley said gently, "but could you be more specific with me? I don't want to give you wrong counsel."

"It's just that when I'm with him, I find myself starting to make allowances for him, excusing his lack of belief. Especially when he — when he makes it increasingly clear how he is beginning to care for me." Celia looked up at Mrs. Chestley, tears gathering in her eyes. "I don't want to hurt him in any way. He's been hurt so much." Could she admit this next to Mrs. Chestley? She finally said, "And I'm afraid of myself, that I'll not say no to further intimacy. That I'll let the relationship go too far — without him coming to terms with God. I'm also afraid that after a while I won't care anymore, that I'll be willing to compromise my beliefs because of my feelings for him."

"I see." Mrs. Chestley turned back to her dishes. After washing another plate, she said, "Do you think you can remain here or should you leave? I mean go home. Maybe you need a respite. And maybe Mr. Lyons needs a little bit of a shock to wake him up to the reality of the situation." Mrs. Chestley turned to Celia. "I know my husband would not like to hear of your leaving, but remember, he said at one of our first dinners any man coming to claim your hand would have to be approved by him first, and I know Mr. Chestley would not approve of Mr. Lyons at this point. Not that he doesn't like Mr. Lyons. He most certainly does. But he would see the pitfalls of the situation."

There was quiet for some moments. "I hadn't considered *leaving* as an option. I don't really want to do so."

"This is *your* decision. It has to be yours."

Celia sighed. After a few more moments of quiet, she murmured, "But you might be right."

Mrs. Chestley held out a plate for drying.

Celia stood and took the plate. "You know, I think I *must* leave."

Mrs. Chestley cleared her throat. "If that's the case, when do you think you should go?"

"The sooner, the better?" Both women

remained silent while Celia dried the plate.

Mrs. Chestley rinsed her hands and wiped them on a towel. "Why don't we go and talk with my husband, see what can be worked out. I could probably fill in for a time until he gets another assistant."

Celia heard voices outside the bookstore. Two familiar ones. She stepped behind the counter ready to help or for refuge — she wasn't sure. When the door jangled, she made herself look casually in that direction. Edward and Charles entered, one following the other. Seeing them this close reminded her of the archery contest. Both men were tall, but there the similarity ended. Charles was lean, Edward's physique brawny. Both men were agile, but one looked as if he could easily overpower the other. Charles immediately headed toward the counter where she stood. Edward made his way toward the stacks and in a moment, was out of sight.

"Just the person I want to see," Charles said.

"I'm glad I'm available. What can I do for you?"

"My mother sent me to ask you to dinner. Before I leave for Boston."

"When are you going?"

"A week from now. What say you to dinner the evening after next?"

Celia felt the dilemma. She hadn't told anyone besides the Chestleys her plans. Not even the man on the other side of the stacks. Should she lower her voice to Charles and tell Edward later, privately? Or just let him overhear what she said to Charles? Edward appearing from behind the stacks answered her question. He walked purposely toward the counter.

"I'm afraid that wouldn't be possible," she answered Charles.

"I know you have a heavy social calendar," Charles said laughing. "Now, why ever not?"

"Well, I'll be leaving that same afternoon. For home."

"For home? Ah, to visit your parents and siblings. Very commendable. Well then, can we make it tomorrow night? I'm sure that would be fine with Mother."

"I was thinking I should have my last night with the Chestleys."

"Your last night with the Chestleys? But surely you're going for just a short visit and the Chestleys wouldn't mind."

She would not answer that in front of Edward. She glanced at him. He was looking at her with an intensity that was unsettling. "They've been so good to me. Would

356

lunch tomorrow be too short notice to your mother?"

"I think that'd be fine with her, she is hospitality personified. You'll be working tomorrow?" On her nod, he asked, "Why don't we ask Mr. Chestley when it would be convenient to leave the store for an hour? Mr. Lyons, you don't mind if she takes a minute to ask, do you?"

Edward said nothing, merely gestured his acquiescence.

Celia smiled her gratitude. Or at least tried to. She felt embarrassment down to her toes. For him to learn of her departure this way!

"Now you see how easy that was," Charles said a couple minutes later as they walked back to the counter. "God didn't make me a lawyer for nothing. Mr. Chestley couldn't say no." He looked at Mr. Lyons. "Thank you for waiting," then touched Celia's arm. "One o'clock, then? I'll come and call for you in the buggy. That will give more time for our luncheon." As he was turning to leave, he stopped and said, "I just remembered, you'll need a way to the station, won't you? Why don't I bring the carriage around the next day?"

Edward took a hasty step forward. "I'm already planning on doing that."

"Oh." Charles looked from one to the other. "I see." He took a step back. "Well, then, I'll look forward to tomorrow. Goodbye, Celia."

The door jangled shut before Celia could make herself look up. When she did, she found Edward's eyes fastened on her. "Celia," he whispered her name. "Why haven't you told me? Is something wrong?"

She looked at him a long moment, swallowed. "I know this seems sudden."

His hand reached for hers. "Has something happened to one of your family? I'm glad I dropped by today."

"No, it's no one in the family. I just need time to think." What could she say? Time to think wasn't exactly true. Time to be away. Her eyes started tearing. She withdrew her hand from his.

"Is this about us?"

"Yes."

Stirrings sounded in Mr. Chestley's office. Celia hoped and didn't hope he'd put in an appearance. She wanted to be alone with Edward, but it was increasingly painful, knowing what she did.

"Celia, can I see you tonight, after work?"

"I don't think so. I have a lot to do to get ready."

"How long are you going to be gone?"

"A while."

"What do you mean? Will it be long?"

"It could be."

"Celia, don't do this to us," his deep voice pleaded. "Don't do this to me."

"I'm doing what is best."

"What *you* believe is best."

"Please, Edward, don't make this harder than it is. I — I wouldn't have chosen this way. Believe me."

He stood for some moments, silent, as if taking in what she had just said, wondering what to do. "So you are leaving the day after tomorrow? What time?"

"My train leaves at two thirty in the afternoon."

"I'll pick you up at one o'clock."

"It doesn't take more than fifteen minutes to drive to the station."

"You'll want to arrive in plenty of time. Besides —"

She couldn't countermand him. Her eyes had been flitting to the side, down to the counter, anywhere but on him. Now, she forced herself to look directly at him. "I'm sorry. I didn't expect news of my departure to come out this way."

Various emotions flitted across his face. Finally, he said, "I'll come for you at one o'clock." With that, he turned on his heel toward the door.

# 23

Celia sat on her bed, alone. Everything was ready for her departure. She had hurried at the end to be early; she didn't want to keep Edward waiting, especially in this instance. She realized she might keep him waiting forever in the larger consideration of his desires. She would not brood over that now, but she was hard pressed to keep her mind from conjecturing about last night. Mrs. Macon had paid her a visit in the bookstore just before closing. Mr. Chestley was holed up in his office.

"Could I talk with you, Miss, while no one is around?"

"Surely."

"I've come because Mr. Lyons isn't himself. When I asked if anything was wrong, he gave me a long, hard look and said, 'Miss Thatcher is leaving.' Then he half slammed the door to his library and I haven't seen him since. His supper has gone cold on the table.

"I heard the scuttlebutt about the flower show and all. And all I've got to say is that he's been misjudged by this town, and I wanted you to know it. His wife wasn't all they thought she was. He wouldn't say this about Marguerite because it would hurt his pride, but she had a streak in her, flirtatious I call it. When they had parties, I'd see her flirting with the men. Subtle-like, while her back was turned to the rest of the party, using her eyes from underneath her lashes, and little smiles. Then, once she entertained a man while Mr. Lyons was away to Boston. That visitor kept staying and staying, and when I finally asked her if it was wise, she told me in no uncertain terms if I told Mr. Lyons, she would see I lost my job. For a long time, I didn't say anything, but then I just had to tell him. I was so surprised when he said he had known for a long time."

Mrs. Macon's hands gripped the counter. "You know, Mr. Lyons was always a gentleman, and never went into that part of her to others. But I thought you should know before . . . Well, I guess I've said enough. I know he wouldn't want me down here, so I'd appreciate it if you wouldn't say anything. But he sets a powerful lot by you, and I didn't want you leaving because of gossip about how he treated Marguerite. The town didn't see her for what she really was. And he has his pride."

Celia had thanked Mrs. Macon warmly, and said no she hadn't realized this, but also, Marguerite wasn't the reason she was leaving. Then she very kindly walked the housekeeper to the door before telling Mr. Chestley he could lock up after her.

But knowing this now made leaving harder.

Her hands twisted in her lap. Edward had specified he'd come an hour and a half before the train's departure. How could she face him? To be with him that long alone? Earlier, she had asked Mrs. Chestley to accompany her.

"Celia, you know I would like nothing more, but Mr. Chestley said he needs me. I'll just say goodbye to you at the house, see that everything's in good order and then must hurry off to the bookstore."

It seemed strange that Mrs. Chestley couldn't come with her to the station, she very much doubted if her husband needed her that much. He had said his goodbye that noon. "Now, you know you will always have a place with us, Celia." He had closed the store for the lunch hour, which he didn't usually do, to be with her as she ate her last meal with them. In this case, he'd seemed casual about attending to the store.

Any minute now Edward would be announced. Abruptly, she fell on her knees, burying her face in her hands. "Oh Father," she prayed, "help me! Help me to be strong. Help me discern what is best for us, for both our hearts. Especially in light of what I learned about Marguerite. And, Lord, I supplicate You for Edward's soul. Do not let him die apart from You. Help me to be both firm and winsome in this battle. I don't want to disappoint You or cause You shame. In Christ's name I pray, Amen."

She waited silently on her knees until some degree of quietness settled on her soul. She then rose to spend the last minutes with Mrs. Chestley. But as soon as she reached for her satchel, she heard a knock at the front door. She exited the bedroom to find Mrs. Chestley rising from her chair.

"That will be Mr. Lyons or his handyman." Mrs. Chestley opened the front door.

"Come in, Ned. We have a trunk and suitcase in the bedroom."

While Ned walked over to the bedroom, Mrs. Chestley took Celia's hands and lowered her voice. "You look very fetching, my dear. That beribboned scrap of a hat adds the perfect touch. Mrs. Harrod has been most generous to you."

"You don't think it too modish for my family?"

"Your family will see a new side of you, certainly. But remember, by looking lovely you do honor to the man escorting you to the train station. Why don't you go out to him now. . . ."

Celia stepped outside. Edward directed Ned where to place the trunk. The last case strapped to the carriage, Mrs. Chestley turned to her. "Now, dear, you must know how much I've enjoyed your time with us. I will not call this *'Adieu,'* as the French would say; that is too final, but rather *'Au revoir.'* "

"You and Mr. Chestley must come for a visit," Celia said. "You know Mother and Father would love to see you. Our family certainly warmed your hearth enough in the past."

"Maybe we will at that. Certainly, if you don't return to us soon enough."

Throughout this exchange, Edward stood respectfully to the side. Celia didn't know how this goodbye with Mrs. Chestley affected him. She hadn't told him how long she would be gone, but she had cleared out her things from her room. In effect, she was leaving for good.

After a hard hug from Mrs. Chestley, Celia allowed Edward to hand her up into the carriage. "Why don't you sit by this window to better see Mrs. Chestley," he suggested, then walked to the other side and climbed in.

As the carriage took off, Celia leaned forward to blow Mrs. Chestley a kiss. A few moments later, her friend was lost from view and Celia sat back against the cushion. Edward had seated himself beside her. After they passed the block of stores and houses, he moved closer to her and quietly took one white gloved hand, then the other in both of his. Celia allowed the fond expression of farewell. She had wondered if such a gesture would happen en route to the station. She had both looked forward to it and dreaded it. She wanted to be strong and not let her guard down, giving him false hope, yet her womanly soul yearned to know he loved her. . . . She could not meet his eyes, however, and continued to look out the window.

Ned turned down a side street. At this she glanced at Edward. "This is not the way to the station."

"Maybe not the direct route, but certainly the most scenic."

How like him to indulge her love of beauty. Sure enough, he had chosen a route on the edge of town where a forest and then a glade showed out her side of the carriage. Even while her heart felt pain, it also felt peace sitting with Edward holding her hands and looking out on all this beauty. She should have trusted him to do something lovely at parting.

Then the carriage turned off to the side of the road and stopped. Edward took one of his hands from hers and leaning over, shut the curtains on his side of the carriage facing the road. "I've instructed Ned to stop for a few minutes so that we could have this time together. Celia, do I need to tell you I dread the thought of your going? This is so sudden, so last minute. I haven't been able to think or plan — Celia, why all this luggage? It looks as if you're taking all your worldly possessions."

"I'm afraid so, at least what I had at the Chestleys."

"But why? Aren't you coming back?"

"I don't know, Edward."

He held her hands more firmly. "Is it as serious as that, our differences in view?"

"It's not only about that. I can't stay — that's all I can say."

"Celia, look at me." She turned, honoring

his request. After a few moments, he lifted one gloved hand to his lips, then the other. As she looked into his dark searching eyes, tears sprang to hers.

He lowered her hands and reached for his handkerchief. After she gratefully took it and wiped her eyes, he put his arm around her and drew her to him, resting her head against his chest. "You don't want this parting any more than I do." He stated it quietly but with a note of triumph. "You will not tell me why you feel so impelled to leave?" He held her closer. "Then I will tell you. Despite our disagreement, you feel the same oneness with me as I do with you. I am the match for your soul as you are for mine. This is something for which we have both longed. We want each other. We need each other. Yet, there is this one barrier, and you have erected it. Religion. God. Whatever you want to call it. But I want to go on record here that it is not I who have erected it. I would take you as you are. You are my soul! What has God to do with that?"

He pressed his lips to her head near her ear and let them rest there. She sensed, felt him drinking in the fragrance of her hair. His words of love were like darts in her heart.

He whispered, "We don't need God to talk

with each other, to share our deepest thoughts, our hearts."

She felt her heart failing. To be this close and hear him say such things. Oh, how she wanted to let go all their contention and be at peace with him. She turned to try to face him, to draw away from his closeness, but he held her fast.

"I cannot talk like this, Edward."

"You can talk very well."

"Edward, I can only reiterate how important God is to me."

"Celia. Celia." He said the words tenderly. After a few moments he raised his head, loosened his hold enough so she could look up at him. "We can agree to disagree. We will disagree on many things. If we disagree without rancor, it will spice our conversation. And then we will call a truce afterward and sit as we are sitting now. I declare it thus."

She couldn't help but smile. "Yes, it's obvious we would disagree on a number of subjects. My parents certainly did." She was silent a moment. "I wish you could meet them, particularly my father. He is a wise man who knows much about God. He would be able to articulate what I have said so poorly."

"Hmm," was all Edward responded. He

held her close once again. Celia could feel his lips once more caressing her hair. She didn't have it in her to deny him. Then a knock sounded on the roof of the carriage. Moments later they started to move. Ned was watching the time.

A low groan came from deep within Edward. "Celia, whatever you may say, the strands of our individual lives are strongly entwined. You may run away from me, but you are mine." His arms tightened around her, but he held her tenderly. They sat the remainder of the trip in silence.

Noises of other horses and carriages increased around them. Their conveyance stopped. Celia pulled away from him.

"One minute," he said. He reached for her left hand. "Let me do this, Celia. Trust me." He removed her glove. He kept her hand in one of his while he reached for something in his breast pocket. He drew out a ring set with a magnificent ruby. For a moment he held it to the sun shining in her window. "See its scarlet glow? The fire of my love burns like the red flame of this stone." He lowered the jewel to slip on her finger. "This proclaims you are mine. When men see it, they will know you belong to another. Some might say, how dare I do this when the woman of my heart has not said yes to my proposal. 'But I know her heart,' I would say to them, 'I know her wishes. She is mine, whether she says it or not.'"

The carriage jostled slightly. Ned had taken off one of the bigger bags. Edward raised her hand to his chest and held it there. Then he lowered it. "I will help see to your bags. Stay here until I return."

Celia sat back on the seat, unable to say anything, hardly able to think. Edward had so mastered the situation. Had she done the right thing? But she hardly cared at the moment. All she knew was that she didn't want to leave. But she must. She could barely cope with his presence at her side, his professions of love.

How she wanted to assure him of her love, hint at the deep yearning he had awakened in her. She felt limp, stunned. Thank God they had arrived at the station, that Ned was looking out for them. Otherwise, she would have given herself away. It would have needed only a little more and she would have exposed her heart to him completely.

How could she be so compliant? She almost despised herself. She had felt the danger, yet wanted to be part of it. Shameful of her. Oh, how glad she was he'd gone to see to the luggage.

As she waited, her head began to clear, her senses returned to normal. What had become of her, alone with him, just a few minutes ago? Had she no conscience? No firmness? For, of course, she could give him no hope — as much as she wanted to. Unless he changed toward God, their oneness was a dream, merely a wish of his.

Should she return his ring? To do so immediately would be the right thing. Looking out the window, she saw a growing number of passengers alighting from conveyances. She didn't know what to do. Rather, she did, but wasn't sure if this was the right place and time. But when would she see him again?

She saw him make his way around a carriage. Saw the seriousness, the determination, the pain etched into his face.

At once, she knew she could not hand back the ring. Not at this moment with the movement and people and animals all around. If she did it now, it would be done too quickly and would be like a slap in the face. And she could not slap the face she loved. Not after what Mrs. Macon had told her last night. She would not wound his pride like that. Later, she could think more clearly and would know what to do.

Edward stepped back into the carriage.

With a quick motion, he let loose the curtains of the side nearest her, dropping them to give them privacy. He settled himself next to her, then drew her to him.

"Celia, in these final minutes I vow my unfailing love for you. I pledge myself to you. I pledge my name, my worldly possessions. I trust you as no other woman and have given you my ring." His arm tightened around her and he said this time with more urgency, breathing the words, "Oh, Celia, how can I let you go?" Gently, he took her hand in his and kissed it, then kissed it again. His kisses were fearfully sweet.

Inside she trembled. She must master herself, take control of self and the situation. God help her!

After a few moments, she resolutely separated herself from him and put her glove back on her hand. "Is my trunk in baggage?"

He gazed at her. "So, you are resolved to leave?"

She nodded.

He reached into a pocket. "Here is your claim." He preceded her out the carriage and handed her down. He was now the gentleman and placed her hand on his arm. He was the *perfect* gentleman, but he was also staking his claim, seeing to her and protecting her.

He went on board the train and helped settle her in her seat. After the final "All aboard!" he took her left hand in his and fingering the ruby through the glove, leaned over to her. His cheek pressed hers. His voice whispered, "You are mine. Remember that, darling." He pressed her hand again, then stepped back, smiled, and turned to leave.

Celia watched him walk down the aisle, his shoulders straight, his head held high. She was glad she hadn't given back his ring, not just now. No sooner would she cause those shoulders to droop than she would disappoint her own father. Somehow, she would find a way to return the ring.

Her heart constricted with the coming separation, but knew it must be so. She would be strong and cling to what was right. She feared that unless she held to her convictions and carried through with this drastic departure, he would have no motivation to examine the very thing that separated them. And she would rather turn the knife in his heart than see him a soul forever damned.

He waited on the platform, watching her as the train started with a jerk. She sat, crushing the handkerchief in one fist, holding a smile on her face as the train picked up momentum. The man on the platform didn't know it, but she was leaving, truly leaving. She held up her hand in a small, impersonal wave, longing to show some indication of her love, but she would not. Then he disappeared from view. Then and only then did she lift the handkerchief to her eyes and wipe the tears.

# 24

"Celia, dear! We received your telegram." Her mother wrapped her arms around her and held her hard. "We'll talk more about that later. First, sit down, and have some soup. The rest of us have eaten."

Celia looked around at her brothers and little sister who'd given her the grand welcome at the station full of hugs and squeals. Now they sat at the table or milled around the kitchen, all with smiles on their faces eager to hear her latest news.

"You've come to stay, you won't be here only a few days?" her youngest brother asked. On her nod, he yelled, "Yea!"

Her sister sidled up to her and circled her arms around her neck. "We've missed you, Celia."

"I've missed you, too." She looked at the curly blond head. This was food for her soul, a family who loved her. She glanced at her mother, pouring out soup from the big pot on the stove, her father now settling himself at the opposite end of the table with a cup of tea. She could talk with them all — oh, the riches of love and conversation she had here in her old home. The sweetness of it was almost too much to realize.

Her thoughts reverted to earlier in the day. Did Edward have anyone who loved him, there where he lived? She had such blessings that he did not. Her heart ached for him but also knew things had to be this way. If he felt his need, maybe it would drive him to God.

"We'll visit Grandma tomorrow, maybe late in the morning," her mother was saying. "You may have one day to sleep in and acclimate to life in this busy family, then you'll find plenty of work to do, my dear. I've been thinking. For the time being, you could help out at the general store. Mr. Jenkins broke his leg and finds it difficult to get around. You probably won't get paid at present, but that's all right. We need to aid our neighbor. The boys can lift the heavy things, but help with the little, detailed matters is what he now needs."

So within a few hours of homecoming, Celia felt she would fit right back into life in the small town. It looked as though mornings through early afternoon she would assist in the store, then help Mother at home. "Having you here late summer will be such a treat for me," her mother said, "especially with all the canning. Best of all, we can talk." Her mother emphasized her words punctuating them with a large spoon. "When you left at the end of canning season last year, I didn't know how I would get it all done this year, but now, here you are. I think the Lord brought you home just for me." The spoon tapped her forefinger. "Of course, I'm joking a bit, but the Lord has a way of working out the details of everyone's lives so they mesh in the most intricate, interesting ways. We can trust Him with the smallest aspect, can't we?"

After supper the following evening, Celia walked down the hallway to the sitting room. The rest of the children would follow later. They were to clear the table and do dishes while Mother and Father spent time alone. This had been a nightly ritual since the children were old enough to do chores. Even when the youngest child couldn't yet help, the older children looked after her while Mother and Father had their time together.

Once her oldest brother Joe asked what his parents did. "We talk," Mother said.

Later Mother explained to Celia that a number of years had passed before she discovered how Father loved time alone with her, that talking with her was his special delight. It brought them closer. "At first, you all clamored for my help in the kitchen. Well, clamored isn't quite the word." Mother laughed. "You were never allowed to do that, as you well know."

Celia remembered. Mother had patiently showed them how to do each required task, then firmly walked out the door to be with their father. When the occasional dish broke, she made herself adopt a *sang-froid* attitude, knowing she was attending to the more important business of keeping her husband happy.

Tonight, Celia had been asked to come in early, ahead of her brothers and sisters. When she opened the sitting room door, she found her parents in a close embrace.

The tender scene struck her in a way she'd never noticed before. Yes, she'd seen her parents' gestures of love and caring before and surmised devoted husbands and wives did the same in the privacy of their homes. And growing up, she'd seen her parents embrace many times, but now it affected her differently. She noticed not only the tenderness in her father, but his — she searched for the right word — desire for her mother. And she for him. She felt herself flush. It was what she had felt for Edward and it frightened her, especially when marriage could not be considered. With strong feelings like these, a whole new world had opened up to her.

"Come in, Celia," her father said. He gestured toward a chair opposite the couch where he and Mother sat. "Now, tell us why you came home so suddenly."

Celia hesitated at the door, then entered. Best make a clean breast of it.

Later that night, she lay in bed, gazing up at the white ceiling. Its blank whiteness was the picture of her future. Mother and Father had made it clear she could stay with them as long as necessary, that under the circumstances, it was just as well she didn't continue to live near Mr. Lyons.

"He seems an interesting man," her mother said. "I wonder what I would think if I met him." That her mother had evinced a degree of sympathy for the man surprised Celia.

"He seems a compelling individual with a formidable mind," her father added. "Because of his kindness toward you, I know that made it all the more difficult to discern what to do." He had looked at her carefully before continuing, "Daughter, I believe you did the right thing in coming home. I'm glad you assured us the Chestleys wouldn't be too inconvenienced by it. So you worked to put the bookstore in good order before you left?"

She replied in the affirmative.

"Taking care of all these details on such short notice was admirable."

Celia was relieved her parents approved all that had transpired. As she rolled over on her side, her mind went back to her parents themselves. She thought of her mother, the way she saw to Father's needs — his desire for time alone with her as well as the other things she did for him in the course of a day. She was starting to see the word *wife* in a new light. No other woman occupied this particular role in his life. It was a special place indeed. Her mother had made it a place of honor and respect, herself loved and desired. A deep longing took hold of Celia. Oh, to be that woman — to someone.

These first days home, while someone was speaking, Edward would suddenly come to mind. What was he doing? Was he thinking of her? And now, with her absence, was Mrs. Adams stepping into the gap Celia had left?

Though terribly curious about that visit Mrs. Adams had made to Edward's house alone, Celia hadn't felt the freedom to ask him about it. But it made her heart ache.

"Celia!" her mother called, "a telegram for you." Her mother held it up as Celia rushed down the stairs.

Carefully but quickly Celia opened it. "It's from Charles!" She glanced at her mother. "He's the friend who attends law school in Boston." Celia could see her mother brimming with curiosity. "He says he'd like to stop here on his way to Boston. Late tomorrow morning."

"Will he need overnight accommodations?"

"He doesn't indicate it but we might be prepared just in case. I saw him only a short while ago. I wonder what's on his mind."

"Well, I'll have a nice meal for him."

Celia smiled at her mother. "His family has been so gracious to me. You remember, his mother invited me to accompany her to Boston? I would like to have things special for him." Regardless of why he was coming, he would provide a diversion from other thoughts that pulled at her doggedly.

The next day when Celia and her brother Joe walked up the steps to the train station, she felt such pleasant anticipation in seeing Charles again. Preparations for his visit had been accomplished in a leisurely and equally pleasant manner.

"You say he's training to be a lawyer?" Joe asked.

"Yes, I believe he's near the end of his schooling. His father is one, you know."

"I've thought that is something I'd like to do."

"Well then, this is a good opportunity to ask questions. What Charles doesn't know from his studies, he'll surely have learned from growing up in a lawyer's home."

The train whistle sounded in the distance. As they sat on one of the oak benches to wait, Celia glanced at her tall, lanky brother. Being with him gave her such a sense of confidence. How proud she was of her family. When the train arrived, there would be the anticipation of seeing in which car Charles sat, what window he might be looking out. She had forgotten the sense of excitement in the small things of life.

The train steamed into the station. "There he is!" Celia spotted his friendly wave at the window.

Charles put his bags in storage and the three of them walked down the road, chatting comfortably. Charles talked so companionably with her brother. How nice to have such friends. And so the visit went. It wasn't until after the meal that Charles asked permission to speak with Celia alone. Her father acquiesced, suggesting the sitting room.

"Now, Celia," Charles began, sitting next to her on the couch, "do you wonder why I dropped by when we just saw each other?"

"I certainly do." She smiled at him.

He returned her look, a light in his eyes. "This sudden change in your address affected me in a way I hadn't anticipated. I thought you would always live near my parents, whenever I came home, I would be able to see you. At the luncheon a few days ago, I suddenly realized I was losing something valuable. Somehow, the place wouldn't seem the same. It would be empty of the woman I had come to esteem and admire in a way I don't feel about any other person of my acquaintance." He reached out to take her hands. "Can you guess why I'm here, Celia?" For the first time she saw a shy, almost sheepish look cross his features.

"I've always been terribly fond of you," he continued. "You have a first-rate mind. You are discreet and do everything well and properly. And, most of all, from a man's point of view, you are a beautiful woman. I remember seeing your blond hair for the first time. It pulled me like a magnet. No, don't pull away from me now. I need to say this.

"I told Mother of this visit and she was delighted. In fact, there's nothing my mother would like more. From the very beginning, she saw the possibilities in you and warned me not to flirt with you unless I was serious, that you were far too nice a girl to trifle with.

"Well, I'm not trifling now. I am in dead earnest." His eyes had lost their hesitant, apologetic look. They were eager and his bearing had the resolute look of a lawyer arguing before the jury. "Celia, you are one of the loveliest women I know, strikingly so. I would be proud of you. You are an absolute dear in the way you approach and handle people. You would make a lovely hostess."

He continued. "You know, when I heard of your leaving, I thought you were going to your parents for just a visit but when I heard you had moved out of the Chestleys' lock, stock, and barrel, it woke me up in short order. It appeared more was afoot than I guessed.

"I wondered why you hadn't said more at the luncheon. That night as I was ponder-ing all this, I remembered that little scene in the bookstore when Edward stepped forward so suddenly after I offered to bring you to the station, how he forcibly informed me that he was already taking you. Thinking back, it had the nature of his staking his claim on you. The more I thought about it, the more I realized I didn't like it one bit."

Charles looked down at the hands he held, then grasped them tighter. "Celia, forgive me for taking you for granted. Now I want to make sure you are mine before it's too late." He looked at her expectantly. "It's not too late, is it?" When she looked down, silent, his voice faltered. "It's not Edward — is it?" He paused repeatedly while talking, as if he was thinking while he spoke. "You're free, aren't you — free to entertain what I'm asking to you consider — free to be my wife?"

He was serious, then all of a sudden, he chuckled. "Nothing like pushing through to the heart of the matter! You know, Celia, you don't have to decide this moment. I realize this is rather out of the blue. I just became serious myself a day or so ago." He grinned. "But you always knew I thought the world of you. You couldn't have missed that. Why even in Boston, during your visit, we got along famously. When I think back on it, I saw then how well you looked in that city. You would make a superb lawyer's wife. Never mind that Mother had worked her wonders with your wardrobe, your bearing said you belonged there. You have style, poise — and loveliness — to suit the most exacting of tastes.

"Celia, you're so silent and here I am going on and on like any lawyer trying to win his case. Have you anything to say?" He bent his head, trying to catch her eyes. "It's not too late for us, is it?"

She lifted her head to oblige him. "I'm sorry to be so quiet in response to your flattering proposal. You do me great honor, Charles, and you are a worthy man. A woman like myself could not be associated with a better family. Your mother has been generous to me from the very first, and your father has always treated me with a kindly deference. Regarding yourself, I could not imagine a better friend, companion. You are just the sort of person a woman values — values most besides a husband."

He pressed his jaw hard as if to control a sudden emotion. "Then it's too late for us, in the way I envision?"

"Yes, Charles, I'm afraid so." She squeezed his hands sympathetically before withdrawing her own.

He sat a moment gazing at her. "Celia,

you are so beautiful. I hate to give you up. Is there no hope for me whatsoever? Does another — does Edward have such a strong claim on you?"

"I want to be honest with you and tell you my heart is already engaged. It remains to be seen whether Edward will ever become the person he needs to be before I can accept him. But let us be friends, Charles."

He reached over, took her hands in his once again, and drew them to his lips, holding them long and tenderly. "Then I will take my leave. Another train leaves in less than an hour." He put her hands down, and rose. "I will say goodbye to your parents and the rest of your family. You needn't see me to the station. Just say goodbye here. I'd prefer it that way."

# 25

Edward looked up at the knock. He had purposely closed his library door so he wouldn't be disturbed.

"Come in," he finally said.

Mrs. Macon appeared. "Sorry to bother you, sir, but someone is here to see you. A woman."

His heart leaped. Celia? "Who is it?"

"Mrs. Adams, sir."

What was she doing here again? But during her last visit, the woman had been kind, offering her help and support after the flower awards fiasco. He should give her a few minutes."

"Is she alone?"

"Yes, sir."

"Show her into the drawing room." Suddenly, he felt caution was in order. "Will you find something to do in the dining room — in earshot? I want Mrs. Adams to know you're nearby."

"I can polish the silver, sir."

"Good."

As soon as Edward entered the drawing room, Mrs. Adams rose and extended her hands in greeting. "Mr. Lyons! How good to see you."

What could he do but take both her hands in his? He saw she had removed her gloves, her hands felt soft and — pudgy. He looked down on them an instant and noticed they glittered with rings. He looked up in the woman's eyes. Did he detect a glitter there as well?

"You were kind enough to receive me the last time I was here. Is your life getting back to normal?" She looked at him, tenderly he felt. And she had held onto his hands rather long. He was grateful for the clatter of silverware he heard from the dining room. He gestured for Mrs. Adams to retake her seat. He walked away to stand over the fireplace.

She arranged her skirt carefully, then looked up and gave him an entreating smile. "I hoped things were better, because I have a proposal to make." Her eyes sought to hold his. "I know that we are both interested in literature, both attending Mr. Chestley's book discussions. I was talking with him the other day, and he seemed to think they wouldn't have them anymore with Miss Thatcher gone. That really is too bad. So I was thinking I might continue them, but I would need help and hoped you might be available to do so."

"What exactly did you have in mind?"

"Well, that we might consult together about the next book to be discussed. You are so much more widely read than I. And then once we've done that, we could meet again to talk about what questions to pose for discussion."

"I don't know —"

"It would be a wonderful way for you to get back into society. After the — well, the flower show, you know. And everyone loved the book discussions."

"I believe Miss Thatcher had a lot to do with that."

"Of course, of course. But I don't believe she is returning, and it would be such a service to the community to continue the discussions, besides showing good faith on your part."

"I don't know if people are ready to accept me."

Mrs. Adams moved forward in her chair. "That is why I am offering you my every support. I'm something of a leader in society, you know, and with Mrs. Harrod as my good friend — we would both like to see you rejoin our circle."

He considered her cautiously. "That is very kind of you, Mrs. Adams." He breathed in deeply. "But I think I must say no. Besides, I believe Miss Thatcher will return to lead the discussions once again."

Mrs. Adams rose from her chair and started pacing the room. "You know, I'm sorry to say I believe you're mistaken about Miss Thatcher. When I talked with Mr. Chestley, he didn't say anything about her returning. I know what a help she was to him in the bookstore, and if anyone would know, he would." She stopped in front of him. "You know how these young women can be. They take it into their heads to try something new, and when they get tired of it, they're off to other things."

Her easy assessment of Celia irritated him. Mrs. Adams didn't know Celia. Yet, her assurance that Celia wouldn't be returning made him wonder, uncomfortably so.

"So you see, Mr. Lyons, it's for us to take up the reins. This would add to the community spirit, and I would lend you my presence, my support — aid you in any way possible. Help you to regain your rightful place in society."

"I don't know as if I would aspire to that."

"But Mr. Lyons, I'm sure you must. Why, after I heard about your place in Boston, your ancestral home, I knew we were the poorer for not having your distinguished company in our midst."

She had been gesturing expansively when talking about his home, and now she stepped close, resting her hand on his arm. "And I would help you get over the initial . . . any embarrassment you might feel. It would be my *pleasure.*"

She said the last word with such emphasis, such a sense of intimacy, he felt himself draw up. There was Marguerite, standing close, just before they married.

These last weeks and months, this woman had been flattering him, much the way Marguerite had. His soul sickened. He'd been lapping up flattery and praise like a thirsty dog laps water. He'd been hungry to be accepted back into society, not for his own sake, but for Celia's. How he had wanted Celia to be proud of him.

This book discussion stuff was just a cover screen for Mrs. Adams to throw herself in his way. He looked down at her hand on his arm. He wanted to shake it off. It seemed to him she wanted to weasel her way into his good regard and eventually into his affections, supplanting Celia in his heart. Well, he would have none of it. Suddenly, she felt cloying, and he wanted to put as much distance between her and himself as possible.

"You are very kind, Mrs. Adams." He moved so that she had to drop her hand from his arm, and reached for the tapestry pull on the wall. "But I believe I will have to say no to your generous offer." He wanted to tell her never to bother him again, but he would treat her nicely, for the sake of Celia, because of course she would be returning. "And as far as future interviews of this sort, if you will be so kind as to leave them to me to initiate, that would be much appreciated."

He looked up to see his housekeeper at the room's entrance. "Ah, here is Mrs. Macon to see you out." He led Mrs. Adams across the room. "Now, if you'll excuse me." He made himself wait until Mrs. Macon gestured for Mrs. Adams to precede her.

"I was only trying to —"

"I understand perfectly. Now, Mrs. Macon —" and he motioned the two women to leave. He caught a flash of outrage from Mrs. Adams's eyes before she stiffly followed his housekeeper, then he turned sharply in the opposite direction to his library.

His first thought was, now what should he do about Celia?

Celia opened the door to her father's study. "Sit down, dear." He held up a letter that had been lying on his desk. "This came in today's post."

Celia felt her heart skip. She couldn't remember when Father had singled her out to tell about a letter.

Her father's eyes contemplated her as he talked. "Edward Lyons has written, asking if he might come speak with me. He outlines certain questions of his. Apparently, he is interested in what I have to say about the Christian faith. Says that he always considered himself a Christian, but you saw fit to disagree. He goes on to write at one point you suggested he talk with me.

" 'Respectfully yours,' he closes. Somehow, I sense he is conveying more than what that sentiment usually means at a letter's end. From the scope and tone of his writing, he seems an unusual person. Even if I didn't know your interest in him, I would be pleased to spend time with that kind of man."

Celia gazed at her father. The possibility of seeing Edward again, here, in her home! She experienced the wildest kind of anticipation, dread, fear, delight — her heart was a mixture of emotions, but she sat quietly.

"You don't say anything, daughter?"

"It is beyond me to express anything. I feel full of conflicting emotions."

He looked at her some moments before speaking. "Would you think me a cruel father if I told you I think it best you see him as little as possible during his visit? Maybe not at all."

"But why, Father?"

"To see how he reacts to such a stipulation. I want him to also have an opportunity to really hear what I say without him being distracted by you. In fact, if he knew at the outset he wouldn't see you, I think it would keep the visit more to the point. But then, he might not come after all. That would settle the matter, wouldn't it?"

The thought of Edward not coming at all pierced her to the heart. She sat for some moments thinking over what her father proposed, then finally said, "As much as I dislike admitting it, I suspect you are right. We wouldn't want him distracted, if there's any chance of him coming to the truth."

"I even thought of traveling to his town, to see our old friends the Chestleys, but then I thought he might better see the circumstances in which you were raised. It might add force to my words." He smiled. "And then I thought, there is blessing in this home, love for each other and love for the Lord. Here, in my study, I feel we can meet as equals. While we live modestly, I know no one has a library equal to mine in these parts. Considering his Boston heritage, I think it would be important."

"Yes, Father, it would be."

"So then, it's decided. I'll consult your mother but I think next week would do. If he needs to stay overnight, I will ask your grandmother to put him up."

Celia left the study in a welter of emotion. To have him here and not be able to see him filled her with dismay. But to have him here at all filled her with joy. Celia immediately sought out her mother to ask permission to be the one to clean her father's study. Then she asked if she might wax and polish the front hall and add flowers to its one small table.

Her mother looked at her and smiled. "Of course, dear. And since he might be staying at your grandma's, you might give a hand over there as well."

In the days that followed, Celia had never loved housekeeping so much. Doing it for *him*. He might not be able to see me, she thought, but surely, I can keep a lookout for him, maybe from an upstairs window.

Thursday of the following week came all too slowly and then all too quickly for all that Celia wanted to do. Her grandmother commented she hadn't seen so much of her granddaughter in years and was delighted with the prospect of meeting this paragon of men. "I imagine he will manage things so that he can stay," Grandmother said. "If he is in love with you, I can vouch for that." Her grandmother grasped Celia's arms, looked laughingly into her eyes, then brought her into a loving hug. "Well, I think I'm almost as excited as you are. I might even put in a word or two; you know, tell him how delightful you are and all that sort of thing. And that he better change his ways if he wants a chance at you."

"Oh, Grandmother, don't get carried away." But Celia felt herself dancing inside. "I want to keep him honest. Although," here she became more serious, "he is, I think, a man who will not compromise his beliefs, even for love. In his own quiet way, he is proud of his noble heritage. How could he go against it? His family passes down customs and beliefs as though they were sacred. They do not easily change, for anyone."

"Yes, but remember, he moved out of Boston, away from all that and, from what I understand, a very close circle of family and friends. Many wish to be a part of his elite group but few are admitted. And here he left of his own accord. Maybe he is more independent in his thinking than you give him credit for."

"I hope so," Celia said with more confidence that she felt. She knew she would not change her views. Why should Edward?

Well, she would do all she could in the way of preparing the house to make his visit pleasant and memorable. God would have to be the One to work in his heart. She looked at her grandmother. But how could he stay hard-hearted around such a darling? In her own way, Grandma could give out point for point in a discussion but do it in such a charming way. And she had the benefit of age and wisdom. Edward would respect that.

Celia thought of his mother, comparing the two women. His mother was a fine woman, highly thought of in the world. However, Edward might see something in her grandmother, a certain vitality of living, a clarity in the way she saw life, an ability to see what was important. And she had the courage to kick over the traces, if that's what was needed. Celia loved her for it. Maybe it would be most advantageous for Edward to stay with her grandmother after all. Something might transpire right here in this house that Edward wasn't anticipating. Celia smiled. That's right, hit him on his blind side. She suddenly laughed.

"What are you chuckling about, my dear?"

"You, Grandmother! That's who! I was thinking it might be very well that our Mr. Edward Lyons is staying with *you.*"

# 26

Celia quickly closed the hall closet door. Dare she leave it slightly ajar? No, she didn't think she'd better chance it. Moments before from the upstairs bedroom window, she had seen Edward come down the road with her father. In this closet near the front door, she could be as near him as possible without being discovered.

She held her breath, holding herself close against the solid wood, her ear near the crack. There! The front door opened. "Welcome to our home, Mr. Lyons," her father said.

"I appreciate your letting me come."

"Joe, please take Mr. Lyons's bag. And tell Mother our guest has arrived, she'll want to bring some refreshment. Won't you come this way, Mr. Lyons? My study is down the hall."

Celia held herself hard against the door, willing Edward to sense her presence, to feel the stir she felt within himself, being this close. She heard their footsteps on the wooden floor, fancied she could distinguish his footsteps from her father's.

How pleasant his voice sounded. Now that she couldn't see him, this quality was a welcome surprise. His stature, his bearing had so overawed her, she hadn't particularly thought about his voice. Now she clung to this discovery with the intensity of a girl with a beloved doll.

When she heard the door shut to the study, she prayed, "Oh Father, by Thy Spirit open Edward's heart to the truth about You and Your son, Jesus. Please!" Every fiber of her being pressed into the words. What did Scripture say about a fervent prayer?

As afternoon evolved into evening, she kept track of Edward's movements, on occasion hovering near the room where he sat, trying to trust the Lord with all that went on.

A three-quarters moon shone in the darkened sky, its white light filtering through the gauzy curtains of Celia's bedroom. Tonight he was at her grandmother's. She knew exactly in which upstairs room he would sleep — the best guest room, its bed quilt the colors of a sunlit dappled forest with its many shades of green and occasional splash of yellow. With the walnut furniture, the room suggested a forest. She had slept in that room many times. A faint fragrance of violets permeated the air. Yes, it was like the woodlands in spring. Just such a place existed in Edward's woods.

It was nearing eleven o'clock. Would he be sitting in the large armchair with a lamp lighted on its nearby table? Reading Pascal's *Pensées?*

Earlier today, her chores finished and no one around, she had quietly approached her father's study. The two men had been talking all afternoon. She felt desperate to be near Edward again, to hear his voice. And to hear what was being discussed. Stealthily, she approached the closed door, avoiding the floorboard that creaked. She pressed her ear to the dark wooden door gently, so no unexpected sound would give her away. Even though she would not disobey her father and see Edward face to face, she felt shy letting her father discover this kind of stratagem. She honored him, but surely he had never been in such straits as hers.

She concentrated on the voices within. "Edward," her father said, "consider Pascal's passionate defense of Christian belief, one of the greatest apologies for religion written since the Middle Ages. Note this section entitled, 'The Misery of Man Without God.' Here, Pascal paints man as puny and weak. When man realizes his insufficiency, then he can discover his need of God.

"Pascal also describes man's mind as simultaneously capable of intellectual power — and moral, spiritual, and intellectual imperfection. This last, the Bible refers to as sin.

"The Renaissance seemed to mark man's liberation from the limits of medieval scholastic thinking; it represented a new spirit of inquiry. Its point of view was sensuous and rational, with man placed neatly in the center of nature. Yet for Pascal the liberation was largely illusion. He discovered the supernatural order of grace and salvation was primary. For him, the rational exploration of this world, exciting and valuable as it was, presented merely one more episode in man's voyage home to God.

"Note the quote at the beginning of the section on the Wager: 'A Letter to incite to the search after God' . . ."

How well she knew what followed. Hadn't she brought up these same thoughts in their last book discussion, the discussion Edward missed? She both wondered and smiled at the Almighty's way of working out things. Who would have thought Edward would be here, sitting in her home, hearing Pascal from her father?

And what was Edward thinking, how was he reacting to one of the greatest scientific geniuses of the seventeenth century — he who so valued the scientific mind — to consider such a one defending God and Christ?

Just then, she heard the kitchen door slam shut and her mother's particular step. Shame and a bit of pique welled up in her. She didn't want to be caught eavesdropping. Quickly, she had turned from the door and glided down the hall.

But tonight the moon's gentle radiance glowed in her bedroom. As it would be doing in his. She scrunched up her pillow and turned over on her side. Yes, he would undoubtedly be reading the *Pensées*. A quotation popped into her head . . .

Lastly, that death, which threatens us every moment, must infallibly place us within a few years under the dreadful necessity of being for ever either annihilated or unhappy.

There is nothing more real than this, nothing more terrible. Be we as heroic as we like, that is the end which awaits the noblest life in the world. . . .

Celia knew such thoughts would challenge Edward to think about his life and eternity. At least so she hoped. Her heart cried out, Oh, Heavenly Father, touch that fine mind of his. Move that true heart of his with the truth about You and the truth about Christ.

Celia rose from the bed to stand before the window. In the moonlight, the path from the house gleamed. It beckoned her to leave the house and walk quietly to the street and then the quarter mile to her grandmother's. She could picture his light on, shining from the window. How she longed —

A floorboard creaked outside her door. Her breath caught. Was someone awake? Father? Abruptly she turned from the window and eased herself back into bed.

What had she been thinking, to sneak up to her grandmother's at night? Foolish and sinful! And what would she be dressed in, this nightgown? If Edward happened to see her, he would think her an absolute — his respect for her would plummet. Foolish thinking indeed, for she valued Edward's respect almost as much as his love. He knew the stipulation her father had placed on his visit.

Besides, how would this help his search for the truth? Would she compromise it by doing such an unseemly act? Would she put her own desire ahead of his eternal welfare? No! No! A thousand times no!

She tucked the cover under her chin, rolled onto one side.

But oh, how she wanted to be near him. She grasped the pillow, holding it hard to her chest, hoping for comfort. How much sleep would Edward get tonight? If her own condition was any indication, very little.

Celia glanced at the clock: ten a.m. Edward was to leave this afternoon. Once more, he and her father were ensconced in the study. She had asked Mr. Jenkins if she could have a half day off. Her parents finally agreed that she could go into work after Edward left. From her heart, she thanked them.

She rushed through her assigned chores in the hope she might spend a few moments outside her father's study. She longed to hear what the men discussed, to hear Edward's voice. Later, her mother sent the children outside and went outdoors herself, leaving Celia alone in the kitchen. Had her mother done this purposely? Whether or not she had, Celia blessed her. Was it wrong to think God had worked this out? She remembered Mother saying He worked out the details of everyone's life, for everyone's good.

She put down the dishcloth, wiped her hands dry, and left the kitchen to tiptoe down the hall. Once more, she gently pressed her ear to the door, closing her eyes, waiting for Edward to speak. Then she heard him say, "I know you believe in the afterlife, heaven certainly. But what of hell? What does hell consist of — that is, if you believe it exists?"

Celia stood very still. What a question for Edward to ask. She listened, hardly breathing. What would Father say?

"Yes, I do believe in hell, but it really isn't a matter of what I believe. As I've said before, my beliefs could be as erroneous as the next fellow's. Rather, it's what God has said in His record to mankind. We've discussed the proofs for the Bible's veracity; there isn't another book of antiquity so well substantiated. Let me show you a verse in Psalm 9. David spoke of hell. In verse seventeen he said, *The wicked shall be turned into hell, and all the nations that forget God.*" Silence ensued. "The question is, are you part of that host of people who have forgotten God?"

Celia heard the pages of the book turn.

"Here, read this from the prophet Isaiah."

Edward read out loud, *Therefore hell hath enlarged herself, and opened her mouth without measure; and their glory, and their multitude, and their pomp, and he that rejoiceth, shall descend into it.*

"Note," her father said, "those having an indulgent time here on earth, those that have glory and pomp, will descend into hell. One can be enjoying one's life, and the very next hour find oneself in torment." Her father paused. "For hell is a place of torment. Let's turn to Mark 9:43, 44. Its description is contained in this verse:

*And if thy hand offend thee, cut it off: it is better for thee to enter into life maimed, than having two hands to go into hell, into the fire that never shall be quenched: Where their worm dieth not, and the fire is not quenched.*

"Edward, hell is a fearful place. Jesus, our Savior, went there. Remember what the Apostle's Creed states. *He descended into hell.* He did that out of love for us."

Quiet reigned once again.

"Let me say this as kindly as I can. Out of love for us — to save us — God poured out His wrath on Jesus on the cross, letting His son experience both death and hell. If you reject such a love, can you expect God to ultimately spare you His wrath — you who are a sinner and separated from Him? If you expect so, I believe you are sadly, severely mistaken."

After washing the lunch dishes, Celia stationed herself near the top of the stairs behind the railing. Her mother had served Edward and Father lunch in the study. They continued talking while they ate and the time was nearing when Edward would leave to make his train.

She heard the study door open. "Can I walk you to the station?" her father asked.

"No, that won't be necessary. I'll pick up my satchel near the front door and be on my way." Edward's voice — just ordinary words — yet how precious when that's all she had of him. Suddenly there rose in her an overwhelming longing to see him, if only for a moment. Could she chance sticking her head around the banister? She dropped to the floor silently, her cheek on the hard wood. She could see the foyer and front door.

Footsteps advanced down the hall. She hugged the floor. Her breathing stopped as Edward stepped into view below her. She raised herself slightly. He looked immaculate in a dark suit and white shirt, his broad shoulders squared back. He reached out to grasp her father's hand. "Thank you, sir, for your time in answering my questions, and reacting with composure to any disconcerting opinion I might have expressed."

"My pleasure."

Edward stooped for his satchel and as he did so, he glanced up the stairwell. Celia drew back. She didn't think he had seen her, but couldn't be sure. Moments later, he exited their house.

As soon as her father closed the door, Celia rose and raced to the front bedroom, darting to the window. Thrusting aside the curtain, she gazed hungrily at the tall, powerful figure walking with purposeful stride down the stone path. "Don't walk so quickly," she whispered. In another few seconds, the tree branches would hide him. Her lips parted to take in more air. She felt faint.

Then without warning, he wheeled around and looked up at the house. For a brief moment, shock made her limbs immobile. Then she quickly drew out of sight. He must have seen her. What must he think? Her hands clasped each other over her racing heart. But a little bit of her hunger for him had been assuaged. Even now, her mind's eye etched the two pictures of him in her memory.

Edward clenched his hand in triumph. He'd seen what he'd desired. When he'd glimpsed a moment that pale, lovely face surrounded by a flaxen braid at the top of the stairs, he'd hoped he would see her again. Outside, he turned instinctively, hoping against hope to glimpse her at a window. As soon as he wheeled around, he saw the same oval face, a slender frame dressed in the color of sky, standing at an upper window. Then disappeared. Ah, she hadn't been fast enough for him!

He was assured of what he most wanted to know — that she was his. And that she, hopefully, felt their separation as keenly. Somehow, it comforted him to think she suffered as he did.

He stood for some moments, his hands clenched, sorely tempted to march back to the house, gain admittance, and demand — no, rush up the stairs and storm the bedroom she was in. His chest heaved.

"No!" His breath exploded the word, then his chest tightened. He would not do it. Would not lose the respect he'd gained from her father. And what of herself? Would she still respect him if he did such a foolhardy act?

The crux of the matter was he didn't know how the gulf between them was to be spanned. She, a believer in the God of the Bible, a God he thought he knew. But what did he really know? Her father had given him much to think about. A worthy man. And she, a worthy woman. A woman he wanted with all his heart.

Taking a deep breath, he turned onto the street. He would make that train.

He grimaced, but at that same moment, a little loveliness settled around his heart. Two fleeting pictures he would keep secure in his memory: an oval face at the top of the stairs, and the blue figure and pale countenance at the upstairs window.

## 27

Mrs. Divers inched her way down the stairs, her legs trembling. She'd had a good rest after that noon meal, but oh, getting old was no picnic. These knees were getting worse. She had to get going though. Loydie would be coming for his list of errands. Besides, she wanted to have the cookies ready for him.

She entered the kitchen and plodded her way to the stove. A cup of tea would hit the spot right about now. She had asked Miss Waul to stoke the fire before she left to visit a friend, told her to use better hardwood so the fire would last a good hour and a half. She slid the teakettle onto the burner.

That scamp Loydie, she thought affectionately. Not every boy would have done the things she'd asked him to do; they saw eye to eye on things. Maybe that's why they got along so well. It sort of bothered her, though, when he'd asked *that man* to help him with his archery. It all came from that contest. She didn't like the boy getting friendly with the enemy. Loydie needed to keep his distance from Edward. She might need the boy to do a little spying again, especially after Mrs. Adams told her about Miss Thatcher coming from that man's house — alone. With all those flowers to boot.

And just the other day Miss Waul was sure Miss Thatcher had done it again. Edward had no business inviting her in. Just went to show the man's morals wouldn't bear much scrutiny. It grieved her to think Miss Thatcher was taking to him. And from all appearances, he to her. Just the thought caused a pain in her chest. Mrs. Divers clamped down her jaw hard. It wasn't fittin,' it just wasn't fittin.' He didn't deserve happiness. And now she didn't know what to think of Miss Thatcher. Hadn't she better sense? She'd warned the girl!

Now, what had she come here for? She stood staring at the pantry shelves. Oh yes, the cookie ingredients for that rascal. Flour, sugar, lard. Yes, that Loydie had a bit of mischief in him, but he'd turn out all right. She'd bet her last dollar on that.

Gathering up the ingredients in her arms as best she could, she turned from the pantry. She would set these by the stove, then pour herself a cup of tea and go over her list. Then bake those cookies. All before Miss Waul came back later this afternoon. She'd amaze her companion and do something herself in the kitchen for once. She might be getting old, but she could still hand out a few surprises.

She set down the ingredients on the little counter by the stove. Drat that Miss Waul! She'd left out the grease from this noon's fried chicken. The woman was getting forgetful. She'd warned her before about grease by a stove, letting it sit so near those burners.

Pray tell, where was her own head? She snorted. Why hadn't she noticed the grease when she'd set on the teakettle? Aw, they were both getting old.

She lifted the grease pan to move it over, but it was heavier than expected. Her wrists felt ready to break. Suddenly, the pan slipped. Grease shot across the stove and onto the wall in back. Faster than she could have thought possible, flames leapt up from the stove.

She could hardly think. What to put out a fire? Baking soda? She jerked away from the stove heading for the pantry. Her foot slipped and she lost her balance, her shoulder hit the floor. Pain shot through her body. "Ow!"

She could hardly get her breath, it seemed knocked out of her. Oh, her shoulder! She'd injured something. Then glancing up, dread overwhelmed her. Flames were spreading to the wall.

Had to get that baking soda from the pantry! Tried to get up. "A-ow-w-w!" She couldn't! Tried to push herself across the floor. Too much. She could hardly move.

Smoke billowed from the stove, curling around the kitchen and down to the floor. She coughed. Everything was happening so fast. Was there no help? Had something else caught fire? The curtains! She had to get herself out.

She tried to push up, but the pain in her shoulder was excruciating. Using her feet, she slowly pushed herself away from the stove, but managed only a yard or so.

"Help! Help!" she yelled. Could no one hear?

She felt so alone. And helpless. Smoke burned her eyes and throat. Starting to feel woozy, her head drooped. All she could do was lie down. Did she have a handkerchief in her pocket? She struggled to get it, fighting unconsciousness.

Just then she thought she heard the door

open. A figure rushed in.

"Mrs. Divers! Mrs. Divers!" Loydie shook her shoulder.

"Oh!" she wailed. Pain snapped her out of her grogginess. "Don't grab my shoulder, I think it's broken!"

"Got to get you out of here!" He caught at her other arm. "Sit up!" he yelled. He coughed. "This smoke is terrible."

She tried to sit up and finally made it with his help. He put his arms around her as best he could and tried to drag her. She couldn't budge.

"I'll go get help! Put your face down! To the floor!" He ran across the kitchen and rushed out the door. It slammed shut behind him.

Was she trapped in here? She sank down, shoved her nose to the floor, trying to keep conscious.

Edward was sitting at his desk when he heard shouts at the back of the house. "Fire! Help!" He shot up from his chair, bolted out the library door and ran into a boy racing down the hall. The boy grabbed him. "Mr. Lyons! Fire at Mrs. Divers's — I can't get her out!" Edward heard his housekeeper clamoring down the stairs.

He turned to her. "Get the fire wagon over

to Mrs. Divers's! She's trapped inside. I'm running there now." He rushed down the hall with the boy. "Where's the fire? How bad is it?"

"In the kitchen. I don't know where else. But there's smoke! Lots of it!"

"Stop!" In the kitchen, Edward grabbed dishtowels and doused them with water and handed one to the boy. "Lead the way."

They ran out the back door and across the lawn, into the woodland that separated the two houses. Edward saw smoke coming out one of the windows.

As they rounded the corner of the house near the kitchen, the boy stumbled. Edward caught him. "Wait!" Edward yelled. "Put that over your nose and mouth. Here!" He looped the ends of a towel around the boy's head and tightened it, then tied one around his own. They ran up the steps, then stopped. "Take deep breaths out here and when you go inside, hold your breath as long as you can!" He grabbed the boy's arm. "Keep low. Show me where she is."

Edward tried to see, but the kitchen was dark with smoke. Fire raged on one wall. Both he and the boy crouched close to the floor, the heat blasting them. On the far side of the darkened room, they stumbled into a figure slumped on the floor. Edward turned to the boy. "Run and get help!" He sucked in smoke-filled air and coughed. "Get Ned! I'll get her out!" The boy hesitated and Edward pushed him hard. This time the boy went. Edward bent over the woman. "Mrs. Divers! Mrs. Divers!" She didn't respond.

Smoke burned his eyes and throat. And the heat! Like hell in here! He rolled the woman on her back, grabbed her under the armpits and started dragging. His eyes burned. He kept them closed as much as possible, then arched his head around to make sure he was heading for the door. A faint rectangle of light off to his left. Had he gotten disoriented? His lungs screamed for oxygen. He drew in the smoky air, started coughing again.

He tensed his body, barreled toward the open door, dragging the heavy limp figure with him. Finally, he reached the threshold where air was less acrid. He lifted the dead weight of the woman over the doorstep onto the stoop.

Half-lifting, half-dragging, he managed to get her body down the steps. All he could think was to get away from the house. His head was feeling fuzzy. With force of will, he hauled her across the lawn and collapsed beside her.

Someone ran up. Several others arrived

right behind. "See what can be done for Mrs. Divers," someone yelled. "And help Mr. Lyons. The fire wagon is coming."

Dizzy, Edward felt like vomiting. He'd never fought flames and smoke like that. Except once when he was a boy.

He shuddered violently.

Edward sat on the edge of his bed and leaned to turn down the lamp, but as soon as it was nearly extinguished, he turned it back up. The dark — that dark, smoke-filled kitchen — he felt it to the core of his being even yet.

He lay back and brought the sheet up to his neck, only the sheet as a light cover. Those flames, the heat —

The memory of fire in his grandfather's summer home leapt up. While he'd slept upstairs, it'd licked up the stairwell. Shouts woke him. In a daze, he half-ran to his bedroom door, opening it, saw the stairwell engulfed in flames.

The smoke! He'd coughed and slammed the bedroom door shut and rushed to the window. His grandfather was bent over below, hardly able to move, but on a neighbor spotting him, he turned his head up, shouted for him to jump.

Neighbors held a blanket, stretched to

break his fall. Wasn't there any other way? He had looked back at the door. Saw the smoke seeping from under it. That terrible fear he'd felt came back with a vengeance.

Without warning his mind reverted to a picture of hell, the hell Celia's father described. Fire that never quenches. Never quenches! Everyone salted with fire.

At the time, Edward had sloughed it off, wouldn't consider it. But now, he thought, if terrible fire and smoke existed here on earth, couldn't it exist — in the afterlife? After what he experienced today, he couldn't *not* think about it.

His body twitched violently. He grabbed the pillow, held it hard, trying to control his muscles, trying to make his mind go blank.

Had Mrs. Divers felt the same? The heat and that awful smoke. Holding her breath, terror stricken. No one should have to die that way.

Edward walked up the sidewalk to the Bakers' home. They had been kind enough to take in Mrs. Divers and Miss Waul. He wondered what arrangements could be made for their future. At present, Mrs. Divers's house was unlivable. The kitchen had been burned out or smoke-damaged to the point of needing major repairs. Smoke had sullied most of the house. Miss Waul's and the guestroom doors had been closed. Miss Waul had tried to sleep there for one night, he heard. Said she'd rather sleep on a cot beside Mrs. Divers.

He knocked. It had been a week since the fire. Maybe this visit would tell him more. Also, he had come to do what he should have done long ago. He'd not been able to forget what Celia said to him.

The mistress of the house opened the door, her smile guarded. "Mr. Lyons."

"Hello, Mrs. Baker. I've come to see Mrs. Divers."

The aperture of the door widened. "She's in the back bedroom."

"You've been very good to take her in."

"Appreciate you saying that, sir." She led him to a long hallway. "She's been very little trouble, though. And Miss Waul sees to her needs most of the time. I just put aside food for them." She tapped on the bedroom door. "Miss Waul, Mrs. Divers. You have a visitor." Opening the door, she announced, "Mr. Lyons."

Miss Waul looked up immediately. Edward saw she had been reading to the woman lying in bed. His old neighbor didn't open her eyes at his entrance, but her hand twitched on the bedspread. Her breathing was forced. She had aged in the week since he'd seen her.

Miss Waul put down her book and rose to meet him. "Mr. Lyons, how kind of you to come. We were just reading a story. You know how Mrs. Divers loves to read."

"Can I serve you tea, Mr. Lyons?" Mrs. Baker asked. "It won't take but a minute to prepare."

"No, don't trouble yourself."

"Well then, Miss Waul, do you need anything? Please, just say so." Miss Waul shook her head. "All right, then." She turned to walk down the hall.

"Won't you sit here, Mr. Lyons?" Miss Waul indicated a chair near his former mother-in-law. "I can take this by the window."

"Thank you." Edward took the proffered seat. He looked at his old neighbor lying silently in bed. "Mrs. Divers?" She continued to breathe in a labored fashion, coughed, not bothering to cover her mouth.

Miss Waul rose from the chair she had just taken and came over to his side. "She isn't too responsive, I'm afraid," she said in an undertone. "But I'm sure she can hear you just the same. She hasn't been herself since the fire. Just go ahead and say what you have to say." She turned to her mistress and said loudly, "Mrs. Divers, Mr. Lyons is here to see you. Remember how he rescued you from the fire? We certainly want to thank him, don't we?" She turned to Edward once again. "We do thank you, sincerely, from the bottom of our hearts. I don't like to think what would have happened if you hadn't come." Her voice caught. She reached over to grasp his hand resting on the chair's arm.

He thought it an extraordinary gesture considering their past association. He looked up at her and smiled.

Edward then turned to the woman on the bed and cleared his throat. "Madam, how are you doing?" When she remained silent, he said, "You weathered quite an ordeal. I hope your condition is stabilizing." He waited for her response. When she didn't say anything, he continued. "The reason for this visit is not only to see how you are faring, but to say something I should have said long ago. It's about Marguerite."

At the sound of her daughter's name, Mrs. Divers's eyes opened and as he waited, her eyes began to water. He stared at the tears. Suddenly, he knew Celia had been right, saw something of the terrible pain of this mother when her daughter died. Had never fathomed it before.

Mrs. Divers had truly loved her daughter, grieved at her passing, and he had — suddenly, his past hard-heartedness shocked him. He saw himself as Celia must have seen him. No wonder she'd misgivings, had held herself off from him.

Sitting there, he hardly knew what to say, but disjointed thoughts started spewing out. "Mrs. Divers, I'm sorry. About your daughter and all that happened. I never understood your pain in losing her." He faltered, but then pushed on. "And I'm sorry for my part in her unhappiness. I didn't love her as I should. And not to let you visit each other more often, that was wrong as well." The room was quiet except for the sound of Miss Waul's quick search for a handkerchief in her pocket. Edward asked, "Will you forgive me?"

His old neighbor stared at him, saying nothing. Tears began welling in her eyes. He reached across the coverlet and took one of her hands. "I am truly sorry."

She closed her eyes.

In the strained silence, Miss Waul abruptly rose and came over. "Mr. Lyons, how very kind of you. On behalf of Mrs. Divers, I want to tell you how much we appreciate your saying this. We appreciate it very much."

Edward looked up at her. "Thank you." Miss Waul was wiping tears from her eyes. Here was one who was glad for his words. If he hadn't come for anyone else, then he had come for her. He was about to say something else, then thought better of it. Instead, he leaned over to his old neighbor. "I will leave you now and hope the good Lord will minister to your healing." He squeezed her hand gently, then rose.

"Will you accompany me into the hall for a few moments, Miss Waul?"

Outside the room, he asked, "What are your plans for the future? Is Mrs. Divers well enough to be moved?"

"Mrs. Baker and I talked that over. As soon as Mrs. Divers recovers sufficiently and can travel, we think it best she go to her sister's. It would be a train trip of some hours. I don't think she has it in her to return to her own home. To rebuild, I mean. You've seen how she is."

"Yes. Do you need things from the house? I could send Mrs. Macon to help you sort through clothes and such to send with Mrs. Divers. And help wash them, I imagine they are smoke-stained."

"I've been to the house for just the necessities. It is disheartening. But I'm grateful the neighbor men have been so good as to cover and board up things where they could."

"If you need help packing boxes or a trunk to send with Mrs. Divers, I could send Ned. And he can take you to the train in my carriage and carry the trunk and boxes in our wagon."

"Thank you, Mr. Lyons, you are most kind. I'd been wondering about these things, but didn't want to burden anyone."

"What are neighbors for?" He smiled. "Ah, something else. Does Mrs. Divers have enough funds for traveling? Do you? I would like to give you money for the trip if you need it. That would be one way I could make amends as her former son-in-law. Help take care of her, you know."

"Oh, Mr. Lyons, that is most generous. I think she has money enough, but thank you, thank you so much. It is such a relief to me personally to think that such a man as yourself is looking out for us."

"Well, it's the least I could offer —" He waved away her thanks. "One other question. After you bring Mrs. Divers to her sister, what will you do?"

"I imagine I will stay a few days to help her adjust and then I think I best move on. I will apply as companion in another situation."

"I'd be glad to write a reference. You have been devoted to Mrs. Divers." He paused, then added, "Anyone who would be companion to Mrs. Divers could attend almost anybody."

Miss Waul looked up at him and smiled. Gratitude shone from her eyes.

"I will send Mrs. Macon over in a day or so. Don't hesitate to ask her to do anything. She will be instructed to help in whatever way she can. I will take leave of you now." He inclined his head in a slight bow. Miss Waul accompanied him down the hallway.

He stood on the stoop a moment after she closed the door. Who would have thought a week ago he would apologize to his former mother-in-law? And have the degree of good-fellow feeling he now had?

It had been that dreadful fire. And Celia's benevolent influence.

The familiar figure of a boy caught his attention, casually picking flowers out of a neighbor's yard two doors down. Loydie. Edward watched, amused. The boy roughly arranged the flowers, and kneeling at a flat rock, took a pocket knife and cut the stems even. Edward strolled down the flagged path, then stopped at the front gate. The boy came up as Edward was undoing the latch.

"Hello, Loydie. I haven't seen you since our adventure the other day. I'm glad you asked for help."

"Hello, Mr. Lyons. Sure glad you were there."

He looked closely at the boy, and remembered something. Mrs. Macon had been upstairs when Loydie ran into the house for help. Apparently, the boy had just let himself in. Well! "Flowers for Mrs. Divers?"

"Yeah. I know she likes them. Might cheer her up."

"I'm sure they will." Loydie stepped aside to let him pass through the gate, then went through himself and walked up to the house.

With a friend like you, Edward thought, I'm sure she'll be well served, even if it's at the neighbor's expense. Suddenly he wondered if it had been Loydie who'd helped himself to his roses. He glanced back at the boy who had just knocked on the door. Mrs. Baker opened and a wide smile spread over her face. Apparently, he'd cheer up more than just the two old ladies. Well, all to the good.

Edward threw his head against the headrest of his desk chair. It had been a hell of a week. His hand involuntarily reached for the letter opener, then threw it back on the desktop. He *didn't* like that word, why had it come to mind?

It was the fire. A hell for him.

He'd told Celia's father he wasn't sure there was a heaven or hell.

"But what if there is?" Mr. Thatcher had asked. "Are you willing to take a chance on something as important as that? And if heaven and hell do exist, are you confident in determining your way of getting to the former?" Mr. Thatcher's pointed look had pierced Edward's soul. "Why not consider what the Bible says?"

The man would brook no evasiveness.

Edward knew Boston Brahmins were a proud, self-sufficient lot. Their place in society, their money were very important to them. That might answer for this life, but what about eternity? Had they, in reality, conceived their own way of salvation? Were they that presumptuous?

He stared across his well-appointed library, at his books. All this knowledge at his fingertips.

Thoughts ran back and forth through his mind. He hadn't felt this confused since very young. How could he gain clarity on this? He wanted someone to talk with, someone wise. Someone — like Celia.

How he respected her. Her sensitivity, her

purity, her quickness of mind. The fineness, the subtlety ingrained in her had drawn him to her. She would stand up to him, but at the same time listen to his viewpoint. Give him respect even when she disagreed. That satisfied something deep within.

Though she was not a Boston Brahmin, she could have been.

Curious that she agreed with beliefs his Puritan ancestors had held, beliefs his family no longer espoused. His family now had a more liberal view of mankind — views he had thought true — but were they? Celia made him question them, examine beliefs he had taken for granted.

He swung around in his chair and crossed the room to the fireplace with its settee and chairs. Scanning the third shelf, he found the Bible Celia had handled.

He purposely sat down on the settee where she had sat. Even though she was miles away, he would invoke the sense of her being here, next to him. He could see her smile, approve what he was about to do. He opened the Bible to Genesis.

# 28

Celia hastily put Mrs. Harrod's letter in her dresser drawer and ran down the stairs. After Edward's visit, she'd been reticent to talk about him, even with Grandmother, but after this letter she felt emboldened, compelled in fact, to do so. She ran out the front door.

When she had begun reading the letter, her eye caught a beloved name. *Edward.* Mrs. Harrod wrote he'd rescued Mrs. Divers from a house fire, and now she had pneumonia and was near death. Something extraordinary was taking place in Edward. Celia wished she could discover what he was thinking. However, she could only wait and pray.

The letter continued: *You know, Celia, my son wrote little of his visit when he stopped at your home on the way to Boston. All he will say is that you are the best of friends. Of course, I had always hoped for more. . . .*

Celia had glanced ahead at the letter's closing, *Your friend*. She was grateful that despite Mrs. Harrod's disappointment, she was keeping their friendship intact.

And then a surprise near the end. *Our friend Mrs. Adams has decided to take an extended trip in Europe. Said her husband had never taken her and she's always wished to go. Strange, I thought she was interested in Edward, and for her to leave now, I just don't understand.*

Relief washed through Celia.

She raced up the steps to her grandmother's front door. "Grandmother!" she called as she opened the door. Grandmother rose from her chair in the front parlor.

"Your coming is well-timed, my dear. I've been sitting here wondering when I'd have you to myself for a good visit." She then gave Celia a significant look. "And you know what I want to talk about. We'll do so over tea and gingersnaps."

Minutes later Grandmother set down her teacup. "That man who stayed here — you didn't do him justice. I declare, Celia, what a gentleman. He looked after me like I was his own grandmother. He didn't stand on ceremony as I expected. Oh yes, I saw his Boston Brahmin upbringing. One couldn't help see his refinement and strength of mind. But his affability and sense of taste, well, I could go on and on."

"What did you talk about, Grandmother?"

"Well, everything, I would think. A lot about family, especially your family, what each of your brothers and sister is like. However, he wasn't being inquisitive in an inappropriate sort of way. With myself, he was interested in what I valued and asked my opinion about things."

Grandmother's eyes twinkled. "Celia, he is the most charming man. I really don't know how you withstood him. I think I've fallen a little bit in love with him myself."

Impulsively, Celia reached out and grasped her grandmother's hand to squeeze. She would have a strong ally in Grandmother. "Did you talk of spiritual matters?"

"I'm getting there. You know, just talking with him, being with him, I could understand how you would admire and love a man like that. Whenever he mentioned you in the slightest way — I could see how much he loved you, yearned after you."

Her grandmother stopped, looked dreamily over Celia's shoulder. "I think he and I were talking about my marriage to your grandfather. I told him your grandfather's love for me was a picture of how God loves those who believe in Him." Grandmother shifted in her chair. "At one point, I looked right at him and told him that a man's love for his wife — well, Christ loves us in the same way, but even more so. He died for us. How can we reject so great a love?"

Tears came to Celia's eyes. Leave it to Grandmother to get to the heart of a matter. How she loved her for it.

The older woman drew a handkerchief out of her pocket and handed it to Celia, "There now." Grandmother looked at her long, then added, "In our talk, we pretty much covered the ground."

"Well, I would think you did!" Celia laughed, giving her nose a hard blow.

Grandmother's eyes brightened. "Changing the subject, would you like to step outside and cut some flowers for your mother? My garden is bursting at the seams and I like to keep cutting to encourage more blooms. Maybe you can take some to poor Mrs. Jenkins. I hear her husband's injury has kept her hopping with hardly time to do anything else. She could do with a bit of kindness, I think."

A few days later Celia closed the door to Mr. Jenkins's store. She had tidied up things to her satisfaction. "Should have broken my leg long ago," he told her, "and had you come over to help. The store hasn't been so well-organized in years."

She was still smiling over his quip. He wouldn't want to break his leg again under any circumstances, of that she was sure, but she loved his sense of humor.

As soon as she arrived home, she spied a letter on the hall table, addressed to her. The envelope was written in a familiar neat hand.

She scooped up the letter and walked briskly to the kitchen. Her mother was washing beans in a large bowl. "Mother, the letter from Mrs. Chestley, could I possibly read it before helping you?"

"Certainly." Her mother's lips curled up. "I'd like to hear anything you can share. I'm all curiosity."

Celia gathered up her skirt and ran upstairs to her bedroom. Mrs. Chestley never wrote her, only to Mother. She settled herself in the chair near the window.

Dear Celia,

I'm writing to say how much we miss you, especially my dear husband. He had thought I couldn't be replaced in the bookstore until you came along. Now, he says you can't be. You had such a way with the display window. I try to imitate you, but you always came up with new ideas. People tell me they came by the window just to see your arrangements. Hooray for you, my dear.

Also, I heard Mrs. Harrod wrote you and I thought, why don't I do the same, particularly when I know something of interest to you, something known only to my husband and myself.

Mr. Lyons dropped by the bookstore yesterday and had a long conversation with my husband. He's been reading the Bible straight through. Isn't that amazing? He'd just finished the gospels. He talked as if Jesus were more than a good teacher. The account of His crucifixion moved him greatly. Now he is on to the book of Acts. I am so excited and will keep you apprised of any developments.

Edward! Immediately, Celia got down on her knees, hugging the letter to her as she knelt by the chair. She prayed his heart would be opening to the truth. Of how the Lord loved him. Dear Mrs. Chestley for writing her.

"Isn't it wonderful our neighbors gave us all these cherries?" her mother said, putting aside a bowl for supper. "There's nothing like eating fresh fruit in summer. And I can't tell you how much I've appreciated your help this afternoon." Celia caught her mother's quizzical look. "You've been rather quiet. Nothing wrong, is there?"

Celia didn't answer right away. "You remember that letter I received last week from Mrs. Chestley? Remember how she wished I would work for them again? Do you think there's a possibility that will ever happen? They are such dears. I'm feeling now as if I've left them out on a limb."

"But there's Mr. Lyons."

"Exactly." Celia sighed.

Her mother wiped out a bowl before speaking. "We are promised the Word is 'sharper than any two-edged sword, dividing bone from marrow.' It does just that in a person's thinking. In his heart. Who knows how Mr. Lyons's perception of life might alter while reading the Bible? Where God's concerned, my dear, there's always hope."

"Oh, Mother, I want it so."

"Here's a few cherries, I kept some aside for just us." Her mother handed her a small bowl of the fruit, then sat down with her own dish.

Celia looked up. How beautiful Mother was. No wonder Father was still taken with her after all these years. How she hoped —

She sighed again.

"Anything else on your mind?"

Celia laughed, felt a blush creep up her face. "I suppose so. I was thinking — when I first arrived some weeks ago and came into the study early, I noticed as if for the first time how affectionate Father was with you. How he loves you and wants to be with you. I had wondered about myself and. . . ."

Her mother pushed aside her bowl of fruit. "What a lovely thing to say about your father and me." She looked at her daughter, smiled, then briskly suggested, "After we finish eating these, why don't you take some to your grandmother. A walk will do you good. There are times in life when it doesn't pay to sit around too much."

Celia blushed again. "This is one of them?"

"Yes." Her mother smiled. "And if it's any comfort to you, I imagine Mr. Lyons needs to stay busy as well."

"Oh, Mother!" Celia rose and hugged her hard.

Minutes later Celia placed a cloth over the basket of deep red fruit. She had wanted to talk with Grandmother again anyway.

She opened the white picket fence to her grandmother's yard and ran up the front steps. Flinging open the door, she shouted,

"Grandmother! I've a present for you."

"I'm back in the kitchen!"

It felt good to be on such familiar terms. Celia cherished the strong, sweet connection between Grandmother and herself, and these feelings had strengthened since their heart to heart about Edward last week.

She entered the kitchen and plunked her basket of cherries on the table. Grandmother was stirring something on the stove.

Her grandmother looked up. "Pudding for you and the family. I had a feeling you might be over today, or soon at any rate, so decided to make some." She gave one last stir and took it off the burner. "There, that needs to cool."

"Just smell it. Our family favorite, old-fashioned vanilla."

"And if it hasn't cooled enough by the time you leave, you can send one of your brothers for it later." Grandmother's eyes sparkled. "But would you like a taste now?"

Moments later they sat by the table, each holding a miniature white crockery bowl containing the dessert. Celia dipped in her spoon, blew on it a little and carefully tasted the silky pudding. "Grandmother, this warms my insides as nothing else. Makes my visit doubly pleasurable." After a few minutes, she carefully scraped out the last of the pudding, put her spoon down and gazed at Grandmother.

"Something's on your mind," her grandmother said briskly.

"Yes. It's about —" Celia hesitated.

"Edward Lyons," her grandmother finished.

"How did you guess?"

"I see it in your eyes. They shine. And there's a restlessness about you. I can see the signs."

"The signs?"

"Of someone in love."

"Oh, Grandmother! I do so love him. But I promised myself that unless Ed— Mr. Lyons changed, I couldn't go back to the Chestleys. I'm too much drawn to him. As hard as it is to be separated by all these miles, I do believe it would be harder to remain true to God and my convictions if I were around him." She rose suddenly. "Those last few times we were together, I felt as if I — physically —" She felt her chest tighten. "I just wanted to be with him. Oh, Grandmother, what am I to do?" She put her hands to her face. Her shoulders quivered. "I didn't want to leave him."

"But you did leave. And it was right to do so, considering your differences. Before I go any further, dear, I want to say that whomever you marry, you will have differences. It's a part of marriage. However, sharp differences in faith are too important to ignore. God's Word must be heeded in this, or more unhappiness will breed than you care to deal with."

"I couldn't disobey God. That's what decided me to come home."

Her grandmother rose and said, "Somehow, I feel sure the Lord has used Mrs. Divers's house fire in Edward's life. We don't always understand God's dealings, but we can trust Him. Even when He uses extreme measures to accomplish His ends." Then she held out her arms and held Celia hard and close.

An hour later, Celia closed the front door, considering what her grandmother had said. Decided, too, that whenever she needed comforting, she would go to Grandma's.

She held the basket with care as she walked down the porch steps. Vanilla pudding had replaced the berries. It was still quite hot, but the basket made it easy to carry. Her brothers would crowd around her, if they were home, and she would be the center of attention. How she loved bearing gifts to her loved ones.

Closing the white picket gate, a flash of scarlet winged over her path. A cardinal.

Edward loved the color red and its many shades. She fancied he loved even the lightest pink because of her preference. The beautiful red of the cardinal struck a strange little chord in her. Was it a sign from heaven? She felt more lighthearted on the walk home.

As she came into view of her own house, she saw her father rise from a porch chair. "Celia!" he called. "A letter!" He hurried down to meet her.

They met at the end of the walk and he relieved her of the basket. "Mr. Lyons wrote me with a short note enclosed for you. Why don't you sit on the porch and read it?"

Edward had never written her. She looked at her name on the folded manila paper. The script was an elegant, strong autograph, but looked as if written in a hurry. She sat with her father hovering nearby. He placed the basket on the porch floor.

She opened the note.

Dearest Celia,
Recently, I came across this poem, one that should be set to music. The words express the song of my heart:

"My faith has found a resting place —
Not in device or creed:

I trust the Everliving One —
His wounds for me shall plead.
I need no other argument,
I need no other plea;
It is enough that Jesus died,
And that He died for me."

I plan to see you as soon as possible.
                    Your own, Edward


Tears sprang to her eyes. She cried, "Oh, Father!" and handed him the note.

After reading he said, "He wrote me he would ordinarily await the favor of a reply, but finds he cannot wait that long. From the date in his communication to me, he will be here tomorrow. You better tell your mother." He handed both notes to her.

Celia took them and hastily opened the front door. "Mother!"

## 29

Celia arranged the large bouquet of orange lilies in the tall vase. Their glowing color would brighten the dark foyer, the flower offering meant to speak a warm welcome to Edward. Her heart sang with the anticipation of his arrival.

Turning from the hall table where she placed the flowers, she ascended the stairs. Next, she would change into her white lawn dress. Mother was giving her the remainder of the morning to get ready. How would she arrange her hair? In a chignon, maybe, with a flower nestled at its side. White with just the faintest hint of pink in its throat.

Standing in front of her dresser, she drew open the top drawer. Nestled in a corner, wrapped in a fine handkerchief, rested the ruby ring Edward had given her. Should she wear it? Her heart said, Yes! Her better sense said, Wait. She had shown the ring to her parents on first arriving then put it away.

Her siblings didn't even know of its existence.

After the noon meal, she stood at the upstairs bedroom window keeping an eye out for the anticipated guest. Her father and her brother Joe would meet Edward at the station. What would they talk about on the walk to the house? The weather? That would be an appropriate topic since the air was balmy this late in the summer, a day surely meant for Edward and her. The graciousness of the Heavenly Father's gift brought tears to her eyes.

There, coming in sight down the road, the three of them walked with Edward in the middle. Her father was slender and her eldest brother looked a mere boy next to Edward. He walked with a vigor that threatened to outstrip the other two. Was he that eager to see her?

The threesome turned into the front walk, her father now leading the way. She saw Edward glance up at the window where she was hiding. Had he glimpsed her? She felt her heart start to race.

She could not miss his entrance. She hurried across the room, out to the hall and skimmed down the stairs. Just as she reached the bottom step, the front door opened. She stopped just there, eagerly seeking his large frame. His eyes searched for hers, speaking a silent endearment. Then he stepped forward, holding out his hands. "Hello, Celia." He hadn't waited for the lady's customary first gesture.

"Hello, Edward," she answered softly. He pressed her hands, holding them long before releasing them.

Her mother appeared from the back of the house. Apparently, she had waited, hidden, anticipating this moment as Celia had. "So good to see you again, Mr. Lyons."

Her glance now included both Mr. Lyons and her husband. "Would you gentlemen like some refreshment? I have tea, coffee, or lemonade. Mr. Lyons?"

"Whatever the rest of you will be taking." He was all affability, wanting to please rather than be pleased.

Her father gestured him down the hall to his study. Last night, Father had made clear he would first speak to Edward alone. Before turning, Edward's eye found Celia again. Her heart went down the hall with him and watched as he and Father entered the study.

Celia and her brother followed Mother into the kitchen. "Since it's a warm day, I think your father would like a cool drink, as would our guest." Mother started pouring lemonade into the glasses. "I have enough for all the children. Would you take these glasses out to the back yard?" Her look indicated her son.

"Would it be too much for me to bring the tray into the study?" Celia asked.

Her mother looked at her fondly. "I know how much you'd like to, but under the circumstances, I think I should. Besides, I want to take the measure of their conversation — what I can hear of it — and I also think I will be less of a distraction."

Celia wanted so to be near Edward, to make him feel welcome and comfortable. An idea came to her. "Mother, may I first run to the garden and cut some flowers to arrange on the tray?" At her mother's nod, she hastened outside with the cutting shears.

What to choose? Something scarlet. She looked at the zinnias and quickly clipped three. Once inside, she cut the blossoms near the head and put all three in a small bowl of water. They filled it to its lip with a cheery splash of color.

"That will look lovely against the light yellow of the lemonade, Celia. We'll put it all on the black lacquered Chinese tray." She added a plate of Grandmother's cookies. "I've always been thankful to the Hodges for giving us this tray as a wedding present."

Celia held the kitchen door while her mother walked through with the refreshments.

She was sitting at the table when her mother returned a few minutes later. "I think everything's going well," her mother volunteered. "Your father said for you to come to the study in half an hour."

Celia glanced at the clock.

"Would you like some lemonade?" her mother asked.

"Maybe a little. I don't think I could eat anything."

Her mother smiled knowingly.

As her mother poured the lemonade, Celia's hand went to her pocket and fingered the ruby ring hidden there. She wondered if Edward would note the color she'd chosen for the tray's flowers.

The next half hour, Celia fiddled around the kitchen, helping her mother with dinner preparations as best she could. Finally, her mother laughed. "It would have been better to send you to your room to wait. You've just been getting in my way. Why don't you get along to the study."

At Celia's knock, her father opened the door and motioned her inside, saying succinctly, "I'll be with your mother."

The door closed behind him. Her father

was leaving them alone. This surprised her. Her eyes immediately sought Edward's.

He stood near her father's desk. Though the study was softly lighted, his eyes shone with the intensity of his feeling. He strode across the room, stopped in front of her, watching her face. "Your father approves of me."

She held out her hands. He grasped them, kissing first one then the other. When his lips rested on her left hand, his eyes met hers, questioning.

"Oh!" She withdrew her right hand and reached into her pocket, fumbling just a moment for the object at its bottom. Bringing forth the ruby ring, she said, "I would take this out every morning, look at its scarlet flame in the sun, believing your love burned as bright for me."

He reached for the ring and gently slipped it on her finger. "Celia!" He drew her close, pressed his lips against her forehead. Holding her tight, he bowed his head and whispered words she had longed to hear. He told of his suffering after she'd left so summarily, of his determination to visit her father and talk about Christianity with as open a heart as he could muster. And his hope of seeing her somehow, some way.

When he finished, they stood some moments, silent. Finally, Celia said, "I cannot tell you how it feels to be in agreement about spiritual matters. Tell me, how did it happen?"

"Here, come to the window seat." His hand slipped down to hold hers while he led her across the room. After seating himself beside her, he began, "The visit to your grandmother's — she has a way about her." He smiled. "When she spoke of God's love — for me — I felt my interest quicken."

Celia's eyes began to tear. "Grandmother!"

"Yes, quite the lady. And you, too, my darling. Your careful explanations about God and then your father's arguments cleared my spiritual pathway of years of debris. But I didn't start walking down that path until your grandmother spoke of God's love. She quoted Him saying: *I have loved thee with an everlasting love.* And then — *Hereby perceive we the love of God, because He laid down His life for us. . . .*

His smile was warm and confident; it lighted his whole countenance. "Oh, the love of God! For each of us! It is deeper than the deepest ocean. But that realization didn't crystallize till later.

"When I returned home, I contemplated all this, trying to piece it together — when

452

that dreadful fire of Mrs. Divers's occurred. It was then I started reading the Bible. Reading it, I began to grasp how great, how monumental God's redemptive plan was, spanning the ages. John in Revelation wrote it began from the foundation of the world.

"Celia, I knew that I loved you, loved you deeply. To think that God loved me like that! Light started dawning in me. You spoke of your life changing. Now I know what you meant. My mind, my heart became light, light, light, mingled with the most glorious love."

He slipped to his knees. "My dear! How can I thank you for being who you are. It was you and my love for you that opened the way to this revelation."

He reached for her hands. "You know the rose that flourished outside the prison in *The Scarlet Letter*? I was a man, standing inside the penitentiary looking out through bars, my eyes fixed on a lovely rose. A rose that spoke of hope and loveliness. You were that to me." He turned her hand over, touching his lips to her palm. Kissed it tenderly.

He looked up. "Dearest Celia, will you do me the honor of becoming my wife?"

"Edward! Yes, yes, with all my heart."

He rose and drew her to him, kissed her

hair, her forehead, her face. Then his lips sought hers.

Finally, she drew away. "These last weeks, I felt our oneness of mind and soul in so much, but was wounded to think we didn't share what was most important: oneness of spirit."

She reached up to tenderly touch his face. "I knew I needed to remain strong and leave the Chestleys, giving God time to work in your heart. Truly, I did not know how it would be accomplished, you with such a fine mind, who holds such strong opinions. I prayed and prayed. But thanks be to God." She clung to him.

"Words sweet to my ears." He laughed softly. "Words like those must be celebrated." He bent down and pressed his lips to hers, long and hard. Then he lifted his head and his eyes looked triumphantly into hers.

Just then a knock sounded at the door, and a little girl's voice asked, "May I come in?"

Celia parted from Edward, but he kept her hand firmly in his. "Yes, come in."

The little girl opened the door cautiously and peeked in. "Mother said it would be all right." The boys followed close on her heels. They all wanted to meet the new Edward, now that he would be part of the family.

"Celia said you're a good archer," the second-oldest brother offered.

"She did, did she?" Edward glanced at Celia fondly, his lips twitching.

"Our friend Willie down the street has a bow and arrow," he added. "We can make a target, so we wondered if you could show us how to shoot better."

"I can see what you boys will want for Christmas," Celia said. She smiled at Edward, then grimaced at her brothers. "I suppose you may have him in a few minutes, but you must remember I've waited to be with him for weeks."

Edward smiled at Celia's siblings. "Could I have her a few more minutes . . . alone?" As her sister and brothers filed out of the room, he said, "I've already talked with your father about staying over Sunday. I want to hear him preach, worship in your church. And see where you went to school, view the town, and the like."

"Edward, how absolutely wonderful. The people in our little town will all want to meet you. Are you sure you know what you're in for?"

"Such eagerness will be a welcome change after the last — what has it been — three years? I wouldn't mind an adoring town."

"Maybe you should move here."

"Well, I have plans you don't know about. I spoke with Mr. Chestley before leaving. He wants you back in the bookstore, and I want you nearby — to court you, my dear. I have yet to persuade your father."

"I'd like to be married here, in my own church," she said softly.

"Of course. We both want your father to marry us." He squeezed her hand. "My mother and whoever else of my family that attend the wedding might stay at your grandmother's a night or two. It makes it very convenient your town is on the train line from Boston. And I'm contemplating a reception at the Harrods'.

His mouth twitched into a half smile. "I think Mrs. Harrod will accept the fact you will not be her daughter-in-law. I'll butter her up with promises of letting the garden club meet in my conservatory. And will generously support their cause. In time, I'm sure it will dawn on her she will see more of you by marrying me than if you had married her son. I hear he is to stay in Boston practicing law."

"You've been a busy man."

"Regarding you, I certainly have," he said. "Am leaving no stone unturned, want no toes stepped on. I want to deserve my wife in the town's eyes, redeeming myself as best I can." He planted a kiss on the back of her hand. "Someday I will be viewed as a paragon of men. People will cease to wonder how I deserved you, but rather think what a lucky catch you made." He laughed and Celia couldn't help laugh with him.

How delightful, she thought, to see him happy and making plans. Plans for both of us. As the day went on, she was amazed how easily he fit in with her family. No stiffness or undue formality. Her brothers adored him. She had to smile. Saturday afternoon when giving them pointers on archery, he used her as a guinea pig. As she held the bow and arrow, he ingeniously put his arms around her to show her brothers how to better aim. She blushed to feel him hold her thus, because, of course, he was the complete gentleman around her family with little or no physical contact. Her family, liking him as they did, wanted to spend as much time with him as his short visit afforded. She could tell, however, he yearned to be alone with her. His eyes would repeatedly catch hers.

Sunday evening after the worship service and their usual light supper, the family headed toward the sitting room as was their custom. Edward stepped up to Mrs.

Thatcher. "As I will be leaving in the morning, do you mind if I take Celia for a walk?"

"Can I come, too?" her little sister asked. As soon as she did, the youngest boy chimed in as well. The two older boys held back. Celia had just given them a quelling look.

"I think a walk would be a nice idea," Mother said. She looked down at her two youngest. "But why don't we let Celia and Edward go by themselves. The night air is mild, perfect for a walk for just the two of them."

Edward held the door for Celia and extended his arm in escort. With the moon lighting their way, they strolled very properly in such a manner, sharing thoughts they hadn't been able to say in front of the family. But as they turned toward home, Edward put his arm around Celia, and as they walked, held her close. The last stretch they said little.

Under the deep shadow of a tree, Edward stopped. He turned and put both arms around her. "You know what I want before we go to your house, don't you?"

In answer, she lifted her arms, encircling his neck. In the near darkness, she saw him smile at her willingness, no, her eagerness to accommodate him. He lowered his head and touched her lips with his, lightly at first, then ardently. At length, he lifted his head, breathed deeply, and said softly, *Thy lips . . . as the honeycomb: honey and milk are under thy tongue.* A quote from the Song of Solomon, my dear. You see I read the *entire* Bible. If you only knew how your loveliness entwined me when I read Solomon's Song."

"Oh," she whispered, "I will have to reread that book."

"Why don't you do so after our marriage. Or maybe right before the nuptials. I would not have you think wayward thoughts before we are married, my love." He laughed. "Then afterward, you can think such thoughts *about me* all you wish."

To hear him laugh! It brought warmth and eagerness to her soul.

He lifted her up at the waist and held her close, planting a quick kiss on her ear. She laughed, delighted, but tried to keep her laugh soft.

"Celia dear," he said when he put her down, "we better return before it gets any later, or your father might take back his blessing." He reached for her hand. "We'll start now, if you promise me one more kiss at the door."

"But if I will not promise?"

"Then I will be forced to —" He seemed at a loss for words.

She laughed. "Promise only *one* kiss?"

"You, my dear, are headed for trouble!" They both laughed again and hurried the remainder of the block to the house. At the door, he stopped, and she made good on her promise.

# 30

"I'm glad our adopted daughter finally came home." Mrs. Chestley patted Celia's hand, sitting near her on the couch. "It took you awhile, but you're finally here. I knew Mr. Lyons, now our dear Edward, would convince your father."

"Well, you didn't sound so confident a week ago," her husband said.

"Don't remind me, I don't even like to think of it. But with her back at her job in the bookstore, I am delighted to be your full-time wife again."

"Amen!"

Mrs. Chestley turned to Celia. "I was just filling in, you know. The whole time I believed you and Edward would get together, that is, after you turned down that Jack fellow." She leaned over to her husband. "Mr. Chestley, aren't you glad now I told everyone she had merely gone home for an extended visit, so that she could return to us without undue speculation?"

"I see you're delighted only you and I know the whole story." Mr. Chestley sat back in his chair and slapped his knees.

"Of course. I like to be in the know on some things. I think Mrs. Harrod guessed, but we *do* have the inside track with you, don't we?" Mrs. Chestley patted Celia's hand again.

A knock sounded at the door. Mr. Chestley rose to open it.

"That will be *him,* I suppose." Mrs. Chestley added in a whisper, "You look ravishing in the rose-colored dress, my dear." As Celia stood, she added, "Be sure not to stay out long. I want to have you home with us. Call it selfish, but there it is." She looked up as Edward entered. "Besides, you know it isn't proper for you two to be out alone too late."

Edward chuckled. "I see I have traded one set of chaperones for another. I hardly saw Celia alone when I visited her parents last month, and now I'm encountering the same obstacle."

"As well you should," Mr. Chestley said. "When Celia first came to live with us, I promised to be her adopted father. In addition, I said to the world in general, and now I say to you in particular, that all men must first get my approval before claiming her hand."

"I hope I have your approval, sir."

"You do. And you have won her heart, we can all see that. So, go along now, but I'll have to second Mrs. Chestley to bring Celia back in a timely manner."

As they walked from the house, Celia said, smiling, "Do you think you can put up with the two hens? Mr. Chestley is as much one as his wife."

"I think I can. It will only be a few months until our marriage. And you, my dear, are worth it."

"Thank you. I suspect as the Chestleys and I get back into a routine, they will ease off a bit. They are just so delighted at my return — but they have you to thank for that."

"I had quite a time convincing your father. He and your mother thought you should stay home and plan the wedding. They finally agreed on our present arrangement, you to help with the initial planning those first weeks, then return home the last month before our marriage." He reached to cover her hand on his arm. "But for now I want you here, near me. We need to become better acquainted. I promise to be the perfect suitor. Neither your parents nor your adopted ones will have any fault to find."

He was leading her toward the road to his home. She stopped as they turned into it. "Edward, what's happened? Where is Mrs. Divers's house?"

"I bought the property. To save and re-build the house would have required a lot of work and expense, so I decided to take away what was left of it. Come to my place and we'll walk the path I made to adjoin the two properties. I want you to see it from that vantage point." A minute later, they entered his drive.

"You know Mrs. Divers forgave me at the end. I never heard her actual words, but Miss Waul told me she whispered them the day before she died. Miss Waul was always fair-minded. I think she tempered her friend's thinking, even when Mrs. Divers hated me the most. Oh, she would always take Mrs. Divers's part out of loyalty, but after the fire I found Miss Waul more than kind."

"What has become of her?"

"I wrote her a recommendation for the companion position she holds in a neighboring town."

Celia looked up at him. How she admired this man.

They crossed the backyard then to a wide

path that adjoined the two properties. As they approached the clearing of what had been Mrs. Divers's place, Celia stopped. "It all looks so different."

"Yes, fill still needs to be brought in and the ground leveled, but we are well on the way. I decided I want a clean slate. Just like my life." He paused, looking over the changed scene. "I must confess, even though I forgave my neighbor, the thought of getting rid of her damaged house and the memories it represented, was a relief."

"The best thing to do under the circumstances." Tenderness swelled in Celia's heart. "What are you going to do with the property?"

"Make it a garden. A friend of mine from Boston will plan the bones, the structure, supplementing it with additional trees and shrubs, and then you and I, my dear, will add to the landscape, choosing our favorite plants and flowers. I'll enlist Ned's help with the planting, of course."

His eyes scanned the property. "The place will need more care than Ned and I can give it. I thought of that young Loydie. As the house was being razed, I came on him standing rather woebegone, gazing at the property. I believe that boy had a soft spot for Mrs. Divers, she seemed a grandmother of sorts. In fact, now that I remember it, the day we sent off her things to her sister, there was a box of junk to be thrown away, and the boy took one look inside and claimed it for his own. I'm thinking of hiring him to help with the gardening, training him to tend the yard."

Edward smiled. "Besides, he seems to know his way around this place. I suspect that boy has been up to more than meets the eye. His energy needs to be turned to good account or he'll get into mischief."

Edward guided Celia back to his home. At the edge of his own yard, he stopped and became pensive. "Are you sure our wedding must wait until the spring? A December one couldn't be managed?" He took her in his arms. "Oh, Celia, sometimes I think I can't wait that long. My bed will seem cold and lonely this winter."

"Edward." She clung to him a long moment. "I had thought about making it earlier, but to ask my mother to do all that work in such a short time, making our dresses and all, I just couldn't."

"I suspected as much." He gently put her from him. "You know as much as my flesh wants you, wants you *now*, I would never dishonor you. The fear of God is in me — after reading the Bible — and I know what

He says about fornicators. More than that, I could not betray the love Christ has shown me." He looked at her seriously a moment, then added, "Knowing all this, another idea has been brewing."

"Oh?"

"It involves the upstairs of my house. When Marguerite was ill, I took a secondary bedroom and let her have our room. Now, however, I think I will knock down the wall between the two bedrooms to make one large room with a dressing room at either end. I want old memories shed there, too. While the work is being accomplished, I can use a room downstairs for a bedroom."

Celia felt wonderful anticipation welling up at the elaborate plans.

"I will purchase a new bed for our room. And other furniture as well. When we travel to Boston to visit Mother, we can choose it all."

Celia knew her family could have never done anything like this. Wouldn't have been able to afford it. How cared for and cosseted she felt.

He looked at her with a twinkle in his eye. "I need to have something keeping me busy this winter, waiting for you. Mrs. Chestley has said she wants you by her side, but I don't believe she knows what it is to feel *need.*"

He laughed ruefully. "Now, I feel the need for a brisk walk. But first —" He chucked her under the chin, then leaned over and gave her a quick peck. "That's all you get for now, Miss Thatcher. Take my arm. Any matron happening to look out her window will see a sedate couple taking the air, deep in discussion. Meat and potatoes first, then dessert."

He placed her hand more firmly on his arm, then paused, apparently thinking better of his hasty decision. "Maybe, a little dessert first," he said and bent down and claimed a sweet lingering kiss. He looked into her eyes, smiled, then drew away with decision and led her across his lawn.

A deep sense of contentment filled Celia . . . to be so loved and desired. A little impatience needled her, too, but she knew a spring wedding would be best. If nothing else, the town needed to accustom itself to this change in Edward. She wanted the townspeople here to appreciate him as much as those in her hometown.

When they arrived at the drive, Celia looked at the maples and oaks on either side. The scene before them had an air of quiet distinction, like Edward himself. Fall had arrived with leaves turning yellow, orange, and red. Just about this time last year, they had met. And not many months hence, they would begin a new life together. This would be her home, and she would walk this beautiful avenue many times.

"Now," Edward said, leading her down his drive at a leisurely pace, "I know Emerson is not your favorite writer, but I read something the other day I want to discuss with you. But looking at this beauty," he lifted his free arm and swept it around to indicate the foliage surrounding them, "I want to first quote Milton."

. . . when the air is calm and pleasant, it were an injury and sullenness against Nature not to go out and see her riches, and partake in her rejoicing with heaven and earth.

Celia stopped suddenly. "Mr. Lyons, I beg to differ with you, and with our dear Milton." She looked up at him with mock horror. " 'Sir, 'tis not an injury against *Nature,* not to go out and see her riches, for who is Nature?' I can see we will have much to discuss in the coming months."

She squeezed his arm affectionately, holding close a little longer. "It is an injury against *God* not to see His riches." Her eyes smiled into his. "Don't you agree, my love?"

# DISCUSSION QUESTIONS

1. Seeing Mr. Lyons is so particular about the books he orders from the bookstore, why did he choose to overlook or forgive the ripped page?
2. How does Mrs. Adams change as the story progresses? Cite specific ways in which she displays a new side of herself.
3. Contrast Celia's belief in God and the Bible with Mr. Lyons's Unitarianism.
4. During this time Unitarianism opened the way for individuals to believe in Transcendentalism. Describe this way of thinking and who represented it in literary America.
5. Why does Celia find the Chestleys' marriage and the marriage of her mother and father so appealing? What specifically strikes her about them?

6. When does the idea of the rose first appear in the story? What is its significance? Where else do roses appear in the narrative? How do they help shape the story?

7. Describe instances where the color red, or shades of pink to deep purple red, are used in the story. What do they add to those particular passages?

8. What do you believe is the main theme of this book? What are some secondary themes or lessons?

9. Which supporting character is a favorite of yours and why?

10 Literature is cited in The Soul of the Rose. How do the examples quoted from books, essays, and poems tell us more about the characters?

11. Tell how the instances of fire help develop the story, especially in regard to Mr. Lyons.

12. What does the French print reveal about Edward and Celia? How does it bring the two protagonists together?

13. Who was the "villain" of the story? Who were other trouble makers?

14. Why did Celia feel so strongly about
the necessity to forgive quickly?